FINDING LIBERTY

B. E. BAKER

Purple Puppy Publishing

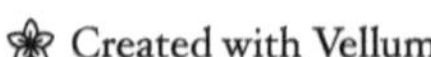 Created with Vellum

For Whitney.

Some people say the men in my stories are too good to be true.

Thanks to you, I know they're wrong.

BREKKA

Every single one of my friends in high school hated something about their bodies. Matilda hated her abs. Sydney couldn't even look at her thighs. Abby wore long sleeves year round to hide these tiny little white bumps she always picked at on her arms. Angie complained daily about the girth of her calves.

Not me.

I loved every last thing about my body. My long, lean legs shifted infinitesimally in whichever way I needed, effortlessly holding up the weight of my torso as I carved the snow, one beautiful slope at a time. My hands gripped the poles perfectly, not that I needed them often. My abs and core muscles held everything else together on the slopes and looked pretty great in a bikini in the summer, too. My lungs never failed me, no matter how high the altitude or how frosty the air. My sharp eyes spotted every indentation in the snow, every stick and branch, every patch of ice.

Unlike all my friends, I was one with my body from

birth, and it performed like my dad's Shelby Cobra 427. Perfectly, with precision, and without complaint.

Until it didn't.

I stare at the useless lumps the doctor persists in calling my legs. There should be a different name for legs when they betray you. You should get a new name for every body part that quits working, for everything that malfunctions and fails you when you need it. When a stallion's man parts are snipped off, they call him a gelding. My legs should be called flegs. Failed legs.

The doc picks up my chart, her eyes squinting to make out the tiny print. I know exactly what it says. Incomplete T10 fracture. Stabilized. Partial function.

That's the biggest joke of all. Partial function. It's like saying a Shelby Cobra has partial function because the interior lights still turn on. The car won't run. It can't do anything that made it useful in any real way, but you could still sit inside of it and, I don't know, read a book or drink a milkshake. It's more like a sofa than a car, but somehow that would be partial function. Similarly, my thighs are more like pant holders than actual legs.

"Miss Thornton," the beefy doctor says, her cheeks ruddy, "I'm not sure why you're here."

"You're the one who sent me to try the aqua treadmill. You still claim I have partial function. I've been doing physical therapy twice a day, or sometimes three times—"

She frowns at me, her crows feet becoming even more pronounced. "You're only supposed to do it once a day."

"I'm an overachiever, so sue me." I wheel toward her a few inches. "I haven't had any improvement from anything. Not a single bit. I still can't support myself with arm braces for more than a step or two. I've been flying out weekly for those treatments in Michigan you suggested. That underwater treadmill, the newest best hope. Still no improvement."

Dr. Captain purses her lips. "Miss Thornton, I told you there were no guarantees. We never know how much progress a patient can make until you've tried as many things and pushed as hard as you can. The fact that you can ambulate from your chair to the toilet and into a shower chair using only hand rails and without any other assistance is tremendous progress."

"Yes." Tears threaten and I focus on my anger instead. Better to rail at her than to break down and sob. "I should be giddy I can go pee without a chaperone."

Dr. Captain drags a chair over next to me, sits and looks me in the eyes. "I understand you're frustrated and disappointed, angry even. You aren't going to want to hear this, but I don't have anything else to offer you. The Hydroworx is what we use for professional athletes and celebrities. It's the gold standard. You're one of a handful of non-professional athletes who has even used one. I'm not trying to preach or anything, but you're very lucky to have the means to try this sort of treatment. If it didn't work. . ."

I can't stop them this time. Tears stream down my face unchecked. As frustrated as I was that everything kept failing, knowing we've reached the end of the line, the last trick in her bag, well. That's even more depressing. "You're saying this is as good as it gets for me, and I should be grateful it's this good."

She nods.

I can't bring myself to meet her eyes. I've been dealing with this for years, and even so, every time I try a new therapy, my hopes soar. Barometric chambers, neuro-stimulation, acupuncture, ChABC injections, and now underwater treadmills. I've tried every single non-surgical option available. There's nothing left to try.

Which means it's time to abandon all hope of ever being normal again.

"You have a good quality of life," she says. "Full mobility in your upper limbs, partial mobility in your legs. Sensation through your pelvis. Intermittent sensation in your legs and feet. You have every reason to expect a long and healthy life, and these disabilities are workable."

"Yeah, thanks." I check out for the rest of the appointment, responding with nods and grunts. I won't be scheduling another appointment here.

What's the point?

When Dr. Captain's nurse tries to push me out of the exam room, I snap at her. "If I wanted to move without making the conscious decision to move, I'd have bought a power chair."

I wheel myself through the door. If there's something my body can still do, I do it. I've grown enough muscle through my shoulders and back and enough calluses on my hands that I don't even notice long treks. My older brother Trig kept trying to convince me to buy something with an electric option at least, but they're so heavy and difficult to transport. Besides, I won't rely on a machine to do anything I can still do myself.

A magazine catches my eye as I wheel past the waiting area. It's not a new issue, but it's one I haven't seen before. Which means Trig worked overtime to make sure I didn't. As my hand reaches for it, the air around me thickens into jelly. Time collapses to nothing and my fingers shake. I press past it all and force my hand to close around the glossy pages of the Outside Magazine.

Winter Olympic Issue.

My fingers trace the face of my former best friend where it smiles at me from the cover. It's not Annelise Mayberry's fault we aren't close friends anymore.

The blame for our withered friendship falls squarely on me. Five years ago, we were both bound for the Olympics, the best two downhill skiers in America. Annelise trailed me by a hair on downhill, and by a wide margin on slalom. I was going to medal in both the downhill and the Super G at the Olympics. Everyone knew it. Even the Swedes cringed when they heard my name.

Until the accident.

Without me on the team, Annelise still snagged a bronze, and at the time she told every news network who would listen she wouldn't have won it if she hadn't trained with me. She was a loyal friend, but I didn't care. I couldn't talk to her, or even congratulate her. It only reminded me of what I lost.

I can't stop my fingers from flipping to the spread on her from the most recent Olympics. Even though it's been more than four years now, I couldn't bring myself to watch any of it. Sometimes I pretend the Olympics died. No one cares about them anymore, and they disappeared. But of course, wishes aren't horses, and other people can still ride.

Annelise's huge, shiny teeth gleam at me from the centerfold. Her cheeks are rosy, her eyes sparkly, and my lungs almost fail me as I read the blurb. "Three time Olympic Gold Medalist Annelise Mayberry has it all: speed, accuracy, and control. That's how she conquered the Combined, the Downhill and the Slalom in this year's Olympics, the first sweep by any woman from the United States of America."

My hand crumples the glossy pages involuntarily, and when I force my fingers to uncurl, it slides to the ground. I wheel out of the office without meeting anyone's eyes and beeline toward my Range Rover without thinking. I open the door and then wheel back in close to the seat. I hit the position two button so the chair leans back, and then I lock the wheelchair in place. I shift my feet out of the footrests on my chair and toward the car, and then I lean forward, and using my arms, I boost myself out of my chair and into the driver's seat. I reposition my legs. Then I pull my seat cushion off and tuck it behind the seat of the car. Next, I pop off the huge back wheels one by one and stow them, too. Finally, I lift the middle section, collapsing the body of the chair and swing it into the passenger seat.

I've done it so many times that I can switch into robot mode as I do it. Somehow the familiar routine calms me down a bit. I drive home a little too quickly, my heart still racing a bit, but I'm not stupid enough to pick up the phone when Trig calls, even if I'd like to hear his reassuring voice. I never use my cell when driving. Not to text, not to call, and certainly not to check any social media. Not since that day.

I call my brother back once I'm at the office, in front of my desk, with the file on our newest acquisition open on my computer screen. "Sorry I didn't answer. I was driving before."

"No problem," he says. "It wasn't a big deal." Except his words are clipped, his tone clearly agitated. He actually sounds about like I feel.

"It wasn't?"

"Nope."

I wait silently, because something clearly was a big deal to him. Eventually he'll spit it out, whatever made him upset. I've learned that when I press him for details, he doubles down like a tick that a vet's trying to evict. Can't go popping my own brother's head off.

"Fine, I'll just tell you." He sighs heavily. "So you know Geo's best friend Rob?"

"The marine with huge biceps and perfect hair?"

He grumbles. "They aren't that big. But yes, that's him, and you know yesterday was Memorial Day."

"Yes," I say. "I mean, I've never met the perfect Marine myself, but I did know it was Memorial Day."

"Well, Geo always spends Memorial Day with Rob, or she has ever since her fiancé died anyway. She asked if it bothered me, and of course I said it was fine. But when I told her I'd like to come along, she looked at me like I suggested she dip her French fries in strawberry yogurt."

"Wait, sweet potato fries or regular ones?"

"Brekka!"

"Sorry, I'm just kidding, okay? I'm listening, I swear."

"She didn't want me to hang out with them," he says. "I could tell, so I didn't go."

"Okay." There must be more to it than this, right? I mean, Trig adores Geo, and she is completely bonkers for him. But her fiancé died in a huge explosion with perfect Marine Rob, so I'm not surprised they'd spend Memorial Day together. It's a little awkward since he's a guy, I suppose, but it's not like Rob and Geo ever dated or anything. I'm not sure what question to ask next. I don't really get why he's so upset.

Trig clears his throat. "I never told you this before because you get a little protective sometimes."

"Me?"

Trig snorts.

"Fine, I might look out for you, but you're just as bad. We only have each other. Which is exactly why you can tell me, no matter what it is. I promise I won't judge."

"After I asked Geo out on our first date—"

"When you stalked her to Macaroni Grill, you mean?"

Trig grunts. "When I happened to run into her and Rob at dinner at a local place, yes. Anyway, after Paul and I left that night, Rob told her he loved her."

Wait, what? "Perfect Marine Rob tried to snatch her out from under you?"

"Not exactly snatch her, since they'd known each other for like twenty years. But he did finally profess his love for her, and he told her he considered their dinners to be dates. He had loved her since her fiancé died, or sometime around then, or maybe it happened after. I don't know. The point is, Geo didn't feel at all the same, but he did like her, or he does, so it made me kind of ... nervous to send her over there alone all day."

"Basically, she wanted to spend all day with a super muscular, caring, fairly rich guy who's besotted with her? And she didn't want you to come along."

"I don't know whether I'd call him super muscular, but sure. That's essentially right."

I lean back in my chair. "That sucks. Why didn't you call me on Friday or Saturday or whenever you first heard about all this?"

"I had it under control. Geo loves me and I know that. If she wanted Rob, she'd have picked him, but she didn't. She picked me."

I lean forward again. "Uh, okay. So then what's wrong? This story reminds me of one of Dad's." His stories meander like a third grader playing right field.

"That's rude."

"Then get to the point."

"I let her go, but then I didn't hear from her. She didn't come home last night, and she didn't answer my calls."

I almost drop the phone. "Is she okay? Did creepy Rob like, kidnap her?"

Trig's voice drops. It sounds nearly menacing. "I'd end him."

"Okay, then what?"

"I drove over to his house, obviously."

"Obviously." But wait, at what time? "When did you go over there? Before or after you called the police?"

"Before. I mean, I didn't even call the police, okay?"

"You suck at stories, Trig. What time did you go over there?"

"Three a.m. I went over at three."

"And?"

"I saw Geo, all curled up and adorable, in Rob's lap."

"Uh, wait, are you saying she cheated on you?"

"No," he practically shouts. "But she was asleep. On Rob. On hot Rob's lap."

I think about Geo. She adores my brother. I don't doubt that. In fact, my brain was trying to reject the possibility of her cheating on Trig, even as I asked. But I can see how this Rob guy would make Trig nuts. He and Geo have been friends for a long time, and they hang out all the time. They've been through a lot together.

"How long have they been friends again?"

"At least twenty years," Trig says. "They lived a few doors down from each other growing up. They met playing kickball or something. I guess Rob beat up some kid who told her she couldn't play."

"What a freaking Boy Scout."

"Right?" Trig huffs. "I know nothing happened, but I'm sick of them having their little club that I'm not a part of."

I wonder if he'd care if Rob was a girl, or a really unattractive guy. Probably not. Even so, it's a valid irritation. At the same time, I can't fault Geo, not really. Especially since she doesn't seem to have many friends. I can relate to that deficit, and it makes the thought of cutting off anyone you care about a painful prospect.

"What are you going to do about it?"

"Probably nothing," Trig says. "Seeing her asleep with him, all curled up, with his arm slung around her shoulder, well. It pissed me off, but I just drove back home. She called me the next morning and apologized. She told me she fell asleep on Rob's couch next to him."

"Which is true. At least she wasn't withholding information."

"Whose side are you on?"

"I'm always on yours," I say. "Every minute of every day of every month of every year."

"I know you are. It actually helped just to tell someone. I love Geo, Brekka, and it's hard. It's so hard watching her care about anyone that much. Someone who's not me, I mean. Does that make me a monster?"

No, it makes him human. "Not at all. Maybe tell Geo how you feel, but try to remember she's lost her dad, and her mom too, essentially. That means she has you, and me of course, and her friend Paisley, and Rob. That's pretty much it. So asking her to not be his friend might be... a steep ask."

"Oh, I'm not doing that, not at all. I can handle it. And I don't need her to think I'm coming unhinged." He sighs. "Did you have a chance yet to look over the comparative analysis and EBITDA on Parker Family Holdings?"

I run him through my assessment, and then hop off the phone, ostensibly to finish digging through our leads. Instead I find myself pulling up the purchase order I recently approved to Franklin Graham Honda, Rob's Honda dealership. Sixteen Honda Accords to use for company cars. My eyes stop at the address.

I should not even consider flying out to Atlanta and giving Rob a piece of my mind. Trig doesn't need my help.

Even so.

I pull up the same purchase order twice. Then I google the dealership and work out a plan to get there. I don't have a car in Atlanta, and I have a little control over my lower limbs, but not enough to drive myself without a modified car. I need at least a push pull or I'd be a total hazard on the road.

I mentally shake myself like a wet dog. I need to let this go.

Trig doesn't need me to get involved. I force myself to review the files, but every time I close my eyes, even for so long as a blink, Annelise's face flashes in front of my eyes.

I was better than her. So much better than her, but I didn't win a single solitary gold medal, much less three. I'm a loser stuck in a metal chair. I can't ski. I can't walk. I can't even crawl using my knees. The best I could manage in a pinch would be dragging my body behind me like crazy Ivar the Boneless in that History Channel show, *Vikings*. The only value I add to the world now is in analyzing companies to determine whether they're a good investment.

Which is exactly what I should be doing right now, instead of imagining I might storm Rob's office in Atlanta and let him have a piece of my mind. I evaluate the file and type my recommendation for Trig. I send it through the ether and glance at the photos on my desk. Trig swinging me around at a dance recital when I was twelve. Trig photo bombing at my high school graduation. Trig and I on the slopes, his arm slung around my shoulder.

My mother is a power vampire who hammered Trig and I like a drill sergeant. If anything, she's grown scarier with age. My father hasn't been in the same room as her for more than thirty minutes in years, and we usually have to photoshop us all into the same photo for Christmas cards.

Dad, on the other hand, always purchases lavish gifts, like a jet for my birthday, or a Porsche Cayenne for Christmas. He even gives gifts for things no one else does, like the Fourth of July, but I wouldn't bet on him remembering my middle name, much less listening to me lament about matters of the heart. I'm not sure he even realized how the accident led to the ruination of my hopes and dreams. He hasn't once asked how I'm doing since I lost use of my legs. I'm sure he cares about me, I'm just not sure he thinks about me much.

In the industrial strength vacuum left by my parents' multitudinous shortcomings, my brother Trig stepped up. He came to every dance recital, every swim meet, every spelling bee, and every important ski run of my life. He cheered me on, he buoyed me up, and he stayed up late to commiserate when things didn't go my way. Trig has been there for me from birth until present day, showering me with love and affection for more than twenty-seven years. He bought me my first pair of skis, and paid a fortune for a custom-made titanium wheelchair when I wanted to curl up and die.

The more I think of everything Trig has done, the more worked up I get that Rob would do anything to hurt my brother. I may not be able to compete in the Olympics, but I can sure as heck survive an unplanned trip out to Atlanta.

Robert Graham is going to rue the day he was so inconsiderate of Brekka Caroline Thornton's brother's feelings.

2

ROB

I run my hand along the satiny finish of the end table and beam like an idiot. At least no one in the world can see that I'm grinning like a loon. I'm just so excited that I finally got the temperature perfect to dry the new polish I concocted. I haven't been satisfied with the last four tries.

It's nice to do something perfectly, even if it's just a piece of furniture.

A bang on the door at the back of my shop brings me back to reality. I spin around to face the intruder. My dad glances from the end table to my face, his expression quizzical. "I figured you'd be at work by now."

If he thought I'd be gone, why did he come over? I don't bother asking, because I know it's his passive aggressive way of telling me I'm not going in early enough. "I'm about to head over. I had a few small things to fix here first."

Dad glances at the end table. "It already looks nice."

"That's because I'm done."

"Well, it's a real good one."

He's said the same thing about everything. From my

clay pinch pots in first grade, to my winning Pinewood derby car in fifth grade, to every piece of furniture I've ever made.

"Thanks."

I close up my sealant and shut off the lights. My dad follows me out. "Are you planning to go to auction next week? Bob mentioned the Pre-Owned stock is a little light at the Marietta location."

"Bob always complains about the quantity of cars on hand. That's his standard excuse when sales dip."

Dad shrugs. "Maybe, but he might be right this time. And no one has as good an eye as you do at auction."

I don't roll my eyes. I don't groan. I just nod. "Sure, I'll go Monday."

"Perfect."

Dad grills me on a few more things before I walk him out of my house so I can head in to my office at our flagship location. I never once mention that I might not need his guidance because our sales have doubled since I took over four years ago. I don't breathe a word about the fact that our profits have tripled. He already knows all of that.

"I'm proud of you, Robbie. You may not be a salesman, but you're the best manager in the family." Dad pulls me down for one of his signature bear hugs. I climb into my old truck and wave bye.

I dread going into the office every day, but at least my family appreciates my sacrifice. It's not like most people in the world love their jobs. My dad always told us, 'they pay you because it's work, son.' And his words are true, after all.

Even so, I pause outside the door to my office and breathe in and out through my nose once, and then twice. Finally I force myself to go inside and squeeze a little more profit out of our family business, tabulating which cars we need to order based on current inventory and profit margins, and which cars I should look for at auction for the pre-owned department.

I'm halfway through the sales numbers from the last week when I hear a commotion outside my door. I'm convinced that Stacey, my seventy-one-years-young secretary, trained in the CIA's black ops division. She scares the pants off of me, and I sign her paychecks. I feel terrible for everyone else who isn't her boss. If someone is tangling with Stacey, there must be something major going down. I'm about to go out to see what it might be when my door opens. I'm shocked when it's not Stacey's white-haired head peeking around the door frame at me.

In fact, I have to drop my gaze nearly three feet to even find a face, and it's the face of a tiny woman in a wheelchair. Her hair's pulled back into a high ponytail and her golden eyes flash like a cat about to pounce on an unsuspecting bug.

"Robert Graham?" She pins me with a baleful glare.

I reassess based on that glare. It could melt sand into glass. She reminds me more of a small, angry dragon than a cat. I can't quite help the smile that pulls the corners of my lips upward. "Yes, I'm Rob. Who are you?"

She inhales and straightens in her seat, shooting toward me in a blur of dark metal and ire. "Your secretary tried to tell me I didn't have an appointment."

"Do you have an appointment?" I glance down at my calendar. Empty until a meeting at eight-thirty a.m. tomorrow with my general managers.

She tosses her head. "Of course I don't. But I don't need one, because I'm not here for business. This is personal."

It's personal? I can't quite help the swell of curiosity her words evoke. What does this adorable woman want from me that isn't business related? "How exactly did you get past Stacey?"

"Is that the octogenarian Nazi's name?"

I raise my eyebrows. "She's only seventy-one."

"Her hair is utterly white and she's pretty quick to grab that cane," she says. "I won't lie and say she didn't make me a little nervous, but this chair hasn't failed me yet."

"Your wheelchair hasn't failed you?" I ask.

She nods. "People almost never get in my way when I play the wheelchair card."

"Exactly what does that look like?" I ask. "The card, I mean? Is it paper, or plastic?"

She compresses her lips into a tight line and glares at me. "Neither. It's hypothetical. I told her I was working for the ACLU."

I laugh. "Which you aren't, I take it?"

She crosses her arms. "I am not with the American Civil Liberties Union, no. I am here to tell you that you're an inconsiderate idiot."

She's not wrong there. I wonder what stupid thing I did to make her mad, in particular. "You're planning to elaborate on that, I hope?"

"Your best friend is who?"

"My best *living* friend is a woman named Geode Polson."

She smirks. "You don't hesitate to pull the dead comrade card, I see."

I grin at her. "I guess I don't."

She frowns. "I'm Trig's sister Brekka. Trig won't tell Geo, but it bothers him that you two are so close, almost inappropriately close. He feels left out of your super special dead compatriot club. And since they're getting married, I came to tell you to get over Geo and let her be happy."

I fold my arms across my chest. "I didn't realize I was impeding her happiness in any way."

"Oh be serious. You have to know what I mean."

"I do?"

"A few days ago you slept with her."

I nearly choke. "Excuse me?"

She looks at the ceiling as if asking for divine help in being patient. "I guess I'm being too literal. You spent the entire day together, excluding her *fiancé*, and then you fell asleep in one another's arms. Does that sound more accurate to you?"

I sit down in my desk chair and lean my forearms on my desk. "Have you ever lost anyone, Brekka?"

"Two grandparents," she says.

"I hope you won't take offense when I tell you that doesn't really count for the purposes of this conversation. If you haven't lost someone before his or her time, if you haven't lost someone you felt was a part of you, then you probably won't understand what I'm talking about. I appreciate your input, I really, truly do. But the time I spent with Geo had nothing to do with eros."

Her eyebrows knit together and her lips compress in the most adorable way when she frowns. "Excuse me, eros? Is that like erotica?"

I snort. "Uh, same Latin base, but otherwise, no. There are four types of love. You're familiar with that concept?"

She stares at me without comprehension, so I explain. "Storge, pronounced store-gay, is one you probably can identify with. Familial love, like you feel for your brother Trig. That's the kind of love and affection that drives you to fly from, say, Colorado to Atlanta to yell at someone because they caused pain to a loved one. Whether the yelling is justified or not, you're reacting to your desire to help someone you love in a familial way."

She sets her jaw and her eyes flash at me. I adore her scowl, but I don't mention that.

"Philia is the type of love you feel for friends, also

considered Christian love. Pronounced fill-ee-uh, but spelled with a ph. You could think of this as brotherly love, but it's not for brothers. It's love between really good friends."

Brekka lifts one narrow eyebrow. "Did you have a point?"

"I'm getting there. Agape is like God's love. Pure, unde-filed, unlimited. But the last love I haven't yet defined is eros. Romantic love, including sexual tension. I'm telling you that my time with Geo had to do with philia, and even storge, but not with eros. So you and Trig have nothing to be worried about."

She rolls toward me and rests her arms on the opposite side of my desk, leaning over it so our faces are less than three feet apart. "I don't much care what you call it. You can't spend all day with Geo and then let her fall asleep on your hot body any more. Got it?"

I can't quite help the grin. "You think I have a hot body?"

She seethes. "Try to listen, meathead. Whether you want to kiss her or not doesn't matter. The point is, she loves her fiancé. That love works because they turn toward each other when things are difficult. If she's turning toward you, Geo and Trig aren't getting closer. They're not bearing one another's burdens, if you want to use Bible speak. So, if you want to keep phillying and storgying my future sister-in-law, figure out how to bring Trig into your little party. Or I'm going to call the cops and get your party shut down."

I lean back in my chair, a little bit floored. Because this spitting dragon isn't wrong. She's spot on. I love Geo, but she's picked Trig, and that means she loves Trig. She's building a life with him. Which means I can be around, but I can't be her support, not like I used to be.

I was out of line.

I hate being wrong, but I always admit when I am. "You're right. I need to figure out how to bring Trig into the knot of pain so he can heal it instead of the two of us just wallowing."

Brekka opens her mouth and then stops, her lips dangling open. She snaps it shut. "Okay, then."

"That's it?"

"I guess so. I didn't expect you to agree with me."

"I didn't agree with you until I realized that Geo needs to let Trig in with all this stuff. If she can't talk to Trig about the past pains that had nothing to do with him, it'll hinder their future."

"What makes you so wise?" Brekka leans back in her wheelchair, which I notice for the first time is not even approaching standard issue. It's not painted black like I thought. The metal itself is black. What's it made of?

"I'm not wise," I say, "but I've spent a lot of time studying trees. Have you ever heard of inosculation?"

She shakes her head.

"Have you seen intertwined trees, two trees that have grown together?"

"We had one that needed to be cut down in our back yard in Colorado. Our gardener said it wasn't safe to have around since it was two trees, not one, and could come down in a storm."

I close my eyes. "Your gardener sounds like an idiot."

"Excuse me?" she asks.

"When trees conjoin, it's because they have entwined and the wind causes the bark to rub away. Once the cambium, also known as the main growth layer, of the two trees touch, the trees begin to grow together. As one. It doesn't weaken them, it strengthens them. Your gardener probably meant your tree had a fork, and if bark was growing in the juncture, it might have been unsound."

"Uh, sure. Why do you know a bizarre and unbelievable amount about this stuff? Are you a secret arborist?"

I chuckle. "Let's call it a hobby."

"Uh, okay. Or an oddity. Both words end in y."

"That may also be true. My point is still a sound one. Once you pointed out the error of my ways, I realized I needed to course correct."

"I've never met a man who . . . course corrected so quickly."

I flex my biceps a little and smirk. "I'm a unique, and some might say hot, guy."

"I can see that," she says. "Well, if you agree that you need to start including Trig and maybe not pining for Geo, then I think my work here is done."

She wheels backward and starts to turn and something tugs at the corners of my heart. Something I haven't felt in years and years. Something I haven't experienced at all on dozens and dozens of dates.

I don't want her to leave.

I want to spend more time with her. She might burn me, or she might scratch me with her shiny claws, but I like this tiny, bright-eyed dragon.

I hop to my feet and jog around to the closed door. "Leaving already?"

She looks up at me. "I am."

"If you agree to let me take you to dinner, I promise I won't mention trees once. Not a single, solitary time."

"I'm sorry?"

"No, I'm sorry. I really don't talk about plant life that much. I'm not sure what came over me. And since you had to fly all the way out here to talk some sense into me about Geo and Trig, the least I can do is buy you dinner."

She squares her shoulders. "I didn't fly all the way out here for you."

"Oh, you didn't?"

She shakes her head. "Of course not. That would be childish. I had a meeting."

Duh. Of course she wouldn't fly all the way to Atlanta just to talk to me. I'm really shoving my entire foot, work boot and all, right in my mouth today. "Look, you said you wanted me to forget about Geo. What better way to divert my attention than having dinner with the most beautiful woman in all of Georgia?"

She blushes and ducks her head and I realize I've said something wrong again, but for the life of me, I don't know what. "Brekka, throw me a bone here. It's hard to ask a woman on a date, and even harder when she's both drop dead gorgeous and absurdly smart."

"I can't go to dinner with you." I can barely make out her words. What happened to my fire-spitting dragon?

"Why not?" I reach down and use one finger to tilt her head toward me. "What did I do wrong this time? We've established that I'm open to course corrections."

She leans into my hand and breathes in and out slowly. "You didn't do anything wrong. I just can't go to dinner. I'm sorry."

When she maneuvers past me, opens the door and rolls away, I want to kick something. What did I do?

❋   3   ❋

BREKKA

Rob is way, way hotter than I expected. I knew he'd have big muscles and great hair, but that's all he was to me, a meaty former Marine who sold cars. I was prepared for a winning smile, delicious biceps... and an empty head.

Geo's smart, funny and sophisticated, so I'm not sure why I reduced her friend to a caricature in my mind. I certainly didn't expect him to school me on horticulture, and I had no idea he'd match me, barb for barb. His willingness to take criticism and accept it straight up floored me.

Which is the reason why, when he asked me out, something went haywire in my brain.

I haven't been out with a guy since before the accident. Which means I haven't been on a date in almost five years. Things may have changed some in that time, but one thing I know for sure must be the same. Hot Marines do not ask out paraplegic girls. Ever. I have no idea what he was thinking. How could he not know that? He must've asked me out from some kind of surge of pity. Or maybe curiosity. Or maybe he felt obligated, since I'm Trig's sister.

No matter his motivation, Mr. Graham couldn't have asked me out because he wanted to kiss me. No one would find me irresistible, much less someone who looks like him, which means he couldn't possibly want to date me for real. No one who takes that much care with their appearance and physical fitness wants to chain a bowling ball like me around their neck and hop into the middle of the Pacific Ocean that is my life now.

I wheel outside to the front curb where my driver's waiting and signal that I'm ready to go. He pulls into the handicap spot so I can transfer into the back of the sedan. It's harder to transfer into the back seat, especially in a car I'm not used to. It's annoying to shove all the parts of my wheelchair next to me in the seat too, but it's not my first time doing it. When the driver runs around to try and help me, I flinch. He has no idea how to do any of it, and he'll just slow me down while drawing attention to me.

I don't need his help, and I sure don't want his pity.

I don't blame him for trying to be nice. No one knows how to react, after all. His mom surely taught him to be gallant and chivalrous and kind, and someone else in my circumstance might not wave him off. People usually mean well. They're often dead wrong about what I want, but then again, I frequently don't know what I want until the wrong thing is presented. For example, I'm currently sick to my stomach with myself for turning Rob's invitation down. Which is insane and delusional and utterly ridiculous.

Nevertheless, I totally wish I was going on a date with super foxy Robert Graham tonight.

Tears well up behind my eyes and I blink them back rapidly. I clench my fists and look at my knees so that the driver won't notice I've gotten all emotional. First I sobbed in a doctor's office yesterday over my lost Olympic dreams, and today I'm about to bawl because some guy asked me out and I intelligently turned him down. What's wrong with me lately? It's not like any of this is new. I gave up on hot dates years ago.

I want to call Trig or text Geo, but I can't ask either of them about Rob. They don't even know I'm in town. And I just lied and told their friend I was here for a meeting. He's sure to mention something to them, which is when things will get weird, and I'll look stupid. I need to at least do damage control on that before it comes back to bite me.

"Don't leave yet," I say to the driver.

I whip out my phone and call the main line for Franklin Graham Honda. "Rob Graham, please."

"Does he expect your call?" the receptionist asks.

"No, but tell Stacey to tell him that the woman who just left his office is calling back. My name's Brekka."

"Hold please."

Less than thirty seconds later, Rob answers. "Hey! Any chance you're rethinking your complete shut down earlier?"

I'm actually only calling to explain that my meeting was a secret and he shouldn't mention it to Trig or Geo. But suddenly that seems like a conversation I should have in person. "Maybe."

"Maybe? That's the best noncommittal word I've ever heard. Are you still here? I'll be right out."

So I can struggle with my wheelchair in front of him, transferring to and from his car? Absolutely not. If he asked me out because he's curious about the girl whose legs don't work, I won't perform for him. I'm not a zoo exhibit.

"We're already on our way out." I point at the driver, who pulls out of the parking spot and toward the exit, bless him. "Name the place and I'll meet you there."

"We?" he asks. "Please tell me now if you came here with your hunky boyfriend."

I snort into the phone.

"Did he take the phone from you? Or are you choking?"

"Uh no," I say. "I mean, there's no boyfriend. We is me and my driver."

"Oh, that's the second best news I've heard today. Now if I can just get that maybe upgraded to a yes..."

I can't suppress the smile that takes over my mouth. "Fine. Yes. Dinner can't hurt, right?"

"With the bar set that low, I feel reasonably confident I can stumble across it. What kind of food sounds good to you?"

"I eat most everything," I say. "As long as it doesn't try to bite me back."

"Beautiful Brekka likes her steak well done," he says slowly, like he's writing it down. "Got it."

I giggle, which horrifies me. It's like I've climbed into a movie reel for a ghastly, poorly written teen love story. I clear my throat. "How about Italian?"

"I make better Italian than any restaurant in the area." Rob's voice is deep and rough and I imagine sitting across the table from him at his house, a candle between us, his bed in the next room. My stomach executes a strange flip and flop move that I don't like at all.

"Actually, I've been craving sushi lately."

"Doesn't want to be lured to a strange man's house on the first date. Got it. Well, Sushi-ology is my favorite raw fish place, and it's on my end of town."

"Can you text me the address?" I ask.

"If you're brave enough to give me your cell phone number." Rob's voice drops even lower and my stomach somersaults again.

I may need to see my doctor soon. Something is definitely wrong with my intestinal tract. "Duh." I rattle off my number.

"Perfect," he says. "I'll text you."

"Great," I say. "But it's only ten minutes until five. When did you want to meet me there?"

"If you head that way now, so will I. I've got some plans later that you're welcome to join me for, but an early dinner makes them easier."

Plans I can join him for? That sounds ominous.

"You might actually enjoy coming along tonight. I'll fill you in at dinner and you can decide."

He'll explain at dinner. A dinner date with a hot Marine. "Semper Fi," I say without thinking, like a complete idiot. I don't even know what it means. Always true or something. "Uh sorry. That sort of just popped out."

Maybe I'm suffering from otherwise asymptomatic heat stroke. Atlanta's much warmer than Denver, and it's the only explanation for me accepting his invitation to dinner and then blurting out the Marine's motto to him, with no explanation or segue. Please let it be heat stroke.

I need a lemonade, stat.

He chuckles. "I'm a former Marine. Did Geo tell you that, or did you notice the tattoo?"

And now I can't think of anything except where he might have a tattoo. I need to see it, although if he thinks I might already have seen it, it's probably not somewhere especially interesting. "Geo mentioned it, yeah."

"Well, you can rest assured tonight's plans aren't anything dangerous. Totally not military business."

I need to end this call before I say something stupid about his hands. "Well, I'll head that way as soon as I get your text." My phone buzzes in my hand and I realize he's talking to me from a landline. "Which I'm guessing you just sent."

"I did. I'll see you soon, Brekka."

The way he says my name, carefully, purposefully, sends a shiver down my spine. Hanging up feels like self-preservation.

I immediately read his text.

SO GLAD YOU RECONSIDERED. Then an address.

I give the address to my driver and tell him to get there as quickly as possible. I need to arrive before Rob so I can already be waiting when he reaches the table. I wrack my brain on the way for reasons I might have to be here without telling Trig.

Maybe I'm making this too hard. Why can't I confess to Trig that I came to chew Rob out? Especially since it worked. Rob's going to leave Geo alone. Oh, right, because I told Rob I was here for business. Think, brain. What could I need to do here?

I text Trig. FLEW IN TO ATLANTA TODAY. FIGURED WE COULD GO OVER THE NUMBERS FOR STARFIRE, AND YOU CAN FINALLY SHOW OFF YOUR NEW HOUSE.

Dots while he's typing, and then, *$^%#*@ YOU'RE REALLY HERE?

I'm a little offended by his shock. I haven't declined his invitation *that* many times. YES.

I CAN'T BELIEVE IT! LET'S GET DINNER. WHERE ARE YOU?

Dangit. I MIGHT HAVE STOPPED OVER TO CHEW ROB OUT FIRST, AND NOW I'M STUCK EATING WITH HIM TO MAKE SURE HE'S NOT OFFENDED BY MY SAGE SISTERLY ADVICE. GOOD NEWS: HE AGREES WITH ME AND HE'S BACKING OFF.

YOU DID WHAT???????

Oh good grief. Sometimes Trig can be such a little girl. DID YOU READ THE PART WHERE IT WORKED?

I ONLY WANTED TO COMPLAIN. YOU'RE SUCH A GUY SOMETIMES, SWOOPING IN TO FIX THINGS INSTEAD OF LISTENING. I DIDN'T WANT YOU TO FIX IT.

Which I totally knew. MAYBE I NEEDED A WIN TODAY.

ARE YOU OKAY?

No. But I can't tell Trig that. He'd worry about me instead of enjoying his new life with his beautiful fiancée. YES, I text instead, I'M FINE.

AFTER DINNER WITH THE NEANDERTHAL, YOU'RE STAYING WITH ME. NOT IN A HOTEL. TEXT ME WHEN YOU'RE DONE.

DEAL.

When my driver pulls up in the parking lot across from Sushi-ology, I reassemble my wheelchair and transfer into it. The only wheelchair access to the restaurant is in front of a barre workout place. I'm glad I don't need to make Rob follow me all the way to the ramp and then loop around past the nail salon just to get inside. This sushi place is small, but it looks fairly promising. Before I can open the door, a woman in black pants and a dark blue shirt opens it for me.

"Welcome to Sushi-ology," she says, her smile barely faltering when she takes in my wheelchair and the fact that I'm all alone.

"Thanks," I say. "I'm meeting a friend. Could you show me to the table first, though?"

"Of course," she says. "There are only two of you?"

I nod.

"That's good. We have a wait for more than two, but I've got a small table open right now."

I breathe a sigh of relief. Once she's grabbed menus, I follow her to the back corner. Perfect. She shifts the chair out of the way and I roll into the space it previously occupied.

Before the waitress has even handed me a menu, I notice Rob at the hostess stand. When he sees me, he beams and nods his head at her. He heads straight for me. My hands shake a little, so I grab my napkin to give them something to do.

When he reaches the table, he holds up one hand as if to forestall some action. "Oh, don't stand up, not for me. We're past that kind of formality at this point, don't you think?"

My jaw drops. He's making jokes about my inability to stand?

He drops into his seat. "Too soon for me to tease you?"

The twinkle in his eye does the trick and a belly laugh bubbles out of me. Not even Trig makes jokes about my incapacity. Somehow, poking fun at me for not standing makes me happy, not angry. He's acting like it's just part of who I am, like he doesn't care. Like he doesn't need to walk on eggshells just because he can walk. And somehow, his joke actually pushed our relationship past the awkward formality of a typical first date, because he felt comfortable teasing me about it.

I slug him in the shoulder and he pretends to be injured. "Ouch. Give a guy a break. First dates are stressful enough, and you turned me down the first time I asked. I'm just trying to lighten the mood." He leans closer to me, near enough that I can feel his minty breath on my face. "I promise to behave from here on out. In fact, I won't even try to kiss you tonight. Scout's honor."

Why does that disappoint me so badly? "Then why are you chewing gum?"

He looks skyward. "You see right through me, but the polite thing is not to draw attention to it."

My grin is back. He's flirting, with me, like he asked me out because he's really interested, not out of some sense of pity or obligation.

"What do you like here?" I ask.

"Other than the company, you mean?"

Heat rises in my face. "Okay, okay, enough flirting. Let's order right away, because I'm starving. I might have skipped lunch in my haste earlier. Someone needed to be yelled at."

He narrows his eyes at me. "I thought you came for a business meeting."

I bite my lip. "I might have made that up." Why am I confessing to him? I had this covered!

The glint in his eye has my stomach somersaulting again. Or maybe it's doing that to keep from digesting itself.

He grins. "So you did come out just to see me."

I lift my eyebrows. "Did you miss the part where I said I came to yell at you?"

"Right." Rob reaches for the menu and his hand brushes mine. He doesn't jerk away. If anything, his hand moves back even more slowly. "I'm glad you did. For future reference, you can yell at me whenever you feel the urge. I can take it."

"You're bad," I say. "And you can't really mean that."

He shrugs his broad shoulders and I look down at my menu to keep from staring. What could he possibly be doing here, flirting with me? What's his angle?

"I have three sisters and a very vocal mother. You could say I've been prepped for criticism from stunning women my entire life. And to answer your question, normally, I think the more things a restaurant has on its menu, the less chance that any of it will be good. If, for instance, a restaurant serves tacos, pizza, and hamburgers, I'm going to turn around and head right back out the door. But somehow Sushi-ology serves ramen, sushi, and teriyaki, and they pull it off. I love the ramen here, and the crunchy yellowtail rolls are close-your-eyes-and-sigh amazing. The spicy tuna's memorable, too."

Food. Right. I gulp and focus on my options. "Maybe we better try them all."

He lifts one eyebrow. "You look like someone who won't be able to finish a single roll order."

I square my shoulders and meet his gaze. "That sounds like a challenge."

"What if it is?"

"I'll eat you under the table, mister."

"I very much doubt that." He beams at me. "But I'd be extremely impressed."

I'm sure he'll eat more than me, but as a very small person I've learned the importance of talking a big game. Even if you have to stuff a few pieces of sushi into the dirt of the potted plant next to you, people take you more seriously when you don't back down from challenges.

In the end, Rob orders a bowl of ramen, and we order five rolls to share.

"So how did you end up finding this place?" I ask. "Geo mentioned you live in Marietta, near where she and Trig just bought a house."

"I do, which is only twenty minutes from here. But have you heard of Kennesaw Mountain?"

I shake my head, an uneasy feeling settling across my shoulders.

"There was a huge battle there during the Civil War. I'm not much of a history buff, but the trails are gorgeous, and the weather is usually really nice during the hot summer months. I found this place after spending most of the day hiking Kennesaw."

That's what I was afraid of. Of course hot Rob, with his bulging muscles, loves hiking and outdoors activities. Which means I really would be an anvil around his neck, just as I suspected. "Cool."

"I'm sure you have much nicer mountains out in Colorado," Rob says.

"We do boast some huge piles of rocks." Not that I ever climb any, not anymore. I glance down at my stupid flegs and grimace.

"Tell me about your work," Rob says. "What do you do?"

I suck in a huge breath. I need to make the best of the hour I'll be stuck on this ill-fated date. May as well talk about something I like. "Trig's a numbers guy. He doesn't need me for that. When he graduated, Mom wanted him to step into an apprenticeship with her so she could mold him into her perfect mini-me."

"I've heard she's . . . intense."

I can't help my laughter. "That's a very diplomatic way to describe my mother. She's a beast. An unstoppable business leviathan who consumes everyone and everything in her path."

"Possibly less diplomatic as descriptions go, but infinitely more intriguing."

I lift one eyebrow. "You like strong women?"

"Exclusively."

I think about Geo, who I know he is, or maybe was, in love with. She's strong, decisive, and competent, so that makes sense. "Well, you'd admire the heck out of my mom then. She steamrolls anything that impedes her progress. Trig had to strike out on his own in a big way, or he'd have been sucked into her orbit and never broken free. He called me. He could have asked for permission to invest trust funds, but Mom manages those."

Rob nods. "She'd be unlikely to release money to enable him to head out on his own."

"She's not a monster, but she likes to guide us. She thought that Trig fumbling around on his own, in her words, was a disaster waiting to happen."

"You told him to try it anyway?"

"I did. Trig has been a mathematical savant since birth, I think. He sees patterns you and I would never spot."

"But you two work together right? If he does the numbers, what do you do?"

"Trig's not as good at seeing how things connect when more than math is involved. That's my strength, though we didn't know it yet."

"So if you didn't know it yet, that's not why he called either."

"Nope," I say. "He's older than me, so I was just starting college when he decided to strike out on his own. He had a pretty big ask."

Rob's eyebrows go up. "Wait, so, did you actually go to college?"

"I did. He didn't want me to come on full time, not yet anyway. He proposed that he and I sell a house Mom and Dad had just given us. An amazing house, a beachfront home in Hawaii. We loved that house. It was, hands down, the best present either of us had ever gotten."

"And you did it?"

I nod. "It was a no brainer. My brother, whom I idolized, needed me to help fund his new enterprise. We'd be fifty-fifty partners, and I'd only be nominally involved. He said he'd send me the paperwork to review whenever I wanted, but he didn't expect me to do anything else unless I asked."

"When did you get more involved?" Rob asks.

I shake my head. "I was at Vanderbilt when Trig started, a starry eyed freshman. I was skiing every day." I suppress the pang of regret and continue on. "I spent every moment I wasn't studying or dating on the slopes."

"I bet you went on a lot of dates."

I giggle. "I did. So many dates with so many spoiled, entitled brats."

"Which means I'm not your typical date."

I shake my head. No one is my typical date, not anymore.

"And now you're heavily involved in Nometry, connecting the dots for your brother."

I tilt my head. "I am heavily involved now, yes." Because it was the only thing I had to do.

"Trig's glad you're involved. He talks about you constantly."

Luckily our food arrives to cover my embarrassment at knowing Trig talks about me to strangers. And even luckier, it looks as amazing as Rob said it would. Rob must notice that I'm eyeing his steaming bowl of ramen, because he catches the waitress's eye. "Can you bring an extra bowl so we can split this? I think my stunning date would like a little, but I can't very well have her hogging the whole thing." He holds his hand up and mock whispers the last part. "I hear she's a bit of an overeater."

"Thanks for keeping that under wraps for me," I say. "But for the record, it's polite not to draw attention to it."

Rob's grin at my dumb copycat joke melts my insides into a gooey mess. I focus on eating a few rolls, and I'm happy to find he's right. Their sushi might not put New York sushi to shame, but for the South, it's pretty impressive.

"You never finished the story," Rob complains. "How

did you end up running the whole company while Trig goofs off and flits around in a jet all the time?"

I shake my head. "Oh it's a far cry from that. Trig still does the heavy lifting."

"That's not what Trig says. He told me he's able to move out to Atlanta because his sister runs Nometry almost entirely alone. He says you turned Nometry into a well-oiled machine."

It's always nice to hear good things someone says about me, but that's a little overstated. "I followed along during college with what our company was doing, but I largely let Trig handle things. Shortly after I graduated, we were driving home and. . ."

"Trig told Geo it's his fault you broke your back."

I swallow hard. "It wasn't, not at all. He harped on me every day of our lives, from the time I was little. I used to claw my arms out of my car seat. And once I was old enough, I'd unclick my seatbelt the first chance I got. It was an ongoing battle between me and everyone I rode in a car with, practically. I was that stupid."

Rob's eyes fill with sadness. "You weren't buckled?"

I shake my head. "Trig came through the whole thing completely fine. He told me to buckle. He badgered me, actually, but I ignored him. I've always been small, so seat belts hit me in a weird place and that was my excuse not to use them. He didn't force me to wear it that day, the day of the accident, and I went through the windshield."

Rob closes his eyes and compresses his lips.

This I'm familiar with, other people's pity. "Trig blames himself when clearly it's not his fault. But after that, I sort of gave up."

"On what?" Rob's eyes open and when I meet them, they burn into mine.

"On everything, other than Nometry."

He doesn't look surprised. It's like he understands. He can't possibly, but it feels almost like he does anyway.

"That's when you started oiling the machine for him?" he asks.

I nod. "We found out that I have a knack for sniffing out deals where the math doesn't reflect the whole story. Deals other people ruled out when they shouldn't have. Trig was already doing really well, and he gets people. He sees patterns but sometimes he misses the bigger patterns. The entire market."

"Which is what you see."

I shrug. "He started with Luke and Paul's company. You've met them, I assume?"

Rob groans. "Geo and Trig make me come to game nights. They invite all their friends, and they don't have very many. It's pitiful, really, that I get stuck going."

I chuckle. "Oh, the horror. Monopoly and Yahtzee and charades, oh my."

"Yep, Lions and Tigers and Bears." He chuckles. "I stink at charades, so I know they're desperate to keep inviting me. I didn't realize Trig bankrolled their company, though. That's kind of cool."

"I told you Trig has a good eye for stuff. He did way before I came along."

"I'm still not clear on what exactly do you do. I mean, how do you find these miraculous companies?"

"It's less about finding the companies, and more about seeing what holes exist in the market," I say. "Wait." I pin him with a severe look. "Are you prying to get me to divulge trade secrets right now? Are you some kind of corporate spy playing a long game?"

Rob splutters. "What? Not at all."

I smile. "Gotcha."

He leans back in his chair and crosses his arms. I lose my train of thought entirely.

"You aren't going to tell me?" he asks.

Right. I was supposed to say how I find the groups we invest in. "Basically I read every market magazine I can, as well as lots of others. Vogue, People, anything that shows me what consumers are thinking about, and what's trending."

Rob frowns. "How does reading gossip magazines help you?"

"Economists frequently overlook the importance of pop culture. If you keep your ear to the ground, you can figure out when a train is coming. It's as important as economic news, knowing what people *want* in life. Trig loves puzzles, but I kind of step back a level from that. I look at the puzzle of the world and try and figure out things that are lacking, or things that people might love if only they were available. Then I try and figure out what's available."

"Like what?" he asks.

"Okay, for instance, a few years ago I realized that wires that connected runners to their tech bothered active people. I pushed Trig to bankroll one of the first wireless earbud companies. The numbers didn't add up, but I knew there was a need in the market. We turned the economics around, which is sort of our specialty, and then we sold that wireless tech to Apple for a bundle."

"So you're a prophetess," Rob says.

I roll my eyes. "Nothing that dramatic, and sometimes my ideas don't pan out."

"Then you're like a human eight ball, only, one that usually works instead of never."

"A what?"

"Oh come on, tell me you had one of those. It was a little toy that told you what to do."

I nod. "Mine gave me the worst advice in the world."

"Really?" Rob mutters under his breath. "That's not promising. My eight ball is what told me to ask you out earlier. Maybe this wasn't such a good idea after all."

"Thankfully for you, we're nearly done eating," I say, too much truth clinging to my words for comfort. "Which means the ramifications of that bad advice are nearly concluded."

"Wait, you're not even going to consider hanging out with me afterward?" Rob glances at his watch. "It's only six-forty. You can't end a first date before the nursing homes tuck in their residents. Think what that would do to my male ego."

I pick up my phone and wave it at him. "Trig knows I'm here. He ordered me to come over to his place as soon as dinner's done."

"He knows you're here... with me?" Rob's lips twist with what I'm guessing is humor.

"He does. Why?"

He shrugs. "No reason other than he's maybe not my biggest fan. I wonder how he reacted to me taking you out."

"Oh you don't need to worry about that. I told him it was to smooth over me yelling at you. He knows it's not a real date."

Rob leans toward me, shifting plates aside to put his forearms down on the table. "Oh, this is a real date alright, as real a date as I've ever had. You disagree?"

My heart races and my right hand shakes under the table. "No, I mean yes. I know you asked me out because you thought you needed to, since I'm Trig's sister."

Rob leans closer still. I notice his eyes are sky blue, and his hair really is perfect, even up close. "I shouldn't have asked you out, *because* you're Trig's sister. I did it anyway.

You dazzle me, Brekka. You brightened my abysmal office in the same way that you improved my entire evening. You should believe me when I tell you that I hope you'll come with me to my appointment at seven."

No one has ever said that I dazzle them, not once. Not even when I was at the top of my game. Not when I was the best skier in America.

"What exactly is this mystery appointment?"

"What would you want to do?" Rob asks. "What might convince you to come with me?"

"Do you not really have anything else planned?" I ask. "Because you could just admit that."

He shakes his head. "I do have plans, unfortunately, but I may need ideas of things you'd say yes to in the future."

"Tell me your plans," I say. "And I'll let you know whether I'm interested. But if I go, you'll have to help me explain why I'm not headed directly to Trig's house."

He holds out his hand. "I can handle Mr. Crabby. Give me your phone."

I laugh. "Absolutely not. What would you say, though?"

"I'd tell him you're too busy swooning over Rob's body to make it over to his place tonight. Then I'd wish I had some kind of camera on location to watch the aneurism burst in his brain."

I roll my eyes. "Out with it. What are you doing next? Fertilizing your urban garden share? Running a poker match? Meeting for a back alley drug deal?"

"Do I look like a back alley kind of guy?" he asks. "If I had to move some cocaine, I'd at least set up the swap at a country club or in a nice restaurant. Give me a little credit."

"Spit it out, goofball."

"Fine, so there's kind of a story behind tonight."

"Okay," I say. "Hit me with it."

"I'm guessing you broke something below T7 in your

accident, based on what I've observed of your mobility level."

"Excuse me," I say. "What in the world—"

"Don't get upset," he says. "The thing is, I know a little bit about spinal cord injuries. See, I broke T3 overseas, as an active duty Marine. The doctors told me it was a complete break."

My brain scrambles to process his words. This tall, strong man in front of me broke his spine?

֍ 4 ֍

ROB

"**I** don't talk about it much," I say.

The waitress approaches. "Would either of you like dessert?"

Sometimes the restaurant industry professionals have such bad timing it feels intentional. "We'll have one of everything," I say. "Thanks."

"One of everything?" Brekka asks.

"I didn't want to deal with her," I confess. "Plus, this way you have to stay for a little longer, and you can make sure you get something you like."

She grins. "Plus my aforementioned overeating problem."

"Right, that too." I've never seen anyone who looked less like an overeater in my entire life. Brekka can't weigh more than a hundred pounds. "But getting back to my point. I was in a Humvee with my best friend a few years ago in Syria. We were attacked and thrown from the vehicle. I was stuck under debris, which is why the rebels didn't kill me. My broken back saved my life."

"You seem. . . healthy."

"That's the most unfair part of all this, isn't it? My fracture turned out to be an incomplete break, and over the course of several months and four major surgeries, I regained function, more and more. The metal they shoved into my spine to stabilize it allowed the bones to refuse, and now." I spread my arms out. "I'm cleared to do most anything except contact sports."

"Whereas I'm stuck in this chair."

He nods. "It's entirely unfair, and I'm sorry."

"What does that have to do with tonight?" Brekka's voice sounds wobbly, but maybe I'm imagining that.

"I joined a group in the hospital and kept going during recovery. When I moved back to Atlanta, I found a group here. Most of the people in those groups didn't recover, or at least, not like I did."

She closes her eyes.

"My friend Clive suffered a complete break of T7. He can't afford a nice place on his pension, and now he can't even cook in his own kitchen without difficulty."

"The counters are too high."

I nod. "He saved for years before he could buy a place. I'm redoing his kitchen cabinets so he can use them. I'm nearly done, if that helps. I told him I'd go every single Friday night until it's finished."

"Okay, I'll do that," she says. "If you think there will be anything for me to do."

"I think I can find something to keep you busy, but there's something else."

"What?"

"You have to promise me something, and I'm serious about this. No matter how tempted you are, you won't ever date Clive."

Brekka blushes. It's cuter than a baby giraffe taking its first steps. "I think I can promise you that."

"Because I happen to know that he has dreamy chocolate brown eyes, and I don't think I could handle watching you flirting with him. Not in front of me."

She blushes again and I grin.

Our waitress brings us a tray full of dessert and sets the check on the corner of the table. I hand her a credit card, but Brekka objects.

"I don't mind paying," she says.

"No, I insist. I always pay when I take a girl on a date. Call me old fashioned."

I try the cheesecake, the apple pie, and the chocolate cake. "I think the cheesecake is the best. What about you?"

Brekka won't meet my eye, and she hasn't tried a bite. She's clearly uneasy about something.

"You can pay next time if it's that big of a deal."

"No, it's fine." She doesn't even make a joke about how there won't be a next time since she lives in Colorado. I'd take that as promising if she didn't look like she was about to vomit up all the sushi she just ate.

"Hey, are you okay?"

"No, I'm fine," she says. "But I may need to go to the restroom."

"Are you sick?" I ask it bluntly this time.

"Just text me the address, and I'll meet you at Clive's."

"I'm happy to give you a ride. Unless you're worried about your rental car."

She shakes her head. "It's sweet you think I might have a rental car. I have some sensation in my feet, but I can't use them to drive. Or really to do anything."

I smack my head. I can be a real idiot. "Duh, you said you had a driver. Sorry." Because she's a gazillionaire, so of course she has a driver. "Or you can send him home, and I'll take you over and then drop you at Trig's. I know exactly where his house is, you know."

"I think I'll keep my driver," she says.

"Why?" I ask.

"You don't let things go, do you?" Brekka glares up at me.

"Not until I know the reason I should let it go."

"I don't transport gracefully in cars I'm unaccustomed to using."

"I can help," I say. "I'm happy to do whatever you need."

She shakes her head. "I don't want help."

Ah, she's embarrassed.

"I'll meet you there," I say. "But you should know, I think you're amazing, whether you're transferring to a car, or wheeling from one place to the next, or sitting and stuffing huge sushi rolls in your mouth."

She doesn't blush this time. She still won't even meet my eyes. I text her the address.

"I'll see you in a bit."

She nods.

I walk alongside her on the way out the door, but I don't try to push her, or open her door. I've learned the hard way around friends in my group. Gallantry isn't appreciated unless you've gotten close enough they trust your motivation and don't mind feeling indebted to you.

The tightness in Brekka's shoulders has eased a bit by the time we reach the parking lot. "I'll head for my car. Text or call if you need anything."

She nods and I walk across the parking lot toward my truck.

"Wait," Brekka calls out.

When I turn around, she's already wheeling toward me. "Is that your truck?"

I glance at my cherry red 1951 Chevrolet truck. "It is."

"I figured you'd drive a Honda."

I shrug. "I like classics. I told you I'm old fashioned. What can I say?"

"It's beautiful."

"Thanks."

"Maybe ... maybe you can give me a ride."

I hide my smile. I don't offer to help her disassemble her wheelchair, but she hands me the pieces one at a time so I can stow the wheels behind the seat and the body in the truck bed.

"What's your wheelchair made of?"

"Gladys is made of titanium," she says.

"I adore that name."

"She's a tough one, Gladys is." Brekka smiles. "A lot of the high end chairs are titanium, but Trig had her specially made to fit my smaller frame. It makes her easier for me to manage."

"I bet. The whole thing's so narrow she might fit behind my seat, almost."

"Fifteen inches," she says. "Eighteen is standard, and sixteen is the typical narrow option. Gladys fits into even tight places, and she stows easier."

"I can see that. Clive's going to be so jealous."

She smirks. "I bet. You know how we paraplegics get about our wheelchairs."

I shake my head. "I guess I'm about to find out."

Thankfully, Debbie starts up on the first try. She runs great usually, but if she's going to throw a tantrum, it's always when I have a guest I want to impress.

"What got you into old cars?" Brekka asks.

I shake my head. "Not sure, but Mom says I turned my head to watch them every time one drove by starting when I was like three years old."

"That's adorable. Does your dad love them?"

My belly laugh startles her. "He hates Little Debbie."

"You named her after a cupcake?"

"Mom wouldn't let us eat them growing up. Dad wouldn't let me get an old car and work on it. The name just made sense for some reason. I'm an adult, so I can do all the things no one wants me to do."

"You're a rebel alright."

"I sense your sarcasm, lady, and I don't appreciate it. Neither does Little Debbie."

"Well, I'd hate to upset a cream-filled treat like her. What other things have you done your parents don't like?"

I scratch my jaw. "Dad wasn't giddy when I enlisted. And I'm not married yet and making bratty grandkids for my parents to spoil."

"You don't like kids?" she asks.

I shrug. "I like them as much as anyone, I guess. My sister has two now, and they're both really cute. I'm glad I'm not getting up in the middle of the night with them, but that's kind of part of the deal, right?"

"Do you ever want any of your own?"

"Yeah, if I ever meet a woman I want to replicate." I wink at her. "My sisters are like miniature versions of my mom, from their Kate Spade bags down to their sassy backtalk."

"You sound like you love them."

"My family squabbles like any family does, but yeah. I love all of them. They're different and the same in the perfect proportions. I kind of think that's what family is all about. Being similar enough we have common ground, but different enough that we're interesting to spend time with."

"How old are they?"

"I'm the oldest by seven years. Mom and Dad didn't think they'd have any more. Then they had twins. Surprise!"

"I bet they were excited."

"I was too, until the crying started anyway." I make my

zombie grimace face. "Suddenly I did all the dishes, took out the trash, cleaned the bathroom and kitchen counters and packed my own lunch. I went from a pampered only child to an indentured servant overnight."

"Did you resent it?" Brekka taps her fingers on the doorframe and I can't help noticing how delicate they are. Her nails aren't long like a witch's, but they're long enough, and they're painted pale pink. Her hands are utterly feminine.

I draw a ragged breath and focus on her question. "I didn't resent it, no. I knew my parents wanted more kids, and I was kind of lonely if I'm being honest. Most of my friends had siblings. They complained about how awful they were, but I wanted anyone to play with, even if it was a girl who dressed me up for tea parties."

Brekka laughs. "Did they really?"

I shake my head. "Nah, but they did follow me around unbearably, insisting I play basketball with them. They were horrible and exhausting and irritating for a really long time."

"I kind of feel bad for my brother now. That sounds tiring."

"I loved every second. And then, when my parents brought Beth home, our house finally felt right, like we had everyone who had been missing. Does that sound crazy?"

Brekka's eyes fall. "I wonder if anyone at my house cared whether we were a complete family or not. By the time I was born, my mom and dad barely talked to each other most days. I do feel sorry for you, for being an only child for so long, I mean. Trig never seemed annoyed about me following him around, which was lucky for me."

"You're younger?"

She nods. "Almost five years, but only four years in school."

"He taught you basketball?"

She shakes her head. "No, I never even tried playing basketball, but he took me skiing for the first time. That one time was all it took."

"Right, I should have known. You're from Colorado."

She turns to face the window again, and I wish I knew what she was thinking.

"Until today, I never once wondered whether Trig was upset about having a little sister. He never acted anything but happy, as far back as I can recall."

"That's because he's a smart guy."

"I thought you two didn't get along."

"Ever seen two magnets?" I ask. "Opposites attract."

"And two similarly charged magnets repel."

"Something like that. I already respect Trig, and I'm sure with time I'll like him well enough."

We pull up in front of Clive's house and I glance at Brekka to see how she reacts. Clive's pension wasn't enough to pay for much. Not everyone was as lucky as me, coming home to a supportive family with means. His father beat him regularly enough that he knew how to take a punch like a pro when we met. He enlisted to escape, which meant he had no safety net when a land mine took out his spine and his future.

"I helped him find this place. It's got two bedrooms and it's close to his job."

"What does he do?" Brekka asks.

"He teaches P.E. at Moorhouse Elementary."

Brekka laughs uncomfortably.

I touch her arm lightly. "I'm not kidding. He teaches P.E. He was a football star in high school not far from here, and he had a lot of friends. The school is pretty good at accommodating him when necessary, but he's got a real way with the kids. They adore him."

Brekka doesn't reply, but she bobs her head and opens her door.

Clive's waiting in an open doorway when we reach his house. Brekka rolls up the ramp and toward Clive like she isn't worried at all that the tiny house with the bowed wood-siding will be below her standards.

"That's an amazing ramp up to your front door," Brekka says.

"Rob made it for me as a housewarming present." Clive smiles warmly at Brekka and then turns to me. "You didn't warn me you were bringing a gorgeous lady with you. My mom taught me not to poach, but I'd have showered, at least."

I roll my eyes. I wasn't kidding earlier. The ladies love Clive's dreamy brown eyes, and he's got at least a PhD in flirting. Part of me didn't want to bring Brekka, but if she's going to dump me for Clive, she may as well do it right away. It'll hurt less.

"Wait, did you really?" Brekka asks. At first I can't figure out what she's asking, but then I notice she's still staring at the ramp.

"Sure, I like to work with my hands."

She cocks an eyebrow at me. "I thought you managed your family's car dealerships."

"My boy Rob is a modern day Renaissance man. Brilliant mind, and a genius with his hands. Did he tell you he restored that gorgeous truck himself?"

"He did not." Brekka eyes me sideways. "But he should have."

"Oh, please. Clive's just being kind. I knew nothing about cars, and we restored that one together. He worked at a mechanic's shop through all of high school. He taught me everything I know."

"How about I admit that I'm now impressed with you

both," Brekka says. "The handiest thing my dad's ever done is use talk-to-text on his phone to call for repairs. I can't even add oil to my own cars. I have no idea where it would even go."

I smile. "Surely Trig's a little more capable than you and your dad."

"Not hardly," Brekka says. "He called his assistant last week to change a lightbulb. At his house."

I store that little tidbit for later. "Did I mention Brekka is Trig's fabulously wealthy little sister?" I ask Clive. "She's the one he chucked his entire family trust at when he decided to take his vow of poverty for Geo."

"Which means you're what? A multibillionaire?" Clive's eyes widen alarmingly. "I had no idea or I'd have been sure to order extra caviar when I sent my manservant to the market."

Brekka rolls her eyes. "Hilarious. You two are so funny."

"Wait, so you aren't really rich?" Clive asks. "Because that's one of my happiest fantasies. That I'll meet and utterly charm Trig's little sister. And now that we've met and I see how beautiful you are, it's my very happiest fantasy."

"Oh please. But the rich part is true enough. Tales of my wealth have been downplayed, really. I exclusively sit on solid gold toilets, and brush my teeth with unicorn hair imported from Narnia. But I hate caviar. It's too fishy for me."

"You brought her to my house with no notice, why again?" Clive asks.

"She couldn't bear to be parted from me," I say. "And I promised to come work here, so here I am."

"Better get started then." Clive wheels his way through the family room and into his modest kitchen. He's already laid out the tools I need to install the remaining cabinet box.

"If you two want to start putting the hardware on the doors and drawers," I say, "I'll be ready to mount the fronts on the boxes shortly."

Clive shows Brekka how to screw the hinges in and lets her use the electric screwdriver. She picks it up quickly. She makes a worthy assistant, and she never once complains. By the time we finish, there's sawdust in her hair and a streak of dust on her cheek, but somehow, even with all that, she's more dazzling than the first time I saw her. I wish this date never had to end, but thanks to Trig and Geo, I've got to get up early tomorrow morning. Way too early.

Once she's in the truck, her wheelchair stowed away, I reluctantly put the car into gear to head for Trig's house. I want to ask whether she had fun, but I know this is probably the worst date she's ever been on. Sushi, hours from any coast, at a chain restaurant, followed by manual labor in a small house for someone she doesn't know.

"Hey, thanks for convincing me to go with you to Clive's house," she says. "I've never spent much time talking to other people who have been through something like that."

I nod, afraid to push.

"He's a really good guy."

"Not too good though, right? Because you promised you wouldn't fall for him," I remind her.

She giggles. "No, not that good. Plus, you'd think his arms might be a little more ripped, what with all the time he spends wheeling around."

"Oh, you can make those jokes, but I can't, huh?"

"After watching what you're doing in there, I think you get a pass on poking fun at wheelchair users like me."

"What, redoing some cabinets for a dear friend?" I ask. "I don't think that entitles me to much."

She shakes her head. "I've never really thought about what life would be like for me right now if I didn't have so much money to smooth the way."

A private jet, a hired driver the very second she wants one. The world is her platinum-dipped, diamond-encrusted oyster. But how would she realize that, from inside the shell?

"I wonder how many people who use wheelchairs don't have the resources to modify their homes, or buy the right equipment."

"A lot," I say. "And it's not a sexy cause like AIDS or PETA."

She barks a laugh. "How are AIDS and PETA sexy?"

"I'm just saying, you don't see a bunch of movie stars pushing for disabled people. After all, most wheelchair users are stable, which means they're 'fine.' It's just their entire quality of life that's at stake."

I wish I could do more for Clive and people like him. One day, maybe I'll have the chance. But it's good enough for now to know that Brekka had a decent time at least, and that Clive's cabinets are essentially done.

BREKKA

I didn't think I'd enjoy building cabinets, but I was wrong. This turned out to be the best date of my life, which doesn't sound very impressive since I haven't been out with anyone in years and years. But it's so much better than any of the ones I remember before, and I used to do far more exciting things. Maybe it really is about the person you're with, not the things you do.

Or maybe I liked helping someone instead of letting other people wait on me for a change. Either way, I'm a little disappointed when Rob starts Little Debbie and heads, I assume, toward Trig's house to drop me off.

"How long are you staying in town?" Rob asks.

"I'll probably leave tomorrow."

He clucks. "That's too bad. I'd love to see you again. If you could stay longer, maybe we could do something Sunday?"

Wait, Sunday? If he wants to see me again, why not Saturday? "What's going on tomorrow? Big day at the dealerships?"

"Trig didn't tell you?" His brow furrows.

I pull my phone out of my purse and realize I've gotten six texts and two phone calls from my brother. "I haven't exactly been chatting with him the past few hours."

Two hours ago Trig texted, WHERE ARE YOU?

Then, ARE YOU COMING?

An hour ago. ARE YOU STILL AT DINNER?

Right after that, he texted, I'M GOING TO KILL ROB. I KNEW HE WAS A PERVERT. WHY AREN'T YOU RESPONDING TO ME??

Ten minutes ago. I'M CALLING THE POLICE IF YOU DON'T TEXT ME BACK IN FIVE MINUTES.

Five minutes ago. I'M DRIVING OVER TO HIS HOUSE AGAIN AND THIS TIME I'M GOING TO KILL HIM.

I laugh. "Trig may or may not be at your place right now, depending."

Rob lifts one eyebrow, pretty unconcerned. "Depending on what?"

"On how far you live from him, and whether he actually called the police."

He chuckles. "I'm around the corner. Which means he's probably already there. So he told you we have plans early tomorrow?"

"Wait, what are you doing?"

Rob turns a corner and I see an agitated Trig in a tuxedo peering into the front window of a small, old, farm-style home, sitting on an enormous lot. The fence encloses an acre at least.

"I'm surprised none of your neighbors called the cops."

Rob grins. "We kind of keep to ourselves. I doubt any of them even noticed. You've heard of neighborhood watch? We feature the 'neighborhood mind your own business club.' We'd meet periodically, but then we'd have to, you know, communicate with each other and that's against our bylaws."

"Cute."

He pulls into the driveway and puts his classic car in neutral, right next to Trig's Vantage. They couldn't be more different. I think about Rob comparing himself and my brother to similarly charged magnets and I wonder about the wisdom of the comparison.

Rob rolls down his window, cranking it one spin at a time. "Hey, Trig! Your sister's whole and hale and completely safe. I was headed for your house when she realized you'd gone full-on creeper and redirected me here."

Trig's frown consumes his entire face as he looks past Rob toward me. "Where have you been?"

"Where have *you* been?" I eye his tux.

"The Berkman party, I'd guess," Rob says. "Geo's been frantically working on last minute details all week."

"Yep, I left her party to meet you at home, but then you never showed."

"And you never changed? Too busy wringing your hands as you waited by the phone?" Rob's trying to suppress his smile, but he's not succeeding very well. "Or are those your pajamas? I will never understand the mega-wealthy and their obsession with penguin suits."

Trig's eye twitches. "I was waiting to change until I found out whether Brekka wanted to hang out with me at home, or borrow something from Geo and go to the party. Pardon me for being comfortable in clothes that look amazing."

"It's more the disconnect between the tux and the crawling through shrubbery to peep into my window that's entertaining me the most," Rob says. "Find anything interesting? I think my next cabal meeting isn't for almost two weeks, but my fridge full of human body parts is always stocked."

I cover my mouth to keep from laughing out loud.

"You can make all the jokes you want, but you took my sister to dinner, and three hours later I still haven't heard word one from her." Trig shoves his hands in his pockets casually, but he must be melting to death. It's far too hot for him to be comfortable outside in all those layers.

Rob sighs dramatically. "We went to my buddy's house to work on his cabinets. I'm sorry I didn't call and check in with you first. Since Brekka's potty-trained, I didn't realize I needed to. But if I'd thought about it, I'd have made sure she checked her phone and made sure you knew she wasn't headed back yet. I really am sorry it was stressful for you. Also, I had no way of knowing Brekka wasn't paying attention to her phone. Mine was in my pocket all night. Maybe call *me* next time before driving all the way over to throttle me."

"Sound advice, as always." Trig circles the truck and opens my door.

I grab one of my wheels from behind the seat and hold it out to him. He takes it, grabs the other too, and starts back around his truck toward the Vantage.

"Uh, hello?" I ask.

Trig stops and turns toward me. "You don't need to assemble the entire chair just to wheel over to my car, right?" Trig glances at Gladys' frame where it rests in the truck bed. "It's like ten feet."

"I guess not." But I need to get to Trig's car, and I'd rather not look ridiculous. Now he either has to carry me like a baby, or I have to act like a baby about him not carrying me.

Before I can object or even think about it, Rob leans down and slides me across his bench seat toward the

Vantage. Then he picks me up smoothly, his breath against my cheek, his voice deep and soft. "Here, I'll help you."

I definitely don't feel like a child, not in his arms.

"I could have done that," Trig complains. But he opens his passenger side door for Rob to set me on the smooth, black leather seat. I hope my wheelchair fits in the trunk. It's probably rude that I haven't come out to Atlanta before this to see Trig's new house, but he hasn't been here that long, and his house isn't exactly accessible, much less his car.

"Thanks," I whisper in Rob's ear. In spite of my own better judgment, I realize that I do want to see him tomorrow. "Hey, what's going on in the morning? Trig never told me anything."

Rob sets me gently in the seat, his hands brushing my lower back and the undersides of my knees as he retreats. The look on his face prepares me for something I won't like. "Tomorrow I'm going on a double date with Trig and Geo."

Except it's not bad. Not at all.

I smile. "You are? So was this whole thing, like, a joke? You've been texting Trig all night to set it up, or something?"

"Yeah, it turns out I forgot about that," Trig says. "Geo's a little annoyed at me, since she never forgets anything. We have been trying to convince Rob and Paisley to go on a date for weeks and Rob finally asked her. We're supposed to go hiking to see the sun rise. Early." Trig groans.

Hiking. Rob's going hiking with Geo's best friend, the one she keeps telling me I'll love. The one who's bubbly, and funny, and smart, and kind, and beautiful. And she hikes, clearly, which is something I will never, ever do again.

"I'm sorry Brekka," Trig says, "but you can totally come along."

Rob nods his head. "There's even a gondola that you can take—"

"It's fine," I say. "I actually completely forgot about a meeting I set up with Mom for brunch Sunday to go over trust stuff, so I need to get back immediately anyway."

"You do? For sure?" Rob asks. "I was going to try and convince you to stick around. In fact, we've got some amazing brunch spots in Atlanta. We could Skype your mom in or something."

"Uh, trust me, you don't want that," Trig says. "No faster way to ruin a meal than inviting dear old Mom along."

"She can't be that bad," Rob says.

Trig's laugh is genuine and hearty. "Said like someone who has never met Mother."

"Guilty."

"Let's hope for your sake it stays that way. I'll have Geo text you a photo so you can avoid her at the wedding."

"She did raise two amazing children. She's got to have some redeeming qualities," Rob says.

Trig pins Rob with a look. "Have you been possessed by an alien? Are you complimenting me? Because I want to know where the real Rob went."

Rob rolls his eyes. "Drive safely."

Trig flinches and Rob closes his eyes. Lots of land mines to avoid around my family, poor guy. "Thanks for dinner, Rob. I'm glad I'll know at least one of Geo's friends at the wedding."

I lean forward and close the door. Which would have been an awesome move, except the frame for my wheelchair's still in Rob's car. When Trig circles around and climbs into the driver's seat, I ask, "Uh, would you mind grabbing the rest of Gladys?"

Trig chuckles and climbs back out. Rob's already jogged

over to help him load the pieces into the tiny trunk. With a little finagling, she fits. Thank goodness.

"Thanks again," I say loud enough that it permeates the glass. "Have fun tomorrow."

Rob frowns and I hate seeing it, but there's no point in even trying to explain. It's not like he and I are a good match. He might understand what I've been through, but I won't sentence him to a life of titanium wheels and access ramps. Helping a buddy on the weekend is very different than staring down the barrel of a life full of accommodations and hike-less Saturdays.

"You could bring Brekka tomorrow," I hear Rob say to Trig. "Or we can cancel the whole thing. I've known Paisley for years. It's not like—"

I want to know what he'd have said next, but Trig cuts him off. "Of course we could. Easy for you to say, as you wouldn't have to deal with the wrath of Geo. We are not cancelling tomorrow. She's going on about this like it's Christmas and the Fourth of July all rolled up and stuffed into an Easter egg." Trig drops his voice, but I can still hear him. "She's even talking about how great it would be to have a *joint* wedding."

Rob rolls his eyes. "Oh please. Geo will get over it."

Trig shakes his head. "Trust me, Brekka doesn't care. She was probably being polite, but she didn't want to stick around anyway. I can't believe she came out at all. She loves being at home. Traveling's such a pain for her."

I close my eyes. Trig loves me. I came out here for him. He has supported me in every single way.

He's still an idiot.

I tap on the glass. "Let's go."

"Sorry," Rob says loudly. "I hope to see you again soon. I had a great time at dinner."

I can't look him in the eye. He'd see how upset I am to leave. I bob my head instead.

Trig slides into the seat and his car roars to life.

"Hey do you have a name for your car?" I ask.

"Yeah," he says. "It's a Vantage."

"No, I don't mean the make. I mean like Fred. Or Tony the Tiger, or something like that."

Trig's face scrunches. "It's not orange or striped. Are you feeling okay?"

"Yes, never mind. I was just kidding." Rob and Trig aren't even in the same state, let alone similar enough to be magnetically repellent. Rob's just wrong about that.

"But seriously, are you okay? You're acting super odd."

"I'm fine."

Trig glances my way sharply. "Now I know something's wrong. People who are fine don't say they're fine. You flew all the way out here with not a word to me. I've asked you to come out here every weekend since March. It's the end of May. What's going on?"

I cross my arms. "Why have you been badgering Rob to ask Paisley out on a date?"

"I'm sorry, what?"

"Did I not enunciate properly?"

"Where is that coming from?"

"You said you and Geo have been trying to set Rob and Paisley up for weeks."

Trig shakes his head. "Rob has known Paisley a long time. Rob is Geo's oldest friend, and Paisley's her best friend from college."

"Yes, thank you. I know how they're acquainted. I'm asking why you were pushing him to date her."

"I don't know, maybe because Paisley's hilarious, smart, and really cute."

"Then why don't you marry her?" I cringe at the

singsong tone I used out of habit. Ugh. I need to refocus. "Why *Rob?*" I ask. "Why are you trying to get him specifically to ask her out?"

"Oh. Well, Geo thinks he's amazing I guess. He's tall and decent to look at. He has an okay job, and if I'm forced to say it, he's a pretty good guy I suppose."

"He's an inch away from sainthood. We spent the evening helping his war veteran friend by building him new, accessible cabinets. Did you know he does that every Friday? That's how he spends his free time."

Trig rolls his eyes. "If you go for that do-gooder thing, then yeah he's fantastic. He loves that kind of crap. He'd be better off writing a check and letting manual laborers do it. The quality would be better, and it would get done faster, but he likes the praise I think."

I don't say a word.

"Fine, fine, it's nice of him. And yes, he also volunteers at a local soup kitchen. He and Geo go twice a month. He loves that feel good kind of in-your-face charity."

"The point is that you like Rob. You find him acceptably impressive and big hearted."

"Sure." Trig huffs. "He makes me feel bad about myself, but yes, I like him. Why are you asking?"

"Because," I say. "You've asked me to come visit you a hundred times, right?"

He shrugs. "Maybe."

"And not once have you tried to set me up with Rob. You've never even mentioned it as a possibility."

"Uh, news flash. You live in Colorado."

"So did you," I say. "And people move."

"Wait, I'm in trouble because I didn't try to set you up with Geo's loser buddy who fawned over her for years? Are you serious right now?"

I close my eyes and lean my head against the window. If

I'm honest, I'm mostly upset that he hasn't tried to set me up since the accident. Not with Rob, not with anyone. He doesn't think I'm a great match, not anymore. He'd rather pressure Rob to take out someone he's known for years and could have asked out any time than ask out his own sister.

The worst part is that I agree with Trig.

I wouldn't set me up with anyone either. Still, realizing that stings. And for the first time since my accident, I'm desperate to change my life, no matter the cost.

❧ 6 ☙

ROB

I don't sleep much. I blame Trig's sister, but that's not entirely fair. She didn't make me stay out late. And she didn't mean to make me toss and turn while dreaming of her face, her laugh, and her smile. Either way, the lack of shut-eye leaves me abnormally crabby. I'm not sure who thought it was a good idea to hike Stone Mountain at five a.m., but they were most definitely incorrect.

Paisley's entirely too perky when I climb out of my truck at Geo's house at four-thirty in the morning, yawning. My eyes are still burning, and her neon pink shirt doesn't help. I rub at my face, and when I reopen my eyes, she's waving at me like a lunatic.

"You guys ready?" she chirps.

"I've got my bag of stuff." Geo pats a small backpack. As always, she looks like she just walked off the set for a skin care commercial.

Trig yawns and hooks sunglasses on the neckline of his Polo shirt.

I blink several times. "Actually, I vote we reconvene at ten a.m."

"Cute." Paisley bounds toward me.

"Is it just me, or is her ponytail bouncing like Rainbow Dash in *My Little Ponies*?"

"Dude," Trig says. "You sound ridiculous. From now on, you need to think, 'Would Vin Diesel say this?' before you speak. That might help."

I roll my eyes. "I'm comfortable with how I sound. I've got three sisters, and I watched a lot of *My Little Ponies*. Besides, yesterday a customer told me I look like a short-haired Jason Momoa, so I can pretty much say whatever I want." I flex my chest muscles one at a time and grin at Trig. He hates that I'm ripped. "If you'd hit the gym once or twice a week, you'd look less like Tom Hanks and more like Tom Cruise yourself."

Trig exhales in disgust and climbs into his Range Rover. "Let's go."

"What? No quip, no witty retort?" I say. "What's going on?"

"Geo made him promise," Paisley says.

I turn my head toward her. "Huh?"

She grins mischievously. "Geo made him promise to stop baiting you. I think mocking your comparison of my hair to that of a famous alicorn was borderline. Anything else would be a direct violation."

"You're kidding," I say. "Geo muzzled him? Yanking Trig's chain is the best part of my day. I'm not sure if this will make today better or worse."

Paisley frowns. "Remind me why we're on this date again?"

"Oh, right." I lean toward her and drop my voice to a whisper. "Because we wanted to get them to leave us alone."

She purses her lips. "That's right, I almost forgot. Not that I'm upset this whole thing is a farce. You're way too poor for me to ever date for real."

I toss a hand to my chest. "That hurts, Pais. It hurts me."

She shrugs. "My family has standards. What can I say? Jason Momoa man-boobs aren't on their list, but they do require a certain level of liquidity. If I tried to introduce my parents to you, they'd lose it."

I roll my eyes. Paisley has been joking about her family demanding she marry a billionaire for years. Not that her family standards stopped her from dating every body builder at her gym over the past eight years.

We all climb in with Trig and he drives a little too fast to the park. The hike is fun enough, but by the time we reach the top of Stone Mountain, Geo and Trig have realized it's not a real date for Pais and me.

"Why did you guys even agree to this, if you weren't into it?" Geo asks.

"At first we agreed as a joke, but then you two were so excited about it," Paisley says. "We figured it might shut you up if we pretended it was real for a date or two. I didn't realize Rob would suck so bad at faking it or I'd never have bothered."

I frown at her. "It wasn't my fault they figured us out. I was doing just fine."

"You're treating me like you treat your little sisters. If that's how you act on a date, it's no wonder you're still single." Paisley swats my shoulder before heading back down the mountain.

"Who wanted to hike this early again?" Trig asks with a groan.

"Paisley," Geo and I say at the same time.

"Because I hate hiking," Trig says. "For the record."

"Mr. Outdoor Magazine himself hates hiking?" I ask.

"I like sky diving. I like skiing. I like snowmobiling. I don't hate jogging. Climbing 700 feet in elevation in an hour and a half on your own power is crappy. And that's the nicest way I can think to say it."

I don't hate hiking, but I wouldn't cry if I could never do it again. There are lots of other ways to have fun outdoors that don't involve as many blisters, bugs or sweaty socks. Paisley loves hiking though, and since it was supposed to be a date...

"This gets us out of Kennesaw next month, right?" I ask.

Paisley spins around on her apparently unblistered heel to scowl at me, and then she turns toward Trig and Geo, too. "You guys are a bunch of whiners, and you're ruining this."

"What did I do?" Trig asks. "I was just wondering who set up this delightful excursion."

Geo grabs Trig's hand and yanks him down the trail. "We better jog on ahead, sweetie. Let's give these two love-birds some alone time."

I fall into step next to Paisley. She bumps me with her hip. "What's up today? You aren't usually this crappy at pretending, and those two are so twitterpated they never would have noticed if you'd put forth even a half-hearted effort. Do you find me that detestable?"

I shake my head. "I'm sorry. It's not you at all. It's that I actually met someone yesterday, someone I like. Probably the first person I've liked since. . ."

"Since Geo?" Paisley grins. "That's exciting. You could totally have brought her today, you know. It would have been better than," she gestures between herself and me, "this weirdness."

I almost choke. "I wasn't weird, and I did ask her to come along. She turned me down flat for the second time in one night and went back home."

"Wait." Paisley stops in the center of the trail. "Just wait."

I glance around. "For what? Is the great Paisley actually out of energy? Or did you get a blister?"

She just shakes her head.

"What exactly are we waiting for?"

"Shut up, idiot. You have no sense of dramatic effect whatsoever. I'm stopping to appreciate the lightbulb moment I just had. You said she went back home."

"How does that constitute a lightbulb moment?" I ask.

Paisley's eyes lock on mine like a heat seeking missile. "You met Brekka yesterday, and she lives in Colorado."

I open my mouth and then snap it shut.

"It's Brekka? The girl you like?" Paisley practically squeals in delight.

"Close your mouth. Good grief, what's wrong with you? They aren't *that* far down the road."

"It's a trail not a road, dolt. And yes, they are. They probably ran down to the car and are making out right now." Paisley taps her lip. "I heard she's got an ethereal beauty, delicate like handmade lace, or the trill of a song-bird." She claps. "So, is it true? Is all of it true?"

"Yes, she looks exactly like a bird. Made out of lace. By hand."

Paisley stomps. "You know what I mean."

"She's prettier than Geo."

"You take that back right now, because I know that's a lie. No one is prettier than Geo."

I cross my arms. "She's delicate and understated, and I asked her out over and over and she still left without a backward glance." Because she's way out of my league.

"Well, do you blame her?"

I don't. Paisley's right. I'm not even a college graduate. I start back down the trail, my hands stuffed into my pants pockets. I kick every rock I see. Paisley's hand on my shoulder startles me. "What?"

"You're mad. Why are you mad?"

"I'm not smart, I'm not rich, and a discharged Marine isn't a catch for a gorgeous, genius heiress. That doesn't mean hearing it said out loud by a friend doesn't hurt. I am human."

Paisley's eyes flood with pity and my hands clench at my sides. "No, don't feel sorry for me. The fact that I liked her at all is promising. It's more than I've felt for anyone in a long time."

"You've always loved broken things," Paisley says softly. "It's one of the things I admire about you. You want to fix the world, one broken-winged bird at a time."

"First of all, she's not broken just because she uses a wheelchair." I shake my head. "But secondly, that's not fair."

"Are you sure?" Paisley bites her lip. "You never even loved Geo. You just wanted to fix your friend whose heart had cracked in two."

"I did love her, Pais. I still do, maybe."

Paisley's laugh is high and clear. "If you did, you could not have hiked with Trig and Geo this morning. You'd be watching him every time he touched her. Every time they shared a glance, you'd be boiling inside."

"That guy does bug me."

"Because he's displaced you as her best friend, but there's no passion in it. You enjoy the exchanges with him, which you admitted earlier yourself. If you truly loved Geo, you'd have moved, changed your name and not forwarded your mail."

I stare at her.

"Okay fine, maybe you wouldn't have gone that far, but

you'd be a far sadder sack than you've been. You were more like a little league player denied his token trophy. You wanted to fix her and another guy came along and did what you'd failed to do for four years. But now a new bird has fluttered into your orbit, and if you object to the word broken, how about a lonely bird, and you see your chance to redeem yourself. You want to befriend this one like you couldn't befriend Geo."

I start back down the hill.

"Trig is not going to like this at all, you and his baby sister."

"Oh shut up, Paisley."

To my surprise, she does. Then in another surprise turn, Trig and Geo agree to skip out on the rest of our plans and head home. After all, now that they know the whole date was a farce, there doesn't seem to be much point.

Even without her talking in my ear, Paisley's words ring in my ears. I do like to fix things. I run my hands over the beautiful ash in front of me. It's an absolutely enormous slab of ash, two trees fused together. It's a piece of inosculated ash, which is why I knew the term when I talked to Brekka yesterday. I'd looked it up a week or so before, when my dealer offered me this piece. I jumped at the chance, even though it cost me half my savings for the month.

It's going to make a perfect wedding gift for Trig and Geo, and there will be plenty left for a few more tables afterward. Well worth it. I lose myself in work as long as I can.

"Rob, son. Turn the saw off and come talk to your Dad!"

I can barely make out the words over the headphones I'm wearing. I shut my saw off and yank them away. "Oh, Dad, sorry."

"What are you doing in here?" He gestures around to

my shop. It's twice the square footage of my house, which is exactly what I wanted.

"Why do you care?"

Dad shakes his head. "We barely see you anymore. Your mother misses you."

He can't just say he misses me, because that's not manly enough. I smile. "I've missed you too, Dad."

I pull him in for a hug. "I'll come for dinner tomorrow, okay?"

"What about tonight?"

I sigh. "I need some time for doing this as well. It matters to me."

My dad lifts his eyebrows. "It's a hobby, son, which is fine, but you're letting it take over." He gestures around the enormous shop, and I look at it as he must see it. I've got a thousand square feet of pieces, stacked and stored... for no one. It has taken over all my free time, and even though I have no reason to keep after it, I do. I hide in here when I'm sad, lonely, scared, or angry. I make and make things, like a bee storing honey. I do it for no reason other than it calms me, and I feel compelled to make something.

Dad may actually be right, but I don't have to tell him that. "It's my life and it's my decision how much time and money I spend on anything. I'm not gambling or paying for strippers, or drugs, so you shouldn't criticize."

"Don't get me wrong. It's cute stuff," Dad says. "I've never seen anyone else fire glass on top of furniture. It covers all the cracks really pretty."

I don't groan or correct him. But I can't help explaining my goal one more time. "It's not covering the cracks Dad. It's about highlighting the fact that flaws are what make us beautiful and unique. It's a statement to the world. We shouldn't be ashamed of what makes us who we are, even if we're fragile or different or strange."

"Uh huh. And that's really nice, too. Your mom has her coffee table on display in the formal living room for everybody to see it. Every person who comes over oohs and aahs, but that sort of oohing won't pay the bills. You should spend less time on blowing glass and cutting wood and more time with friends and family." Dad grunts. "At the end of the day son, this wood is never going to love you back."

He's right again. I know it won't love me, but Paisley's wrong. I don't just like Brekka because she's broken. I don't think she's broken at all. She's a work of art. I meet countless broken people every week, people who have given up, people who need major repairs. They ask for special financing, knowing I can't approve it. Or they ask me to forgive inexcusable behavior in the workplace. None of those people, the shattered people I deal with and manage, none of them have appealed to me, not like Brekka did.

I like Brekka because she's unique, not because she needs my help. She doesn't. But if one of the things that helped shape her into the unique beauty I met was her accident, well it's an important part of her story.

I grab my dad's arm and squeeze. "I know I said I was coming to dinner tomorrow, but I think I might not make it. And I'm going to need you to go to auction for me on Monday if things go well enough."

My dad's eyes widen. "Why?"

"You were right. Your advice helped me realize that I need to do something I've been ignoring. We sent a big shipment of cars to Colorado and I never followed up to make sure Nometry was happy with them. Vertical sales are much easier than horizontal, right?"

My dad nods dumbly. "Wait, you're going to Colorado?"

I nod. "Tomorrow night. That way I can go see Trig's sister first thing Monday morning."

"Okay, well, it's refreshing to see you taking an active

interest in big orders. It seems like you've sort of been running things on autopilot lately."

I nod. "You're exactly right, and it's time for that to change in a major way."

❄ 7 ❄

BREKKA

An hour after my plane lands, I'm shocked when Dr. Anthony's name shows up on my caller ID. I didn't think he'd return my call until Monday at the earliest.

"Hello?"

"Is this Brekka Thornton?" a quiet voice asks.

"It is," I say. "Is this Dr. Anthony?"

"I was delighted to get your message," he says. "Your brother has been funding my program for years now."

That explains the speedy call back. He's probably heard that Trig passed his share of the trust to me, and now he's worried I'm cutting off his meal ticket.

"What can I help you with?" he asks. "Are you interested in hearing about any of our recent developments? Many of them have been quite successful."

I swallow the giant lump in my throat and force out the words. "Actually, I am."

He spends the next half hour talking to me about two of their front runner programs. One centers on an exoskeleton of sorts that bypasses the dead portion of the spine, which sounds a little too science fiction to me. In fact, just thinking about an exoskeleton circumventing my spine gives me the willies. The other option he mentions combines scar tissue removal with application of stem cells to stimulate new spinal cord growth and repair. Nerve cells in the spine don't regrow, but it sounds like they've developed a method that tries to do the impossible.

Of course in my experience, things that sound too good to be true generally are.

"How risky is the stem cell procedure?" I ask. "On a scale of one to ten?"

"It's hard to quantify it like that," Dr. Anthony says. "If you're asking whether you might die, that's always a possibility with any procedure, from something as simple as a dermal filler to open heart surgery."

"But obviously the risk of death is dramatically different, and that's certainly quantifiable," I say. I could pull the last ten thousand incidences of dermal filler, and I'd probably find that none of them died. Whereas, I'm sure that's not the case with open heart surgery."

"You're absolutely correct. In this case, the mortality rate is quite low. If we put it into percentages, it's less than a half percent risk of death when you undergo the procedure that combines the stem cell therapy with the scar removal. I know that sounds terrifying, but we have somewhat more complicated patients than your normal dermal filler patient. In spite of the added complexity of our patients' various other medical issues, we are consistently bringing our rates down."

How stellar. Only a one in two hundred chance of never waking up again.

"If you're asking about loss of function, well, that's higher."

"I'm sorry, you're telling me that there's a half a percent

chance I'll *die* if I undergo one of these procedures, but beyond that, instead of gaining function, I might lose it?"

"Any time we test new treatments on patients, we need to make sure that they understand all the possibilities. The procedure may not work at all, as it does not on over half of our patients, and while more than twenty percent of our procedures result in improved sensation and mobility, another twenty percent or so complain of reduced sensation and usage. It can also exacerbate existing deficits in patients such as yourself with incomplete injuries."

Dr. Anthony has just articulated all the reasons I always run the other direction when Trig suggests I look into something like this. I might improve, or I might exacerbate existing deficits, reduce sensation and lower my usage. Translation. I might never feel my toes again, or I might lose the limited amount of function I've got.

"Thanks for the information," I say.

"I'd love to send you more details," he says. "I've got numbers, case information and other hard data. Can I email it to you? We've had some very promising cases lately, and in one case from a month ago, the patient has been restored nearly to full function."

Wait. "Really?"

"Absolutely," Dr. Anthony says. "He suffered an incomplete break to T8, and following three rounds of the stem cell and scar removal procedure, he's walking with the use of a cane. We're hopeful that he may be able to walk unassisted soon."

Talk about dangling a carrot. I close my eyes and imagine walking on my own. Running. Hiking next to a handsome Marine.

"Send me what you have." I hang up, but instead of feeling hopeful, I'm more depressed than before I reached out to him.

I spend the afternoon binge reading the first book that snags my interest on my kindle. In retrospect, a love story might not have been my best call, but I'm desperate to experience a happily ever after, even if it's only vicariously.

None of that puts me in the best frame of mind for brunch with my mother on Sunday morning. And as always, Mom can tell I'm upset about something and zeroes in on it like a drug sniffing dog at the airport.

"You're anxious," she says two seconds after I wheel up to her table. "You have stress lines over your eyes, and those puffy bags make you look twice your age."

Oh good grief. "Maybe I was stressed about seeing you. I knew you'd criticize the fluff level of the skin under my eyeballs or something equally unimportant." I scowl, until I realize that's probably deepening my stress lines. "I'm just tired. My head hurt last night and I didn't sleep well. That's all."

She frowns. "Did you text Dr.—"

"Mom, I'm almost twenty-eight years old. Lay off the micromanagement."

She frowns again, and her forehead actually crinkles up.

"You must be late on your Botox," I can't quite keep myself from saying. "You're going to get wrinkles with all that unhampered frowning."

Her hand flies to her forehead. "I am late. You're right." She whips out her phone and starts tapping away. I imagine the blistering text she's sending to her assistant. WHY HAVEN'T I GOTTEN INJECTED WITH MY FISH TOXIN RECENTLY? I NEED YOU TO FREEZE MY FACE, STAT.

I giggle.

"What's so funny?" she asks.

"Nothing, nothing," I say. "Just thinking about something Trig said."

"I heard you went to Atlanta. Down one day and back the next sounds like a grueling trip. What was that about?"

I shrug. "I went to see Trig's new house. It's nice."

Mom's face channels a storm cloud this time, wrinkles popping out all over the place. "It's a shack in hillbilly hell."

Her annoyance makes me smile, but I don't dare laugh again or I'll be facing bamboo shoots under my nails for sure. "It's a five thousand square foot mansion in a beautiful suburb of Atlanta, Mom. Let's dial down the melodrama please."

"I still can't believe he dumped our family for that girl."

"Her name is Geode, not 'that girl.' You meant to say he dumped our family for Geo." I can't keep the smile off my face.

Mom meets my gaze. "You would like her, in spite of her horrible influence, and Neutrogena commercial face."

I cross my arms.

"I'm being irritating, aren't I? I'm sorry. I can't seem to help it. I've worked my entire life to expand the family legacy for the two of you and he spat all of my hard work back in my face like I'd created a pile of fecal matter."

Fecal matter? Really? She can't say poop like the rest of the world? "It wasn't like that, Mom. He didn't want his kids to grow up with so much pressure and such high expectations."

"You can't tell me your childhood was miserable." Mom practically pouts.

"It wasn't bad, and Trig knows that too, but it was stressful. He and Geo want something different for their kids, something a little more low key. Can you really blame them for making their own decisions? That's who you raised us to be. Brave, independent innovators."

"I suppose not."

"Which reminds me. There's sort of something I've been wanting to talk to you about."

Mom's face clouds. I've scared her. "Nothing dire, Mom, calm down."

"What then?" She pins me with her patented focused gaze.

"I won't ever have kids, but Trig and Geo almost certainly will."

"Unless she's barren."

"Mom."

She folds her hands in her lap. "Sorry. Go on."

"If I refuse to formally accept Trig's share, what happens to it?" I've read the documents three times, but they're confusing. I want to be sure I'm understanding it correctly.

"They'd go to the next heir..." Mom's eyes light up. "They'd revert to any children he has." She beams at me. "Are you considering refusing his half?"

"You don't have to act so delighted."

"Your brother will be furious with you."

I shake my head. "You can't groom them for taking over, because Trig's their guardian. You won't be able to meet with them even once until they turn eighteen, unless Trig allows it."

Mom's eyes flash, but I can tell that doesn't deter her pleasure in hearing my plan. "You'd do that to your brother?"

"You make it sound like I'm defying him in some way," I say. "I don't see it that way. I see it as taking part of the deep impact out of his rash decision. He was trying to impress Geo and show her he was sincere, and in doing that, he walked away from a lot. That's fine, because it was his choice to make. But what if Nometry fails? What if his kids are more like you than we were? What if they want to manage family assets? I would hate to deprive them of that opportunity."

Mom's an absolute peach the rest of the meal. Except she's signing the receipt for the check when she casually asks, "Why did you say you won't ever have kids?"

I shrug. "How would I?"

"Well, I'd hardly encourage you to visit a sperm bank or anything, but I'm sure you're capable."

I shake my head. "You can't possibly know that. I've never even asked myself."

Mom tilts her head. "You can feel your toes. It was an incomplete break. I've done quite a few internet searches. In almost all cases like yours, the woman can still bear a child, and even if you couldn't feel your feet, even with complete breaks, it's often still entirely possible."

Yes, it's that simple.

I can bear one, therefore I will. Never mind I'd have to sit, pregnant, in a chair for nine months with all the circulation problems that would create. Never mind that I'd need biweekly or more frequent visits and special physical therapy to avoid clots. Never mind how I might feel, being a mother who can't chase her toddler around without fearing I'll roll over him or her. And none of that even contemplates the added risk to the child or me.

If I can even conceive at all.

And in order to find out, I'd need to sleep with someone, which hardly seems likely. Although if I had to pick someone to be a father for my kids, a certain face comes to mind. A handsome face, an attentive face.

I shake my head to chase away my mom's nutty idea. I need to think about something else. Instead of heading back home, I drive in to work. On a Sunday, like a lunatic. I dive into the files I need to finish before tomorrow morning's project meeting with the staff. We've got more cases to review than usual. I've been spending a little too much time picking up Trig's slack lately.

I'm early for the meeting Monday morning, and I'm wearing my favorite suit. It's a chocolate brown wool blend, shot through with gold threads. Miuccia Prada custom made it for me herself as a gift after my accident. I'm halfway through the meeting when I notice my secretary's head poking through the back door. I glance past her through the window and almost drop my notepad.

Robert Graham smiles when I meet his eyes and my stomach spins like an overeager pinwheel on a mountaintop. He points at an empty chair in the back of the room and I realize he wants to know whether he can come inside and sit in the back.

He wants to watch me conduct the meeting.

I drag a breath into my boycotting lungs and nod. Brooklyn follows him in and watches until he sits down. Perfectly harmless, except my brain stopped working when he walked in, and I need to sound rational for the rest of the meeting.

Brooklyn backs out of the room, and I do my very best to ignore his classically beautiful face while I discuss cannibalizing one of our poorly performing companies and buying another to consume it.

"We'd double our profits by Trig's last projections," Calvin says. "And I think they may be a little conservative."

"Company morale?" I ask. "Has anyone taken that into account? The entire model only works if the new divisions can work with the old."

Every time I look down at my notepad to cross another item off my list, my eyes scan past Rob. Every time he shifts, I lose my train of thought. He smiles every time I flub, like he knows he's causing my lack of focus. My stomach doesn't flip anymore, but my leg bounces and my hands tremble like I've had too much coffee. It feels like I've got a test next period, or like I'm about to go on a date with a guy I've been dreaming about for days.

Which is stupid. I don't even know why he's here.

I finally dismiss everyone. Before the last employee has even walked through the door, Rob's walking toward me.

"I missed you," he says simply.

My heart contracts, the traitor. "I missed you, too." My mouth is fired. Fired without a severance package. "What I mean is," I scramble to say, "I shouldn't have left in such a rush. Brunch with my mom sucked, and I should've postponed to spend more time with my brother."

Rob pulls a chair over next to me and straddles it. He takes my hand in his. "Let me take you out tonight."

"You flew all the way to Colorado to ask me on a date?" I ask, a little breathless.

"I told my dad I came out to review the purchase order and make sure you were happy with the large shipment of cars we sent."

"Is that why you came?" I ask.

"No."

"Then why did you come?"

The corners of his mouth turn up, and my stomach cartwheels. "I flew out to yell at you."

Which is almost exactly what I told him on Friday. I beam at him. "Well, get on with it."

"I've been thinking about this a lot, and you can't just fly away whenever you get annoyed by something."

"What makes you think I was annoyed?" I arch one eyebrow.

"Your face when my date with Paisley came up."

"And you're an expert on my facial expressions?"

"I'm an expert on women who are annoyed."

"Why is that?" I ask.

"I've got a mother and three younger sisters. I've caused my share of annoyance, and I've learned to recognize the symptoms."

"Fine." I huff. "Read this."

"You're not really annoyed this time. You're pretending to be annoyed, but really you're flirting, which is promising."

"Are you done yet?" I ask.

He shakes his head. "From now on, you have to talk to me about how you're feeling. I can't afford to jet all around the country, you know." He winces then, like he stepped on a landmine I don't see. "You got mad when you heard I was going out with Paisley, which is dumb. Because I've known her for years and years, and I never asked her out until Geo and Trig badgered me to do it. You're smart, so you'd know that, which means you know I don't actually like Paisley. We agreed to go out on a mock date to get Geo and Trig to leave us alone."

"Or maybe you never realized she was so amazing because you were blinded by Geo."

He snorts. "Yeah, that's not it."

"Fine, I might have figured out that it was something like that," I admit.

He drops my hand, and it's like I'm a patient on life support whose oxygen was shut off. "Then why'd you leave?"

"I had brunch with my mom," I protest pathetically. "And I didn't want to deal with her freaking out if I canceled."

"Liar."

"Fine. It was the hike," I say. "I can't hike, and I'll never be able to hike." I choke up a little, so I clear my throat. "I can't even do a fake date like you and Paisley had, not if it involves climbing mountains, or even hills."

"Sure you can," he says. "I could carry you. It would have been a much better work out for me that way."

I roll my eyes. "Be serious."

"I am. But if you don't want to do that, I could push you. Or you could wheel yourself. Or you could have taken the Gondola. We would have worked something out, but I can't work anything out if you leave."

I close my eyes. He's missing the point. When I open them, Rob's nose is only an inch away from mine. I inhale sharply.

"Not that it matters. I don't even like hiking all that much."

"But you set up a double date to hike Stone Mountain, and at Sushi-ology you mentioned you found it after hiking Kennesaw."

Rob shifts toward me slowly, so slowly my heart stops in my chest. I'm suffering a catastrophic heart attack and I don't even care. I only care whether he keeps moving toward me. Please keep moving.

His lips brush against mine and my insides melt into a puddle of goo. He pulls back until his mouth's only a millimeter away from mine. "I practically hate hiking." He presses his lips against mine again and talks against my mouth. "Compared to how I feel about this right here."

My heart hammers in my chest and I realize that I like it too. I like it more than I have any right to like anything, especially with someone like Rob. He could wink and have almost any girl he meets. Danger, danger, a little voice in my head screams. This won't end well. The voice is right. I should listen.

But instead, I tell it to shut up. I grab Rob's face and kiss him back until I can't breathe at all.

Which is about the time Brooklyn clears her throat behind me.

"You're fired," I tell her.

Rob laughs like he thinks I'm kidding, which I suppose I ought to be. After all, I'm the one acting like a high school sophomore. But I've never wanted to kick someone out of a room so badly in my entire life.

❧ 8 ❧

ROB

"So that's a yes to going to lunch with me?" I ask after Brooklyn leaves.

Brekka smiles against my lips.

"And you're not really firing your assistant, right?"

She leans back in her wheelchair and groans. "I guess not. She's pretty good at rearranging my meetings for things like a last minute lunch."

"Men storm your office unannounced and demand you go to lunch with them pretty regularly, huh?"

"Daily, sir, daily."

"Oh really?" I ask. "Well, I'm lucky none of those guys showed up today. Because I'd hate to be arrested for assault, and I might punch anyone who tried to take you away."

"Me Tarzan, you Jane," she says, sticking out her bottom lip.

"Maybe I'm a little old fashioned, but I'm not quite a Neanderthal," I say.

She smirks.

"Admit it. You like me, at least a little bit."

She blushes.

"And while threatening to fire someone who interrupted our kiss is flattering, I think we're going to be doing this a lot. Which means you can't really fire everyone who clears his or her throat to interrupt us. You'd spend all your time interviewing new candidates."

"Are we going to be doing this a lot?" Brekka leans forward and brushes another kiss against my lips. It's better than the first bite of Blue Bell ice cream, or the first line of text written with a freshly sharpened pencil, or even the perfect glaze on a gorgeous walnut shelf.

"I hope so," I whisper. I could live on the feeling of her smile against my mouth forever.

"If it's going to be a normal thing, I guess I can let the infraction slide."

I pull away slowly so I can see her face. "This time we're on your side of the world. I googled a couple options for lunch, but I'm happy to let you pick the place if you have any preferences. You seem like someone who might be a little particular about where you eat."

"What's your plan?" she asks.

I lift my eyebrows. "Are you testing me again?"

She shrugs. "Maybe a little."

"Alma Cocina is supposed to be good if you're in the mood for tacos," I say, "or Ray's in the City if you want seafood. Their website promises they fly the fish in fresh daily."

She bobs her head. "Not bad at all. I like taco salad better than tacos, but Alma Cocina has both. Let's go there. We had fish last time we went out."

"True." A little zing runs up my spine at her mention of 'last time,' like we're a couple already.

I follow her out to her Range Rover, almost identical to her brother's, except it's equipped with a push pull on the steering wheel. I don't offer to open her door or help her load her wheelchair, even though every single fiber of my body rebels at the omission. I walk around to the passenger side and climb in, my hands fisted uselessly at my side. After a moment, I whip out my phone so she won't feel like I'm staring at her. She's fast at transferring, especially impressive since she's driving an SUV. She's faster than Clive, and she does it all in the nicest suit I've ever seen, with spiky brown high heels on her feet.

"Graceful," I can't help myself from saying.

She doesn't respond, but the corners of her mouth tilt upward. I'll take it. She doesn't make much conversation between the office and Alma Cocina, but it's not far. Once we've reached the restaurant, the stress lines around her eyes relax and she appears much happier.

"Brekka," the hostess greets her. "Your normal table?"

She nods, and inclines her head toward me. "But for two this time."

The hostess smiles at me and we follow her over. The extra chair's already been moved so Brekka can wheel right up to the table.

A heavy guy with a thick mustache hands me a menu without a glance. "Shredded chicken taco salad, no cheese, dressing on the side?" When he smiles at Brekka, his eyes sparkle with genuine affection.

"You know it," she says. "Cactus ranch."

He winks. "Like I needed the reminder."

I clear my throat. "I'll have—"

And... he's already walked off.

"He'll come right back," Brekka says. "He probably went to put in my order first in case I'm leaving early. I'm usually in a hurry."

"They clearly love you here," I say.

"I order for the office pretty often when we're swamped with work. They value my business as a client."

And they like her as a person. People can't fake that well. It doesn't surprise me, but it's good to know she's kind to people who work for her. Not everyone with means treats subordinates with respect and consideration. A few moments later, the same waiter returns and takes my order for three tacos and tortilla soup.

I'm actually surprised when our food comes out at the same time.

"This looks amazing," I say.

"You won't be disappointed," Brekka says. "It may not be as authentic as you'd find in Mexico, or even Texas, but it's pretty good. Especially for Denver."

"It's nice to have decent food options that are close to the office."

"Where do you usually eat lunch?" Brekka asks.

I shrug. "At my desk. Is that pathetic?"

"Not pathetic, but a little sad. You don't meet friends?"

I think about her specifying her table is for two this time. I'm guessing she isn't meeting friends too often either. It's hard to be the boss sometimes. "Not for lunch, not usually. I'm not really friends with the people I work with. Being the boss doesn't help, or at least, that's what I tell myself when I get down about it."

"It can be lonely sometimes, especially now that Trig's gone, but I still get along with several of my employees pretty well."

"I can see that you do, but I don't have much in common with most of my employees. I don't even drive the kind of car we sell."

Brekka grins. "Traitor. How can you call yourself a car salesman?"

I shake my head. "I never would. I doubt I could sell a car if I had to in order to save my life."

She tilts her head. "How'd you end up managing all those dealerships, then?"

"My issue is that I like most people when I meet them, and I want to give them the very best deal I possibly can. I don't have that problem in general, but when I get specific my empathetic guilt kicks in." I wave my hands. "So management is easier for me than a one-on-one sale. I had too much guilt at making a profit off of a person I'd met."

"How did your family end up with car dealerships? I'm guessing your dad wasn't like you?"

"My dad was a good old boy car salesman when I was a kid. He moved more cars than anyone, and ironically, I think it was because he liked everyone just like I do. Only, he didn't feel guilty about making a little profit on the service he provided."

"What do you mean he liked people and that's why he did well?" Brekka asks.

"I think people could tell Dad was genuine, and he really wanted to find them the best car for their lifestyle. He did well enough they bumped him up to manager, and then he saved his money and opened a used car lot. It mudded along for a few years, but he saved everything he earned. Eventually he bought a franchise and opened his first Honda dealership. He wasn't pleased when, instead of dedicating myself to learning the art of car sales, I enlisted."

"He wasn't ever a military man?"

"Nope, not even close. He was probably closer to protesting Vietnam." I laugh, because I can totally see my dad, knee deep in mud, holding some hand written sign as a twenty-something.

"Why'd you go that route?" Brekka asks. "Marines are impressive, but most people are encouraged that direction by friends or family."

"And I was," I say. "My lifelong best friend worked on me for years. His grandpa had been a Marine and his dad talked about it nonstop. He didn't want to do it alone, so I decided to try it."

"And you were better than he was."

How could she possibly know that? "We both did fine."

She smiles knowingly. "You miss it?"

"Sometimes. Mostly I miss Mark."

"You weren't passionate to join the Marines, but you did it anyway for your friend. And then you came home... and even though you didn't want to sell cars, you're running the dealerships. How many?"

"Four now. Three Honda dealerships and an Acura one we just started a year ago."

"Pretty impressive. Is the management different enough from sales that you actually enjoy it?"

I shake my head. "Not really, no, but no one else in my family can do it, so I don't have much choice. My dad's got arthritis in his hands. It got bad enough that working at a desk and doing paper and computer work was a misery. He muddled through with the help of his assistant, now my assistant, but it's hard for him in today's world. Technology has changed a lot, and as you noted, my assistant is no spring chicken either."

"The dealerships struggled?"

Brekka sees a lot. "Yeah. They were in the black when I stepped in, but barely. I had to learn quite a bit, but I still managed to double our profits in the first year. We're making ten times what we made that first year now."

"I bet your parents are proud."

I shrug. "I guess so."

"Which is why you're doing it, right?"

"I always do what needs to be done."

The corner of Brekka's mouth turns up. "For some

reason that conjures an image in my mind of you hugging a puppy with cancer while you slowly suffocate it."

"You're a little disturbed. You know that, right?"

"Maybe." She smiles. "Probably. But tell me this. What would you do with your life if you could choose anything? If no best friend, or dad, or mom, or anyone was telling you what to do?"

I think about the enormous pile of furniture sitting in my shop, slowly disappearing under a thick layer of sawdust. "That's a conversation for another time."

"Like when?" she asks.

"The next time you visit Atlanta," I say. "I'll show you what I wish I could do if I didn't have a family or any other obligations."

"Your family should support you, not weigh you down," Brekka says.

"That's where you're wrong. Your family lifts you sometimes, but you lift them too, whenever you can. I can right now, so I do."

"Don't you want to love what you do for work?"

"What do you mean? Like I should be a professional ice cream taster?" I wink. "Or maybe I could watch movies all day and call myself a film critic. I mean, sure. I have a pie in the sky job, and it's about as realistic as either of those."

She lifts one eyebrow. "What is it? You said it's a conversation for another day, but I think there's no time like the present."

I can see why she'd feel that way, but I'm strangely nervous to disclose details about my goofy hobby to this accomplished titan of economics.

"Come on," she says. "If you don't tell me, I'll imagine you're designing lingerie, or like, braiding dog hair. Or wait, I know, maybe you wish you could be a figure skater and I have to wait because your tights are all back home!"

I groan. "Stop. I make furniture, that's it. If I didn't have to run the family business, I'd spend more time doing that. I might even, I don't know, try to sell some of it. But it's not like normal furniture. I experiment with things, like adding blown glass, or crackle glaze, or epoxy. I put a river running through split wood, or I use raw edges with multiple wood types."

She beams at me. "I can see that, absolutely. Those cabinets you made for Clive were exceptional, and I imagine he was on a budget."

I chuckle. "Yeah, my budget. I got that wood for cheap and decided it wouldn't work for what I initially intended."

"Did you make every part of them, including the cabinet boxes?" Her eyebrows rise.

"Yep, right in my shop."

"You should be doing that, right now."

"Says the woman who's never seen my work. My dad says it's fine, but he's my dad. What's he going to say?"

"I'm sure your dad is right, and the added bonus is, that's something you could do anywhere."

"What do you mean?" I ask. "I couldn't do it at my real job, if that's what you're saying. It's not like I'm a whittler. I need tools and space, and it's loud."

She shakes her head. "Of course not. Actually, never mind. So your dad likes it? How much longer does he think you need to run the family business before you can switch to woodworking full time?"

I clear my throat. "Umm, forever?"

"Wait, does he even know you'd rather make furniture?"

I laugh. "Oh, he knows. He's the first one who pointed out what a monumentally bad idea it would be to try and sell 'my little wooden projects.'"

She frowns. "I'm no expert, but based on the caliber of

those cabinets, I'm sure your work is better than the average hobbyist."

What is wrong with me? Talking about how I wish I could quit my job and tinker with wood is definitely not going to impress the woman who was just carving up companies and tripling their worth. She led that meeting like a pro, and fifty well-educated, sharp people bobbed their heads along as she laid out an attack plan I couldn't even follow. I never should have mentioned any of this. I need to figure out how to end this line of conversation quickly.

"The point is that I know it's a hobby and not a business plan. I'm not delusional, and I'm okay with having both a job and a hobby."

"Where did you even learn how to make furniture?" she asks. "If I tried to build so much as a card table, I'm sure it would collapse."

Actually, based on what I've seen of Brekka, she'd probably craft a work of art on her first go. "It was part of my therapy after I broke my back. There was a veteran's group in Florida that taught skills for handicapped people, and one of the things you can do quite well, even from a chair, is specific woodworking tasks."

"Really! I would never have thought of that."

"You need an equipped shop, but yes."

"That's kind of amazing. It's like you drifted along in life, pleasing other people, like your best friend with enlisting, and then when things went completely south, you found your real calling by accident."

Drifted along? "I'm not sure I've ever heard anyone describe joining the Marines as 'drifting along.'"

"I didn't mean it as an insult. You're clearly a pleaser."

"What now?"

"Someone who cares about the feelings of those he loves and puts their needs before his own."

I can't quite help my scowl. "I'm plenty selfish. Believe me."

"Really?" She folds her hands in front of her. "This should be good. In what ways are you selfish, Robbie Graham?"

"Well for one, I take care of no one but myself. I work out when I want, eat when I want, and make furniture whenever I want."

"Except when you're running a business you don't like for your family."

"For which I'm being paid pretty handsomely." Probably not an amount she'd consider impressive, but it's a lot for me.

She shrugs.

"My point, before we got sidetracked, was that making furniture is a little like painting. A handful of people make money at it, but the majority of the poor saps painting their hearts out barely cover their costs. So not only would it leave my family high and dry, but it wouldn't pay my bills either. It's just not feasible as a real career, no matter how much I wish it was." My dad used those exact words when I came back from Miami able to walk, but barely 'recovered' from my broken back a full year after the accident.

She stares at me for a moment. "You do know that my job is making the unfeasible into something that's feasible."

Great. Now I'm one of her broken companies and she wants to save me. That's hot, I'm sure.

"I don't need help," I say. "I'm perfectly able to manage my own life. And my family matters more to me than anything. They matter way more than any hobby ever could. So thanks for offering to help, but I don't need it. I'll keep managing the car dealerships until I'm so old I can't see my computer screen, if that's what my family needs."

"And Geo?"

"What about her?" I shift a little in my seat, suddenly uncomfortable.

"Is she family to you?"

"Essentially," I say. "She's my oldest friend, and now she's my closest friend. We lost someone together, and then we recovered together, emotionally for her, and physically and emotionally for me."

Brekka grunts softly. "Speaking of, how was your fake date with Paisley?"

I lean forward in my seat enough to shift my hand closer. I don't want to spook her, so I don't take her hand, but my fingers brush hers. "It went so well that I booked a flight to Colorado after I got back home."

Her small smile brightens the entire room. "I'm sorry to hear that."

"Liar."

"Why'd you agree to go on a date with her if you didn't want to?"

"Maybe I did want to. Maybe I tried to kiss her and our teeth banged together and she slapped me."

Brekka rolls her eyes. "Be serious."

"Geo has been trying to set me up with Pais since the day I stupidly confessed my love for her." I want to suck the words back the second they fly out, but Brekka doesn't look surprised.

"And?"

"I've known Paisley for a long time and never shown any interest. She hasn't either, but for some reason, Geo saw her friend as the perfect solution to her own guilt for crushing my poor heart." Again, no reaction from Brekka. I shouldn't be annoyed, but for some reason I am. Why isn't she upset that I liked Geo?

"What about Paisley?"

"She feels the same. No interest."

"Are you sure?"

I shrug. "None I've sensed, and none she's ever expressed. She was mildly annoyed when I utterly failed at convincing Trig and Geo that I had an interest in her on Saturday. If she actually liked me, I think she'd have been angry, not annoyed."

Brekka purses her lips.

"When I told her about you, she reacted. Not with jealousy, but she wants me to videotape the interaction when I tell Trig that I like his sister."

Brekka laughs out loud. "Actually, I'd like a copy of that too."

"Hey Trig. I just wanted to tell you that your sister's lip gloss tastes like sugar plums, and I can't get enough of it. We cool?" I make air guns with my hands.

Brekka laughs harder. The people around us glance our way. "Then once you've videotaped that, can you tell my mom next?"

"I'm glad it's so hilarious, the thought of me telling your family we're dating."

"My mom calls Geo the Vixen," Brekka says. "As though she somehow entrapped Trig with her face. As if a real gold-digger would have encouraged Trig to abandon his family money. It would be hard to imagine a more adorable daughter-in-law than Geo. So if my mom can criticize her, I could bring the president's son home and she'd be upset he wore a blue tie."

"Fair enough. I'll let my dad know to prepare to run for office, and I'll stock up on red ties."

"Great plan. I'll pencil in your first meeting with my

mom for..." Brekka glances down at her phone as if looking at her calendar. "Did you want three years from now, knowing I'd have to bump that, or never? Both are currently available."

"She can't be that bad. Moms love me, you know, just for the record. I think it's the purple heart, but it could be this winning smile." I flash a cheesy grin at her.

"Oh my gosh, did you just flex your pecs?"

My face heats. "Absolutely not. If they drew your attention, it's just their general fabulousness, I'm sure."

"You totally did."

"I can neither confirm nor deny your outrageous allegations. But I will note for the record that you've been staring at my chest ever since I arrived."

This time Brekka's face turns red. "Guilty." Her phone rings and when she glances down at it, her mouth drops and she grabs the tabletop with her left hand.

"Is everything okay?"

She doesn't take the call.

"I take it that dear old Mom's ears were burning?"

She shakes her head. "It's nothing. I'll call them back."

Now I'm curious. "It didn't look like nothing."

Brekka lifts her eyes to mine slowly. "It's a doctor. I guess it's a doctor who works for me. I had a call set up with him that I forgot about."

"A call scheduled for right now?" I ask.

"Yeah, but it's okay."

I guess skipping out on scheduled meetings is less horrifying when you're worth twenty billion dollars. "I don't mind if you need to talk to him."

She shakes her head, her face and hands pale as cream.

"What's the call about?" I ask. "You seem pretty worked up. You don't have to tell me if you don't want to, but I'm a decent listener."

"You like hiking, right?" Brekka asks.

This again? "Uh, we've been over this. I'll lodge my formal response as 'sort of.'"

"Imagine if you could never hike again."

"I don't need a crystal ball to figure out what you're getting at here."

"I guess not. But it hit me hard on the weekend that I couldn't go hiking. If I'm being blunt, I can never so much as go for a stroll around the block."

"You can go around the block in your wheelchair," I say. "I know that's not exactly the same, but there are still other ways to do what you want to do. Right now."

"I can't ski."

"They have sit skis," I say. "Or something like that. You could totally still carve down a mountain."

"You're intentionally missing the point," Brekka says. "Or you're just being argumentative. I'm not sure which is more irritating."

I sigh. "I take your point. And the call from the doctor has to do with that?"

She nods. "Trig's been after me to talk to docs about alternative treatments for years."

"And you're considering them?" I ask. "Now?"

"I am."

"I don't want to overstep here, but can I ask why you're considering them now when you haven't before?"

"If you're implying it's because of you," Brekka says flatly, "it's not. If I try something experimental, it's for me."

I throw my hands up. "Relax, okay? I was just wondering what prompted it. I looked into a lot of those when I was lying in a hospital. They didn't have great rates of success a few years ago."

"You're right. But the fact that they have success some-times, albeit limited, might be enough."

"They're risky." I've inched forward on my chair, and my fists are clenched tightly. I've gotten a little more upset than I should. I force myself to lean back in my chair. "I understand the attraction, okay? But what exactly are you considering?"

Brekka lifts her chin. "There have been some amazing things coming from stem cell treatments."

"Only when the spine is opened up and stem cells applied locally, in conjunction with scar cell removal protocols."

She nods. "You know a surprising amount about it."

I shrug. "I keep up on it. A bunch of my friends are still wheelchair users, you know." I keep my voice as level as possible. "From what I've heard, those are very, very risky."

"That's your opinion. And the risk is only as high as the quality of life you're putting in jeopardy."

I don't even try to keep my voice even this time. "Are you implying your life isn't worth much?"

"What if I am?" she asks. "It's my life to value."

I rub my face with my hands to try and calm down. "Yes, it is, and you're alive for it, and mobile, and healthy. That can all change."

"That's true for you, and for those people right behind us, and our waiter, and everyone else in this restaurant."

"That doesn't mean they should go lay down on train tracks," I yell.

Our waiter appears at Brekka's side. "Is everything okay, Miss Thornton?" He scowls at me.

"It's fine." Brekka's lips compress tightly. "We were just finishing. Can you send the check to my office?" The stress lines around her eyes are back, and this time it's my fault.

"I'm sorry," I say. "I shouldn't have gotten so upset. You're right, of course, and you're unbelievably bright. I'm sure you're evaluating the risks and benefits and the most up to date clinical data. I'm sure I don't have all the information."

"I am, and you don't."

She doesn't say much else when we head for her car and return to her office.

Her assistant greets her with several messages.

"I guess you have a lot of work to do?"

She nods brusquely.

"Did you want to meet me for dinner tonight?" I have no idea how we went from brushing fingers and flirting to this awkward, anger filled space.

Her face softens infinitesimally. "I can't, unfortunately. I had no idea you were coming, of course, and I'm speaking at an awards banquet. Nometry provides scholarships for a few local kids every year."

Of course they'd want one of the founders to speak. It's probably icing on the cake that she's so smart, beautiful and talented. I've never had an out of body experience in my life. Even when I was thrown from the Humvee, or when I laid in a hospital bed wondering if I'd ever feel anything but pain. I never experienced anything like that during my never-ending surgeries, or when I saw the vacant eyes of my dead best friend from a stretcher next to me. But suddenly, here in the middle of the Nometry building, I see myself as if from the outside, as if I'm floating above my own body.

Robbie Graham is a washed up Marine. He never went to college. He runs a few car dealerships, but he doesn't even enjoy doing it. And to top it all off, he wants to glue wooden sticks together and sell them. Even his Dad knows a hobby like that can't support a single guy with very limited wants, much less a family. Such a clear loser could never impress the valedictorian of the entire college of economics at Vanderbilt. There is no way that Robbie

Graham could ever be worthy of Brekka Thornton, much less impress her.

She'd never have even glanced my way, except that my friend is marrying her brother.

I think back on the time I spent with Brekka. It's short, so it doesn't take long. I asked her out and she turned me down. I asked her to stay and she flew home. I mentioned 'another time' when we'd have a date in the future and made a joke about it. Then she almost died laughing when I mentioned the idea of telling her mom or brother we were dating. Because it's such a stupid idea.

I'm an imbecile.

She's trying to kindly brush me off. She wants me to go home. She's been telling me she's not interested from the very beginning, and here I am, flying out to Colorado, kissing her in her own office. I even convinced myself that she threatened to fire her assistant for interrupting a great kiss, and not because she wanted to keep her assistant from telling anyone about it.

Of course I would misinterpret everything. I've never been to college, I have no business expertise, and my dream is to build custom tables and chairs. I'm Little League and she's pitching for the Majors. This entire trip, or actually, my entire pursuit was completely hopeless from the start.

"Well, I guess I'll head back to the airport then," I say slowly.

Stop me. Object to my statement. Ask me to stay, please. Anything. I'll run with any encouragement at all.

She doesn't even blink.

Maybe I can preserve a tiny shred of pride so I can face her at the upcoming wedding. "I should've gone to auction today, but I imagine I can rectify that tomorrow."

Brekka's eyes widen, but she still doesn't argue. She doesn't tell me to stay. She doesn't even look upset that I'm leaving. Even if it hurts, that's my final answer. When I walk out of the office, I try not to look back, but I can't help myself.

When I turn around, she's talking to someone in the office, and she's still the most beautiful woman I've ever seen, which only twists the dagger deeper.

9

BREKKA

I should never have brought attention to the fact that I can't hike or do anything fun at all. Rob obviously can't push me to take medical risks, and he clearly hadn't thought about how dating me would ruin his life. He'd never hike again without feeling guilty. He'd never even be able to so much as go for a jog without leaving me behind. We couldn't ever do any normal couple things together. We couldn't take casual strolls, or hop into a car without thinking or planning ahead of time. He'd have to wait for me to break down my wheelchair and consider what car I might fit in every single time we traveled anywhere, even for something as simple as grabbing coffee.

Forever.

I don't even blame him for racing home, because I'd probably have done the same thing if our roles were reversed. I mean, how stupid am I? One dinner together, and then halfway through our second date, I suggest he quit his job and move to Colorado? When he doesn't warm to the idea, I try to bludgeon him into admitting he'd rather build furniture?

What did I expect him to do? If he had asked me to move to Atlanta... Well I might actually consider that since Trig's there. But if he'd suggested it a year ago, I'd have asked security to remove him from the building. And I tried to convince him to quit helping his family and stop being a pleaser for them... so he could do it for me instead? I made one catastrophic mistake after another.

What I wouldn't give for a lunch do-over, but by now he's probably taking off on a flight back home.

I pick up my phone and call Dr. Anthony back.

"Hello?" he says. "Did I have the time wrong?"

I clear my throat. "Uh, no, I'm sorry. Something came up."

"Oh, it's no problem. In fact, I've still got the other doctors here, if you'd be willing to have the meeting now."

I shoot a quick email to my assistant and ask her to push back my other meetings. "Sure. I'd say I'm even more motivated right now than I was when we last spoke."

I sit through their video presentation, which on the whole is pretty convincing. There aren't consistent results yet, but ten percent of patients have had dramatic improvements, and another fifteen percent have reported some kind of positive shift. Of course, the risks aren't nominal, either.

"You're saying there's nearly a fifty percent chance I'll lose all sensation and mobility from T_{10} down if I do more than one procedure, and over thirty percent from just one?"

One of Dr. Anthony's fellows, a rail thin man in his thirties with sparse hair asks, "You currently report sensation through your trunk and pelvic region?"

"That's correct. Intermittent sensation in my legs and feet. Usually I can feel things fine in the morning, but by the time I go to bed, I typically can't feel much anymore."

He nods. "That's not unheard of, but yes. You could lose

that sensation. Anywhere from the injury site down, as a result of the attempts we are making to restore function, we could worsen the damage."

I gulp. "I can move my legs a little, and my feet. It varies based on the day and time, but what about that?"

He nods. "The same. I'd say a fifty percent chance. The surgery will most likely either worsen your current situation or improve it."

I steel myself for my last question. My most important question. "Could I lose bladder function?"

Dr. Anthony nods. "If you lose sensation, you'll likely lose bladder control as well."

Oh my gosh. "Half the people who had bladder control lost it?"

Dr. Anthony shakes his head. "Maybe it's not quite that dire. It might have been closer to one in three."

My hands shake. I could lose every bit of sensation I have. I could lose bladder function. I could lose balance in my torso. "And you guys have sort of danced around this but what exactly is the mortality rate for the study currently?"

"Well, we had a handful of participants who didn't meet criterion," the fellow says. "But they lied to gain entry. We didn't discover the omissions or outright falsifications until after the procedure."

"What does that mean exactly?" I ask.

Dr. Anthony scowls. "It means that they suffered from undisclosed complicating factors, and we would not have included them in the study had we known."

Which means their numbers are bad. "You said less than half a percent. How many total procedures have you performed?"

"We have completed over fourteen hundred procedures," Dr. Anthony says.

"And how many deaths?"

"We have only performed this procedure on four hundred and thirty-eight different patients, because most patients required several procedures."

"Okay." Answer the question.

Dr. Anthony's voice sounds appropriately funereal when he says, "We've lost thirteen patients, but only four of those met the requirements of the study. The other nine falsified their admittance paperwork."

"We hired a private investigator to verify the reports after the first few bad outcomes resulting from the medical history omissions," the fellow says.

Everything is so relative. A hundred is a pretty big number if you're talking about elephants, or if you're counting pimples on your face. It's a substantial number if you're discussing something like cookies you might eat in a day. But if you're talking dollar bills, it's not enough to get you from Colorado to Georgia, for instance.

For some reason, when Dr. Anthony admits that nearly one in a hundred and twenty people who have the stem cell procedure performed in conjunction with a scar cell reduction *die*, one hundred and twenty feels like a very small number.

My odds of dying seem quite high.

Last month I'd have politely declined. Last week I'd have said heck no. But today, my future without the use of my legs seems bleaker than it ever has before.

"I'll let you know."

"We'll need you to come out for a pre-operative battery of tests," he says. "Before you can proceed. You don't have to make any final decisions in order to do the testing, but you should know that I can only hold this particular slot for another two days. After that, we're looking at the late Fall."

"Understood." I end the call.

When Brooklyn opens the door, I jolt in my chair.

"I'm sorry," she says. "I didn't mean to startle you. Your brother's on line one, and I saw you were finally off the phone. Should I push the strategy session back again?"

"Push it. I need to talk to him." I pick up the line. "Hey Trig."

"Brekka," he says. "I hear you're kissing someone in your office?"

Oh come on. "Since when do you believe gossip?"

"Since Jack from accounting sent me a photo of you kissing a guy. I just texted it to you, because that looks a *lot* like someone I know. And while I badly want to punch him in the nose, if it's who I think it is, I might need to subcontract that job."

My cell phone dings. I'm a little too eager for the image. It's grainy and clearly been blown up way too far, but it's definitely Rob, his huge, defined arms resting on my wheelchair, his head angled toward me, our lips barely brushing. My heart hammers at the memory of it.

It was the best kiss I've ever had.

And my wheelchair takes up a full third of the frame. I text Dr. Anthony and let him know I'm coming out for the testing.

"I take that silence as an admission."

"I'm an adult, Trig."

"That guy is a menace," he yells. "You flew out here to yell at him, if you recall, for sleeping with my fiancée!"

"Letting her fall asleep on his lap is not the same as sleeping with him."

"You're splitting hairs. And how are you on his side, now? I hate this guy, I swear I do."

"You don't really hate him," I say.

"What makes you say that?" Trig practically growls into the phone.

"If you really hated him, you'd be planning how to destroy his car dealerships. You'd be ruining his life, not grumbling at me on the phone about how awful he is, and how you'd like to hire someone to punch his unbelievably handsome face."

"His face is not handsome. It's practically paunchy."

"I don't think you're using that word right," I say.

"Of course I am." Trig sulks better than any preschool kid I've ever seen. "It means baggy and blotchy or something like that."

"I think it's kind of specific to the belly region."

"Like you know. You've never used the word paunchy in your life."

"Did you join a vocabulary club or something?" I exhale. "Wait, did Geo get you one of those calendars? Is paunchy the word for today? No, wait, that can't be it, because then you'd have used it correctly."

"Brekka, focus. Why are my employees sending me photos of you making out in the boardroom?"

"You mean *former* employees?" I scowl, not that he can see it.

"Oh please. You aren't going to fire them. You've probably already printed it up onto a poster and tacked it to your wall. Once I hang up, you'll reapply your lipstick and smoosh kissy lips all over the border."

"You're such an older brother. You're irritating in the extreme, you know." And I totally want to print it on to poster sized paper, and I might, if the resolution was better. Of course, I'd need to crop myself out...

"Do not print that image up."

I smile. He knows me too well. "Some ideas are too good to ignore."

"You can't date him, Brekka."

"I already did," I say.

"So it's over?"

My heart twists into a knot and I can't breathe. Is it? Did I destroy it already?

"Is silence an admission or do you not know?" Trig grunts. "Hello?"

I still don't know what to say.

"He's there now, isn't he? Oh my—are you on his lap right now Brekka? Brekka, say something."

I splutter. "Knock that off. I have the scholarship dinner tonight, so he flew back home already." My voice cracks on the word already and tears threaten behind my eyes. "I think I screwed it up, Trig." I hate the wobble in my voice. I hate it so much.

"Oh B, I'm sorry. I'm sure you didn't. It's not like Batman could screw up with Robin. And that's the problem. He's not good enough for you, not by a long shot."

"Okay, first, Robin's a guy."

"Um, Rob IS a guy. And am I the only one feeling how perfect this comparison is?"

"Yes, because it's not. What I meant was, Batman's a guy. And I'm a girl. And secondly." Fury floods my chest. "He's not good enough for *me?* How dare you say that?"

"He's not even a college grad, B. I'm not trying to upset you. He's not smart enough, he's not rich enough, and he's not impressive enough in any other areas to make up for those things."

"Yes, I was just thinking I need to marry someone richer than me. There are forty-three men on earth that qualify, and thirty-nine of them are already married. The other four are over sixty-five. You're right though. I shouldn't let age stand in my way. After all, if they're ancient, I'll just inherit their dynasty sooner. Good call."

"Oh, knock it off. My point is that he won't be able to

bear up under that kind of strain. It'll eat away at him. It's part of being a guy."

"Maybe your type of guy. Stop being a moron, Trig. Shut off that spigot that's spewing jealousy and competition and look at it objectively. He's kind, he's bright, he works hard, and he cares about his family, including your future wife. He considers her to be part of his family, you know. I'm positive he wasn't lying when he told me that."

"I'll consider my wife family, too," Trig mutters. "And I still want to kiss her."

"Oh, stop. Of all my concerns, Geo isn't even on the list."

"So you do have concerns."

I grit my teeth. "Of course I do. Don't be stupid." I breathe in through my mouth and out through my nose, although that might be backward. I can never remember what I'm supposed to do to calm down when I'm actually upset. "I told you, I think I already messed it up. I might or might not have suggested he move here." I bite my lip.

"You *what?*"

"Not like, explicitly. But I might have mentioned that he could make furniture anywhere."

"I think I have bad reception. Did you say make furniture?"

I close my eyes. He told me that in confidence, and now I'm blabbing it to Trig. I need to shut my mouth. "I told him something else that really upset him." This should distract the heck out of Trig.

"What now? I can't keep up with this conversation. Is there like a Cliff Notes version you can email me?"

"I told him I'm thinking of doing the stem cell procedure."

Only the sound of breathing comes through the phone.

"Trig?"

"Were you serious?"

"I've spoken with Dr. Anthony's entire team about the details and booked the battery of testing. I'm flying out for all of that tomorrow."

"This was Rob's idea?"

"He's pissed, actually. We fought about it before he left."

"I told you he was stupid."

"You won't ever call him that, Bernard, or I'll never talk to you again. I'm not kidding. Not to me, not to anyone."

"Fine, geez. Calm down."

"No. Words have meaning. You'll promise me."

"I promise, sheesh."

"He's upset, but Trig, I'm only doing this because of Rob."

"What does that mean?" he asks.

"When I met him, I can't explain it." I wrap the phone cord around my finger. "For the first time since the car crash, I long for something."

"You what? I couldn't understand."

"I long for ... I don't know. Something. More than I have. I'm longing for a future, I guess."

Trig's tone is flat, emotionless. "With Rob."

"With Rob or someone like him. I realized I'm tired of sitting on hold in my own life. I'm tired of mourning my old dreams. I want new dreams. I want to move ahead. I want to move on my own, even if it's in arm braces or whatever. I'm going to try whatever it takes to wrestle my life back."

"Maybe I can try and deal with the idea, if he makes you this happy."

I wouldn't describe any of my feelings as happy. I turn the phone over and look at the photo of Rob kissing me. I'm pissed Jack snapped a photo of me, but I'm grateful to him, too. Now I have this moment to hold and cherish and look at over and over. I want to fire him and promote him at the same time. But even my feelings when our lips met for the first time weren't happiness. I felt torture and anguish and unadulterated joy and exultation and longing all at the same time. A chill runs from my toes to my scalp, just thinking about that moment, that one perfect moment.

"I fly out first thing tomorrow," I say. "And I was thinking about coming by Atlanta on my way home."

"To see me or your new boyfriend?"

"Oh, stop sulking. To see you. We didn't really get to hang out last time. I need some face time with my most obnoxious sibling."

"I'm your only sibling, unless Dad has some true confessions to make."

"Which is why you're also my funniest, my smartest, my dumbest and my most beloved brother. And I wouldn't have it any other way."

"I'll clear tomorrow for you," Trig says.

"What? You're going to cancel your massage, your facial *and* your pedicure? I'm so honored."

"Oh, the massage is early enough I won't need to cancel that, thankfully."

I snicker. "Bye Trig. See you tomorrow afternoon or early evening."

"Brekka, all joking aside, I'm really proud of you. I know this is a hard thing to do, not just because of risks. I know the hope is ...hard to deal with."

He and I both know it's not the hope that hurts, but the death of it. "Thanks."

"It's the right call."

I really hope he's right.

❧ 10 ❧

ROB

Auction starts early, brutally early. But the good news is that it ends pretty early too, typically. Today was no exception. I text Geo when I'm done.

LUNCH?

SURE. I JUST FINISHED A MEETING UP NORTH. ARIA?

Geo always knows the best new places. I google the menu, and when it doesn't look too strange, I reply. BE THERE IN THIRTY.

She's wearing a beautiful blue sheath dress that has Trig's name all over it. The hostess seats us right away, probably because we're a little late for the lunch rush.

"Love the new dress Trig bought you," I say.

She smooths her hands down the line of the bodice. "It's too low cut and too tight, isn't it?"

I shake my head. "You look great. He has good taste. It's just predictable."

She frowns. "You need to do better. It's like you're trying to piss him off."

"Have you ever seen brothers?" I ask. "They don't sit around complimenting each other. They snipe."

When she exhales, her side-sweep bangs blow upward. Of course, when they fall back down they do it in perfect order. Geo's like a non-clumsy, real life, romantic comedy heroine. Never a strand of hair out of place. Never a spill on her dress. Never a zit on her chin. Never a wrinkle in her clothing, and never ever any lipstick on her teeth.

That kind of perfection must be exhausting.

"Trust me," I say. "We're making progress."

"And part of your grand plan to endear yourself to my fiancé is what? Kissing his sister?" Geo taps her foot.

"She told Trig?"

Geo grins mischievously. "Even better. Someone snapped a photo of you two in the conference room."

Oh crap. "And she knows that?"

Geo nods, an impish smile on her face. "Trig said she almost sounded pleased about it. I gather she hasn't kissed very many guys in the last few years."

"Really?" I ask. "That's nuts. Why not?"

Geo tilts her head. "Think she's an easy wheeler? She wheels around?"

"Huh?"

"Never mind. That joke didn't transfer like I thought it might. My point is she doesn't really date, or that's what her brother says, not since the accident. Remember, I told you she didn't even want me to know she used a wheelchair until we'd had a chance to visit for a while first. I don't think she's entirely comfortable with who she is right now."

Her accident was almost five years ago. It seems unlikely that someone as strong willed as Brekka, as bright and talented, would still struggle with value, confidence or self-worth issues. Would she really not date because she's using a wheelchair? I think about our interactions. She certainly seemed embarrassed about transferring in front of me, when she should've been proud. I was amazed at how gracefully she did it and how easy she made it look. It can't be a snap, and it must have taken a lot of work for her to be so quick and efficient.

Could Brekka be embarrassed of being paraplegic? Still?

She did make a big fuss about not being able to go hiking. I thought she was upset that I couldn't understand what her life is like. Or maybe even mad that I healed when she didn't, but maybe it wasn't that at all. Maybe she somehow thinks being unable to walk makes her ... damaged?

I know gossip sucks and social media's a plague, but sometimes I wish people could see themselves like everyone else sees them. If she could log in to someone else's life, someone else's account and look at herself from the outside, she'd never worry again. If Brekka saw herself through my eyes, she'd realize that she's a supernova. If people blink and stammer around her, it's not because she's sitting in a wheelchair. It's from the glare she casts. Dealing with her is a little much for most of us normal humans.

Geo spends the next half hour talking about her wedding plans, which are taking longer for Geo to sort out than you'd think, since it's kind of her forte.

"I gave Trig a deadline," she says. "I narrowed the wedding down to two venue options: Hawaii or Atlanta. He has to decide by next Friday so we can firm up our date and send out invitations."

"Won't Hawaii be tricky with your mom?" I ask. "Or would she just miss the whole thing?"

"There are a lot of impossible things that become doable when you have money," Geo says. "It seems that's one of them. She'll need people around she knows, but we can swing it. Speaking of..."

"I'll be on Mom duty?"

Geo's nose scrunches up. "Would you mind terribly? The thing is, she knows you and she remembers you from before. Plus, you remember all our family stuff. So if she freaks out, other than me, you probably have the best hope of calming her down."

I bob my head. "Of course I'll help her. Whatever you need. You know that."

She puts her hand over mine and it warms my heart she trusts me, but my pulse doesn't race like it would have last year. My heart doesn't pound either. In fact, I haven't been a stitch nervous around Geo. I haven't been antsy or eager or sad. All I've felt for the entire duration of lunch is the warm comfort of a friend.

Paisley's words niggle at me when I walk Geo out to her car. Did I only like Geo because she was broken? Did I just want to fix her? Now that she's got Trig to heal her injuries and soothe her broken heart, is that why the attraction is gone? I shake my head. That can't be it, can it? When I hug her goodbye, I don't suffer pangs of remorse, or jealousy, or resentment for Trig. I'm genuinely happy for her.

Is it because I believe Trig's a good guy? Or I've accepted she's happy? Have I moved on, or did I never love her to begin with? The transience of feelings when they aren't fed bums me out a bit, but I guess it's also a healing mechanism for the human body.

"Oh, and by the way, I hear Brekka's coming into town again today." Geo tosses that bomb over her shoulder as I walk away from her car.

I pivot on my foot. "Come again?"

"Yeah, she's coming out tonight. Twice in like four days. Got to be some kind of record for her, since she's never flown out here in the entire time I've known Trig. Actually, her dad bought her a private jet the same time he got one for Trig, but she almost never uses it. She's only traveled once since we met. I think she kind of hates it."

"Why is she coming?" My heart's pounding so hard now that my pulse beats in my ears. "Did he say?"

"He told me they're doing sibling bonding tonight. That's as far as we got."

"Well, you're the world's worst wingman."

"I'm not a man at all."

"That's probably the reason. Any man would have known to ask."

"Oh for Pete's sake. You're a lovesick mess, aren't you?"

"Who gives a crap about Pete?"

She grins at me. "I'll see what I can find out."

"You do that, because I hear your best friend contract is coming up for renewal. I'd hate to sign with Paisley, but I feel like she'd never let something that critical slip."

"Shaddup." Geo slams her door loudly, effectively cutting off our conversation.

I try to focus at work, but the third time I type Brekka's name into a report by mistake, I throw my hands up in the air and pass the reports off to the GM at my flagship store. He can handle them for a few days, I'm sure.

I make a beeline for my workshop, not even stopping to grab dinner. My shoulders are a little sore from this morning's workout, but I forget about that as I work on Geo and Trig's wedding gift. The table will be perfect for a breakfast room, or maybe even a game room.

Now for the trickiest part. I left the edge raw, smoothing out only the roughest patches. Carefully, one painstaking letter at a time, I burn the words 'fortiores una' into the outer circumference, over and over. It's Latin for 'stronger as one.' The fused ash plus the message might have been a little obvious, so I decided to bury the phrase in a dead language. Art's really about hidden meaning that reminds someone of promises they've made, or realities they've uncovered. At least, to me it is.

Three rounds of the words complete the perimeter, and I step back to make sure I won't need to cut the entire thing down another level to erase a catastrophic error in judgment.

The burned letters stand out beautifully, and the gothic font perfectly matches the overall look. I'm sure I'm smiling like a halfwit, but I think that when I'm done, this may be my most stunning piece ever. My hand's hovering over the tabletop when a loud crash yanks my head toward the entrance to my shop. I very nearly drag the tip of my wood burner across the pristine surface.

Once my adrenaline spike calms, I realize it's only my dad. I should have known. He's almost the only person who ever comes in here. "I'm going to make you a collar covered in bells, Dad. You won't be allowed in here without it. One of these days you're going to scare me to death, or I'm going to kill you for ruining something critical."

"What's critical about furniture? You can buff out any problems, or glue broken bits back together."

I don't bother correcting him. "Come over and take a look."

Dad peers at the table from the left, and then from the right. "What do those letters even mean?"

"Stronger together," I say. "Or maybe stronger as one."

"This is for Geo and her new boyfriend?"

"It's a wedding gift for Geo and Trig, yes."

"You think they are? Stronger together?" he asks. "Or you're just saying that?"

Patience, Rob, patience. "I really think it's true. But what do you think about the design?"

Dad frowns. "The table's not symmetrical. You noticed that, right?"

"Actually, it's exactly the same on this side," I point, "and on this side. That's kind of the definition of symmetrical."

"What I mean is, it's not a square or an oval, or even a circle. It's not a very normal table, honestly."

Which means he hates it and can't think of anything nice to say. "It's unique Dad, like their love." I mentally strike through my notion of making Mom and Dad a table like this with another slice of the trunk for Christmas.

"Well, I think it's different than anything else they'll get from their rich friends, that's for sure. Definitely no wonky shaped tables on the registry at Nordstrom's!" Dad whaps me on the back.

He's right, of course. Which is precisely why I took the time to make them this. It's not something they can run right out and buy. I hope they'll appreciate that. Trig called yesterday to commission me to make Geo a jewelry box with a tiny inscription on the inside. He said Brekka mentioned I make wooden stuff.

He wants a simple wooden box that says, *I'll shower you with jewels until this box can't hold them, because you're the most precious gem in my life.*

It's a little cheesy, but it's cute. I worked on the main components for that piece half of last night to give me something to do, but I'm not going to complete the details until I've decided what to use for lining materials. I may need to subcontract that part. None of my furniture is upholstered in any way. It's all wood and iron.

"I heard you had a surprisingly good day at auction, especially for a Tuesday."

I bob my head. "I found several big block trucks way below the typical reserve."

"I heard you had great hammer prices all day."

I nod. "It went great, Dad."

"I sure am glad to hear that," he says. "I really miss going to auction."

It shows. I wish he could still go, but the last few times, he paid far above market rate on a few cars. We took a straight up loss on a dozen of the vehicles he bought.

"You know who might be decent at auction?" I ask.

"If you say Mel, I'll never listen to another word you say."

One of our veteran salesmen, Mel, could sell bark to a tree, but he's not the sharpest crayon in the box. He's more like the crayon with the paper pushed down erratically. "No, I was thinking about Jennifer. She's smart and level headed."

"Don't you mean her husband Jarod?"

I love my dad, but sometimes he's a little misogynistic. I think it's unintentional. I hope so, anyway. "No, I didn't mean Jarod. I meant Jennifer. She's smart as a whip, and she bargains like a leprechaun."

"Do leprechauns bargain well?" Dad asks. "I thought they chased pots of gold around."

"Don't you remember *Darby O'Gill*— you know what, never mind. Yes, they bargain well. My point is that she'd probably be great at running the dealership."

Dad collapses onto an oak captain's chair. "This is like basketball all over again."

"Dad, running a family business is nothing like basketball."

"You wanted to quit," he says, "and I wouldn't let you. I was the horrible monster who made you keep going to practice every day and games every week."

I'm sick of this story. "You wouldn't let me quit. I stayed in for you, and then we won the championships." I hold up my arms in the air and wave them around. "Yay," I yell with lukewarm enthusiasm.

"Your team won, thanks entirely to you!" my dad shouts. "You were epic! You destroyed those other boys. What was that team's name? The Challengers."

Except I hated it, every day, every week, every year. If I could go back again, I'd still choose to quit. Even knowing that we'd win. I can't get that time back again.

"Son, you don't think you love running the car dealerships, but you're a natural at it. If you quit, how will you pay the bills? People don't buy tables with words carved into them. They want shiny, plastic, new furniture these days, not solid wooden things crafted by hand in America. People buy foreign crap, or solid teak wood from India because it's cheap."

I don't bother correcting him. "There's no championship in car sales, Dad."

"What does that even mean?" he asks.

It means there's no end. I'll be going to practice and enduring games until I die. "Nothing. You're right."

"Of course I am. You'd be a handyman within six months, and then you'd have to move in with your mom and me. You'd have to donate all this stuff to Goodwill, and that would be depressing. Better to stick with what you're good at and get a trophy than to quit over a pipe dream."

I head over to Mom and Dad's house after I've put my tools away. Mom makes beef stew, and Beth has a new piece to play for me. She's the most exquisite pianist I've ever heard. By the time I'm ready to head home, I'm not even annoyed at my dad. He's a good man who loves his family. He worked hard his entire life and provided well for us. I glance around our house, from Beth's baby grand in the entry hall, to my mom's Bernina sewing machine in its own room. The things my family loves surround us. And if I'd loved it when I was a kid, Dad would have given me an entire garage space for my woodworking tools. He's that kind of person, and I shouldn't resent that. I should emulate it.

When I get home, I brush my teeth and I'm drifting off when I hear a tiny bing on my phone. I almost ignore it, but who would text me this late?

One glance at Brekka's name and I bolt upright in bed. Drowsiness gone.

I'M IN ATLANTA.

I HEARD THROUGH THE GRAPEVINE. Because you didn't tell me yourself. I didn't call or anything because I don't want to cross the line from eager to creepy.

Minutes army crawl by, their heads down, their beady little eyes staring at me accusingly. I should say something. I want to text her back and give her more to work with. But what can I say that isn't pathetic? I can't think of anything. If I get too excited, I'll be Yosemite Samming her again. If I leave things as they are, she might assume I hate her, because it sounds like that. I need to find some neutral ground. Maybe a white flag about something that made me cranky before will open a window.

LET'S SAY SOMEONE WANTED TO OPEN A FURNITURE BOUTIQUE. WHAT WOULD YOU TELL THEM TO DO?

I stare at my phone like an addict waiting to hear back from his dealer.

Eventually my focused attention pays off. IF THE SOMEONE IS A HUMAN PERSON AND NOT A CYBORG, HE OR SHE COULDN'T MAKE LIMITLESS QUANTITIES. THAT MEANS HE OR SHE WOULD NEED TO CREATE A HIGH DEMAND. LIMITED GOODS MEANS YOU CAN FORCE HIGHER PRICES.

HOW WOULD I CREATE THAT KIND OF DEMAND?

WAIT. A HYPOTHETICAL PERSON, OR YOU?

SURE, I text. LET'S DROP THE PRETENSE.

THEN A FRENZY IS WHAT YOU NEED TO CREATE.

HOW?

FIRST, IDENTIFY WHAT MAKES YOUR PRODUCT UNIQUE. IF IT TRULY IS ONE OF A KIND, YOU CONTROL SUPPLY. A LA, DEBEERS.

Debeers? I google it. Apparently diamond companies created the frantic demand for the clear stones by creating an image and controlling production lines. Diabolical.

AND THEN?

YOU CREATE THE MARKET FOR IT.

HOW?

THAT'S MY SPECIALTY.

I grin. SO I PROBABLY NEED TO MEET WITH YOU. MAYBE SEVERAL TIMES TO GET THIS KIND OF INFORMATION.

ABSOLUTELY.

YOU FREE TOMORROW?

I MIGHT BE ABLE TO CLEAR MY BUSY SCHEDULE OF SITTING AROUND TRIG'S HOUSE IN MY PAJAMAS.

PAJAMAS ARE ENCOURAGED, I text.

Laughing emoji. MAYBE YOU CAN TAKE ME SOMEWHERE.

She wants to go out? IF YOU NEED TO ESCAPE, SEND ME THE LAUGH EMOJI TWICE. I'LL KNOW WHAT YOU MEAN.

Laugh emojis flood my screen.

I'LL BE RIGHT OVER.

SERIOUSLY THOUGH, IF TRIG TRIES TO MAKE ME PICK HIS VENUE FOR HIM ONE MORE TIME...

GEO TOLD ME SHE GAVE HIM AN ULTIMATUM.

I'D OBVIOUSLY FAR PREFER HE HAVE THE CEREMONY HERE IN ATLANTA, BUT I CANT FORCE THAT ON THEM. TRIG AND GEO NEED TO DO THEIR WEDDING WHEREVER THEY WANT.

YOU'D PREFER *ATLANTA* TO HAWAII? SOMETHING IS WARPED IN YOUR PRETTY LITTLE BRAIN.

WHEELCHAIRS AND SAND DON'T MIX. She sends me a gif with car tires deflating.

Now I know exactly what we're doing tomorrow. Brekka needs to see that she can still have fun. She needs to see that the world really is her oyster. It's time she gets over all these hang-ups about going fun places, especially with me along to lend a hand.

Life is better with Rob. That's my theme for tomorrow. Let's hope Brekka agrees.

BY TOMORROW NIGHT, WE'LL HAVE PUT AN END TO THIS BACK AND FORTH BICKERING OVER THE VENUE.

IF YOU CAN DO THAT, I'LL CALL YOU MIRACLE MAN.

YOU SURE? IT'S KIND OF A TONGUE TWISTER. MAYBE YOU SHOULD PRACTICE TONIGHT A LITTLE BIT.

MY TONGUE IS PRETTY DEFT.

I almost can't sleep thanks to her last text. But when I do drift off, they're some of the best dreams I've ever had.

11

BREKKA

"How many bridesmaids do you plan to have?" I ask Geo.

Geo wipes off her stunning, darkly veined granite counters while we talk. "You, Mary, Mary's sister Trudy, and Paisley."

"Wait, is Trudy the one dating Paul?" I ignore a tiny twinge of jealousy. I may have had a secret crush on Paul for years.

"Yeah, I didn't know her very well, and she's still really busy with her son Troy and her job, but I've seen her at a lot of game nights. She's actually quite bright and a genuinely kind person. She's had a rough go of things, but it sure seems like that's turning around."

"Is she good enough for Paul?" I ask.

Geo lifts one eyebrow. "I think the question ought to be asked in the reverse, but yes. I think Paul has risen to the level that he's now worthy of her."

"He's that into her?" I ask.

Geo grabs a broom and starts to sweep, even though the dark wood floor already looks spotless to me. "Something about her really turned that guy inside out. I've never seen a man put forth such dogged effort, or change in his general demeanor quite so much. I mean, with me and Trig, your brother sort of smoldered at me and I swooned. From what I hear, Mary had a few hang-ups, but once Luke realized how much he liked her, he shoved right past those. Trudy, on the other hand, gave Paul the cold shoulder for months. Her ex was a real piece of work, and she took a long time to believe he really liked her and was a decent guy, from what I can tell."

"I've always thought Paul was a really good person," I say. "But now that you mention it, in years and years, I've never seen him put forth much effort for anyone."

"He went to kickboxing every day so he'd see her," Geo says. "And he started going to church every Sunday and helping her entertain her toddler, Troy."

Wow, he's really smitten. My jealous twinge shifts into something closer to yearning. I want someone to want me that badly. "So you've got four bridesmaids, and Trig has four groomsmen?"

Geo plonks down into a chair next to me at the smooth, shiny wooden table.

"Yeah, and four is a pretty standard number I guess. It's strange to me, though. When I really think about it, I don't have many close friends. I wouldn't have asked Mary or her sister Trudy except Paisley loves them so much and they're either dating or married to Trig's old friends. For me, I'd probably just have asked Paisley, and you of course, but I only knew you through Trig. This wedding is exposing me for the social loser I am. Two friends: Rob and Paisley."

"Honestly, Trig doesn't have so many friends either," I say. "He's too arrogant for that. I'd really just say Luke, and by extension Paul. Who else did he ask?"

Geo grins. "Paul, Luke, and I'm forcing Rob on him.

He's also asked some guy I apparently met at Luke's wedding and don't remember very well. Bradley somebody. He had a few other people he thought about asking, but when I asked him why he wanted them, he said they kept things 'interesting.' That didn't seem like a compelling reason, and he said they won't be offended not to be included. James Fulton, and Adam something or another."

I nod. "I'm surprised he picked Bradley, but I suppose it's nicer for photos if we have an even number." I just hope I can sit next to Rob. If this procedure goes well, maybe I can stand next to Rob. My hopes soar momentarily, until I recall the risks. I really don't want to be sitting next to Rob in a diaper. I close my eyes.

"Paisley really is a hoot." Geo clearly didn't notice my internal panic. "I think you two will get along really well. Speaking of, I thought we might host a game night here Friday, if you'll still be in town. You could meet Paisley."

"How did their date go Saturday?" I ask compulsively. Half of me doesn't even want to know.

Geo giggles. "It was a complete disaster, which was only alright because apparently it was some kind of cover the two of them concocted to get me and Trig to drop the whole thing. They were supposed to fake the date, and then fake some big fight so we'd back off. Rob was too tired and crabby to pull it off."

"He didn't enjoy the hike?"

Geo lifts one eyebrow. "I think he liked it as much as he ever would have. Rob rarely goes hiking. He's more of a jog along the beach kind of guy."

He is? "He said he hiked Kennesaw—"

"Paisley's fault too. She's always badgering us to go enjoy nature, to soak up the grandeur with her."

Which means he really wasn't upset about my inability to hike when we spoke. I try to think back on our conversation. If he didn't have an epiphany about my inability to do things he loves, then the progression went something like this. He and I didn't see eye to eye on my surgery, and he was upset about it. Then he asked me out and I was busy, and he left. I stifle a groan.

"What do you think about that?" Geo asks.

I realize I wasn't listening to her while I processed my own stuff. Crap.

"It would be a good excuse to see Rob..." she continues.

"Uh, what would?"

Geo tilts her head. "The game night. Will you still be here Friday? I can set one up. It's our turn to host anyway."

My cheeks heat up. "Rob's coming by later today, actually."

"Wait, he told you about that?" Geo asks.

I frown. "Told me about what?"

"He's dropping off my mom's birthday present in a little bit."

He didn't mention he was coming for Geo on our text chain last night. Another twinge of jealousy strikes, this one stronger. Obviously Rob texts Geo, but why didn't he mention to me that he was coming over to see her? Do we really have a date at all, or is he just coming by for Geo? I wish I could step into his brain for just one moment and feel what he feels. Why hasn't technology made that an option? It would really clear up a lot of dating confusion.

"Uh, well, he told me he'd come over today to visit since I'm here. I didn't realize he was already coming." I wish I could sink into the floor. I look as pathetic as I feel.

Geo puts her hand over mine. "Brekka, Rob texted me late last night to tell me he'd drop off Mom's desk. I didn't have plans today so I figured I'd come over early to wait here until he brought it, that's all. He didn't even know whether I'd be here since I'm keeping my place until Trig and I are married. That means I'm the afterthought here, not you. Two birds, one stone and all that."

The sun shines again. And I can breathe, which seems like a generally good thing. "Why does your mom need a new desk?"

"She's allowed a bed, a dresser, a nightstand and a desk in her room," Geo says. "I asked Rob to make her one because she's using the really depressing one they provided. The top of it isn't even real wood. It's that painted on laminate stuff."

"Rob mentioned that he enjoys making furniture."

Geo beams at me. "He almost never talks about it. The fact that he's telling you about his hobby at all is a good sign."

"Is he decent at it? What do you think about his work?" I feel a little guilty asking, but I'd love to prepare if I'm going to need to fake my praise.

"Honestly? He's never really shown it to me. I know it's his favorite thing to do, and he spends all his free time in his shop. The enormous size of that shop's the only reason he bought that old dump of a house to begin with, but he's not very forthcoming. Confession time. I actually asked him to make Mom a desk so I could see whether he's decent! I figure anything he makes will be an improvement over the monstrosity she's got now, even if it's sloppy or wobbly."

"I guess we'll find out together," I say.

"Just... don't be too critical," Geo says. "Not that I think you would."

"You're worried it's not going to be very good?"

Geo shrugs. "He did it for a few months during his recovery in Miami in between surgeries. He hasn't had much formal training, and Rob's the kind of guy who loves to try all sorts of different things. I don't think of him as a perfectionist, and don't you think furniture sort of calls for attention to detail?"

I think about the meticulous care he took with the cabinets at Clive's house. Every detail seemed perfect on that.

"Maybe I just feel guilty," Geo says.

"Why?"

"A few years ago, a startup furniture builder actually offered him a job. They saw an end table he made in therapy. Rob really wanted to take the position, but I didn't want to stay in Miami anymore. Mom and Dad needed me, and we didn't have any real connection to Miami other than each other. I should have stayed, or convinced him to do it without me, but I didn't. When I decided to move home to help my dad with my mom, he came too. Once he moved back to the area, he pretty much had no chance. He was doomed to work for his family."

"He doesn't enjoy it much."

"It's sucking the life out of him. His dad made him spend a few weeks on the floor in each dealership trying to sell cars. Two months of that and he never sold a car. He's not much of a salesman."

"Which is probably part of why he's scared to try and sell his furniture," I say.

"Wow, I'd never thought of that, but maybe."

"He seems good at running things, though," I say.

"He doesn't hate the management of the dealerships nearly as badly as sales, but he struggles with aspects of that, too. Part of him wants to find a job for every unemployable person he knows, while another part of him desperately wants to succeed. Those two components of his personality battle with one another. He needs to make his family proud and earn them a good income, but he's also desperate to help all the Sally Sob Stories he meets."

"I met Clive. It's clear that he's a really good person."

"He's one of Rob's best friends, so make sure you never imply Rob's doing a favor by being his pal."

"I never meant anything like that," I say. "Just that most friends don't spend their weekends building kitchens for each other."

"Huh?"

Rob didn't tell her? "He's been putting in cabinets for Clive at his new house, at a lower height that Clive can reach himself from his wheelchair."

"Huh. That sounds like him, so I'm not surprised." Geo leans a little closer. "How'd they look?"

I smile. "Beautiful. They fit the space, but were definitely nicer than everything else inside."

"Glue streaks and corners that didn't line up?" Geo asks.

I shake my head. "No."

"That's promising."

The doorbell rings and my heart decides I'm sprinting a race. I drag in a deep breath and brush crumbs from my pants. I swivel Gladys around and wheel toward the door.

"Oh, Geo, I didn't realize you'd be here." Rob's voice reminds me of fresh bread slathered in melting butter, a puppy licking my face, and sliding underneath clean, crisp sheets. I could listen to him all day.

"That's funny. I still live at my apartment for now, but my name's on this deed. It is my house, and yet you didn't expect me to be home." She taps her lip.

Rob brushes his hand over the stubble on his jaw. "I figured you'd be at work, but Brekka would let me in to the house to drop off the desk."

Geo's eyebrows wiggle up and down. "We pieced together your sneaky plan, Mr. Sly."

"Are you ready for it?" he asks.

She nods. "Can you carry it yourself or do you need a hand?"

He lifts one eyebrow. "You said a small writing desk, right?"

"Right."

"I can manage it myself."

He must be able to, or he wouldn't have been planning to bring it without Geo around. Clearly I'm useless.

Rob ducks out, and a few moments later something taps on the door. Geo swings it open, and Rob carefully angles two wooden legs through the door. He pivots and then walks forward and then pivots again, and he's through. He sets the desk down carefully in the entry hall. I wheel over to get a closer look.

"Morning, Rob," I say a little nervously.

He grins at me. "Brekka, you look as lovely as ever."

Geo's running her hand across the top of the desk, and when I look up at her face, I notice a tear running down her cheek. I wheel a little closer.

The dark wood grain is stunning, and the area where the simple legs join the top of the desk is seamless, but the edge of the desktop somehow manages to be both smooth and raw at the same time.

Geo's fingers gently touch something on the left corner. I notice something on the right corner, and words span between. The numbers connected with hyphens on the far right should look out of place and yet they don't. They seem to frame the workspace of the desk. It's a date, I realize. The words read: The Heart Remembers.

Geo's mom suffers from Alzheimer's and can't always recall much of anything that matters.

"What are the dates?" I whisper to Rob.

Geo wipes the tears from her face. "It's my parents' anniversary and my birthday," she says softly. "Days we always celebrated together. Days I still go see Mom, no matter what." She throws her arms around Rob then and squeezes him tightly.

My faith wasn't misplaced. His work is beautiful, and meaningful and unique. The desk is rustic and classic at once, and the words look like they were somehow burned and carved, the finish accentuating the message, not detracting from it.

"I should never have made you leave Miami," Geo says. "I'm really sorry."

Rob shrugs. "It was the right call. This is fun, and I'm glad you like it, but you were right back then. My life is here, with you and with my family."

His life is here, and I live in Colorado. I try not to read anything into his words since he wasn't even talking to me, but it's hard.

He turns toward me and beams. "You ready to go, Brekka?"

"Wait." My heart beats a staccato rhythm in my chest. I wasn't wrong. We do have a date, and he's taking me out somewhere. He has plans. "Where are we going?"

"It's a surprise," he says.

I shake my head. "I don't like surprises. I'm a planner."

He shrugs. "Surprises are good for the soul. Take it or leave it."

As if there was any chance I'd leave it now, looking into the eyes of my very own Adonis. I exhale in exasperation. "Fine. I'll just head to the restroom and grab my bag."

"When you put it that way, my surprise sounds unbearably romantic," Rob says.

Geo laughs.

And then we're on our way.

❧ 12 ☙

ROB

"That is not your truck," Brekka says when I open the door and she sees my extended cab Ram 1500.

"Actually," I explain, "I don't drive that to work, but it is mine. And since I'll be on a date, I thought you might want air conditioning."

She lifts her eyebrows. "You have an old Chevy and a brand new Dodge Ram? Does your dad know?"

I can't help smiling. "He isn't too enthusiastic, but honestly, the Honda Ridgeline isn't really a truck. It's a modified SUV they're trying to market as a truck to the guys who want to look manly while driving into an office or commuting."

Brekka nods. "But you need yours to do actual manly things, like hauling wood and desks."

"Exactly." Wait. She might be making fun of me. I study her for a second, but I can't tell.

"That desk is amazing, by the way. Your parents are wrong. You're the real deal, the painter who makes cash."

I swallow hard. "It's nice of you to say that."

"People call me tough, they call me bright, they call me shrewd. No one ever says, 'wow Brekka, you're so nice.' Because I'm not. I'm the kind of person who can't bring herself to compliment someone's ugly baby. I end up saying, 'Hey! You had a baby!' and then I hope they don't notice it's not a compliment."

She's nicer than she thinks, but I don't argue with her. "Well, then your compliment means even more. I hope Geo's mother likes it."

"I can tell you that Geo loves it, at least."

I duck my head a little, embarrassed at her plainly spoken praise. Her comment scratches an itch I didn't realize I was suffering from. It's nice to have someone independently confirm that my furniture's high caliber. My parents act like they're displaying a preschool finger painting, talking loud and smiling too big whenever the topic of the coffee table I made them comes up.

When I open the truck door for her, she looks up at the seat, her eyes taking in the straw sunhat resting on it. "We're going outside?"

I shrug. "It's a surprise. What did that mean to you growing up? 'I'll tell you in three minutes'?" I toss the hat up on the dash so the seat is clear and tap her gently on the nose. "You'll find out soon enough. Be patient."

"Patience isn't one of my virtues."

"I'm learning that." I point at her wheelchair. "I know you're completely capable of doing this alone, but my truck sits pretty high. Any chance I can assist you with Gladys?"

Brekka nods, but she pops the brakes on and swings herself from her chair up onto the truck seat smoothly. "You've seen me do it. You remove the seat cushion—"

"Let's see how I do without coaching," I say.

I've done it for Clive whenever we take my truck. The chairs aren't identical, but they share a lot of things in common, and I saw where the brakes were located already. I pop the seat cushion up and slide it behind the seat, leaning dangerously close to Brekka as I do. My nostrils fill with the smell of lilacs and I inhale deeply. I force myself to focus on Gladys. I need to impress Brekka with my competency here. Surely I can do what she does alone every day, right?

I'm supposed to pop the wheels off next, but I can't find the release. I shift Gladys right and then lift her up without luck.

Brekka's smirking at me.

"It's here." She points at the very center of the wheel. Apparently the decorative flame symbol is the button I press to release the wheel. Clever.

I slide the wheels into the back seat one at a time, and then I do find the release to collapse the frame. Once it's stowed on the back seat, I close the doors and circle to my side.

"I could have done that myself about twice as fast," Brekka says when I climb in.

"I'm a guy. We like to feel like we're helping, even when we're slowing things down. It's a universal principle you'd do well to learn since you'll be spending time with me."

She shrugs. "I'm a woman and I never like to feel like I'm slowing things down."

"In this case, I think I'm undeniably the one to blame for the delay." I slide into the middle seat and don't stop until my arm is touching her shoulder. She's so much smaller than me. "But sometimes it's nice to slow things down a bit."

Brekka turns toward me. She's biting her bottom lip, and I can't keep my eyes off of her mouth. I dip toward her, my heart hammering, my pulse pounding in my ears so loudly I worry she can hear it. Movement out of the corner of my eye alerts me to Geo's hovering presence.

She's waving at us with a knowing look on her face. "Have fun, you two."

I slide back into the driver's seat like a child caught with my hand in the candy dish. "You ready to go?"

"As ready as I can be without knowing where we're going or what we're doing," she grumbles.

She's apparently not nearly as discomfited as I am by Geo's appearance. I slam the truck into reverse and peel out of the driveway. I head for I-16. We've got a long four hours in front of us, but I'm looking forward to all the time to talk.

"Today's road trip game is called interrogation," I say. "We alternate questions, and you have to answer whatever I ask. If you absolutely refuse, that gives me a pass, too."

Brekka's eyes widen. "Uh, okay." She picks at her pants.

I pause for a moment, because nervous Brekka is adorable. When she starts looking around at the roads, I start. Can't have her figuring out our destination. "What's the most fun you've ever had with your mom?"

She frowns.

"Hey, you shouldn't be upset. You're thinking about something fun. And don't tell me there's nothing."

She pokes my ribs, which I did not expect.

"What was that for?"

"Stop staring at me and watch the road."

"Sorry." Inattentive driving probably scares her. Understandably.

"I'm not nervous because of my accident," she says as though she can read my mind. "I don't feel like things could get a lot worse for me, but I'd hate it if you were injured too." She pulls on her seat belt strap. "Both of us are buckled this time at least."

I keep my eyes trained on the road dutifully, but I wish I was staring at her instead.

"You asked about my mom. Here's the hard truth. I love my mom. She's a difficult person to love, but I do love her. She's driven, and brilliant, like beyond what most people could possibly understand. She has this natural intuition for business, and she worked hard to refine it beyond that point. She's unparalleled at what she does, and no one ever questions whether she's the right person to captain our family's financial ship."

"But?"

"But that's not someone who hugs you when you scrape your knee."

I think about her childhood. "Who hugged you?" Please don't say no one.

"Until I turned five? A woman named Nelly Lopez. She was unfailingly kind and a hard worker, and she loved me. She hugged me and snuggled me and taught me to read. Thanks to her, I spoke Spanish and English."

"And then?"

"I ruined it," she says simply.

I wait, but she doesn't elaborate.

"I seriously doubt that a five-year-old could have ruined anything," I nudge.

She looks out the window and when her words come, they're small and quiet. "I called her Mom where my mother could hear me. Only one time, but she was gone the next day. Nelly had warned me to keep it our secret that I called her that, and I forgot."

"You were a kid. That's not your fault."

Brekka's voice wavers. "It is." Her eyelashes flutter. "I said I forgot, but that's a lie. I was a pretty bright five year old."

I believe that.

"I said it on purpose, to hurt my mother. To show her that I loved Nelly and not her. I didn't realize it would ruin everything. I thought it would grab her attention."

"If your mom actually cared about you like she should have, it would've worked."

"I guess," she says.

"When Nelly left, did you see her more?"

I shake my head.

"I'm sure your mother loves you, Brekka."

"Absolutely she loves me. If I ever need it, I firmly believe she'd shoot someone in the face, consequences bedeviled. I think she'd trade all her riches and power to save my life, or Trig's." She turns toward me. "I think if it was put to her like that, she'd make the right decision."

"But?" I ask.

"Dramatic choices are easy. It's the day to day that's hard, right? Like the camel in the tent that keeps creeping in more and more until the tent collapses, Mom never understood that she was choosing the trust over us every time she worked from before we woke up until after we went to sleep. She would have traded it all if she had to in a big, drama-filled gesture, but she didn't give us any of her *time* when we needed it."

That's rough.

"So you ask what my happiest memory of her is? Mom wasn't mean or unkind. She held us accountable and kept us on a routine. She made sure we studied and were taught everything that matters. We had the finest clothes, the best connections, and I'm really grateful. I know I'm probably the least enviable person in America, but we didn't spend much time with her. In a lot of ways, I understand why my dad's such a frivolous mess. He never mattered to her. None of us did."

"She didn't come to your school stuff, at least?"

Brekka shrugs. "Sometimes. I mean, she'd be there for part of some things, or she'd hire a professional to film our performances and awards and then watch a highlights reel. She'd compliment us occasionally too, but it felt like something she did so she could check it off her list."

"That's terrible."

Brekka licks her lips. "I think it's part of her DNA. I think plenty of kids have dads like that. It's sort of unfair to fault her for doing what men have done to their kids for hundreds of years."

"I'd have faulted my dad the same way for the exact same thing. My dad was on the front row of every single basketball game I ever played, yelling way too loud and trying to coach from the front row. When he wasn't the coach himself, which was really just high school, and only because they wouldn't let him." I blow air from my lips in exasperation. "I hated playing, but every cell in my body knew that I was my dad's top priority, every day and every night. My mom, too. They were both at all my games, without fail."

She smiles at me. "That sounds amazing, but I guess every coin has two sides."

I guess so. I feel like she got tails on this one, though. "There's not a single time you recall your mom connecting with you? Because that's tragic."

"Oh," Brekka says. "No, that's different. You said the most fun. Mom connected all the time, especially when we did case studies."

"Huh?" I ask.

"She had this thing she did with us every night. It started when we began kindergarten, and she really did adjust it appropriately based on our age."

This doesn't sound promising. "Okay."

"She'd describe a scenario, and we'd have to fix it. It

started out with, like, bullies on the playground. We'd have to explain whether we'd defend, attack, or deflect, and then how, and why. Then as we got older, the scenarios grew harder and harder. Plus, as we learned some of the basic principles, a lot of the case studies had to do with economics."

I must be making a strange face because she laughs out loud.

"That sounds kind of odd I suppose, but think about it like this. Some families read the Bible every night. Those families cared about the word of God and their immortal souls, right? Mom's agnostic, but she believes strongly in the rules of economics. So we read *The Wealth of Nations*, and *Das Kapital*. And then we studied what worked and what didn't."

No wonder she's a genius. "That almost sounds like child abuse."

"It wasn't so bad, because it was what we did with Mom. Dad took us to get ice cream. Or tiaras. Or go-karts. He was a little more fun, but Mom made us feel important. Like she valued our answers and they mattered."

"Tiaras?"

Brekka laughs.

An image of Trig in a tiara surfaces in my mind. "I'd kill for a photo of Trig wearing a crown while licking an ice-cream cone."

Brekka snorts. "Me too. But seriously, we both eagerly tried to please and impress Mom and it felt good when we could manage to do it. And when we weren't being grilled, we had the means and time to do whatever we loved."

"Which for you was skiing, I hear."

She stiffens.

"Sorry, is that a sore topic?" I know it is, but I'd love if she would tell me something about it. Anything.

"It shouldn't be, I guess." She stares out the window, but at least she's talking. "Skiing was everything to me. We had a house near Vail and I spent as much time there as I possibly could. Mom humored me, and Dad fawned over me. I was kind of a big deal on the slopes when I was a kid."

I can totally imagine that.

"Your Mom didn't ski?"

She shakes her head, but she turns back toward me and I notice her eyes have softened. "I forgot about this, you know. She did ski with me once, and she was absolutely awful." Brekka's lips curve into a half smile and I want to quit driving and pull her into my arms. That would probably ruin the moment, so even though it kills me to do it, I turn my eyes back to the road.

"She came out for the weekend to celebrate... something. I don't remember. But she was so happy, and when I asked her to ski, for once she actually agreed. We stayed on a green hill."

"I've never been skiing," I admit.

"Oh! Well, a green hill basically means there was no downward angle to it at all. You could sort of just glide over it, propelling yourself forward at a snail's pace. And still, Mom looked horrified the first time we stood at the top."

"Go easy on the scorn there," I say. "Because when we go skiing, that's going to be me."

Brekka opens her mouth to argue with me, I can tell. But she closes her mouth and shakes her head instead. A beat later, she continues. "Mom wanted me to stay next to her at all times, never more than two feet away."

"How old were you?"

Brekka shrugs. "Not sure. Ten, maybe?"

"Go on."

"There's not a lot to tell really," she says. "I laughed a

lot, and for once, she laughed too. It shifted something, to have her somewhere that I was the teacher and she was the student. I think it gave her an appreciation for what I did up there, especially as I grew older. She realized that the runs are steeper than they look. She talked about it all differently after going down a few hills herself."

"That might qualify as fun," I say.

She beams. "I guess it does. We got hot chocolate afterward and she even spilled it on herself." Brekka meets my eyes this time, the sparkle in them contagious.

"Perfect answer." I pull off the freeway to fill up my gas tank. I should have done this before, but I wasn't thinking. I hope she doesn't figure out where we're heading.

Brekka sighs. "My turn, I guess." She glances at me sideways. "I don't want to upset you, but I really want to know something."

I pull into a gas station and cut the engine. "Let me refuel real quick. Pause that thought."

Once I'm done, I climb back in and buckle. Then I reach over slowly and cover her hand with mine. "Ask me anything. I promise I won't get upset."

Her hands interlace with mine, her slender fingers smooth, and I pull back onto the road.

"Why did you get angry when I offered to help you with your furniture company?"

I breathe in and out slowly before answering. "I wasn't angry. More like embarrassed."

"Embarrassed?" She tilts her head like a sparrow.

I gulp and look at the road, but I don't release her hand. "I won't lie. I'd love to try and sell my furniture, but part of me is terrified no one will want it. And even if they do, that I won't be able to turn a profit from it. And beyond that, my family needs me. I don't have time to focus on manufacturing anything. I've stockpiled quite a bit, but it's been over three years or so, which means the earlier pieces aren't as good."

She squeezes my hand. "You were angry that you don't think it will work?"

"I wasn't angry, remember? But I was frustrated, thinking that I might need help to succeed with it, and not just from you. From anyone. It's a dumb guy thing, I guess."

"There's no shame in using the connections you have to do well," Brekka says. "Some people don't have access to them, but when you do, the dumb move is to refuse them."

"My parents have always been my only support, my only connection. And my dad's number one value in life is to work hard and do things yourself. Don't rely on the government or anyone else to support yourself or your family."

"And yet, now he relies on you."

Brekka's right. Everyone needs someone else eventually. "It's dumb, I guess." The winding road back to the freeway is taking forever. I clearly got off at the wrong stop.

"You've heard of Van Gogh," Brekka says. "I assume."

"I have. Thanks for the vote of confidence in my cultural competency."

She laughs. "How much do you know about him?"

"I know he painted beautiful flowers, and blobby looking people, and everyone only loved him after he died. I know he hated himself, and cut off his own ear. People aren't sure quite why, but maybe to spite someone else, right?"

She shrugs. "We don't know the details of that whole incident, clearly. It's pretty likely he suffered from a severe type of mental illness. But the reason he was able to bring so much beauty to a world that didn't yet appreciate him was the tireless efforts of his brother. That brother sold an awful lot of what he painted, and supported Vincent so he could paint more, learn more, and grow as an artist.

Without Vincent's brother, we wouldn't have any of his work today."

"So Vincent was nothing without his brother?" I ask.

"I wasn't suggesting that you'd fail without me, and certainly Van Gogh's genius came from within him, not from someone else," Brekka says. "I only meant that I might have a fresh perspective to add that could help you succeed in pursuing your goal. And my crazy mother could add a valuable perspective. And Trig. And probably Geo, and maybe even the famous hiking aficionado, Paisley. People love you Rob, and you should let them lend a hand when they can. It doesn't lessen your accomplishment. It simply leverages it."

She listed herself, and then said that people love me. Of course, she also listed her mother, who would probably be disgusted with my desire to sell handmade wooden stuff.

But more importantly, I'm sure she doesn't love me, not this early. I have no idea how I feel about her myself, but her support is promising all the same, and her words warm my heart. "You're right. Foolish pride is foolish. I'll try and stamp it out next time."

It's the second time I've talked about a 'next time' with her, and when I glance sideways, she's smiling at me.

A tantalizing aroma rolls over both of us at the same time. I know, because her mouth drops open too. She and I both turn toward the windows, searching frantically for a likely source.

"What is that?" she murmurs.

"Only one thing it can be," I say. "Barbecue."

She closes her eyes. "Can we stop?"

"Oh, I think we have to stop. But where is it?" My eyes scan another hundred yards up before I see it, a tiny red stand on the side of the road with a black smoker on the side. My mouth waters when we pull up. The ground isn't paved, and the gravel crunches as I walk around to her side of the truck and open the door.

"Hear me out on this," I say. "I know you can whip Gladys together in two minutes flat, but do you want to wait that long for—" I sniff the air. "Whatever that is?"

She shakes her head. "What did you have in mind?"

I spin around and back slowly toward her. "Piggy back?"

When I glance over my shoulder, she shrugs. I take that as agreement. Her arms reach over my shoulders, sliding slowly around my neck and clasping. I shiver a little, and I hope she doesn't feel it. Or maybe she felt the same shiver as me, which would be even better.

"You ready?" I ask.

She grunts. I slide my arms around behind her thighs and wrap her legs around my waist. "Off we go. The pursuit of deliciousness has begun."

I bounce her a little and she laughs, which I take as a good sign.

"This reminds me of a fireworks stand for some reason," I say.

"No kidding." She points and I follow her finger to where the advertisement, 'Buy one get ten free,' has faded, but is clearly stenciled on the side.

I chuckle. "As you can see, I'm clearly an observational genius."

She leans her cheek against mine. "You're very smart, Rob. Please don't make that kind of joke."

I don't mention that she might not feel the need to defend my intelligence if it wasn't questionable in the first place.

"Hey there." I release one of Brekka's legs and wave at the man I notice standing near the smoker. "We smelled your barbecue and had to stop. It's one of the best aromas

I've ever experienced. Are you open for business yet?" It's only eleven a.m., so I hope we're not too early.

A man with a really long beard and a soot-streaked face turns to face us. "Menamhimnum Bliggaty momnifun."

I have no idea what he said. "Hmm. I couldn't quite understand you, sir. I'm sorry. Did you say you're open?"

"Flinermuffin bifflin nuffelhaven."

I turn to look over my shoulder at Brekka. She looks as horrified as me.

"Did you understand a single thing he said?" I whisper.

She shakes her head. "Not a word."

I turn back to face the man who's watching us, alert and waiting for a response. I have no idea what to say next. It's a stand, and he clearly sells what he makes. He's got stacks of Styrofoam plates behind him. On the one hand, he sounds like a lunatic. On the other... the smell. He doesn't seem to be shooing us off. In fact, he wipes his hands on something I hope is a dingy apron like he's ready to take our order.

Further, he hasn't given us any indication he can't understand what we're saying. I decide to roll with it. "Uh, we'll take two of whatever you recommend."

He turns around and sets two plates on a counter in front of him. He fills them with what looks like a variety of different meats, and then a big spoonful of beans. He yanks something that turns out to be two rolls out of a bag, and plops one on top of each plate. Then he turns around to hand them to me. I clearly can't take the plates while simultaneously holding Brekka, and there aren't any tables or chairs. Obviously the smell addled my brain and I didn't think this through.

"Gunderfulgin warren blonkerstien."

Uh huh. I imagine he's suggesting I put her down. I'm afraid if I take her back to the car, he'll think we're leaving without the food. I let go of one leg again and pull my wallet out. I yank forty bucks out and plonk it on the counter. Then I point at the car just in case he can't understand me either. "I'll take her back to the car and come back to grab those plates. Thanks so much."

I jog back with Brekka. I hope I didn't just embarrass her, but she's smiling when I set her on the seat.

"Wow, that guy is completely unintelligible," she says. "I wonder if he's speaking another language, or a dialect, or whether he just doesn't make sense."

I grin widely. "No idea which it might be, but that smell." I shake my head. "I'll be right back."

When I grab the plates, the man tries to hand me change. I shake my head. "No way. If this tastes half as good as it smells, we're already cheating you."

He beams at me and I notice that he's missing several teeth. I wish I'd tossed another twenty on that counter.

"Thanks," I say.

When I pass Brekka her plate in the car, along with a fork and knife in a plastic bag, she leans over and sniffs the food.

"I really hope this is beef or pork or chicken. Or maybe turkey," she says.

I glance down at the delicious, delicious looking food. "Uh, wait. What else could it be?"

She shrugs. "Possum? Raccoon? Dog?"

My lips curl back, exposing my teeth. "Not really, right?"

She laughs. "I'll risk it if you will?"

Neither of us talks for several minutes. They're some of the best minutes of my life.

"If that's possum," Brekka finally says, setting her plate on the bench between us, entirely empty, "we've been missing out all this time."

I pat my stomach. "Part of me wants to go back and ask

for more, but I doubt I could eat anything else, and it won't be good if we leave it sitting in the car."

"Speaking of," she says. "You were just about to tell me where we're going."

"Nice try," I say.

I pull back onto the freeway and ply her with more questions, albeit less invasive ones, until we're within a mile of our final destination. I approached from the back so she wouldn't see loads of signs.

"Any guesses?" I ask her.

She shrugs. "I figure you're driving me into the middle of nowhere so it'll be easy to dispose of my body if my family refuses to pay the ransom."

"Dang it. You are too smart." I grin.

She glances up then, and her eyes widen. I follow her gaze.

Crap. She's just seen a seagull, and she does not look pleased.

❦ 13 ❧

BREKKA

"Please tell me that's not actually a seagull, but some kind of land bound relative."

Just last night I told him how much I hate the beach. Plus, we were in Atlanta. What place on earth is less beachy than Georgia? We've only been in the car... I glance at my watch. Four and a half hours, including the barbecue from heaven pit stop.

"Hmm. I can tell you whatever you want me to tell you."

"I want it to be true when you say it." I think about the straw hat and close my eyes. I assumed we'd be doing a picnic. Or maybe a walking tour and he'd insist on dragging me along, pushing me when my arms grow too tired. It never occurred he'd drive me to a sandy nightmare.

"Are you really upset?" he asks. "You don't trust me?"

"I barely know you." I think about the amazing conversation we've been having. The sideways glances and the flirting. The feel of his hand on mine, of my fingers tangled in his. I'm not being fair. "I'm sorry I'm cross. I don't love beaches, as I might have mentioned."

"Which is exactly why I'm taking you with me to Tybee Island."

I sigh resignedly. Today is about to suck. I don't say another word while we drive the last few minutes to the beach. I count that as a win for me. I don't complain or whine or grump, even though I want to do all three.

"You are going to love this," Rob says. "I promise you will."

It's hard to nod and bite my tongue, but I persevere.

"You know, some things aren't as awful when you face them with someone you trust," Rob says.

I snort. "I think that's the motto of the Khmer Rouge."

Rob turns into a lot that's labeled, "Beach Parking." He impressively slides his enormous truck into a tiny spot and shoves it into park.

He turns toward me and crosses his arms. "I'm going to tell you an embarrassing story now. You're going to understand my point, and then give this a chance."

I cross my arms and lean back exactly like he is. "Okay, go ahead."

"When I was a kid, I was terrified of the dentist. I went once when I was five or six, and it turned out that I had three cavities. The man came at me with a drill like the murderer in a cheesy made-for-television horror movie. The numbing shots didn't work and I swear, it was the worst thing that ever happened to me by a factor of ten, or maybe even one hundred. I flatly refused to ever go again. In fact, when my dad dragged me into the dentist's office at the age of ten, I yelled so loudly and for so long that the dentist eventually refused to treat me. My dad beat me when we got home." He closes his eyes. "I still remember the feel of that lash across my backside, and you know what I thought? Better this than the pain of the insane dentist's drill."

I'm not sure how much he's exaggerating.

"You're thinking it wasn't really that bad." He shakes his head. "You're wrong. It was awful. When I turned thirteen, I still flat out refused to go back. My parents tried everything. They grounded me. They took everything away from me they could think to take. I couldn't get online. I couldn't hang out with friends after school. They even canceled Halloween one year, and no matter what they threatened, the dentist still seemed worse to me. And the thing was, I built it up in my mind. As time passed, I convinced myself it was far worse than it must have been. I knew it was irrational, and yet, that fear clawed its way up my spine whenever someone said the word. Dentist." He shudders.

I lift one eyebrow. I know a sell job when I hear one. "And then what? You overcame your fears and that's why now you have the best teeth of anyone I know?"

"Oh, no. I never overcame it." He forces a smile and points at his teeth. "These are all caps. My real teeth rotted out and they filed them down to tiny nubs while I was under general anesthesia and crafted these fake ones."

My jaw drops.

"I'm kidding." He laughs.

I slap at his knee. The rest of him is too far away for me to comfortably reach. "That was mean. Just finish your dumb pep talk so we can get my figurative root canal over with."

He bobs his head. "Now you're getting ahead of me. See, I got a horrible cavity. In this tooth." He opens his mouth and points at his back, right, bottom molar. "It hurt. It started as an ache, and then it grew, more and more each day that passed. I didn't say a word of course, because I knew the dentist was worse than a toothache. Way worse.

At least, until the throbbing in my head got so bad that I couldn't see. It's called referred pain. When I went blind, I was still afraid of the dentist. I still didn't want to go. Thinking about it sent me into fits."

He leans toward me. "This isn't a very manly story, so I wouldn't normally tell someone I liked as much as I like you."

A shiver runs down my spine. He likes me. A lot.

"And then what?" I ask, invested in spite of my dedicated skepticism and principled annoyance.

"My little sisters, Christine and Jennifer. They were twins, you recall. They came up on either side of me. I couldn't see them, but I knew their voices. Each of them took one of my hands." Rob chokes up a little and my heart goes out to him. "I was sixteen years old. I wasn't afraid of bullies, or a burglar, or the all-state basketball tournament. But I was wet-your-pants scared of the stupid dentist."

This time I'm the one who reaches for his hand. He clasps mine eagerly.

"Just like that," he says. "My sisters took my hands that day and promised me they'd stay with me the entire time I was at the dentist. They'd never let go. I might not have been able to see them, but I believed they would protect me. My nine-year-old sisters would keep me safe from the boogey man. It sounds ludicrous, but it was enough. I went to an endodontist and he gave me a root canal and a crown. After that, I went to the dentist for cleanings, but every single time I set up an appointment, at least until I graduated from high school, one or the other of my twin sisters went along too."

He slides over next to me, tucking my elbow up against the warmth of his body. "The idea of the beach is awful. Or maybe you've been a time or two and it truly sucked. Or maybe you're afraid people will stare. I don't know what scares you, but I promise that I know your fear is real and valid. And ultimately, if you stick with me, if you hold my hand, we will vanquish it together."

His words are utterly and completely cheesy. They should be the inspirational line in the middle of a Hallmark card, and yet, he's sincere. He's not mocking me. He's not belittling me for my irrational fear of going to the beach. And he didn't tell me he knows my hatred masks my fear. He just knew it was true without me saying it, and without pointing it out.

I lean my head against his shoulder. "My legs used to be long and tan and lean and perfect."

"They're still long and perfect."

"I notice you left tan off the list."

He shrugs. "I've only seen you in pants. The one time you were wearing a suit skirt, you had pantyhose on. I can't speak to tan, so you'd know I was lying. But to long and perfect, I can attest."

I roll my eyes. "They're thin. I do my physical therapy religiously, but I can't do enough with them to build any real muscle tone. The curves I had have melted away and now—" I choke up. "They look like sticks. Or like toothpicks." I gulp in air to shove back my tears. "People wear shorts and swimsuits at the beach. I'd look repulsive in anything like that."

Rob gathers me into his arms and pulls me up onto his lap. His right hand strokes the left side of my face. "You could never, ever, ever look repulsive. Never. No part of you will ever repel me in any way. Not your nose." He kisses the tip of my nose and my heart takes wing. "Not your eyes." He kisses each of my eyes and my hands shake. "Not your cheeks." He kisses the tears from my face. "Not your mouth. Never your mouth."

He kisses me with dedication and resolve then, and I forget about time and space. I forget about legs and arms and feet and toes. I forget about sand and sun and salt and spray. The only thing that exists is Rob's hand in my hair, and his mouth against mine and his sigh against my cheek when he pulls away.

"No part of you is anything but perfect to me. But if you're concerned, keep your pants on." He chuckles. "That is just not a phrase I was preparing to say to you today, or ever really. But, please. Please keep your pants on. Whenever and for however long you want to. You don't need to impress anyone here. The person you came with already thinks you're flawless."

I draw in a shaky breath and nod my head. "Fine. We can go to the stupid beach."

It's almost worth the misery I know is coming, to see the utter delight on Rob's striking face. "You will not be sorry."

Rob reaches behind me and grabs a backpack, but instead of slinging it over his shoulders, he holds it against his defined pecs and loops the straps over his shoulders backward.

He grins at me, and puts on a pair of sunglasses. "Let's go."

He slides out of the car and pats the driver's side seat. "I'm giving you a ride."

I shake my head. "No way. It's got to be hundreds of yards to the beach from here."

He drops his shoulders in exasperation. "You said we could go. I have this planned. Besides." He slaps his right arm with his left hand and his left arm with his right hand. Then he slaps his legs. "What's the point of all the hours I spent at the gym if you don't let me show off my muscles?"

I smirk. My turn to be obnoxious. "I'll agree to a piggy back ride on one condition."

He lifts an eyebrow. "What?"

"Take your shirt off. We are at the beach."

He grins. "Done." He whips his shirt off in one smooth movement and I can't breathe. Like at all. I'm going to die of oxygen depravation, but oh man. I'll be happy. He has the most impressive chest I've ever seen. And the tattoo I've only seen the edge of on his arm is completely clear. Semper Fidelis.

"Ready?" he asks.

My eyes snap back to his face. "Sure. Yes. A deal is a deal." My fingers itch to run themselves over his shining skin. He turns around so I can climb on, and I notice another tattoo. "Wait, what's this?" I lean closer and realize there are words written in a circle on the left side of his back.

"Words have meaning," he says so quietly I can barely hear him.

"Do you mind if I read these?" I ask.

He shakes his head.

I bow toward the circle. *Broken, but never beaten.* My breath catches. "What does this mean?"

"It says Broken, but never beaten." He lifts his chin defiantly.

"I know." I don't press any further.

"They told me my break was complete. They told me I'd never walk again. I worried I might never regain function of my arms. I wasn't paraplegic, Brekka. I was quadriplegic. I gave up in that hospital bed. I prayed to God that he would let me go. I begged him to let me die, like my best friend Mark already had. I wanted it all to be over."

He clears his throat. "I came to terms with the fact that

I had nothing to look forward to, ever. I had no hope and sank in a puddle of despair, stuck inside my own head. It went on like that for nearly a week, which doesn't seem long, but it was an eternity to me."

He draws in a ragged breath. "God decided one day to answer my prayers and I blacked out. My lungs stopped working, and they had to go in to try and clear out a clot to save my life. When they did that, they found tiny fragments that hadn't shown up on the scans. Somehow, when they removed those, it set me on a path to recovery. I began to feel my toes, and then my knees. One day, I flexed my calves. Both of them at the same time."

He glances toward the beach and away from me. "I decided then, without knowing exactly what function I might one day regain, that no matter how much I improved, I'd be grateful. After all, anything at all was a miracle. I was broken, but I would never give up again. That IED may have broken my back, but I was not defeated, not anymore."

He bites his lip. "I also realized that I was wrong."

"About what?"

"I gave up in that bed. I thought that without the life I had, life wasn't worth living."

"I can relate to that sentiment," I say.

He shakes his head slowly. "I was wrong. It was a miracle that I regained function, but I really hope that even without that miracle, I'd have come to the same conclusion, that my life had value even if I couldn't move my arms and legs. I know a lot of people who live fulfilling, rich lives without the use of their legs and arms too. We humans naturally resist change, but I hope I never again surrender my life because of it."

I wrap my arms around his perfect back, glancing downward at the pattern of scars around his spine. I want to trace them, but I don't. He's not broken, not to me. He's perfect. Actually, he's stronger than perfect. He's an overcomer. When he carries me to the beach and eyes turn toward us, I know what they see. A plain girl being carried like a child by an Adonis of a man.

They wonder why he's carrying me. They wonder why he's paying attention to me at all. The girls around me on the beach, jogging in bikinis, throwing Frisbees, laying in the sun, they're all jealous of me. They should be. I don't deserve Rob. But then again, none of them do either.

I decide to let go of my anger. I may be broken, but I'm not defeated either. I never miraculously flexed my calves and learned to stand and walk again like Rob, but the same sentiment applies to me. Those girls may be able to run and splash and flirt and hit a volleyball, but I'm not throwing in the towel.

I open my mouth to tell Rob about my surgery. In a few weeks, maybe I'll be flexing my calves like he is. I can get the same tattoo, and we can jog along this beach together. Then I'll deserve him. I'll get my life back. I'll dream about the future again.

It's worth the risks. It's worth any risk. Rob sets me down on a chair underneath an umbrella. A man in a white button down and cutoff shorts jogs toward us. Rob pays him and he salutes me. What's going on?

"These chairs and the umbrella are rentals," Rob explains. "These guys come set them up, and we can use them until sundown."

"It's that easy?" I ask.

He nods, and a smile creeps slowly across my face.

"Not so bad, right?" he asks.

I shake my head.

"Geo gave me this for you." He pulls a book from his

bag. "She thought you might like it. It's the first in a series, *Marked*. She said 'the science stuff is kind of boring, but the guy the girl ends up with is hunky.'"

I roll my eyes. "Is this that author she loves? The one with all the kids and the yappy dog and the chickens?"

He grins. "Yep. They're Facebook friends and you know Geo. She's unswervingly loyal."

I sigh and take the book. "I'll read enough to tell her I did."

"She's going to badger you to leave a review. Apparently authors check those like lunatics and smile every time they get a five star."

Oh good grief. "Hey, before you get entirely settled..."

Rob's eyebrows lift. "Yeah?"

"I might need to go to the restroom."

He slaps his forehead. "Duh."

"See, this is why I hate the beach. Now we're here, and we're all settled and I don't have my chair and you can't give me a piggyback ride *into* the ladies' room and set me on the toilet."

"I can't?"

The horror must show on my face because Rob laughs. "Relax, I'm kidding. I'll jog back and grab it. Remember how annoying I was about figuring out how to put Gladys together? I had a reason for it. Two minutes."

I sit by myself on the rented lounge chairs and look around at the beautiful beach. Kids dig in the sand and throw handfuls at each other and squeal. Mothers plod along behind toddlers, scooping them up in their arms when they've gone too far. A group of twenty somethings dive for volleyballs in a spray of sand and cheers.

Sure, plenty of people lay around and read, but even those people hop up and walk to where the water meets the sand and dip their toes in. I'm sitting here in my pants, hiding my legs, afraid to look different. I'm sick of being afraid. I'm sick of being different. For years I've been too nervous to try these surgeries Trig funds. It's past time for me to get over it and take a gamble. It's time for me to be brave enough to live my life again.

"Uh yeah," the girl next to me says. "A total hottie."

I turn to see two girls laying on towels ogling a guy headed our way. When I follow their eye line, it's Rob. Of course it is. He's carrying the pieces of Gladys gracefully, striding toward me quickly. When he notices I've seen him, he beams at me and waves. He doesn't even seem to notice all the female heads that turn toward him as he walks over.

"Here we are," he says.

I reach for Gladys, but he stops me. "Uh, nuh-uh. I need to learn so I'll be fast if I'm ever going to be helpful, and guys need to be helpful, remember?"

I glance around at all the people watching us. He assembles Gladys like a pro, but then I point out the issue. "And now we're here, on the sand, and the bathroom is over there." I point. "How are you going to get me and Gladys from here to there?"

"If you're not worried about theft, I could carry her over, and then carry you over." His voice rises at the end of the statement, almost making it a question.

Am I worried someone will steal my custom, tiny wheelchair? Not really, no.

"That's fine, but it seems like a lot of work." And now every single person here at the beach knows I'm a freak and they're staring. Check out the weirdo and her bizarrely hot boyfriend. 'Maybe it's her brother' they think. Which explains the flirty smiles and waves they keep shooting his direction.

Not that Rob has even noticed any of it.

"Or, wait, look." Rob collapses Gladys sideways and she

folds in half. "I'm clearly a novice. I should have assembled her at the car and carried her over this way. I'm sorry, but I will improve, I swear."

I shrug. He's already learning fast.

"Funny story. I babysat for my sister Jennifer recently. Her son Liam is the cutest toddler, and she was pregnant with her second, and she had to rush to the doctor's office for a UTI. Her husband was out of town and my mom had the flu. Long story. Anyway, I swung by her house and picked up Liam. I got a car seat, a stroller, a high chair and like three bags of crap. At first I couldn't figure out up from down. I ended up putting the stroller in my truck fully assembled. I had to lash it down so it didn't fly out. But I ended up having Liam for two days. By the end of that time, I looked like his dad. I could collapse that whole stroller with a button. I slid him in and out of the high chair like a champ."

He's comparing me to a baby.

"You look annoyed right now, and I get it. I'm not saying I'm babysitting you. My point was that I didn't know how to use any of that stuff, but once I got past the steep learning curve, it was a snap. If you can be patient with me like a teensy bit, I swear, trips like this will be super fun. I just need to get the hang of it. I'm willing if you are."

I hate being compared to a toddler he babysat. I hate needing his help. I hate being an invalid.

But none of that is Rob's fault.

I nod. "Totally, it's fine."

He leans over then and kisses me. Slowly, mesmerizingly. I'm breathless when he finally pulls away. "You hate being dependent on anyone else because you are so strong. You're a force of nature in a tiny little frame. A tempest in a teapot is a phrase I never understood until I met you. But sometimes the best things in life require us to do them with others. You can't do anything on a teeter-totter if you're alone. Let me do my part, and try not to hate me for doing it."

I reach for him, and he flips around so I can put my arms around his neck. He stands effortlessly, like I'm a rag doll or a, well, a toddler. Then he squats down and snags the side of Gladys and carries her along with us. Once we reach the hard packed sand, I tap his shoulder.

"You can set me down here."

He does.

"I'll text you when I'm done."

"Oh," he says. "Smart."

The entire thing is actually pretty simple. And when I'm done, Rob crouches down so I can hop on his back, collapses Gladys and stands back up, jouncing me a little up and down as he jogs back to our chairs.

He doesn't even mention it again. He just sets Gladys next to his chair as if she's his. Rob pulls sunblock out of his bag and offers me some and a tiny part of me wishes I'd worn shorts. It's not too hot in the shade, but it might have been nice to get a little sun on my pale, stick legs. I coat my arms and face and pass it back.

He pulls out a medical thriller that doesn't appeal to me at all and leans back, nose in the book.

I lay back and listen to the surf for a moment, but eventually I crack the book Geo's been talking about. It's actually pretty engaging. A few minutes later, Rob pokes me and I realize with a start that the sun is setting.

"Uh, I wouldn't have given you that book if I realized you'd check out on me entirely," he says with a half smile.

I grin sheepishly. "Sorry, but Geo was right. The guy *is* hunky."

Rob flexes. "But nothing to me, right?"

The mixture of false bravado and boyish insecurity in

his eyes melts my heart. How can he not realize that every single girl within two hundred yards walked past us fifteen times hoping to catch his attention? I mean, I didn't notice while I was reading, but they did it before, so I'm guessing it didn't stop.

"The fictitious hunk has nothing on you." I intend sarcasm, but even I can't hear any in my tone. No one is anything compared to my Rob.

He reaches over and lifts me from my chair, hauling me into his lap again. He smells like sunblock and hot dogs. Wait. "Why do I smell hot dogs?"

"Because I bought some." He waves two foil wrapped rolls at me. "It was all the stand over there had. I hope you'll eat them, because the corndogs looked pretty burned, and there isn't anything else close." Rob wraps his arms around me and tucks my head under his chin. "Be honest. You didn't even realize I got up and walked over there."

"The book was pretty good. What can I say?"

"Oh, well," he says. "Don't let me keep you from it." He lifts me back up like he's going to dump me in my chair again.

"No, wait. I like it here." I'm glad he can't see me blushing.

"You do?"

I snuggle down against him. "I'd have had to stop reading in a few minutes anyway," I say. "The sun's almost gone."

He reaches around my arm to hand me a hotdog. "Here. Eat this. The real show's about to start."

I lean back against Rob's broad, warm chest, feeling the rise and fall of his lungs and the rhythmic thuds of his heart. I eat the disgusting hot dog and think about how I'll play this day over and over in my head from now on. This perfect, beachy day.

"Thanks for bringing me all the way over here for this sandy nightmare," I say. "With you along, it really wasn't as bad as I thought it would be."

I feel his chuckle through my back as well as hearing it. "What a winning endorsement. Clearly my work here is done."

Kaboom. Fireworks go off over my head, and I turn upward like a tiny child, my heart full of wonder.

"How did you know they'd have fireworks?"

"It's a tourist thing they're trying this summer," he says. "I read it online. They're trying to draw new people to spend money here."

"Didn't work for us."

Rob grabs my empty hot dog wrapper. "I beg your pardon. I may not be a high roller, but I spent money. I bought hot dogs and rented these chairs." He tosses the wrappers into the open top of his backpack and leans back, pulling me back against his chest again.

A purr like a contented cat escapes my mouth, and when I glance back at Rob, he meets my eyes knowingly. He wisely doesn't mention it. When the fireworks finally finish, Rob takes me to the restroom again, and then we head back to the truck. I wish the night didn't have to end, but eventually even perfect days come to a close.

We talk just as much on the way back home, but when Trig calls Rob to demand he return his sister, I take the chance to email Dr. Anthony and confirm the date of my procedure.

I've always been greedy, but I'm not ashamed of my greed this time. Every single person I know would want a million more days just like this if they could get them. And I intend to, no matter the risk.

Rob may have gotten upset the first time I mentioned it, and I may be hiding it from him, which might seem bad, but once it's done. . . Once I'm fine and I'm gaining mobility, once the stem cells work and I can walk beside him, he will get it. Rob will be as giddy as I am.

I'll be broken, but not defeated, just like him.

14

ROB

I wake up to a binging sound. I fumble around to silence my phone, until I realize it's binging because of a text. From Brekka.

THANKS FOR ABDUCTING ME AND SUBJECTING ME TO THE BEACH YESTERDAY.

I rub my bleary eyes and grin like a halfwit. SO YOU HAD FUN?

I TOLD TRIG TO JUST PICK HAWAII ALREADY, AS LONG AS YOU'LL BE THERE WITH ME.

With me. I read the words several times, and each time I feel the same surge in my chest.

Until I remember that I told Geo I'd help with her mom. I'll figure something out. I WOULDN'T MISS IT.

WILL YOU BE SAD?

Sad? I've never been to Hawaii, but I can't think why I'd be sad. ABOUT WHAT EXACTLY?

She sends me a heart eyes emoji. I'm not sure what that means. Does it mean she loves something or she sees something she likes? Or does it mean she's happy? And how would that in any way address my statement that I didn't understand her question?

Women make no sense sometimes.

I type, I HOPE MAYBE YOU'LL TRY SHORTS AT THE WEDDING. OR A DRESS, AT LEAST. Then I get nervous that she will take it wrong and delete it without hitting send. Instead, I text, HEADED HOME TODAY? OR ARE YOU STICKING AROUND?

I'M AT THE AIRPORT NOW, WAITING TO TAKE OFF.

I sink back in my pillows and pull a blanket over my head. Why now? BOO, I finally text back.

Heart eyes again. It's like her favorite emoji. I really need to find out what it means.

I MAY NEED TO HIRE A TEXT INTERPRETER.

WHY?

I HAVE NO IDEA WHAT THE YELLOW FACE WITH HEARTS FOR EYES MEANS.

Laughing faces, a whole line of them. Great. She thinks I'm stupid.

I head for the shower. When I'm out and dressed, I see that she has replied.

TAKING OFF, she texts, BUT I HOPE I DIDN'T HURT YOUR FEELINGS. I FORGET SOMETIMES THAT NOT EVERYONE SPEAKS TEENAGE GIRL. I TEXT WITH GEO A LOT, AND TRIG'S NEARLY AS BAD.

Then she sent a heart eyes emoji.

IT MEANS I LOVE SOMETHING I'VE SEEN, USUALLY A TEXT REPLY. I WAS GLAD YOU'RE NOT SAD GEO'S GETTING MARRIED. THEN I WAS GLAD YOU WERE SAD I'M LEAVING. I HAVE TO GO, BUT I WISH I COULD STAY. IT'S JUST THAT I ALREADY MISSED A TON OF MEETINGS.

THANKS, I text back. YOU SAVED ME $199. I WAS ABOUT TO ENROLL FOR REMEDIAL TEXTING 101, AN ONLINE COURSE.

We text off and on all day, which vastly improves my outlook at work. Even my secretary notices.

Trig calls me while I'm driving home. To say he doesn't call very often would be an understatement. In that regard, dating his sister has moved our relationship ahead by leaps and bounds. I'm hearing from His Royal Highness almost daily. "Hello?"

"Hey Rob. I wanted to see if you'd made any progress on our special project."

"Are you with Geo right now?" Because if he is, why is he calling me? And if he's not, why not just call it the jewelry box?

"No, she's working. Why?"

"Never mind. Yeah, it's almost done. I've got someone coming over tomorrow to show me some samples for the ring cushion and inner lining. I tried doing it myself, but it's definitely not my forte. I hope this will go better. It should match Geo's eyes. He brought three different cobalt blue linings, and I picked the one I think you'll like best."

"Sweet. Could I come see it? I'm with the jeweler now, trying to design a few things to put inside, and I want to know what the space looks like."

"Wait, we still have at least a month, right?"

"Yep, we finally settled on the weekend of July Fourth."

"Oh good. You had me sweating there for a minute."

"Jewelers take their sweet time on custom stuff, that's all."

"Then sure, you're welcome to take a look. I'll be home in fifteen minutes. Meet me whenever."

"If you're hungry, I can pick up some burgers."

I frown. This feels like some new Geo directed initiative to make Trig and Rob friends. "Are you sure Geo's not there twisting your arm?"

Trig laughs. "I'll be sure to tell them extra mayo." He hangs up.

I hate mayo, so that makes me smile. Business as usual.

Trig shows up later with a burger doused in mayo, but he brings me a large fry. It almost evens out. "Thanks for dinner."

He shrugs. "Thanks for being willing to make me something that will have some extra meaning to her."

"I'm happy to help."

"If I like the lining color, when will it be ready?"

"Another two weeks, probably. Better it's right than fast. I'm not McDonald's, after all."

Trig smirks. "I certainly hope not. But after today, I'll know. Let's see this thing."

I head for my shop and Trig stomps along after me, slurping on his soda. The sound annoys me, but I don't say a word. I'm not as irritated as I'd usually be. Geo would be giddy at that news.

"This place is huge," Trig says when he follows me through the door of my shop.

"Bigger than my house," I admit.

"Not hard to do," Trig mutters.

Trig winds around the furniture as we walk over to the jewelry box. Except, I realize he's not behind me anymore and turn around. "Hello? It's over here."

He's running his hand down the side of a small, dark wood chest of drawers I made to go with a crib. Is Trig one of those guys who are freaked out about the idea of having children? "Uh, Earth to Trig."

His head snaps my way. "Sorry. I got a little distracted. What did you say?"

"I said the jewelry box is over here by me." I point.

He takes a few steps toward me and looks at the crib as though he hadn't even noticed it. He runs his finger down the side post.

"Freaked out by the idea of having kids?"

Trig's head whips toward me again. "Kids? No, not at all. I love the little boogers. We babysit for Luke and Mary all the time."

"What's up with you being all dazed and loopy, then? Are you high?"

Trig opens his mouth and then closes it and then opens it again. "So the thing is, I have trouble saying good things about you. You know, without at least qualifying them or making it into a joke."

"Uh huh. I've noticed," I say.

"And I love when I can get a good jab in."

I nod. "Yep. Also true."

"You don't even seem to mind so much."

I shrug. "I've got thick enough skin."

"But this furniture." He waves his hand around the room.

I swallow even though I don't need to. I'm inexplicably nervous about what he'll say next. I brace myself for something snarky, something barbed. Or maybe even something downright rude.

"You have, what? A hundred pieces in here? A hundred and fifty?"

"I don't keep an inventory. Probably over a hundred, yeah." He thinks I'm insane. Like a little old lady who suffocates under her own pile of crocheted baby hats and newspaper clippings, except in my case, a carved wooden chair leg will impale me.

"It's all *staggeringly* good. Like, the hair on my arms is rising right now, as though I'm in the presence of greatness. How have you not sold any of this already? Geo said the desk you brought for her mom was amazing, but I sort of figured she was being nice. She and Paisley loaded it up and took it over right away, she was so excited to give it to her mom."

I have no idea what to say, but then something occurs to me. "You didn't come over to see what jewelry might fit."

Trig's face turns red.

"You came over to see if you needed to buy something else instead, and give yourself enough time to do it if you needed to."

"Who cares why I came? The point is, you need to quit your dumb car management job and do this all the time."

I shake my head. "I have no idea who would even buy any of it."

"Me," Trig says. "I'll buy all of it. But I imagine you would do better, like, auctioning it off. And then I wouldn't have to feel horribly guilty for swindling my soon-to-be wife's best friend."

If it really is good, maybe I could hold a charity auction. Clive's warm smile flashes through my mind. "I actually have an idea. You might be able to help me with it."

"What's that?" Trig asks.

"You have a lot of rich friends, right?"

Trig nods. "I guess so. You know Luke and Paul too, and they're well off. And as connected as I am, or close."

"I've been trying to figure out for a while how to fund an idea for a charity," I say. "I wonder if this might be a good way to get it off the ground."

"A charity?" Trig's eyebrows rise. "Why in the world would you do that? Then you don't get any of the money."

"That's kind of what charity means, yes."

"That's great, but maybe split the proceeds at least. I mean, you've got to have something to live on."

"I know a half a million a year is nothing to you," I say, "but

I live pretty well on that. I do a decent job at my family's business. I can afford to donate everything I make in my free time."

"Why wouldn't you quit that job and do this all the time?" Trig taps the shelf of a bookcase. "This is clearly your calling, and I don't say that lightly."

"I can't leave my family in the lurch like that. Trust me, there's no one else who can take my place. I've asked."

"Ask again," Trig says. "You wouldn't make Mozart spend his life playing the kazoo because no one else wanted to do it. There are plenty of people who can manage a car dealership. If there weren't, you wouldn't see them everywhere you can throw a rock."

"Duly noted," I say. "Now can we check out the jewelry box?"

Trig sighs. "You should listen to me, man. I know what I know."

Profound.

Trig meanders to where I'm standing and I point at the armoire. I made a base table for it that I have no idea whether he'll want. He said he'd fill it up for her, and filling it up felt like something that was supposed to take time, so I made it big. Maybe too big.

The center has seven slim drawers, the top three for rings, then three for bracelets and one that's open space. Then three larger drawers at the bottom are made to fit larger pieces like bulky bracelets, hair clips or jewelry she wants to keep in boxes.

"I made the center of the box of this honey colored quilted maple because I love the marbling. I wanted a darker contrast color for the waved doors in the front, and the legs, and the sides, so I used bubinga. It's a hardwood from Africa, and I love the contrast of the reddish tone against the pale gold of the maple."

"These open?" Trig points at the doors in front of the drawers.

"Yep, they just swing out."

Trig opens them gently, the doors swinging out so he can pull out the necklace holder slide bar. But when they're open, he doesn't pull out any of the ten drawers, or the necklace sliders. He bends down to read the engraving and exhales.

"You've already carved it."

"I know," I say. "I put your inscription across the lid, but then this just felt right. I can redo the doors if you want me to. I probably should have asked you first. Sometimes inspiration just strikes me."

I carved the words, "What I promise..." on the top left of the left side door. And on the bottom of the right, I carved, "I do."

"I thought about 'What I promise... I fulfill.' It sounded more poetic, but since it's a wedding gift, I do felt like the proper way to end it."

"It's absolutely perfect." Trig slides the necklaces holders out and back in. He opens the drawers slowly and they glide smoothly.

"I probably have time to redo anything you don't love. We could change wood colors, or——"

Trig grunts. "Nothing. I wouldn't change a single thing. It's immaculate. So delicate and refined and yet sturdy." He whistles. "Don't get mad, but I was expecting a little wooden box. This." He shakes his head. "I don't even know what to say, because it's even more impressive than the rest. You outdid yourself. Your suggested price is far, far too low."

"Oh no," I say, "A thousand is very generous."

"I'm not even going to bother arguing with you. I'll tip

you if you want to call it that." Trig points to the table the armoire jewelry box sits on. "What's this?"

"The base table is optional, and it's my gift if you want it. The jewelry box has so much hardware and solid wood that it's heavy, like almost sixty pounds. I worried it might be too heavy unless the base was made with that weight in mind. And I had this idea that Geo might stand in front of it to pick her jewelry, and then want to grab a scarf or gloves..." I trail off.

The base table matches, with the same two toned wood, and long carved legs, leading up to five large drawers out of the quilted maple again. It's about eight inches wider than the box, so it looks like it was designed to support it, like the box is a crown on top of a princess's head. Or maybe that's only in my mind.

"I want both. I'll pay you double the price of the box for the table."

"I insist on the table being a gift," I say. "Geo is my oldest friend. Remember?"

Trig sighs. "We can work that out later."

I drag him over to look at the samples for the interior of the box and Trig agrees with me on the color swatch I picked.

Half an hour later, he's still poking around at all the furniture I've stored up. "Hey, by the way, I've been meaning to tell you thank you," Trig says. "Brekka said you took her to the beach as an experiment and it wasn't as bad as she thought. She gave me the green light to do the wedding in Hawaii. Geo and I are delighted."

"About that," I say. "Geo asked me to sort of keep an eye on her mom. I'm a little nervous that I won't be able to be there for Brekka like I'd want to, since I'll be making sure Geo's mom is okay. Is there anyone else Brekka might trust to make sure she has whatever she needs on the sand?"

Trig leans on the partner's desk he was looking at. "I'm sure we can think of someone, but hopefully she won't need it. That may be overly optimistic, but you never know, right?"

"I'm afraid I don't understand," I say. "Why wouldn't Geo's mom need assistance? Is the clinical trial over? Has she been approved for daily doses?"

"Oh no, I meant Brekka."

"Why won't she need assistance? Her wheelchair won't roll in loose sand."

"Well, I mean, if the surgery goes well, Dr. Anthony said a full recovery takes time, but they encourage patients to be as mobile as possible as soon as possible. He knows when the wedding is and said we have every reason to hope—"

No. I shake my head. He can't be serious. "Are you saying Brekka's getting one of those stupid, risky, dangerous surgeries she mentioned? Now, after four stable years?"

Trig frowns. "Are you saying she didn't tell you?"

I can't meet his eye. Why didn't she tell me? "She mentioned she was talking to a doctor, but not that she scheduled anything."

Trig taps his fingers on the desk. "She confirmed the date while you were at the beach. She copied me on the email. I thought surely you were the one who convinced her. I wanted to offer to take you to dinner as a thank you. I've been trying for years without any luck."

I stiffen. Take me to dinner to thank me? For endangering her life on a snipe hunt? For gambling her current safety and quality of life on whispered prayers? "I'm the last person you should thank. I told her I thought this was the worst idea I'd ever heard. We fought about it, actually. I'd never want anyone to think I support this, not in any way."

"You're kidding, right?" Trig asks.

"Not remotely."

Trig sits in a wooden chair that's next to the desk and runs his hands through his hair. He's clearly overdue on a cut. "You didn't know Brekka before the accident. She was intrepid. Nothing scared her. She was the bravest person I know. She's always been small, but she didn't seem... I can't think of the word for what she is now, but—"

"Fragile. The word you're looking for is fragile," I say.

He throws his hands into the air. "Yes. That's exactly it. She was small, but she was never fragile, not like she is now. Brekka was a firecracker that would blow anything that got in her way into smithereens. It was a sight to see."

"She's still a firecracker." I think of the day she stormed my office to yell at me for interfering with Trig and Geo. It feels like an age, but mentally I compared her to a dragon.

"Right, you'd think so, but comparatively, she's—"

"No," I say. "Stop that right now. Stop comparing. Stop wanting her to be exactly the same as she was before. Things change and life changes us and we're different. We take a beating sometimes, and that alters us, sometimes profoundly. Those changes aren't always bad, and even when we think they are, they teach us and that strengthens us in a different way."

"She broke her back, Rob. And you know as well as I do that the stupid platitude 'what doesn't kill you makes you stronger' is rubbish. If I break my arm, that bone will always be weaker there. It never remodels as strong as it was before the break."

I pace from where we're standing toward the jewelry box and back again. "I know that biological fact, yes, but you're missing everything else."

"Like what?" Trig asks. "I've never broken my back, but you have. That gives you a unique perspective, but tell me this. Let's say your break hadn't healed. Wouldn't you jump at any chance to regain mobility?"

I would have. I absolutely would have. But I hate the idea of Brekka doing this and I can't articulate why.

"Look, my sister has been cowering in the corner since this happened. We had a cat once that got attacked by something. We didn't know what. But it huddled in the corner, completely fine other than a tiny scratch on its shoulder. We couldn't get to it and figured it would crawl out. It didn't. That poor cat would have hidden back there in shock until it died. Brekka's like that poor cat. She's been hiding. Before you came along, she was content to keep hiding. You've woken something in her, something that she needed to find again."

"She didn't need anything at all when we met. She was already dazzling," I say.

Trig rolls his eyes. "Spare me the besotted drivel. My point is that my sister's being brave again, for maybe the first time in four years. I'm going to support her, and if you're smart, you'll do the same thing."

Trig stands up and walks toward me slowly until he's inches away and we're eye to eye. "What you will not do is call or text her and freak out about it. You will not tell a woman you barely know what to gamble on or what to do with her life. Do you understand me?"

His order raises my hackles and my chest swells. I'm about to tell him where he can shove his advice until I remember what Brekka told me.

Trig blames himself.

He's a wounded animal, too. He needs Brekka to do something, anything to save herself. He needs atonement, and she's refused to give him any hope he'll ever have it.

I lower my voice as much as I can, trying to defuse the situation, not torque it any more. "Are you sure this isn't about you, Trig? Your guilt? Your hopes?"

Trig stares at me for a full minute, pivots on his heel and walks out of my shop.

I collapse onto a chair and put my face in my hands. I hate that she's doing this. I want to call her and yell. I want to rant about what a horrible idea it is. I want to discuss the ramifications, the risks. I want her to believe that spending time with me is precious and she's endangering it.

I want to be enough for her.

But if I'm being honest with myself, Trig's right. I barely know her. I need to mind my own business. It should be easy to do, since Brekka didn't even trust me enough to tell me she's having the surgery in the first place.

I whip out my phone and text Trig. I WON'T SAY A WORD. I WON'T EVEN TELL HER THAT I KNOW ABOUT THE SURGERY.

THANK YOU.

BUT I HAVE A CONDITION.

Trig's emojis may be borderline girly, but his talent at creatively using swearwords offsets it. I grin and push ahead.

YOU'LL TELL ME THE LOCATION AND LET ME BE THERE FOR THE SURGERY. YOU DON'T NEED TO TELL HER, AND I WON'T SEE HER BEFORE OR INTERFERE AFTERWARD, BUT I WANT TO BE CLOSE.

I CAN AGREE TO THAT, he texts back.

I breathe a sigh of relief. Now just ninety bazillion more breaths in and out before that feeling of an anvil on my chest will clear. I can do this, right?

❦ 15 ❦

BREKKA

I'm sick of wearing this flimsy open-backed surgical gown already and I've only had it on for eight minutes.

"Hey, can I ask you something?"

Dr. Anthony turns to me, a clipboard in his hand. "Anything."

Anything? Really? A bizarre, twisted part of me wants to ask him something strange, like what he ate for dinner last night, or whether he likes trying on women's shoes in the privacy of his own home. But I don't. I focus on what matters.

"In your opinion, is it likely I could ever have children?"

Dr. Anthony lowers his clipboard until it rests against his legs. "Well, I'm not an OB, but we did quite a few tests recently. We have every reason, based on everything I saw, to assume that you could, yes. You aren't pregnant currently, however. We did confirm that."

My belly laugh surprises him. "You have to engage in intercourse to get pregnant," I explain. "So it's funny, because there's no way I could possibly be pregnant."

Dr. Anthony frowns. "You have sensation throughout your pelvic region currently, so there's really no reason you couldn't be—"

"Never mind," I say, wishing I had never brought it up.

"You should know, since it's on the paperwork you signed, that there's a twelve percent chance you'll lose this ability should this procedure go poorly."

Twelve percent. If I had a twelve percent chance of having a zit on my chin tomorrow, I wouldn't be concerned. After all, odds are against it. I may not be Trig, but I'm good with numbers. But twelve percent chance I can't have kids tomorrow, when I probably can today seems steep. A vision of a baby pops into my head.

Goofy, it's so goofy, but I can't shake it.

The baby has my tiny hands, but Rob's big blue eyes. It has my thick hair, and Rob's aquiline nose. When she smiles, I can see Rob's dimple, just on the right side of her face. A single dimple, just like her dad. And I realize I've lost my mind, thinking about having a baby with a guy I barely know.

I want this surgery so I'll be good enough for Rob. But what if having it ruins our future? My stomach hurts thinking about it.

"Can I still make calls?" I ask.

Dr. Anthony's eyes widen. He brushes the hair that's combed over the top of his head sideways, as though that might increase its volume. "If you have calls to make, you need to make them immediately. We're in the final stage of pre-op right now." He glances at his clock. "I can give you ten minutes. Is that sufficient?"

I nod. "Thanks."

He slips out the door and pulls it closed behind him. My finger hovers over the call button, my eyes staring at the name saved for the contact: Robert Graham. He doesn't even know I'm going in for surgery, but if he did, what would he tell me? He'd probably yell and tell me not to do this. If he were close enough, he'd probably scowl, his big blue eyes flashing, and wave his hands in the air. That's what he did last time I mentioned it in passing. And he had barely kissed me then. I didn't even know the shape of his back and shoulders, or the feel of his skin under my fingers. I didn't know how he taps his lips when he's reading. I know him so little, and yet he's all I think about.

My finger nearly presses the button. I want to hear his voice one last time, if I happen to be one of the tiny few who doesn't survive the procedure. I want to imagine him standing next to me, holding my hand. He'd be so angry, I doubt handholding would be a likely reaction for him, but it's what I want more than anything.

Of course, being mad at me for doing this would be idiotic since I'm doing it for him, or more specifically for us, so we have some semblance of hope for a future. So we could have a real family, not some poor facsimile of what we might have been. He admitted that he gave up when he thought he wouldn't ever walk. He admitted he threw in the towel entirely.

I want to call him and convince him that I'm making the right decision.

Or maybe I want him to convince me. But of what?

I've been fasting since yesterday at five, and somehow my stomach churns anyway. Should I go through with this? They're going to slice open my back, and then cut into my spine and dig around.

I shudder.

They'll inject a compound that has been proven to destroy scar tissue. Once that has had time to process, which varies depending on the severity of the scarring, they'll inject stem cells. Then more stem cells. The idea is to stimulate the areas of the spine that have died to grow anew. Then they'll shift down and repeat the entire thing again below the highest point.

My spinal cord will pulse there, exposed. My nerve cells are going to be attacked by outside forces, in the hopes they will regrow, heal, and I'm the one sending in the troops. Before I can decide whether to call Rob or not, my phone rings. I nearly drop it.

I swipe without thinking, sure somehow that it's Rob. He could feel my angst. The universe has connected us and he's going to tell me what to do, I know it.

"Hey Brekka," Trig says. "I wasn't sure whether I'd catch you."

"Where are you?" I ask.

"I'm in the waiting room outside," he says. "Duh. Where else would I be?"

I look at the ceiling. "What are you calling for?" I wipe away a tear. I'm not sure whether I'm crying because I'm afraid, or because my brother called and I love him, or because he's not Rob.

"You came in too early," he says. "I came by your room, but they said you'd already left. I was going to give you a ride over and hold your hand."

"I didn't need that," I lie. I could really use him here right now. My hand needs a solid squeeze.

"I had this dream last night, Brekka," he says, his voice dropping lower, so quiet that I can barely hear him. "It was my wedding, and we were walking along the white sands in Hawaii, hand-in-hand."

"You and Geo?" I ask.

He snorts. "No, you and me, goofball. Why would I call you to tell you about Geo and me? That would be fruitless. I wouldn't even be able to see you roll your eyes."

"So you had a dream of us on the sand, walking, and

instead of thinking it's a memory, you assumed it's a prophecy?"

He groans. "Not you too."

"What does that mean?"

"Nothing. Look, my point is that I feel calm about this. I feel amazing, actually. How are you feeling? Are you nervous at all?"

I can't bring myself to speak.

"Brekka, you've spent four years paralyzed physically, but emotionally too. You've been hiding in the office out in Denver. I've been following along and watching all these amazing miracles coming from Dr. Anthony's research, and every single time I've thought, that could have been Brekka. She could have her life back. But now you're finally doing it. I am so proud of you. Have I mentioned that? I'm so proud."

I mumble something. No idea what, and then I hang up.

When I hear a tap on the door and Dr. Anthony pokes his head inside, I force a smile. "I'm ready. Thanks."

"Good to hear. If you hand me your phone I'll put it with your other belongings. Then lie back here, and we'll take you down."

I lie down and close my eyes. I hope it's not the last time, but I can't bring myself to open them again the entire way to the operating room.

16

ROB

I'm almost thirty, and this is my first time in New York City. My redeye flight lands right on time and I have no trouble hailing a cab. It takes me straight to the hospital where Brekka's having her surgery. I'd never have snagged a cab this fast at four in the morning in Atlanta. If I could even find one at all.

I pay my bill by credit card and step out to the curb. Technology amazes me these days. But the lights and sirens and bustle of people at this hour baffle me. New York certainly qualifies as the city that never sleeps. Then again, the streets in Atlanta don't smell of fecal matter and vomit. At least, not the parts I've visited.

The hospital smells marginally better than the road behind it. Not as much better as I might have hoped, but it is a place sick people come for care. I imagine that brings some legitimate explanation for the lingering puke scent.

I sit in the waiting room for half an hour before Trig arrives. He puts an arm around my shoulder and pulls me in for a side hug, which I didn't expect.

"Who would ever have believed a few months ago that

you and I would be sitting in a waiting room together?" Trig asks.

I shake my head. "Certainly not me."

"Well, I sure like you a lot better than I did back in February."

"Your opinion really had nowhere to go but up," I say. "If we're being honest."

"I didn't like you," he says, "but I actually started to respect you when you took my call before my Valentine's Day grand gesture. If our positions had been reversed, I'd probably have declined the call."

"Your curiosity would have won out," I say.

"You think?"

I shrug. "I think we're a lot more alike than you realize."

Trig scratches his chin. "You might be right. Some days I wish I had a decent mom, but then I'd probably have been as big a wash up as you."

I don't laugh.

Trig frowns. "You know I'm kidding right? You got a little defensive about the car dealership before. I know you're smart, and I know you do a great job running your dealerships. I even know you make a lot of money by most people's standards."

"Thanks." I can't bring myself to be more effusive. I don't need his compliments. I know my own worth. I grab an old issue of *Car and Driver* and pretend to read it, flipping a little too fast to be convincing. I force myself to slow down.

"You're nervous," Trig says. "You're wound up even tighter than normal."

"No."

"You are." Trig knocks the magazine out of my hand. "You don't need to be. She's going to be fine."

I lean toward him and my voice comes out a little rougher than I expect. "You don't know that."

"It's a simple procedure, really. They disclosed the official percentages and risks, but all the people who died were a lot sicker than Brekka, and way older too. No one her age and in such great health has had a bad outcome."

"Do you even hear yourself? No one her age has *died*?? I'm not just worried she'll die."

"Then what? What's got you wound tighter than a trampoline spring?"

"She could have things a lot worse than she does," I say. "A lot worse. If you'd spend even a few hours with people with disabilities, you'd know that."

"Oh, and where would I do that? It's not like there are clubs."

I close my eyes. "There are clubs, Trig. They call them groups, but it's the same thing. There are groups for people with disabilities where they can talk about how life changed, and groups for their loved ones."

"Did your family go to those groups?"

I nod. "All three of my sisters did."

"Geo?"

"She did in Miami, and she took me to my meetings, too."

Trig slumps in his chair. "If you're going to be all gloom and doom, can you sit over there?" He points to the far corner. "This side is for the Cheer Bears of the world, like Paisley."

I pretend to clean the inside of my ear out with my finger. "I'm sorry, did you say Cheer Bear?"

"Brekka loved Care Bears. I got stuck watching it sometimes."

"I have three sisters and I can proudly say I have no

idea what any of them are called. But I assume Cheer Bear is an actual character? Your favorite, maybe?"

Trig throws a magazine at me. I snag it. Cosmopolitan. I toss it back. "I'm sorry, you must have thrown that by accident. I'm sure you want to read it, at least until you've looked up your horoscope, Cheer Bear."

"Shaddup."

"Make me."

Trig grins. "You're like a five-year-old kid today."

"Maybe I am nervous."

"You can say it," he says.

"Say what?"

"You're a nervous wreck, because you like her." Trig's pats his throat with one hand and then clears his throat. "Me me me. I think I'm ready for my solo performance. Now how does this go? It's a classic. Oh, I remember. Rob and Brekka, sitting in a tree. K-I-S-S-I-N-G."

I ought to ignore him. Or stand up and pace. Or bean him with another magazine. Instead, I feel my cheeks heat.

"Wait." Trig grins. "She didn't tell you that I know?"

"Know what?"

"One of her employees sent me a photo of you two in the board room." He leans back and closes his eyes. "It was really gross to have to see the guy I hate kissing my little sister."

I roll my eyes. "Now who's wound up?"

"You are proving to be a decent distraction." He glances at the clock on the wall. "Twelve minutes down. Just another three hundred and eighty-five to go."

"Wait, how long do they really think this will take?" I ask. "I thought it was a simple procedure, like an injection and nothing else."

"Well, there are stem cell injections, but between you and

me, they aren't very effective. Dr. Anthony's team thinks the scar cells inhibit the growth of any new cells in the spinal column. They employ the use of a scrubber to remove the scar tissue. That's the reason their results are so much better."

It's also the reason their side effects and risks are worse. Trig doesn't say that, but he doesn't have to. I want to argue about how stupid he sounds, but I can't sit here and bicker with him for six hours. I'll probably end up strangling him if I do, and then no matter how the surgery goes, Brekka will never speak to me again. Which won't matter much, since I'll be in prison.

"You hungry?" Trig asks.

"I already ate."

"What did you eat?" Trig asks. "Nothing's open. So much for New York's vaunted fanciness. Nothing in the hospital, and nothing between the hotel and here was selling food. I've had a Snickers bar, and that's it. But the crappy coffee kiosk opens in ten minutes. I can grab you something. Bagel, muffin, banana, whatever you want."

"I'm good."

"How can you be good? What did you eat?" Trig asks. "Don't turn me down from frustration. Hangry Rob has got to be worse than regular old cranky Rob."

"I brought a bag full of protein bars." I unzip the outside pocket and pull one out. "I'm happy to share. I might have over packed, honestly."

"Are you kidding me right now? I thought you had like an amazing metabolism or something. Do you really eat that crap? Ugh. I bet you wash those blocks of chewy protein powder down with a glass full of raw eggs like Gaston."

I can't quite help my grin. "For someone who made fun of me for my Rainbow Dash reference, you sure seem to know your Disney princess stories."

Trig frowns.

"And for the record, protein bars aren't that bad."

"They aren't good either."

"You're such a foodie. I have neither the time nor the patience for that."

Trig stands up. "Well, I've got news for you. You've got nothing but time today."

I walk around the empty waiting room a few times. Then I drop down and do a hundred push-ups. Old habits.

"Are you secretly an alien? Because no human person just does push-ups randomly in hospitals. And PS, that floor is nasty."

I roll my eyes. "We're stuck here waiting. What do you care how I pass the time?"

"You just told me you're making out with my sister, and I can't have her dating a crazy person."

"Doing a few pushups gets the blood flowing."

Trig's mouth hangs open.

"You should try it."

"You're odder than I thought," Trig says. "But if I had half your energy, I might look a little more like you. I guess I should be glad Geo prefers slim guys."

"She told you that?"

Trig scowls. "Actually, no. She never said that. Why? Did she tell you something else?"

I shake my head as quickly as I can.

"She told you I'm too skinny?" He hops to his feet.

"You know what?" I ask. "I think I'm going to go for a quick jog."

"At six a.m.?"

I shrug. "Nothing else to do, and it's not hot out yet."

"You're wearing khaki shorts and a Polo shirt."

I lift one foot. "I'm wearing sneakers. I won't go far enough to get sweaty and gross."

Trig shakes his head.

Three miles later, if my Fit Bit is to be trusted, I circle back around and head for the waiting room. Trig's typing away on his laptop.

"Everything okay?"

Trig shrugs. "I guess so. No news here."

"So. Want to play a game or something?"

He brightens up. "Do you like chess?"

I laugh loudly. "Oh, absolutely not. Anyone who can beat Geo occasionally is far, far beyond my level. I always have to ask for a reminder of how exactly that dumb horse piece can move."

Trig stuffs his hands in his pockets. "What kind of game were you thinking, then?"

"They have a basketball hoop outside, and there are a few local kids out there. I'm sure they'd love to school some old guys."

"If you aren't going to play chess, I'm sure not about to play Mr. All State at basketball."

I smirk. "Geo told you?"

"Nice try Mr. Sneaky."

"Well we need to think of something," I say, "or we might kill each other before Brekka makes it to recovery."

In the end, we find *The Godfather* on TV, just a few minutes into the very first one. A dozen other people filter into the room as the movie progresses, even though it's a Saturday. Luckily, it's a Godfather marathon. We're nearly through the second one when a lady in a white coat approaches Trig.

He shoots to his feet, and I'm only a second behind him.

"Mr. Thornton?" she asks.

"Trig, remember?"

She nods. "Trig. Brekka's surgery is finished."

I breathe a sigh of relief and the doctor glances sharply my way. "Who's this?"

Trig waves his hand through the air. "It's her...boyfriend. Or sort of her boyfriend. It's complicated."

She bobs her head. "It almost always is. In any case, she's through surgery and in recovery."

"Can I come see her?" Trig asks.

"Not yet. People come out of anesthesia at differing speeds, depending on the type and duration of surgery. Also, everyone reacts in different ways. We'll let you know once she's ready to see you and her, Mr., what did you say your name was sir?"

"She doesn't know I'm here," I say. "And I promised her brother I'd keep it that way."

She yawns and shakes her head. "Whatever, then. I'll come let you both know."

She turns to leave, but Trig touches her arm. "How did it go?"

"It's early yet." She doesn't say more, but her feet shuffle and she glances at the door eagerly.

Something is wrong.

Trig's as sharp as me. Smarter, probably, and he notices it too. "Do you have preliminary findings of any kind?"

She shakes her head. "This isn't my responsibility. Dr. Anthony will be out to talk to you soon."

"It didn't go well?" Trig asks. "The surgery didn't work?"

She licks her lips nervously. "It frequently takes several surgeries before we know whether the patient will respond to the therapy."

"The therapy?" I ask. "Did Brekka know that?"

"We've had several instances where there was improvement with the first procedure," she says.

"But?" I ask.

"But she had more scar tissue than we anticipated."

"And?" I press.

"And our attempts to mitigate were unsuccessful. Dr. Anthony isn't hopeful the stem cells had anything much to work with."

Trig punches the chair and then kicks the end table.

"I'll be back when there's more to report." The doc hurries off.

"Well, I'm glad you got her hopes up. I'm sure if she can't move her legs at all, or if she can't feel her abdomen, or if she needs an ostomy bag, she'll feel it was well worth it for the unproven chance of possible improvement that's more like a Star Trek show than actual science."

Trig sits down and puts both his hands in his hair. "You heard her. They frequently need several tries before there's improvement. She has a lot of scar tissue. A few more rounds and they'll make better progress."

I clench my hands into fists. Several attempts? Brekka will be risking her life, not to mention her quality of life, every single time. "You may be the single most selfish person I've ever met."

"Excuse me?" Trig leaps to his feet. People around us shift and a few of them move to the other side of the waiting room, darting glances back at us worriedly.

"You heard me. You feel guilty for being the driver when this happened. You feel guilty for not making her buckle her seatbelt, and I get that. It's not your fault, but you think it is. It's time now for you to put on your big boy pants and let that go. Because if you don't." I pause. I should quit talking right now. I'm too upset for this to be helpful. But one look at Trig's jaw convinces me he'll never let this go. "Will you really kill your sister, just to assuage your own guilt?"

Trig grabs my collar. "Say that again, I dare you."

"I don't have to repeat it. You know it's true or you'd already have thrown me against that wall."

Trig lets me go and picks up his phone. "I don't need to do a thing to you. You're nothing to Brekka and me. Listening to you rant is a waste of my time. But for the record, I'm already looking at the next open dates on Dr. Anthony's schedule. I finance the entire study, so I can check the protocol to see how long we have to wait, and then drop her into any open slot."

"You can't possibly be ethically allowed—"

Trig's face brightens and his eyes darken. "Allowed? You think I care about what's allowed? For the first time ever, my sister's fighting. She wants to fix her back so she can move on with her life. She hit pause the day of that accident and she hasn't ever resumed. She wants to repair this, and I will move heaven and earth to help her. I'd never give up after one single procedure, because I don't run from things that are hard. Now I know why you didn't want her to know you're here. Because you're not in this for the long haul, for better or worse."

I suddenly realize what's been bothering me. He treats Brekka like she's broken, and what's worse, she believes him. She thinks she needs to be fixed, in part because everyone acts like she's not okay exactly as she is.

My fist connects with Trig's cheek before I have time to think my anger through. Luckily, I pull back at the last moment and my fist doesn't break his skull or even his nose. Geo would probably never have spoken to me again if I'd permanently damaged his pretty little face.

Trig flies back against the wall from the force of the blow, blood spewing from his aristocratic nostrils.

I bend over him ominously. "I didn't break anything that won't mend. But if you ever imply to me or anyone else, but most especially to your sister, that she's broken, or less than, or lacking in any way, I will rectify my mistake. Your sister is beautiful, and she is magnificent, and she is fierce. She may be fragile, but that's only because of her fear. And I'm not talking about her rational and logical and natural fear of signing up to do more surgeries that will only leave her with additional loss to process."

Trig moans.

I hope he can hear and recall what I'm saying. "Hear me when I say this, Trig. Brekka can't fix her back now, and she doesn't need to. That's not what's holding her back."

His eyes flash and I know he's paying attention. He wads the bottom of his shirt up and presses it against his nose to stop the bleeding.

"The fear that's eroding Brekka's bravery, sapping her strength, and leaving her as unsure as an adolescent is that she's not enough anymore. That fragility will eventually fade away and reveal the iron underneath, but not if you keep telling her through your words and your actions that she really isn't enough. It's time for her to face who she is now and accept it."

I storm out of the waiting room before Trig says something else and I end up getting arrested for assault.

17

BREKKA

My eyes flutter open, but the room beyond my nose is blurry. When I close them again, I find that I can focus on the world around me better without trying to see it. Machines beep behind me, people murmur, and something whirs. My back has been stabbed with a hot poker. The throbbing, oh, the throbbing. I shift my shoulders and it worsens.

I cry out and hands press against my shoulders.

I want to go back to the utter darkness where nothing hurt, and no one was telling me to open my eyes and stare into the blazing light of the sun.

"Brekka?" A hand squeezes mine. "Brekka, it's me."

I know the voice somehow, but my head feels like it's full of pudding. Why do I know the voice? I swim through the pudding toward the movement, the light, and the beeping.

"Ouch," I moan.

"She's awake," the voice I know says. "Brekka's awake."

Brekka. That's me. I blink and blink and blink, but there's so much light and my eyes burn, and my back screams at me, and my throat feels raw, like someone cheese-grated it.

"I'm so happy to see your beautiful face," the voice says. "How do you feel?"

Like I've been swimming in Jello and someone threw vodka in my eyes, you idiot. Like I'm impaled on a spike through my spine.

At least my legs don't hurt.

"The surgery was long, but it's over."

A surgery. I had some kind of surgery. That's why I'm here. That's why my back hurts. Is it why my legs don't hurt? I try to wiggle my toes and I can't. My heart rate accelerates and the machine starts beeping loudly. Much louder than before.

"It's okay, Brekka, I promise. Calm down. Dr. Anthony said you'd be a little out of it as the drugs wear off, but they've cleared you, and you're stable."

"My feet," I croak.

My fingers tingle and my head weighs three hundred pounds, and my back's throbbing, but I can't move my feet. Nothing else is quite as pressing as that. I open my mouth.

"You don't need to talk. Your throat probably hurts from the intubation. It's fine. We can talk as much as you want later. I'm here for you."

I open my eyes again with real intent this time. I need to see what's going on around me.

A face swims in front of me, a face I know as well as my own. "Trig." I finally tie a name to the voice and the face. "You're here."

He squeezes my tingly fingers. "Of course I am. I'd never miss something like this, never. I'm always here for you, now, forever. No matter what."

"Look at this reading here," someone behind Trig says.

He turns to see whether she's talking to us and I gasp.

His eye is swollen and puffy and the side of his face is bright purple.

"What happened?" I rasp. "Your face!"

"Oh, nothing," he says. "A little misunderstanding, that's all."

"You look awful." I cough. "Did you do that to make me feel better about my surgery?"

Regret fills his face. "Brekka, I can't even tell you—we don't have time to talk about it now. But we do need to talk. I've been stupid."

I reach for his face, the uninjured side. "I love you, Trig. You're my best friend, always."

For some reason that makes him cry. Big, fat, messy tears, and then he winces, like crying hurts his face. "You're my best friend too, forever. I would never hurt you on purpose."

I struggle to push myself up, to sit, but people converge on me from every direction, hands pushing me back down, mouths clucking, and other people shushing. An older nurse with a severe frown ushers Trig from the room and someone else pushes some buttons.

They must have pushed some kind of medicine into my IV, because I flop back to the bed like a marionette with cut strings and everything goes extremely hazy. Someone wheels me into another room a few moments later with much less noise, lower light, and only one tiny beep every few seconds. I breathe a sigh of relief.

A few moments later, the same stern woman who shooed everyone away, including Trig, returns with my brother in tow.

"Don't forget," she whispers to him loudly, "you agreed to keep her calm."

He nods and sits on a chair next to my bed. He reaches

for me and then freezes and drops his hand back into his lap.

"My surgery didn't go well." I'm not asking. I can tell from the expression on his face.

"They won't know how it went for at least twenty-four hours. They'll let you recover and then begin a series of tests." His voice is flat.

"But those are a formality." My voice sounds angry. Which is strange. I don't feel angry.

"Dr. Anthony said you had more scar cells than he expected based on the scans."

I turn to look at the wall, but it's completely bare, and utterly boring. Which is exactly what I need to focus on tonight. A blank wall. That's how I feel. Like I'm a hollowed out bowl, empty, alone, and useless. Suddenly I'm spiraling, and I don't know how to stop it. My face crumples and I begin to weep silently.

I may never pee on my own again. I may not ever feel my stupid, weak, disappointing toes again. Having intermittent feeling didn't seem like a big deal yesterday, but now, the idea of never feeling a single thing below my waist guts me. I'll never ever feel Rob touch my feet, or grab my knees, probably. Which is a stupid thing to think at all, because now I'll never be anything to Rob. Even the best doctors in the country couldn't fix me.

I'm Humpty Dumpty.

I'm so tired of being freaking Humpty Dumpty. I hate my life, my half-life. Work, work, work. That's all I'm good for anymore. And suddenly, out of the blue, I hate the idea of working ever again. I hate the idea of that being the only way I'll ever add value. I never wanted it, I never asked for it, and yet somehow, here I am.

I am my mother.

Trig's body sinks next to me and his arm wraps around my shoulders, which makes me cry harder.

"I'm so sorry," he says. "I didn't realize I was making you feel like you weren't perfect and amazing and magnificent. You are. You impress and shock and inspire me every day."

I turn my head and sob into the fabric covering his shoulder. "You didn't do anything wrong, Trig. You're the one person who has never let me down, never. You're always here. The only one who's always here for me, no matter how pathetic I am." Even when I'm a failure and I can't even do surgery right. Even when nothing in the world can glue me back into something worthwhile.

He mumbles something I can't understand.

My head is clearing, my eyes work fine now, and I can move my head and shoulders without pain. I wonder if my ears are inexplicably on the fritz. "Trig, I can't hear you."

He clears his throat. "I said someone else was here for you, too."

I scowl at him. "Did you tell Mom? You promised not to tell her."

He shakes his head. "No, not Mom."

I groan. "Oh my gosh, Dad is worse. He's going to order me a pony or something and march it right into the hospital. Or dump a hundred boxes of bon bons into this room. He truly believes French chocolate fixes everything."

"I could totally go for an eclair right now," Trig says. "Oh, or some macarons!"

I drop my head back against the pillows. Dad's always got good intentions, but he's like a kid in a candy store with an unlimited black Am Ex. "I can't handle him. Please don't let him in here, at least not until tomorrow."

"I didn't tell Dad."

I turn toward Trig again. "If Geo's here, she can come inside. I thought you said she was working."

Trig won't meet my eyes. "It's not Geo."

"Who else is here? Just tell me." I'm suddenly exhausted. It feels like laying here on a hospital bed is too much work. Breathing in and out, and interacting and thinking, it's all so very difficult.

"I might have accidentally mentioned to Rob that you were having surgery, and—"

"Rob's here?" I slap Trig, which I guess means I've got complete control of my arms, even if I didn't mean to do it. "Why are you just now mentioning this? Where is he?"

Oh, please God, do not let him see me like this. Please.

"He left, right after he gave me this black eye."

I close my eyes and count to ten. I'm not sure what that's supposed to do, but everyone says to do it when you're upset. Now I feel exactly the same as before I counted, except I feel a little silly for expecting something that stupid to work. Should I do it again? Or count higher, maybe?

"Say something," Trig says.

"Like what?" I ask. "I've been counting in my head. I'd love to shove you off the bed, or give you a matching black eye, but I don't feel up to either one of those things right now."

"Why are you mad at me, exactly?" he asks.

"Why am I mad? Let's see. First you tell Rob I'm doing a surgery he was dead set against, and then you don't confess to me that you told him, and then he flies out here while I'm at my absolute worst and waits with you in the waiting room, punching you for unknown reasons, and then you don't mention any of that to me, and simply drop this bomb as soon as it's too late for me to decide what I want to do about it."

"Wait, he was dead set—"

"No," I say. "You don't get to talk yet. I'm not done, because I still don't know where he is, or why he punched my loud-mouthed brother. You tell me my boyfriend's here, and then give me no details that matter."

Trig's jaw drops and his eyes bug out of his head. "He's actually your boyfriend?"

He kissed me. A lot of times. We text daily. He calls me before he goes to bed at night. I smile every time I hear from him, even if it's a stupid text. And most of all, he's been sitting in a waiting room in New York City for who knows how long because he knew I was in a surgery he didn't want me to have. "I think maybe he is, yeah. Wait, did he fly here with you?"

Trig shakes his head. "No, he flew commercial."

I close my eyes. He bought a ticket and flew commercial, and then took a cab at who knows what time in the morning. And then he gave Trig a black eye. "Why'd he hit you?"

Trig scowls and then winces. I'm guessing that frowning like that pulls on some sensitive skin. Rob really belted him good. I hope it's healed up before the wedding. There's a month. I'm sure it'll be fine. I hope. Either way, Geo's going to be pissed.

"Are you ever going to tell me?"

"We might have had a disagreement when the doctor told us your surgery probably wouldn't result in any improvement to your condition."

I can imagine Rob, roaring at Trig like a lion, calling him selfish or something like it, I'm sure. It makes me smile, because I'm a complete hot mess. In almost twenty-eight years, no guy has ever punched anyone or done anything even remotely similar because of me. I know that's a stupid thing to smile about. But I love the idea that he's so worked up over something that he feels he needs to defend me.

Officially, I'm outraged, of course. "What a Neanderthal," I say. "I'm so mad." He did admit he was old fashioned to me. He apologized for it, I think.

Trig frowns again, and winces. He's not really learning quick on this one. "So you're really mad at him?" Trig asks.

"Don't I sound mad?"

He shakes his head, "Not really, no." He grunts. "You can't possibly condone violence, and against your only brother, of all people."

"What exactly did you say to him?" I ask.

Trig looks at his hands and mumbles again, which is how I know he's feeling guilty.

"Can't hear you."

"I said, it wasn't as much about what I said. It's more what I was doing. I may have been looking at times we could schedule you for a follow-up."

My face blanks, but my heart breaks. "Your wedding is in a month. You wanted me to have another surgery before then?"

Trig's hands ball up in the sheet on my bed. "No, I don't know. I don't want you to do anything, not anymore."

I'm so confused.

"I was so encouraged," he says. "I was so ... hopeful. I've felt like I ruined your life ever since the car crash, and there was nothing I could do about it, no way for me to fix it. No way to take back my mistake. Nothing I could do. I felt helpless, as paralyzed as you were, but in a different way." His eyes meet mine. "Can you understand what I'm saying at all?"

I nod. Of course I understand. Poor Trig. He makes mistakes a lot, but he always does anything and everything he can to make them right, up to and including giving away several billion dollars, all without ever looking back. He has a heart as big as New York City, or Texas, or even China. But he's not always the best at thinking things through. And personal introspection is practically his kryptonite.

He closes his eyes. "I guess when you said you'd do this, and they have that kid who is *walking* again, Brekka. I guess my hopes might have flown a little too close to the sun."

"You want what I have always wanted," I say. "A rewind button. Or a reset button."

He nods. "I want it for you so badly. I want you to be able to go back in time and live your dreams. I want the Olympic Gold medals and the media coverage and the accolades. I want you to dance at my wedding, and then at yours. I want the sun and the moon and the stars for you," Trig says. "It's all I've ever wanted."

I laugh. The sun, the moon and the stars, that's all. It's such a Trig thing to say. He just wants every single thing in the world, plus a cherry on top, pretty please. But at the end of the day, he'd have settled for me being able to walk again.

So would I.

And now I'm just hoping I won't be wearing an adult diaper tomorrow. A tear trails down my cheek. I'm so stupid.

A knock at the door sends my heart racing. Is it Rob? Is he here? I wipe at my face frantically, and my fingers fumble for my drape to make sure I'm covered, then fly to my hair. What does it look like? A bird's nest, I'm sure. Oh, gosh, this is a nightmare.

"Delivery," a man's voice says.

Not Rob's voice.

I should be relieved. I should be grateful. So why does my heart feel broken, like I was promised a bowl of ice cream and I got unsalted, mushy peas instead?

The man sets a huge vase of flowers on the counter against the wall. Birds of paradise. Most people send roses, or carnations, or lilies. I've never seen anyone send birds of paradise. The man then hands me a white box with a card poking out of the top.

"Who sent these?" Trig asks.

The man shrugs and heads for the door.

"It's probably from Dad," I say.

Trig reaches for the box. "Want me to open it?"

My hands are shaking. I should pass it off and let Trig manage it, but I shake my head as the delivery guy walks out. "I can get it."

My fingers open the box, the card falling to the bed and then sliding further down and dropping to the floor. I swear under my breath. Trig climbs off the bed to retrieve it. I open the box while I'm waiting.

It's the cutest little red crab stuffed animal I've ever seen. It almost looks like it's winking at me, its red pincers chubby and cartoon-esque. Trig hands me the card.

My fingers feel like sausages, but I finally open it.

Brekka,

I'm sure you're crabby with me right now. I shouldn't have punched your brother in the face. I hope you can forgive me. Heaven help me, but I'm still so mad at him, I don't really care whether he ever does.

I wasn't sure if you'd want to see me or not. I figured it was safer to send a stuffed emissary than to show up without an invitation to a hospital bed. If you want a hug from me, he can give you one, and if you don't, you can throw it in the trash can as hard as you want to without injuring anyone else. The birds of paradise are because you're the most beautiful bird I've ever seen, and the most unique too. You don't need to be like anyone else to be breathtaking, and you've stolen my breath since the moment you shoved your way past my frightening secretary and into my office.

I have an ulterior motive for my choice of gift. It's a reminder of our last date and an invitation to another rendezvous at the beach. I know you'll need time to recover, and I'll give you all the space you want, but I am counting the minutes until I can see you again. And I want to be your date to Trig and Geo's wedding, if I'm still invited, that is.

Yours longingly,

Rob

I hug the crab against me and wish I was hugging the man instead. But if he'd come himself, I'd have been a bundle of nerves. He's probably right. I'd have been edgy and felt stupidly self-conscious. Better he sent an adorable emissary.

One glance at Trig tells me it was smart of Rob not to come back quite so soon. Still, it means a lot he came and sat here for the entire thing.

"Rob," Trig says.

I nod.

"That guy is a plague."

"He's not."

Trig circles the bed and sits in the chair. "You really like him."

I nod. "I do like him. I thought maybe I'd ruined everything, but he followed me, even here. He always does just the right thing."

"He's all wrong for you, though."

I roll to one side, my heart in my throat. I've thought it a dozen times, but hearing Trig say it hurts. "Why exactly do you say that?"

He holds up his index finger. "He's never been to college. He has no education, and no degree."

I clench my fists. "What do you care? You're such a snob."

"He's a former Marine."

"How is that a bad thing?" I huff. "I'm impressed by that."

"He broke his back, too."

My heart lurches. "What does that have to do with anything?"

"He could have issues from it later on in life. You don't know."

"Again, so what? I have issues now. You didn't date Geo because she was a promising horse to bet money on or to breed. You didn't have her genetically tested. Her mom's got Alzheimer's. What if she passes that gene along to your kids, or gets it herself?"

Trig's lips twist in fury and I know I've finally gotten through to him.

"Before you yell at me, you need to acknowledge I'm right, even if it's silently to yourself. Rob has recovered, and being injured while serving his country isn't a black strike against him."

Trig clicks his mouth shut. "You're right, but he sells cars, Brekka. He's a car salesman."

"Oh? And you're what? How is a butcher any better?"

"Huh?" Trig asks. "What does that even mean?"

"We invest in some companies," I say, "but we slice up others and slap them together. Are we butchers? Is that what we do? No, we aren't. We manage companies, we improve and optimize and encourage. Rob's company sells cars, but he doesn't sell them himself. That's not his job. But even if it was, there's nothing wrong with selling a product, especially something people need, like a vehicle. When did you become such a superior brat?"

He throws his hands up. "He's beneath you, Brekka. Tell me you see that."

I shake my head.

"Mom and Dad will never approve of him."

I lift one eyebrow. "Because Mom approves of Geo?"

"She will, if Geo ever gets pregnant." Trig laughs.

"For a woman, Mom's surprisingly sexist," I say. "But what do I care whether Mom or Dad approve? We aren't in Victorian England, and thank goodness for that, because I'd be marrying cousin Mike."

"Oh man, not Mike." He shudders. "Hey, there is someone I like less than Rob."

"Is this because he totally dominated you in that waiting room?" I whisper. "Because I promise never to tell anyone that my boyfriend completely destroyed you with one punch."

I expect another tiresome scowl or angry words. His belly laugh surprises me. I may never understand men.

"Fine. I don't hate him. I'm mad right now, but I don't hate Rob. But that doesn't mean I think he's good enough for you, and I won't be the only one who doesn't get the whole thing."

I may have finally reached a point where I don't care about what anyone else gets about my life.

I may not be able to feel my legs, but that, at least, feels pretty darn good.

❦ 18 ❧

ROB

"How did you like New York?" Paisley asks just before taking a huge bite of her cheeseburger.

She picked me up from the airport with almost no notice when I was too nervous to call Geo, so I figure I owe her dinner. "No one mentioned that the big apple is rotten and has worms."

She sets her burger down. "Wait, what? Are you talking metaphorically, or like you really saw worms and stuff?"

I chuckle. "Maybe not the worms, but I really did smell pee in the streets."

She rolls her eyes. "Every big city smells like urine. What else you got?"

"The pizza isn't as great as they say. It's kind of flat and underwhelming."

She shrugs. "I'm beginning to suspect you didn't really go to New York. Did you see the Memorial where the Twin Towers were?"

I shake my head.

"How about the Empire State Building?"

I shake my head again.

"The Statue of Liberty?"

"Nope."

"Okay." She shoves her hamburger toward me. "I'm not eating this last-minute-ride-from-the-airport bounty until you tell me why you went and what's really going on."

"I went for work."

She shakes her head this time. "Try again. You'd have gotten someone from work to pick you up."

I should have just called an Uber, but I don't have the app. Downloading it seemed daunting. "Fine, I didn't go for work." Or maybe I wanted to talk to someone.

"Are you going to tell me why you went?"

I study her face carefully. "Geo didn't tell you anything?"

"Does it look like I know what's going on?"

Not really, no.

"And why didn't you just call Geo? I've never picked you up or dropped you off anywhere in my life."

"I punched Trig in the face, so I wasn't sure whether she'd answer my call."

"Wait, Trig was there?" She leans forward with a half grin. "And whoa! Are you serious? You punched pretty boy in the nose?"

"I'm completely serious."

Paisley leans toward me, her hamburger forgotten. In fact, the corner of her elbow is squishing it and I don't think she's even realized it. "Did you tell him you're still in love with Geo?" Her eyebrows rise. "Oooh, did you challenge him to an MMA fight to win her back? Because you would totally destroy him! Or wait, could he hire someone to, like, fight in his place? Oh my gosh, did you get a video? I need to see this myself, like so badly!!"

"Paisley, do you ever breathe? Calm down. There was no cage fight or proclamation of love of any kind."

She frowns. "Oh just tell me the story already. You're such a tease."

I roll my eyes heavenward. Whoever ends up with Paisley will need to be very, very patient. Like, a circus trainer for a sloth kind of patient.

"I went to New York because Trig let it slip that Brekka was having a surgery. I wanted to be supportive, but I wasn't supposed to know about it. Although, I did kind of send her a gift at the hospital that will give away that I punched her brother and I was present. I have no idea how she'll take that. But I told Trig I wouldn't pressure her to let me come see her, and I kept that promise."

"And is Brekka okay?"

I nod.

"Wait, so you went to support Brekka, but didn't see her, and she's fine. That's it? That's so boring. So why did you punch Trig, if everything was so utterly and completely civil and fine?"

"That's complicated," I say.

"Oh yay. I'm so glad we're getting to the good part. Finally." Paisley rubs her hands together, and I realize the pickle has stuck to her elbow and it's dangling, distracting me. "For the record, you suck at stories. Now, go ahead. I'm ready to hear it."

"It's not a juicy tale of anything. Trig's not keen on me dating his sister. I'm not keen on him encouraging her to have risky surgeries for pie in the sky treatments that won't work."

"You're a real Debbie Downer, aren't you?"

"At least I don't have a pickle stuck to my elbow."

Paisley snatches the pickle off and then pops it in her mouth. Ugh, how did Geo ever think we might hit it off? "Look, none of this can be shared with anyone else, okay?"

Paisley grabs her smushed burger, rearranges the

innards so they line up, more or less, and takes another huge bite. Speaking around the food, she says, "Fine, yeah, whatever. Not that I need to, unless I was telling a bedtime story to put someone to sleep. Look, the big news here is... you like someone." She wiggles her eyebrows up and down. "And she's someone we know. And she could buy and sell you like 500 million times and have enough left over to buy a few small islands."

"Yes, that's the point. Nicely put."

Paisley grins. "What are you going to do about it?"

I shrug. "Slow and steady, right? I'm going to make sure she knows I like her and that I'm thinking about her, but I'm also going to give her space so she doesn't panic, or whatever girls and wolves do when they're caged."

"Did you just compare all women to wolves?"

I shrug. "Maybe. You're all a little unpredictable, you're beautiful in a wild way, and you can be hugely feral."

"And your plan to win the queen of all wolves is what? To ... tell her you think she's pretty every day?"

"Something like that."

Paisley's mouth hangs open and I nearly have to look away. Finally she swallows. "Yeah, that's what I usually hear. 'Oh that guy is so swoony. He swept me off my feet and stole my heart by how consistently he sent me text messages letting me know he was there for me.'"

I slam my hand down on the table. "You're pissing me off, Paisley. Brekka's been through a lot, and she doesn't need me to badger or push her. She needs space to recover from the surgery physically, and to realize she's enough for whatever she wants out of life, emotionally."

"Yep. Like I said. You were totally patient and kind with Geo too. And it got you friend zoned. You can slam the table and growl all you want. I'm trying to help you, dummy."

I glance down at my bag, thinking about the beautiful piece of Kintsugi pottery I found for Brekka at a shop while I wandered the streets thinking about what exactly I hoped to accomplish by punching her brother. I think I'm right. I think she needs time and space. But what if I'm wrong? What if I heal her up, only to send her off to the arms of some rich, suave, billionaire, just like I did with Geo?

Paisley was the one who told me Geo was engaged.

"Hey how did I look when you told me Geo was marrying Trig?"

She purses her lips and looks sideways. "Like you'd eaten yogurt past the expiration date and your stomach was protesting."

"Sick," I say. "That's how I looked?"

"Not quite sick? Like you were thinking about being sick. Then you looked angry."

I think about how I'd feel if I found out Brekka had a fiancé and was lost to me forever. The only word I can think that might describe my feelings is gutted. Completely and totally hollowed out.

It would kill me.

"So you think I should, what? Fly to Colorado again? Quit my job and move to Denver?"

Paisley holds up one hand. "Whoa there, partner. Not quite so fast. Man, you're hot or cold, huh? I mean, don't just 'be there' for her. Be *there* for her, if you know what I'm saying." She winks.

"You're saying, be sexy about it?"

"Oh my gosh, you are such a dork. Yes, that's what I'm saying. Don't friend zone yourself. You can give the girl space, but make sure she knows what you want from her as an end game. You're not a teddy bear. You're Fabio meets David Beckham and you're coming to play."

My brain can't even process her mixed metaphors. "Uh huh. So give her space just like I said, but be flirty while doing it?"

She sighs. "And if she doesn't act like she's opposed, then yeah, go see her."

"Got it."

Paisley dings me almost the whole way home with more stupid questions, but I decide her advice is mostly sound. She is, after all, a girl. And a fairly astute one at that.

I think about the tone my text message to Brekka should take the whole way home, which probably explains my distraction and Paisley's mounting annoyance.

"Thanks for the ride," I tell her.

"Yeah, no problem. That'll be fourteen dollars, plus tip."

"Wait, what?" I ask.

Paisley holds out her hand.

"Seriously?"

"Dude, I'm a licensed über driver now. I have expenses to pay."

I pull out my wallet and she laughs heartily, shouts, "Got ya!" and speeds away, the force of her momentum slamming the door shut. There's a screw loose in that girl's head, I swear.

I don't even unpack. I whip out my phone the second I'm through the door.

MISS YOU. THINKING ABOUT YOU. HOPE YOUR RECOVERY IS COMING ALONG, I type.

Then I delete it. That's a text from a teddy bear, or her older brother.

WISH WE WERE WATCHING FIREWORKS AGAIN. HOPE YOUR RECOVERY IS A QUICK ONE.

That's better. She was on my lap during the fireworks, and we kissed. Or, I think it's better. I read it four more times, by which point the words start to look funny. I can't think of anything else, so in the end, I send it.

Nothing.

I watch my phone for almost an hour while I unpack, and then I glance at it off and on during an episode of Daredevil. I hold my phone on my lap so I can feel it buzz if she replies while I review some work email. I basically stare at it all night, like a dog watching a rabbit burrow. Hopeful and then desperate. I'm beginning to think I need to punch myself for being a sissy, because this is not how a man should behave.

She still doesn't reply.

The next morning, I decide to up my game. I read reviews, and then call around and order breakfast for Brekka. At the last minute, I tack on some food for Trig too. After all, I may have some fences to mend there.

Then I wait. When I still haven't heard from her around ten o'clock, I text again.

THEY SAY THE WAY TO A WOMAN'S HEART IS THROUGH HER STOMACH.

No reply.

Fifteen minutes later I text her again. CRAP! I JUST LOOKED IT UP. IT'S THE WAY TO A MAN'S HEART. I BET AFTER THE BREAKFAST I SENT, TRIG'S DESPERATELY IN LOVE WITH ME. SEE IF YOU CAN LET HIM DOWN EASY.

Still nothing.

At what point does persistence cross the line into stalker territory? I feel like an uninvited trip to wait during surgery, a huge bouquet of flowers, a gift and note asking her to a wedding, a flurry of texts, and breakfast for her and her brother might be dangerously close.

Oh crap.

Did I already cross it? I peek out the window. Are the police about to show up at my door with a court order?

I put my phone on the counter and walk away from it. This is all Paisley's fault. She turned me into Yosemite Sam, guns a blazing. Why did I listen to her to begin with? She's as terminally single as I am. Blarg. I'm going to call her and give her what for.

What does that phrase even mean, 'what for?' I run my hands through my hair and wish it was longer. It's not a very satisfying gesture when you keep your hair barely longer than a military buzz cut.

I'm losing my mind.

I jog back to my phone, but before I can check it again, I decide to go lift weights. I haven't maxed out in days. By the time I've done legs and chest and I can barely move my body, I feel much better. I head back inside and force myself into the shower before checking the rabbit burrow, I mean my phone, again.

When I'm clean, dry and dressed, I finally let myself unlock the screen with a swipe. And there's a text. I pick up my phone with shaking hands and focus, because it's from Brekka.

I LOVED THE BANANAS FOSTER PANCAKES, AND THE CRAB, AND THE NOTE. I WISH I'D SEEN YOUR FACE WHEN YOU WERE HERE, BUT I LOOKED SCARY. LIKE THE CRYPT KEEPER, SO MAYBE IT'S FOR THE BEST YOU LEFT.

She sent the text twenty-eight minutes ago. Twenty-eight minutes! Will she still have her phone on her? Will she be awake? Did I miss my window to interact with her? My fingers tremble and fumble and mess everything up as I try to type a reply. It takes twice as long as it should.

WHAT SHOULD I SEND FOR DINNER?

Heart eyes emoji.

I breathe a Texas sized sigh of relief. I'm not a stalker. She likes what she sees. Which gives me an idea. I hold the phone away from me and take a selfie to send her.

I check out the photo before sending it, and realize I look like I'm constipated. Oh, come on. How do my sisters make this look so easy? I try again. And again. Tired, angry, depressed, cheesy. I hate every single photo. Finally, I just close my eyes and pick one at random. I click send and then type, CAN'T BE THERE TO SEE YOU, BUT NOW AT LEAST YOU'VE GOT A PHOTO.

YOU DIDN'T ASK WHAT I'M WEARING, BUT I'LL TELL YOU. IT'S GOT SOME QUESTIONABLE STAINS ON IT, AND IT'S COMPLETELY OPEN UP THE BACK.

A hospital gown. She's hilarious and hot. I collapse in a chair and grin ear to ear, because that's some high quality flirting. She wouldn't send that text to someone in the friend zone, right?

A knock at the door sends me to my feet. I slide my phone in my pocket and answer.

Geo smiles at me sideways. "I'm here to yell at you."

"For punching your boyfriend?"

She nods. "My *fiancé*, but yes."

"And are you going to? Yell, I mean?"

She breezes past me and heads for the sofa in my small family room. She takes up her usual position, far right corner, and crosses her legs. "Do I need to?"

I shake my head. "I'm sorry I punched him, but he deserved it."

Geo grins. "I imagine he did. He's not very rational about his sister, or his perceived guilt about her current disability."

"No, he's not, but it's hurting her."

Geo's lips compress. She looks down at her hands and

then slowly back up at me. "Has he told you we've fought about the same issue?"

I clear my throat. "Nope, that didn't come up." I sit down a foot away from her.

"I told him the surgery was stupid. I told him to accept her as she is, and let her make her own decisions. But he can't seem to let go of his hope. He couldn't seem to accept that she didn't need to be fixed anymore. From what I can tell, it's either a God complex, or a big brother thing. Maybe it doesn't matter. I know he loves her deeply and would do anything for her. He's not like their parents, but he's not perfect either." Geo puts her hand on my knee. "Everyone is flawed in some way. He's well intentioned, and officially I'm mad at you, but unofficially, I'm hopeful your punch is the wake up call he needed."

I lean back against the couch and close my eyes. She's right. We're all flawed. "I guess my problem is that there are so many problems that can't be fixed in this world, sometimes I try to fix the ones I think are within my control with my fists. And then I always regret it, because fists don't fix anything."

She laughs and it sounds like a cascade of water. I've always loved Geo's laugh. It would lift anyone's spirits.

I sit up and face her. "I'm sorry I hit him, and I'll apologize when he's back home. Just let me know when he'll be here and I'll drive over."

Geo shakes her head. "He's embarrassed. I think he feels he should apologize to you."

"Well, far be it from me to—"

"It would be nice if you both said sorry."

"Oh, fine. I can do that."

She beams. "Good, glad that's settled. Now. I have something else to talk to you about. I went to see Mom, and she's not coming to Hawaii."

My heart lifts at the thought that I'll be able to focus on Brekka, but then it sinks under a half ton of guilt. "Wait, why? Not because I punched Trig or anything, right? I swear, I'll be perfectly behaved on your wedding day. No punching of any kind. Unless one of Trig's crazy relatives shows up or something. I'll only punch on demand. How's that?"

Geo shakes her head. "You could help during the ceremony, but the flight over and back, even if you escort her, will be brutal. She'll be stressed and confused, and you know she gets angry when that happens. She can only get one injection the entire weekend. Hauling her out there, well, it was selfish of me."

"So she's going to miss your wedding?"

"The nurses have offered to set up the wireless streaming video and make sure she gets her injection just before so she'll be lucid to watch it."

"That's a smart compromise and a sound plan. I think you're being wise about this." I lean toward her this time, and put a hand on her shoulder. "But I know it sucks your mom won't be there in person. I'm sorry. Face punching of the groom aside, you know you're my sister in every way I can imagine other than blood. I can walk you down the aisle, if you want."

A tear forms in her eye. "That was my next question."

I pull her close for a hug, and I realize I don't feel a single twinge of jealousy, regret, or sorrow. I'm genuinely happy for Geo. She deserves all the good things the world has to offer, and although he's flawed like the rest of us, Trig loves her and he never gives up.

Which is probably part of the problem with how he treats Brekka. Hopefully he's figured that out.

Geo pulls back and stands up, spreading her hands

down to smooth her pants. "I am sorry I can't stick around, but I've got so much to do."

"Work?" I ask.

She shakes her head. "Fun stuff this time. Last minute wedding plans."

Only an event planner would consider anything she's doing a month out 'last minute.' "Well if I can help, please don't tell me."

Geo giggles. "Yeah, I'll be sure not to call."

"Perfect," I say. "Looks like we're on the same page."

"Go slow with her, Rob."

I swallow at the sudden change of direction from the plan I developed with Paisley. "I will."

"I'm serious. She's ... delicate."

"I know she is, but she's stronger than people give her credit for, too."

Geo bobs her head. "You're right, I'm sure. Maybe the truth is somewhere in the middle."

I walk Geo out, and then I remember I left Brekka hanging on the text chain. And after her flirty text.

SORRY, GEO CAME BY, I type. Then I wonder whether that will make her feel bad. I delete it. What can I say to excuse my lag?

BRAIN COMPLETELY SHORTED OUT AT THAT IMAGE. FINALLY REBOOTING.

Laughing emoji. I KNOW YOU'RE BUSY. YOU DON'T ALWAYS HAVE TO REPLY RIGHT AWAY. NOT EVERYONE IS STUCK IN A HOSPITAL BED.

HOW'S THE RECOVERY?

IT SUCKS. I KNOW YOU WON'T SAY I TOLD YOU SO, BUT...

I'M SORRY IT ISN'T FUN. I HAVE CERTAINLY BEEN THERE.

IT'S HARDER THAN I EXPECTED, she texts.

YOU ARE BEAUTIFUL AND STRONG.

I'M NOT STRONG RIGHT NOW. Sad face.

YOU ARE BEAUTIFUL AND STRONG.

YOU ALREADY SAID THAT.

YOU ARE BEAUTIFUL AND STRONG.

ROB? I THINK YOUR TEXTS ARE FRITZING OR SOMETHING.

NOPE. YOU ARE BEAUTIFUL. YOU ARE STRONG. NOT AN ACCIDENT. I'M GOING TO KEEP TELLING YOU UNTIL I KNOW THAT YOU BELIEVE ME.

No response.

YOU HAVEN'T ANSWERED MY CARD INVITA-TION, EITHER. WILL YOU BE MY DATE TO THE WEDDING OF THE YEAR?

No response.

BREKKA? YOU ARE BEAUTIFUL AND STRONG. PLEASE BE MY DATE. PLEASE.

I AM GOING TO NEED EVERY BIT OF THE NEXT FEW WEEKS TO PREPARE FOR THE WEDDING. AND I'VE GOT AN INVESTMENT WE ARE FINALIZING AT WORK.

IS THAT A NO? YOU CAN TELL ME. I'M NOT BEAUTIFUL, BUT I'M STRONG ENOUGH. (I'M NOT PROMISING IT'LL BE THAT EASY TO GET RID OF ME, BUT YOU CAN BE DIRECT IN YOUR EFFORTS.)

YOU ARE BEAUTIFUL AND STRONG, ROB.

THEN WHY WON'T YOU AGREE TO BE MY DATE?

I'LL BE YOUR DATE IF YOU PROMISE ME SOMETHING.

ANYTHING.

YOU WON'T FLY OUT AND SURPRISE ME. YOU WON'T SEND ME GIFTS AND FOOD.

CAN I TEXT YOU?

Heart eyes emoji. YES.

BUT I CAN'T CALL?

YOU CAN CALL TOO.

I dial her number and she picks up.

"Hello?"

"So your offer is," I say, "that you'll be my date at the wedding, for all three days of the trip, but I can't fly out to surprise you or send you gifts before then?"

She giggles. "Yes."

"But I can call you."

"Yes."

"And I can text you all day long."

She giggles again.

"Then it's a deal."

We talk for three hours. When she finally gets off to pay some attention to Trig, I send her a text message.

ALL DAY LONG. YOU PROMISED.

She texts back an emoji that's rolling its eyes heavenward. YES, I DID.

This time, I'm the one who sends the heart eyes emoji.

❦ 19 ❦

BREKKA

My T10 break is rare. Typically the rib cage provides some protection to the thoracic area. And if being in a rare location wasn't enough for me, my break was also incomplete.

Usually incomplete is a word reserved for bad things. You didn't finish your coursework in a college class? You got an incomplete. You didn't explain yourself well? Your explanation was incomplete. You never finished your project, or a race, or a piece of art? Your attempt was incomplete.

But a complete break in neurological parlance means the patient has lost all sensory, motor and autonomic function below the level of the break. Up until my recent surgery, I fit neatly into the category of an incomplete break. I had limited sensory and autonomic function below T10. I even had limited motor function on good days. Some days I could stand unassisted for almost a minute.

I haven't felt my toes on the left side of my body since the stem cell procedure. I haven't felt my calves. I haven't felt my thigh. Not one single time. When the nurse poked me with a needle yesterday and the day before, I felt no pain.

"Just poke me really hard and get it over with," I say. I'm sick of telling my physical therapist 'no, no, no' over and over. "I can't feel anything."

"We need to check it every day," Linda says. "You're lucky you haven't lost bladder control. Or the ability to sit up easily."

I don't feel lucky.

"Maybe I should do a commercial or something," I say. "For kids, to encourage them to wear their seatbelts. It practically writes itself. 'Hey kids! Wear your seatbelt! If you don't, you could end up like me. And I'm one of the lucky ones who doesn't need diapers. Never mind that I can't feel my entire leg.'"

Linda is exceptionally well trained, because she doesn't even scowl at me. "Are you ready for the treatment?"

I nod, and she hooks the electrodes up and down my leg. Before she turns it on, I ask her. "Do you think we're wasting time?"

Linda won't meet my eye. Because she does. She doesn't think I'm getting any more feeling back.

The doc said it could come back for two to three weeks post surgery. I cling to that timeframe. Eight days isn't three weeks.

I grit my teeth and signal her to turn on the shocks. I can't feel anything in my leg, but I can feel the electrical current in the rest of my body, pulsing and buzzing like angry bees. The electrodes are working the muscles I can't in the hope that I won't lose what little muscle tone I have.

It may be a giant waste of time, but I really hope it's not.

I didn't think being able to stand up and shift my legs a little, even if it wasn't much and wasn't consistent, was a big deal. Until I couldn't do it anymore. And the loss was for nothing. The treatment didn't help at all. My spine is apparently chock full of scar tissue, which will probably preclude any stem cell benefit, at least, without a lot more scar cell scrubbing, and that would likely cause more damage.

It's been eight days and I'm doing physical therapy twice a day, and I haven't had a glimmer or a spark to console me. Thanks to the loss of sensation, I can't stand up at all, and my exercises with my right side are harder than they were before. My left side was always the stronger side too, which is the sting in the tail.

At least I manage to wait until Linda's gone this time before I turn onto my side and cry.

My phone rings and I answer without thinking. I need to hear Rob's voice. It always pulls me together. I can't have him thinking I'm depressed, especially when he was so opposed to the surgery in the first place.

"Hello," I say without a trace of tears or even hiccups.

"Brekka," my mom says.

My heart sinks. I should have checked the screen before answering. "What's up, Mom?" I hope she can't hear the note of disappointment in my tone.

"I'm just calling to tell you that I pulled the trust documents as you asked. I wanted you to review Section seventeen, subsection c. If you don't ever produce a biological child, and you go through with your plan to transfer half of the trust back to your brother's children, they would inherit everything. A blood heir takes precedence over an adoptive one if they're in the chain of succession."

My heart sinks. "You're saying if I return Trig's share to his kids, my future kids could be disinherited? That makes no sense."

"It is nevertheless true. If you would like to rethink the transfer, I'll tell the lawyers to put it on hold."

"Can't we change that?" I ask.

My mother clucks. "It requires the vote be unanimous."

"Right, and right now, that's you as acting Trustee, Dad, and me."

"That's correct."

"So?"

Mom sighs. "Nothing with your father is simple."

"You think he'd block me giving his son's kids their money back while preserving my share for mine?"

"I think he might object to changing the rules to give preference to adoptive children."

"I'm sorry, did you say preference?"

"Well, treating them as though it's the same as a blood related child."

My heart freezes. "It *is* the same. Adopted or not, they'd be my kids. Your grandkids."

"Depending on the circumstances," Mom says.

"I don't even want to know what you mean."

"Adoptions can take place as adults, or when the children are older. They're not always what you might think, and it's a slippery slope to just allow anyone to adopt an heir and have them be treated the exact same."

So it's not Dad who will be the difficult one, or at least, not just him. I wish I could throw something just to hear it shatter.

"Did you really just say an 'heir'?" I ask. "We're not discussing the throne of England here."

"They don't have nearly the kind of liquid capital we do, you're right."

I roll my eyes. "I'll look over the trust, okay?"

"You do that and get back to me."

Once I'm off the phone, I look over the clause and she's

right. I have no idea whether I can have kids, if I ever even meet someone who's fine with the prospect of having children with me. I won't be able to easily chase a toddler, or manage a baby if I want to go out and about. I'm a useless lump, and I'm even worse now than I was before. Hearing that if I can't physically create kids of my own, my children won't even be eligible to inherit anything from my family hurts. Knowing my mom is fine with that hurts more.

I click attach to the family trust file and send it to lead counsel for Nometry. I mark the email CONFIDENTIAL.

Laney:

I know this is outside of the scope of your employment, but I'd like to retain you personally. Please review this trust and tell me if there's a way to get around section 17 sub c. I'd like to revert half the trust back to Trig's kids, but I can't do that without disowning mine, if I ever adopt any. Trig doesn't know any of this. Please keep it that way.

B

I stare at my ceiling for a few minutes. Then I tap out a text to Rob. MISS YOU. I delete it without sending.

It's too pathetic. Besides, what's my plan here? If the wedding goes well and he likes me, then what? If he wants me to move to Atlanta... the thought of moving horrifies me. I've lived in Denver my entire life. My business is here. My parents, at least during the summer and part of ski season, are here. And I love the mountains, the crisp air, and the restaurants.

But Trig dropped everything and moved without batting an eye. He'd be okay with moving Nometry, that's for sure.

I shake my head. It's a pointless thing to worry about now.

But since I finished my work for the day, and I don't have my second round of physical therapy, I have nothing else to focus on. I close my eyes and think about how Rob carried me at the beach, and how he'll carry me again. He didn't care who stared or whispered. He paid attention only to me.

I remember the feeling of my legs against his back. A feeling I'll probably never have again, at least not on the left side. A tear trickles down the side of my face. Linda's been harping on me to practice my car transfers and wheelchair transfers, now that I have no feeling or control on that part of my body.

I decide to try it. At least it gives me something to do. I push myself up into a sitting position and grab Gladys. Her brakes are on, and I shift my right leg over the side of the bed. Then I use my arms to shift my left leg over, hating that it feels like an alien limb. I used to have no feeling by bedtime most nights, but now it's all the time and for some reason that's different.

I breathe in and out of my nose and shift over to my chair. Then I place my right foot on the footrest, and use my hands to position the left. I wheel my way out to my car and open the door. I ought to be trying this with my Mercedes first since it's lower and easier to transfer into, but I've always tackled the biggest problem first. I go for the harder transfer. The tallest car I have is my Range Rover.

I push the door open all the way. I hit the right side brake on and press the button on the car seat so it moves to the back most position. Then I shift my right leg into the car, which I didn't used to need to do. It should help me to drag my left leg easier, I think. Then I reach up, grab the seat, and haul myself up toward it. Except my left leg catches on the handle and Gladys spins. I should have put both brakes on.

I swear under my breath. It's too far for me to reach her

easily. I shift halfway out of the car, my left side dangling off the seat. I hold on to the armrest with my right hand and swing out toward Gladys, but she rolls even further away. I lunge for her, unwilling to admit I'll need to crawl across the floor to reach her, and my right hand misses her by a millimeter. I fall to the ground, knocking the air out of my chest.

How can I be struggling to do something I've done now for four years? I'm lying on the floor of my garage like a toddler, and something inside my chest breaks. I realize that I don't even want to see Rob at the wedding.

That's a lie.

I am desperate to see his gorgeous face, his beautiful body, and his winning smile. I just don't want him to see me. I don't want anyone to see me, not anymore. Not like this.

I know Rob will be nice about it, patient even. He'll help me like he helps Clive, like he helps his family, like he helped Geo. He'll do what he does with everyone in his life. He'll nurture and tend to things. I love that he cares for everyone around him. I love that he tapes up torn things and glues together shattered ones. I really do.

I want to be different, though. I don't want to be a project to him.

And if I see him at the wedding, that's what I'll be. He'll feel obligated to date me, like he's obligated to go to Clive's every Friday, even if he wants to go on a date, or take a night off. Because that's who he is. Steady as a rock, kind, caring, and giving.

Before I can talk myself out of it, while I'm still lying on the floor of my garage with tears streaming down my face, I whip out my phone and text Geo.

I'M NOT GOING TO BE ABLE TO MAKE IT TO THE WEDDING. PLEASE DO ME A FAVOR AND

DON'T LET TRIG OR ROB KNOW UNTIL THE DAY BEFORE. I KNOW THAT'S A BIG ASK, BUT THEY WON'T UNDERSTAND.

Geo doesn't reply, but the text shows as read.

Will she just ignore me? Will she tell Trig? I want to text her again, but I don't want her to think I'm being a big emotional baby. I don't want her to think she can talk me out of it, either. But really, if I can't even drive to the store to go shopping without having to crawl across my garage floor to get back to my wheelchair, I shouldn't be going to a wedding.

Even Trig's.

The thought of missing his wedding tears my heart in half. But Geo mentioned they'd do a live feed for her mom, who's sick. I'm sure I can piggyback off that feed, and it'll be like I'm really there. The more I think about it, the more right it feels.

By the time I've finished my second round of physical therapy and dealt with a barrage of emails, I feel better about things. If Geo was going to tell Trig, he'd have called already. It's been hours and hours since I texted her. Maybe she's just trying to figure out how to respond. Surely she'll understand my wishes, or even if she doesn't, honor them at least. That's always been one of the things I love about Geo. She gets me and my reasoning, and so far, she's never pushed me past where I can handle. In fact, with her history and her former fiancé, if anyone will understand I have limitations, it's her.

A ring from my doorbell surprises me.

When I open the door to Geo's smiling face, I have no idea what to say.

"Good evening, Brekka." Her eyes widen slightly when they take in the pasta sauce stain on my shirt and the dirty yoga pants I haven't bothered to change since I went facedown on the garage floor. "How are you feeling?"

I close my eyes. What is she doing here?

Geo marches through the door, pushing past me and spinning Gladys around in the process. She yanks the door shut behind her. "Why yes, I'd love to come inside. Thanks for asking me. And yes, I'd be happy to wheel you over to the kitchen table after I close the door." She grabs the back of Gladys, since she has no handles, and shoves on the back frame, pushing me quickly toward my kitchen.

I sputter. "Excuse me."

"Sure, I will." She doesn't miss a beat, spinning me around and plopping down in a chair next to me. "Now that we're here in your kitchen, all cozy and best friends, future sisters even, let's chat."

My lips open, but no words come out.

"I can see you're not sure what to say. That's okay, because I have plenty of things to discuss. I'll go first."

I click my mouth shut.

"You're depressed. I figured you would be. I hoped your mother or your father or someone would do something about it. But no one else stepped up, and you asked me not to tell Trig, so you're stuck dealing with me. I know I'm not your sister or your mother or your father, but I'm the best you've got, apparently. Did I ever mention that I went to a year of therapy after my fiancé died? Well, I did. It's mandated by the military. Not that they could really make me, but it's covered and I thought, great. I'll let them fix me."

She stares at me. I still have no idea what to say.

"I'll take your silence to mean that you didn't go to therapy."

She pauses again and I stare right back at her.

"Okay, that's fine. Because guess what? That therapy

didn't help me much, not really. But I did learn some things. Some coping mechanisms, and some other stuff. But one thing that stood out to me was what the therapist told me about depression. I'm going to share it with you. Roger told me that there are two types of depression. Clinical depression is about a chemical imbalance. There is medicine they can prescribe to help even that imbalance out, and it frequently works fairly well. Over time you may need to change it or tweak it, or someone with a chemical imbalance may even want to try new options. There are side effects, but in many, many cases, medication is the best way to go. Or sometimes they encourage a mixture of medication and therapy and work or exercise. Some kind of regimen, tailored to the person, to treat the illness."

I nod.

"Good, you're reacting like I'm actually here. That's progress. But the point is that, I never had clinical depression. What I suffered from was situational depression. Something awful had happened, like a hole ripped in the fabric of my life. I had to learn how to stitch my life back together and move ahead, dealing with the scar tissue of that hole. I didn't need medicine, since I didn't have an imbalance. I had an unsightly hole and the fallout from that trauma. Make sense?"

I nod again.

"You're not dealing with a chemical imbalance, or at least, I don't think you are, but you had a cannon blast a few years ago, and now you're dealing with a smaller version of the same in the aftermath of the failed procedure."

Trig knows I lost feeling on my left side. I guess he told Geo.

"You may have sewn the raw edges of your life's fabric back together, but it's hard when something else comes along and puts a hole through things again." She leans toward me and takes my hand. "It hurts. Maybe even more than the first hole, because that major trauma left you numb at first."

A tear runs down my cheek this time and I swipe it away as quickly as I can.

"You, Brekka, are absolutely, positively gorgeous. I know it. Trig knows it. Rob can't stop looking at your stupid photo on his phone. How do I know that? Because he smiles this idiotic smile whenever he does. You're also funny, and smart, and breathtaking. That's what Rob says about you. You took his breath away. You are reeling, and hurting, and grieving, and you're scared."

"I fell on my face today." I hate how uncertain I sound. "My stupid, dead leg caught on the edge of the wheelchair and I fell on my face on the floor."

"You will be fine by the wedding," Geo says softly, her eyes pleading with me. "But if you're going to fall anytime, doing it when Rob is around is a pretty decent time to do it. He's always been there to catch me, you know."

I shake my head. "I don't want that. I don't want him to catch me."

Geo's eyes look pained. "What if it's all he wants?"

My frown lines deepen. "Too bad. It would destroy me. I cannot be a charity project."

She sniffs. "Look, you need to accept that you have value. You have great value, right now, exactly as you are. And it's time to stop pretending you don't. I won't let you. Have you seen the cartoon Spiderman movie? With the pig?"

I nod.

"Do you remember what they ask him at the end? They tell him the most important part of being Spiderman is what?"

"Trust in yourself?" I ask.

She shakes her head. "It's that he always has to get back up, no matter what happens, no matter how many times he's knocked down. And I found you here in your chair. You answered the door. So when you fell on your face?"

Another tear rolls down my face.

"You had already climbed back up. That means you're already doing it. Every time you fall, no matter why or how hard, you always get back up. Rob sees that. We all do. It's one of the things we admire. So do it now, do it for him, and do it for yourself."

I turn away.

She turns my chair until I'm looking her in the eye. "I'm not that easy to ignore. And you can tell me or show me exactly how you're feeling. Always. I'm about to be your sister. I've never had one, and I cannot wait. I love you, Brekka. Just as you are. Believe in me that you're worth it."

I nod my head and she pulls me in for a hug.

Once she finally pulls back, I ask, "How'd you get here?"

"I stole Trig's jet."

I raise my eyebrows. "He didn't ask why?"

She shrugs. "I told him it was emergency wedding stuff. He didn't press."

"Trig's pretty decent sometimes."

She grins. "Most of the time."

I bob my head. He's lucky to have her. "I'll give you that."

"Okay, now that you've suffered through my pep talk, what did you want to do?"

"Re-watch Spiderman, for one," I say.

She laughs. "Good idea." Then a half grin sneaks onto her face. "And how would you feel about a little girl time?"

I never trust anyone who's sporting a half smile. "What did you have in mind? Be specific."

"I can help you pick out what you're going to wear to the wedding. Now that you are coming after all. Right?"

I roll my eyes. "Fine."

She follows me to my room and then walks through it to my closet. Before I can stop her, she's browsing through the racks and racks of clothes. She starts to snag things here and there, sliding them over her arm. "Where do you get all these?" she asks.

"Giovanni," I say.

She lifts her eyebrows. "Is that supposed to mean something? Is that a store?"

I suppress a laugh. "He's my personal shopper."

"Of course he is," she says. "My personal shopper is called the internet."

I laugh. "It has no idea what shape you are, or what colors flatter your skin."

"But I can print return labels up myself, and the internet is free. Or at least, I already pay the $87 a month, whether I shop with it or not."

"You are eventually going to figure out that some extravagant things improve your life," I say. "But for now your frugality is adorable."

She puts a long navy blue maxi dress over her arm.

"Not that one," I say. "Way too dark for a wedding. People will think I'm mourning your addition to the family."

She laughs. "Can't have people thinking that." She snags a hot pink, flowing dress next.

Five minutes later, Geo has piled thirty dresses on the edge of my bed. "This is way too many, you know."

She shakes her head. "Not at all. You need options. And don't forget, it's two days of events. Rehearsal dinner, then a late wedding the following day. So you'll need three outfits, really. One for the dinner, one for whatever you do the morning before the wedding, and then what you plan to wear to the ceremony."

"What about the bridesmaid dresses?" I ask. "I've been expecting something monstrously ugly any day now in the mail."

She shrugs. "I want you all in sky blue. I don't care what you wear. Anything you like is fine."

"That's not nearly obnoxious enough," I say. "I'm disappointed, honestly."

She tosses a yellow, button-down dress at my head. I laugh as I try it on.

Seven outfits later and there are seven outfits wadded up in the corner. "At this rate, we'll go through my entire closet and still have nothing to show for it."

Geo flops back on my bed. "I'm not trying to be difficult. I'm just committed to finding the perfect outfit."

"Okay, I'm ready," I say.

She sits up and I wheel Gladys around so she can see dress number eight. It's a coral sundress with tiny orange and green flowers embroidered along the bodice and skirt.

Geo inhales sharply. "Oh, that's perfect. You have to wear that."

"For which thing?" I ask. "It's not blue, so the wedding is out."

"Rehearsal dinner, then. Unless you want to look *really* good and really formal for hanging out with Rob at the beach Saturday morning."

I grin. "Maybe a swimsuit for that."

Geo's eyebrows bob up and down suggestively. "Now you're talking! We can look through those next."

Joy bubbles through me. I don't know whether it's having a sister, or a friend, or knowing I will be seeing Rob in a few weeks, or having a dress that Geo thinks looks great. Maybe it's all of it. Somehow that elation spills out through my hands and I spin Gladys around in a circle.

Of course, I don't realize my left leg has fallen out of the footrest and I slam it into the foot of the bed. "Ouch!"

I freeze.

Geo leaps to the foot of the bed. "What happened? Are you okay?"

A smile spreads over my face, widening as the pain grows.

This time the tears are happy ones.

"I hit my foot on the edge of the bed," I say.

"Oh, I'm sorry. Man, that stinks. Do you need, like, ice or anything?"

She doesn't get it.

"I hit my left leg," I say. "And I felt it."

Her eyes widen. "Oh, you did?"

I nod.

"Wait, does that mean maybe the surgery did something?"

I shake my head. "No, it doesn't. But I hope very much that it means it didn't."

20

ROB

HOPE YOUR DAY WAS GOOD, I text Brekka around seven. It's earlier where she is, so I've noticed that if I text before seven my time, I don't usually hear back until around now.

She texts back right away tonight. NOT UNTIL I HEARD FROM YOU.

My heart swells. She's gotten more and more positive over the past week. We text intermittently all day long now, and talk most nights.

CALL? I text her.

GIVE ME FIVE MINUTES. FINISHING UP A WORK THING.

A knock at my door surprises me. I'm not expecting anyone. I jog to the door and pull it open.

Trig's eye healed up well.

"Hey man," he says.

He's not scowling, and he didn't swear at me, which I think are good signs. We haven't talked since I left NYC. I missed his bachelor party last weekend, in fact, but no one texted or called, not even Geo.

"Hi." I'm not sure what to expect next.

"I came by to pick up the jewelry box. Didn't you say it would be ready by now?"

I step back and gesture for him to come in. "It's ready."

"Great."

I don't say anything, but I head for the shop and he follows me. I wonder if he plans to simply pretend nothing happened. But when I unlock the door to my shop, he clears his throat.

"I also wanted to apologize," he says.

I stop and turn around, unable to read much on his face in the low light. I flip the switch behind me, flooding the shop with light. Some of it pours out onto Trig and I think he's embarrassed.

"You didn't need to—"

He walks past me into the shop. "I did, though. I'm stupidly late, but I don't process things quickly all the time. I'm working on it."

"It's really fine, man," I say. "Seriously."

Trig shakes his head. "I didn't need to process the fact that you hit me, or the reality of knowing you could completely destroy me. I kind of already knew that, ever since we met. What took some time were the years and years of interactions to think about with Brekka." He meets my eyes. "And you were right. It's hard to accept that you've been hurting someone you love. Every day, maybe. I had to realize I've been a pretty horrible sibling."

I put my hand on his shoulder. "Brekka loves you, and she knows you love her. She knew you were supporting her the best way you could."

Trig's face crumples. "I didn't realize I was making everything worse on her. I didn't know I was doing damage." He breathes in and out deeply. "You have to believe me that I never would have—"

I pull Trig against me for a hug. "I know that."

I haven't hugged a guy other than my own dad since Mark died, and I thought it would feel bizarre, but it feels... right somehow. Like Trig needed this and I helped him.

He finally stiffens and pulls back. "Anyway, I needed to tell you that I'm done with all that, and if you tell me what to do or say, I'll do it. I want to help her like you have been."

I shake my head. "I'm not helping her. I'm in awe of how strong she is, how brave, and not because she uses a wheelchair. She's the exact same person she always was. It's important you realize that. People aren't stronger or weaker because they're dealing with a disability. They're who they are, and all I do is stand back and watch and clap when she succeeds. That's all."

"Well, I'm sorry I didn't get it before, and that we fought at the hospital," he says.

"I'm sorry I punched you." I'm not, but at least I can say it now.

"You don't need to be sorry," Trig says.

"It did get me out of going to the bachelor party to hang out with all your rich friends."

Trig glances around the shop and my enormous stockpile of furniture. "Dude, don't take this the wrong way, because you know I think your work is mind blowing, but you need to get out more. You could use a few friends, even if they're rich jerks."

I snort. "I've got friends. Not your kind of friends, but I've got plenty of friends."

"Alright," Trig says. "Well, I was sorry you weren't there. That sentiment surprised me, but I was. I respect that you care about my sister, and if I'm being honest, I think you're good for her."

My smile is genuine. Brekka may not adore her parents,

but she thinks the world of Trig. It means a lot that he likes me. "Well, let's get this jewelry box all loaded up." I take a sharp left and head for the corner where I wrapped it up for transport.

I lift the box. "I assume you want to give her the stand back here, and not try to take it to Hawaii."

Trig shrugs. "Hadn't thought about that part, but yeah. That's probably right. The jewelry I picked out is for the box, not the stand."

He tries to lend me a hand, but I shake him off. It's fifty pounds, not two hundred. "I got it. Thanks."

I head back for the front of the shop and step out the door before I realize he's not behind me. I spin around. "Trig?"

He's stopped by a table I've been working frantically on. Thankfully it's not his wedding gift he's studying. I put that away a few days ago when I finished it to avoid anything like this from happening.

"What's this?" he asks.

My cheeks heat up. "Nothing."

He crouches down and runs his hands along the edges. "It's really different than everything else I've seen. It's like a bunch of tiny boxes sunk into the surface, but you can hardly even tell they're there." He looks up at me curiously. "Will they be open like this when you're done? Or covered? Maybe hidden? Or, you could have glass over them, showing what's inside?"

I'm not going to tell him anything about his sister's surprise. "I'm kind of carrying something here. Something heavy."

"Right. Duly chastened. I'm coming." This time he follows me out the door and to his car, where I load the box into the back of his SUV.

"Alright, well," I say, "whenever you're ready for the base

table, I'm happy to drop it off. Or you can come grab it. Either way."

Trig hands me an envelope. I take it, but I don't bother looking inside. It's not like he'd short me.

"Does this mean I'm your first paying customer?"

I nod. "My very first. Unless you count the little doodads I made for my sisters when they were little."

"They paid you?"

I grin. "In hugs."

"Then I don't. I'm taking credit for being your first sale."

I smile. "That's fair."

"I doubt I'll be your last. Say the word and I can sell everything in there, I swear."

"I'll keep that in mind," I say. "But maybe don't suggest anything to Brekka."

"Speaking of," Trig says. "I thought I ought to say this now. I told you that I like you in there, and I mean it. But I am Brekka's brother, and so help me, if you hurt her—"

This should be good. I lift my eyebrows.

"You already know I can't beat you up, but I do have capital. Even without my trust, I can still afford to hire the best hit man that money can buy. And I won't hesitate to do it, either."

The thought of Trig trying to figure out how to hire a hit man is absurd. My laugh startles him. "Very convincing. I've been appropriately threatened, thanks."

He bobs his head. "As long as you know I mean business."

"That I do." After I see Trig out, I notice Brekka called. Twice. I call her right back.

"Sorry about that," I say. "Your brother came by to pick up a gift he paid me to make for Geo. For the wedding." I open the envelope and gasp.

"What's wrong?"

"He paid me too much. Way too much."

"Oh, I wouldn't worry about that," she says. "It's not like he'll notice the difference. You can buy something fun."

"No," I say. "I told him a thousand. This is more than ten."

She giggles. "He clearly liked it, whatever you made. Trig's not usually the biggest tipper."

"I can't keep all this."

"Of course you can," Brekka says. "Because if he tipped you that big after you punched him in the face, he really thinks you deserve it."

"He apologized for that," I say. "And I think he really loves you."

"That's one of the few things I've never doubted, not in my entire life."

And that would be enough for me to forgive him if I was still mad, which I'm not. It was only ever on Brekka's behalf I was angry, and she's obviously let go of any anger over his misguided pressure.

"I hope you two will get along eventually," she says.

"I think we're well on our way."

"What are you doing now?" Brekka asks.

I don't tell her, because it's a surprise. "You'll see when you meet me at the wedding in a week. I'm nearly finished."

"You can't say something like that and then leave me hanging!"

"I had an idea when we hit the beach up last time, and I have no clue how well it will work." I shift the wheelchair I borrowed from Clive, one of his old ones, and collapse it. I slide it into the harness I made from leather straps and lift. It fits easily and I don't even need to struggle. I sling it over my shoulder. Clive's chair weighs more than Gladys, and it's bigger, but I think this will work. I made the connective tissue adjustable.

"Okay, but if I guess what you're doing, you have to own up to it," she says.

"Fine." There's no way she's going to guess that I'm making a harness to carry her more easily, or an extension to it so I can carry her wheelchair easier when I'm carrying her. And now that I have the harness created, I'm planning to add a storage pouch.

"You're making me a necklace out of wood."

Not a bad idea. "Well now I feel guilty I'm not doing that."

"Oh, Rob."

"Rob can't talk now," I say. "He has to go work on a necklace."

She laughs. "Don't do that. I have plenty of jewelry."

"Nothing made by your boyfriend," I say.

She goes utterly silent.

"I'm sorry, was that the wrong thing to say?"

"No," she whispers. "It was perfect."

"Only eight more days until you see said boyfriend," I say.

"That feels like an eternity."

"I can fly out tomorrow and come see you for the weekend. Say the word."

"Eight days will blur past."

My heart sinks. Why doesn't she want to see me now? "Oh, fine."

"You're sewing your own tuxedo."

"Huh?" I ask.

"I was still guessing what you're doing."

I set the harness and chair down and collapse onto the couch. "I'm done with that. Now all I'm doing is closing my eyes and imagining you're here next to me on my horrible seventies era couch."

"We need to take a lot of photos next week."

"There will be a paid photographer, but I agree. I'll badger you to smile for a million selfies."

"You won't need to ask me. I'm always smiling when you're around."

I'm certainly smiling now.

21

BREKKA

I smooth the skirt of my coral dress down over my knees for the third time in five minutes. I don't even move my legs, so it's not like it could have become suddenly rumpled.

Clearly I'm a mess.

And it has nothing to do with the magnitude of the step my brother's about to take, because I'm not a very good sister. I'm way more concerned about myself and whether my heart is about to give out.

The first time I ever saw Rob, I fully expected him to be a cretin, a meathead. I figured I'd yell at him, and I'd feel better. In fact, if I'm honest, I flew all the way out to score a win. I needed one that day, and if it meant that I turned Geo's poor friend into a punching bag, well I was willing to do it.

And now I haven't seen him in more than a month because somehow I thought it would be easier to handle the idea of seeing him again with a little time to prepare for it. Boy did that backfire. I arrived at the resort a day early with Geo, ostensibly to help her prepare for the wedding. Really, I wanted to make sure there wasn't anywhere I'd be unable to navigate, or look like a fool for getting stuck.

"Good afternoon Brekka," Ethan says with a winning grin. "Is there anything we can get for you?"

A defibrillator in case my heart gives out? A muzzle for my mother? The first time I'm seeing Rob again, and both my parents will be in attendance. My hand shakes and I still it with a thought. I shake my head at Ethan. After all, there's nothing he can do to help.

"I'm great," I say. "Thanks. The hotel is almost as beautiful as the venue."

"I'm surprised you're staying on site," Ethan says. "I figured you'd be with Trig at your house."

My cheeks heat up. I could have stayed there, but Mom and Dad are there too and it felt crowded. Plus, Rob's going to be here, but Ethan seems to have misconstrued my reasons.

"I wanted to be close in case Geo needed help with anything," I lie.

"I'm so glad you bought this hotel, Ethan," Geo says. "It's made everything so much easier, since I can coordinate the venue and the accommodations with the same person, and they're conveniently located. You've really been a dream to work with."

I haven't seen Ethan since before my accident. I expected him to be weird about it, but he's not. At all. In fact, he's been flirting with me. A little too much.

"When are you going to let me take you on that private tour I promised," Ethan asks. "We have a lot to catch up on. And did I mention our hotel has a killer hot tub? I'd love to show it to you later tonight."

I wish I hadn't kissed him at that summer camp so many years ago. If he brings up the new hot tub one more time, I might sock him. "Uh, actually, I've got a party of guests I should be waiting for near the front of the hotel. The dinner starts soon and a flight just arrived."

"You don't need to worry about that," Ethan says. "I'll send Fiona to wait up front and show them to their rooms."

"No," I say a little too sharply. "I'll go."

Geo tilts her head and laughs. "Don't take it personally, Ethan. Brekka's boyfriend is supposed to be arriving any minute and she hasn't seen him in a while."

Ethan's face blanks. "Right, of course. No problem. Well, I ought to go make sure everything is lined up for the dinner." He spins around and heads for the back of the hotel.

"Poor Ethan. No one ever picks him."

I knew he was flirting, but it's not like he was serious. "That's because Ethan's 99 percent fluff. No way was he serious about showing me that hot tub."

Geo frowns. "If you say so."

I roll my eyes. I know so. No one wants to meet a cripple in the hot tub. Please.

Geo crouches down so we're eye to eye. "If you're implying no one would like you in earnest, stop it. Not ever again, not around me. I'm your best friend, so I can safely say this. I'm not lying or trying to make you feel better. I'd rather spend the afternoon with you than with anyone other than Trig. Guys can see the same flame inside of you. They have the same genuine desire to be in your presence, so stop acting like you're a charity case. You aren't."

Geo spins on her heel almost exactly like Ethan did and heads the opposite direction, her phone in her hand. Probably texting my brother. Those two have gotten gushier as the wedding approaches. They're nearing critical levels of sappiness, so it's good that the ceremony takes place in less than 24 hours or we might all drown in the cheese.

I head toward the hotel lobby, my wheels sinking a little into the plush hotel carpet. I'm sure it's nice to have high-end carpeting for most people, but it makes my life harder. I've barely reached the edge of the huge circular room with its vaulted ceilings and abundant potted plants when I hear a voice. And it's not the voice I wanted to hear.

"Brekka!"

I close my eyes and inhale through my nose. I exhale through my mouth and open my eyes. "Mother, why are you here, in the hotel lobby, almost an hour before the dinner even starts?" Something looks off about her, but I'm not sure quite what.

She shakes her head. "My idiot assistant missed her flight and now she's seven hours late. She's got my lipstick with her."

That's it. Her current lipstick is way too pink. My mom never does pink. I should have immediately known. I'd normally be laughing, but I really don't want to see Rob again with Mom hovering. An attack dog mother is the last thing I want around the first time I see my boyfriend in over a month. At first I was scared, and then I thought I needed time, but now. Now I think I've created this absurd sense of anticipation that no one could ever possibly fulfill.

I'm worried I've ruined everything by imposing some dumb timeframe on seeing him.

"You don't have to stick around, Mom. I'll tell Fran to head over to the banquet hall as soon as I see her."

Mom shakes her head. "I'm not going in there until I've fixed my lipstick."

A shuttle pulls up outside and I realize it's too late. The crash has already begun.

"Sweetheart!" I crane my neck around to see my Dad walking into the lobby from the far corner. "Trig mentioned you were probably in the lobby, and here you are."

My dad strides across the enormous room, arms spread wide. He ducks down to give me a hug as people begin streaming through the front doors of the hotel.

"I've missed you so much! It feels like you've been avoiding me for a month," Dad complains.

I didn't tell either of my parents about my surgery. One of the perks of being an adult.

"I've been swamped at work," I say.

Mom nods in understanding and my Dad's eyes cloud. He's never been stuck at work a day in his life. "Well, I hope everything is going well there."

I smile. "Extremely well," I say. "In fact, Trig and I are doing well enough we might even impress Mom someday."

Dad smirks. "I wouldn't get carried away now, sweetheart."

I giggle. Dad's a mess, but I love him.

"And hey, I've been meaning to tell you," Dad whispers, but not very quietly. "Your Mom mentioned you might want to change that clause about the adoption. While I know it may be hard for you right now, I don't think you should throw in the towel on ever meeting a guy and having a kid of your own. You never know what the future holds."

His words stiffen my spine, but before I can reply, the air shifts. Rob's here. I know it.

"Brekka," a deep voice says, sending a shiver up my spine.

I turn and look up toward the voice. Rob's wearing an athletic cut button down shirt with a coral and blue striped tie loosened at the neck, almost as if we coordinated it. He's holding a carry-on rolling bag a few inches off the ground, and the weight of it bunches his bicep visibly, even through his shirt. I wish I could take a photo and relive this feeling every single day. The first sight of Rob after a long,

long drought. It's like collapsing back against a fluffy pillow. My heart contracts and I smile.

"Rob."

"Hello, Rob?" Mom asks.

"Hey there," my Dad says. "I don't think we've met."

Rob sets his suitcase down and holds his hand out to my Dad. "I'm Robert Graham, Brekka's boyfriend. Nice to meet you."

If I wasn't sitting in a chair, I'd have swooned. Brekka's boyfriend he says, just like that. Plain, simple, straightforward.

Mom's eyes bulge, Dad's eyebrows lift meaningfully.

"Throw in the towel." I roll my eyes.

Dad barks a laugh and takes Rob's hand. "A delight to meet you, young man. Graham, did you say? Like the shipping Grahams?"

Rob grins. "Not even remotely. My family owns a few car dealerships that wouldn't cover your transportation costs for a year, I'm sure. I'm utterly beneath your daughter, but so far she hasn't objected."

"Oh pish," my Dad says. "Brekka knows where true value lies."

Mom narrows her eyes at Rob. "I'm Mrs. Thornton. Nice to make your acquaintance."

Rob pivots on his heel and beams at my mother, who stumbles back a step. "I've heard so much about you, and none of it prepared me for how much you resemble your remarkable daughter. It's truly a pleasure to meet you, Mrs. Thornton."

In a few weeks shy of twenty-eight years, I've never heard my mother giggle. Not once. Until this very moment. She touches her collarbone with one hand and holds the other out to Rob, her eyes soft, her mouth turned up in one corner. "Well aren't you well spoken?"

"Thank you, but I assure you, I'm like a fine wine. I'll improve with time."

I'm not sure he could improve much. He's practically shining right now. Except I'm feeling a little forgotten, maybe.

Rob glances from my mom to my dad and then down to me. "If you will excuse us, we've got less than an hour until the rehearsal dinner and I haven't set eyes on Brekka in more than a month. I might need a few minutes alone with her. Do you mind?"

Dad beams like his stock car just took first at NASCAR. "Not at all my boy. Not at all."

Even Mom doesn't seem annoyed. It helps that Fran shows up just then, holding a small package toward her. "No, go right ahead. We'll see you two in a few moments in the banquet hall."

Rob drops to one knee and takes my hand in his. My heart accelerates. Why's he on one knee? He drops to both knees and I can take a breath again. Stop being crazy, Brekka. He takes my face in his hands. "I've missed you more than fish miss water. More than spacemen miss gravity. More than dogs miss jerky."

He shifts even closer and covers my mouth with his. I close my eyes and surrender to the feeling, forgetting there are people in the lobby, maybe even my parents still. My hand rises to his chest, his pec muscles shifting slightly under my fingers.

Too soon, way, way too soon, Rob pulls back and stands up. "I better get checked in."

I nod. "Yes, you should. I'll come with you."

He grins and I'm relieved. I hoped he wasn't wanting some time to himself before the dinner. I wheel behind him to the front desk. He passes them his ID and we wait.

Every time he glances my way, the smile creeps back onto my face.

"Stop," I whisper.

"Stop what?" he asks.

"Stop looking at me like that."

"Like a little boy in a candy store? Or did you mean like a lion eyeing his dinner?"

Heat rises in my cheeks and I swallow. "Yes."

"I can't stop. You starved me of Brekka for an entire month. I'm finally breaking my fast."

I look half-witted, smiling incessantly in spite of the corniness of it all.

The clerk hands Rob his key and I wish we could head for his room and skip the dinner entirely. Which of course, we can't.

"Rob," a deep voice across the room calls. I turn to see Luke and his adorable new wife Mary. "You made it!"

Rob nods his head.

Luke's eyes drop to me. "Brekka, so great to see you again. We were sad you couldn't come to our wedding."

"I was sad to miss it, too. You must be Mary," I say. "It's great to finally meet you."

Mary smiles and offers me her hand. "I've heard so many good things. Sometimes it's like Trig can't talk about anything else. He adores you, and I'm sure I will too."

Paul walks through the door, a sweet-faced brunette on his arm. A small child barrels through the door right after, leaping upward and grabbing Paul's arm. He swings back and forth a few times and lets go, shooting out in front of them. Luke's children follow him, Chase grabbing the other child around the waist and spinning him around.

"No fair," Luke's son Chase says. "Amy got in the way. I would've beat you so much. Because I have new shoes and they make me super fast."

The other little boy shakes his head. "My shoes are the Flash shoes. Dad said so." He looks up at Paul expectantly.

"They are," Paul says. "Straight from the Flash himself. No one can beat you with those."

"What?" Chase whines. "Dad, I need the Flash shoes too. I need them. Troy keeps winning me."

Luke glances at Mary. "Why did we have to bring them along again?"

Mary taps him on the arm. "It's my first time in Hawaii, and I didn't want to miss seeing it with them."

"You'll change your mind tonight around eight, I promise," Luke mutters. "Well, we better check in. See you in a bit."

Luke and Mary walk toward the check-in desk and Rob and I move aside.

"Brekka," Paul says warmly. "It's been way too long since I saw you." He leans down and hugs me a little awkwardly. "Let me introduce my fiancée, Trudy. She's actually Mary's sister."

I smile at Trudy. "Trig sort of filled me in on the developments as they came along. I'm so happy for the two of you." I would have been lying a few months ago, but Rob takes my hand in his as if he knows that, and my heart expands. I am happy for Paul, and Trudy too.

Paul snags Troy and swings him above his head, settling him on his shoulders. "Stay put here for a moment little man. Can't have you destroying the lobby before we check in, can we?"

Troy giggles and blows a raspberry into the air. "Fine."

"Brekka, it's so nice to meet you," Trudy says. "Mary wasn't kidding. Trig has told us so much about you that it feels like we know you already. We only wish you lived near Atlanta so you could come to the game nights." Trudy laughs, and the sound brings a smile to my lips, it's so silvery and full of joy. "Or maybe not. I already lose every single week. Which Paul hates, but he hasn't fired me as his partner yet. From what I hear, you'd be another Game Night Megalith."

"Hey, you beat me most of the time," Rob protests.

That's when I realize Rob knows all these people already, of course he does. They're his people. He's been going to game nights with them, and hanging out with Paisley and Trig and Geo every week at dinners and parties, probably. I'm not the old friend they're happy to see. I'm the outsider in this circle.

"If I can convince her to come down a weekend or two a month," Rob says, "maybe my luck will change. Surely her genius can counteract my mediocrity." He leans down and presses a kiss to my forehead and my feeling of exclusion evaporates.

"You should come," Trudy says. "Mary and Luke have been practicing cooking all sorts of things, and Trig and Geo always buy something amazing. The snacks alone are almost worth a trip."

Troy looks down at me. "I *never* get to come. And no one even brings me snacks at all."

I laugh. "I'll definitely consider it." I wink at Troy. "And I'll be sure they take snacks home for you if I'm there."

Troy rewards me with an ear-to-ear grin. "Hooray!"

Rob grabs his suitcase again and points at the elevator bay. "I'm going to go drop this off so we won't be late for the dinner."

"So much for alone time I guess. I'll meet you there," I say. "I should make sure Geo doesn't have any last minute questions."

"See you shortly."

Mary and Luke and their kids pour into the elevator with him, and as the doors close, I see him pick up Amy with a smile. My heart constricts. Rob's a good guy. And he's my boyfriend. My boyfriend. I didn't think I'd ever have a boyfriend again.

I wheel into the banquet hall where Geo's talking to guests who are trickling in early. There isn't an empty area near the front of the table where I might belong, but Trig jogs over when he sees me.

"Brekka!" He leans down to kiss the top of my head. "Thank gosh you're here. Mom and Dad are both pelting me with questions. I guess you and Rob came out of the metaphorical dating closet?"

I roll my eyes. "Rob outed us, yes, but he didn't have much choice. They were both standing in the lobby when he arrived. It was confess, or pretend he didn't know me." Which would have broken my heart, so I'm glad he didn't. "But hey, speaking of, where am I supposed to be sitting?"

"Right by me." He points to the front of the table. "I put you just to my left."

"There's a chair there," I point out.

"Right. Usually you want to transfer over. I'll take Gladys into the storage room whenever you're ready."

I shake my head. "Not anymore. I'm done with that. It's too annoying. Besides, everyone here knows I'm in a chair, or if they don't, they will soon."

Trig's eyes widen. "Got it. Let me get that chair out of the way, then." To his credit, he says nothing else and trots over right away to move the chair. I wheel over to the table and realize Rob's placard isn't next to mine.

"Uh."

Geo notices my face. "What's up?"

"Where's Rob sitting?" I ask.

Geo smiles. "He's right across from you, next to me. Since I don't have any siblings, I thought you might loan him to me. Plus, you can stare at his handsome face easier this way."

I try to suppress my disappointment. "I guess I can make that work." I notice the nameplate next to mine. Mother. I groan.

"Since she insisted on paying for the entire thing, she sort of got to choose where to sit," Geo says. "Your dad was fine with being a few guests down and didn't want to sit near your mother, whereas your mother insisted on being right by you and Trig."

Of course she did. Ugh. "Okay, that's fine. Rob seemed to manage her reasonably well."

"Does it make me a horrible person if I hope you and Rob draw some of the fire away from me? She's still not my biggest fan."

I gape. "She practically gushes about you non-stop to everyone we meet."

Geo lifts one eyebrow. "I find that hard to believe."

"It's true," I say. "Geode Poulson, her soon-to-be super-model daughter-in-law, who completely dismissed her looks and focused instead on building the highest caliber event planning company in the state of Georgia. You haven't heard her whole spiel? Really?"

Geo shakes her head. "Not even a hint at it. When we talk, she's always unhappy with something. The colors I chose, my dress, the veil, the seating, the venue for the wedding ceremony, this hotel. And she strongly hints I should have them all under control since, hey, it is my job, which I must clearly stink at doing."

Mom's kind of a bear.

"Look out. Two o'clock," I whisper. The bear's heading our way, perfect lipstick back in place.

Geo's million watt smile amps it up a few thousand more watts and I have to look away or risk going blind. It must be exhausting looking so perfect all the time. I suddenly wish I'd headed by the restroom on the way here, just to make sure there's no lipstick where there shouldn't be, or hair sticking straight up. I run my tongue over my front teeth and smooth my hair with my hand.

"You look perfect," Rob whispers from the side. "Don't stress."

The perfect symmetry of his face takes me off guard again, and my breathing hitches. He's redone his tie, and smoothed his shirt a little, but his smile is as perfect as it ever was. "Tell me where we're sitting."

I wheel forward into my empty space, and point across the table at his spot.

"Oh, no. I'm sorry, that won't do." He grins wolfishly at me.

"Why not?" I ask nervously.

He slides into my Mom's seat and whispers. "How am I supposed to hold your hand under the table from over there?" His hand reaches for me and our fingers interlace effortlessly, like we've been apart mere hours instead of weeks. "Surely your mother can be bargained with?"

"I'm a reasonable woman," Mom says behind me, "but I'm also sure you can survive without holding my daughter's hand for a few moments."

Rob doesn't flinch or back down, and the grin on his face shifts from wolfish to charming.

"The rumors of your poise weren't exaggerated," Rob says, "And I'm duly chastened. But you must place some value on young love."

My heart leaps. Young love?

Mom meets my eye before she says, "I think the truly valiant heart strengthens in the face of adversity."

"Touché." Rob stands and releases my hand. "But don't blame me when you have to watch me mooning over

Brekka like a lovesick puppy all night. You did this to yourself."

Mom sits down next to me. "He's a real piece of work."

I don't argue, because he's my piece of work. And he can defend himself.

22

ROB

Brekka's mom isn't nearly as bad as she said. She may be a little prickly at first, but by the end of the rehearsal dinner, she's giving me stock tips and offering me the end of her cheesecake.

"I'm okay with just the one piece, but thank you so much for the offer." I lean toward Brekka and her mother. "Besides. Between you and me, if I eat much more cheesecake, Brekka might dump me. Trig told me she only likes me for my washboard abs."

Brekka blushes, which I adore. "That's not true at all. I'd love you the same, even if you were squishy around the middle."

I freeze like a deer scenting the hunter. She'd love me? Does that mean she loves me now? Or was it a simple turn of phrase? I've never wanted to ditch a gathering so badly in my life. But I can't leave Geo's rehearsal dinner to interrogate Brekka about her meaning, no matter how badly I might want to. I'm the only real family Geo's got left.

As if she senses my desire to leave, Geo pats my knee.

"You've been awesome tonight, and drawn all the attention away from me. I can't ever repay you."

"Exactly the opposite of what most brides would want," I say. "No attention for them the night before their wedding would probably have them snarling."

She laughs. "I'm not most brides."

But she does look like they all wish they looked, I imagine. And she's marrying a guy they'd all love to marry, too.

For Geo's sake, I wait things out. But when the band strikes up a number and couples start pairing off on the dance floor, my heart races. I should have thought about dancing. Where will that leave Brekka and me? I glance down the table at where Troy's asleep on his mother's shoulder.

"That's how I feel right now," I say. "Between the long flight and the time change, in another five minutes, I'll be drooling on your shoulder, Brekka. Any chance you're tired? Because I don't want to be the only loser who can't stick around to dance, but—" I yawn.

The lines around Brekka's eyes ease and she beams at me. "I'm exhausted." She glances over at Trig and Geo, swaying on the dance floor. "I doubt they'll even notice if we sneak away."

Brekka's Mom winks at me. "Yes, you two better get some sleep."

That's one way to take the magic out of it, a knowing wink from your girlfriend's mom. Ugh. I stand and circle around the head of the table. Brekka's as speedy as me, backing out and spinning around toward the door.

"I've never seen anyone captivate my mother like that," Brekka says when we reach the open hallway.

"I told you parents like me."

"I wouldn't have believed it if I hadn't seen it myself. She hated my last three boyfriends, and they all—"

She cuts off short, but I'd be willing to guess she was about to say they could have bought and sold me. How could her mother like me, when I'm so clearly unsatisfactory by everything that matters to a woman like Mrs. Thornton? She didn't say the words, but they sting all the same.

"People are still people, no matter how much money they have. If you connect with them and discuss things they care about, they'll respond to you."

"I doubt any of my last three boyfriends had as much insight in their entire bodies as you put into that one comment."

I shrug. "Knowing people is kind of what drives sales. You only sell well when you can provide a person something they need. I may not be able to sell individual cars well, but I understand people most of the time."

We reach the elevators and I push the button. Brekka reaches for my hand. "You were spectacular. Thank you."

"For what?" I ask, lacing our fingers together happily.

"For being you. No matter what, no matter who you're with, you're always the same. Strong, steady, kind."

"I think everyone is always the same, by definition."

She shakes her head. "Not even close. Most people show off to some people, act humble to others, and to people they think beneath them, they're mean. You're always the same Rob and it's refreshing."

"You haven't seen me around my family yet," I say.

"True. Maybe you're a monster around the people you love so much that you work day in and day out at a job you hate for them."

The elevator dings and Brekka releases my hand. I'd never thought before how many aspects of small interactions the wheelchair impacts. No simple strolls down the beach, casually holding hands. No simple travel plans, last minute or on a whim. How complicated even things like a destination wedding make her life, and Clive's and everyone who's differently abled than me.

Or how strong you have to be to navigate it all without giving in to anger and irritation.

Brekka presses button number four.

"I'm on six."

"At least see me to my room."

My breathing hitches. "As long as you're only asking for protection from intruders. Because I wasn't kidding earlier. I'm so tired I might pass out as soon as I'm horizontal."

Brekka looks down at the floor and I realize she doesn't know I'm teasing her.

"I am tired, but I'm kidding, Brekka. I'd love to come talk in person for a while." I drop a kiss on the top of her shining hair. Her face turns toward mine and my lips move to hers.

But the doors ding open too soon, and I stand upright to follow her out. My heart races so quickly, and my brain's so fuzzy from exhaustion, that I can't string words together easily. I don't speak while I walk down the hall to her room. Four oh six.

She swipes her card and opens the door, shoving it and swiveling quickly, to back through. I reach my hand up to hold it open so she can move through more easily.

"Thanks." Her voice is small, so small, just like her. A tiny person with a huge soul.

I follow her into her room and turn in a circle, marveling at her space. It's huge. Accessible, clearly, and about three times the size of my room. She rolls through to the sitting area and lines Gladys up next to the fluffy sofa. She moves her legs off her chair one at a time using her hands. Then she shifts her bottom until she's sitting on the sofa, and pats the space next to her.

"I promise I won't keep you up very long, but I've been wanting a hug since the moment I saw you."

Her wide eyes tell me how much it cost her to admit that. I practically sprint across the room and sit down next to her, wrapping my arm around her shoulders. I close my eyes and savor the connection between our bodies, all along my side, her shoulder tucked under my arm, the side of her body pressed against mine.

Something I'd been missing my entire life clicks into place.

Like the last small fragment of a thousand piece jigsaw puzzle. Like attaching the doors to the front of an otherwise perfect cabinet. Like drinking a tall, cold glass of milk after I've inhaled four cookies. Like breathing after a long swim underwater.

Pulling Brekka's body against mine repairs the parts of me Mark's death shattered. It repairs the pain from Geo not loving me. It repairs the fear I've had that I'm not enough for her. Because clearly she's the yin to my yang, the creamy peanut butter to my dark chocolate.

I sigh, and her head tucks underneath my chin.

"You shouldn't have kept me away."

"I wasn't ready to see you until a few days ago." She breathes softly against my chest and I wish I could capture this moment in a bottle and savor it when things are hard. When I'm lonely. When the ache inside my chest feels like it'll never ease.

"Why not?" I need to know. Why did she hold me at arm's length for so long when we clearly fit so well?

She ducks her head even lower, her voice muffled against the fabric of my shirt. "After the surgery, I lost sensation in my left side."

I don't swear, but I want to. She's been hurting and I didn't even know. Why didn't Trig tell me? Or Geo? They had to know. Or why didn't Brekka tell me? Doesn't she trust me yet?

"I had to learn how to navigate without it. I doubled down on physical therapy. None of it helped, and I was spiraling a little."

I hook one finger under her chin and lift her face so I can see her soft golden eyes, her fringy lashes, and her high cheekbones. "I can't be there for you when you don't tell me what's going on."

She shakes her head. "Only I could fix it."

"You can't fix everything. Sometimes you adjust instead."

She bobs her head. "I know that. But in this case, the sensation came back, or at least most of it has."

I exhale a breath I didn't realize I was holding. "Oh, I'm so glad for you. Not that it matters to me, but I'm sure that was rough."

She looks down again and this time I let her. "All I could think about was how I'd never feel you touching my left leg. I'd never feel you, not there. Not ever, because I didn't listen to your advice. Because I was trying to make myself good enough for you."

I shake my head, sure she can feel my vehement denial in the stiff line of my body. "You're already way too good for me."

Her eyes meet mine of their own volition this time, and my head closes the distance between us. I capture her soft lips with mine.

She's the first bite of a crisp grilled cheese. She's the first dive of summer into a cool pool. She's raindrops on my face after a hot day. I could kiss her all night, her presence eradicating any exhaustion I felt. She shifts in my arms and her hand cups my face, rasping across my five o'clock shadow. When her other hand slides across my stomach, my abdominal muscles tighten.

"You really do have a six pack," she murmurs.

"You've been to the beach with me," I say.

"It's different to feel your stomach myself."

I'll say.

But before her hand can slide under my shirt, I force myself to sit up and shift slightly away from her. It nearly destroys me.

"Why are you pulling back?" Her eyes fill with uncertainty and doubt and I want to shove ahead without thinking. I want to yank my shirt off myself, but that's not what Brekka needs. Fragile, perfect, painfully beautiful Brekka. And what I want always comes second to what she needs.

"We can't," I say. "Not tonight, not now."

She swallows. "Why not?"

I look up at the ceiling. "Because when we do, it's going to be earth shatteringly perfect. It's going to change everything for you, and for me, and for us." I look back at the face that would make Madonna cry with envy. "I love you Brekka Thornton. I've loved you since you stormed into my office to tell me I couldn't love your brother's fiancée. I've loved you since you utterly confused my life, and turned everything on its head. I love your defiance, your vulnerability, your doubt, your strength, your bravery and your care for the people you love. I love your anger, your frustration and your hope."

I take her hands in mine, not letting go when she tries to pull away. "And I love when you kiss me. I love the feel of your body next to mine." I kiss her nose. "I love everything about your face." I kiss her neck. "I love your collarbones, your arms." I place one hand on either side of her knees and squeeze. "And I love your legs, exactly as they are. I love all of you, just as you sit in front of me. And I'm sure I'm not the first guy who has touched your nose, your arms, or your legs." I drop my voice until I'm positive she can barely hear me. "But I think I'm the first guy who has touched them since your accident."

She bobs her head, her eyes full of unshed tears.

"Which means we'll be learning together. And it will be breathtaking, and fun, and maybe a little funny."

She leans toward me. "Why not, then?"

"Because I know you, Brekka Thornton. You're like a rabbit in a clearing, looking for the slightest excuse to duck back into your warm, dark burrow. And I'm not going to let you."

She purses her lips. "What does that mean?"

"It means," I say, "that my washboard abs are off limits to you until we're committed."

She frowns. "Are you proposing?"

I shake my head and laugh. "I'm confessing that I love you. And waiting in agony for you to say it back. But believe me, if I were proposing marriage, I'd be on one knee, and you wouldn't need to ask me whether I'm proposing."

She sighs dramatically and slumps back against the sofa. "Okay."

"Was that an 'okay I really do love you, you big old hunk' kind of okay? Or the 'okay now get out of my sight, you great big disappointment' kind of okay?"

Brekka rolls her eyes and bites her lip before answering. "Maybe a little bit of both."

"That's fair," I say. "But I still think I'm right, and I'm not willing to risk you ducking back into hiding."

"I may never have kids," Brekka blurts out. "I may never even be able to have sex. Are you saying you don't want to find out until you're already stuck with me?"

I shake my head. "That's precisely what I'm saying. Because I don't care."

She doesn't believe me. That's clear.

I squeeze her hands. "You're saying you may not be able to have sex." I snort. "Pardon me, but if you can go to the bathroom alone, you can have sex, even if you can't do it the way you're used to doing it. You may not love your limitations at first. We may have some work to do, and we may need to be creative." I smile. "You haven't seen my shop yet, but if you had, you'd realize that I'm very, very creative. And at its heart, sex is about the expression of love between two people. That's it. The rest is just details. I'm also very, very good with details."

Brekka's mouth turns up just a hair.

"And with the kids, I already told you. I don't care whether you can have kids. You're enough for me."

"You love kids. I've seen your eyes light up around Amy and Chase and Troy. I've heard you talk about your nephew, too."

I bob my head. "I love kids."

"You don't want to give that up."

I shrug. "I'll do it, if you don't want any. But I've seen your eyes light up, too. I'm not worried."

"I might get pregnant one day, or I might not. But I don't want to spend the rest of my life feeling inadequate if I can't."

"If you want kids and we can't conceive, we can always adopt."

She shakes her head. "Why doesn't that prospect bother you, like not even a tiny bit?"

"My sister Beth, who you haven't met yet, is adopted. I love her at least as much as the twins."

Brekka blows out her breath so hard her bangs fly up in the air. "Fine. But, how can you be fine with *waiting?*"

She says it like it's a dirty word. I don't even justify that with a response other than raised eyebrows.

"You own car dealerships. You're familiar with the idea of a test drive. It's standard practice to drive something before buying it."

I pull Brekka up on top of my lap so we're eye to eye. "The dating *is* the test drive, Kiki."

"Wait, who's Kiki?" she asks.

"I was trying it out as a nickname for Brekka. See, I'm trying things. I'm guessing from your face that's a veto?"

She smiles. "Maybe not. It surprised me, is all. But don't you want to try out the whole car? You'd make sure you got up to highway speed before buying something, right?"

I laugh. "You are tenacious. I'm adding that to my list. Look, you're the most beautiful car on the lot. You handle like a dream, and your acceleration is impressive. I don't need to take you zero to a thousand to know that you're plenty of car for me. Some things are safer to practice when you're beyond the three-day returns window, and for me, this is one of them. I don't want you getting rid of me. Got it?"

When I kiss her goodnight a few moments later, the anger is gone, and the frustration too, replaced by what I hope is understanding.

I stand up. "I'm headed to sleep. But if you want to meet me for breakfast around nine, we could spend some time together before the ceremony."

Brekka nods. "I'd love that, but I promised to have breakfast with Geo. Can we meet at ten?"

"Of course. I'll see you then. And bring a bathing suit if you want to get in the water." I turn to leave, but she grabs my hand. "Wait."

I turn to face her, but it's clear she's struggling to say something, so I keep quiet.

"I love you too, Rob. I'm not as good at listing all the reasons, but you've glued me back together in a way I thought wasn't possible."

I want to stay the night with her so badly it stings, but I drop another kiss on the top of her head and see myself out like a gentleman.

23

BREKKA

Geo's face shines the next morning, like she's lit from within. I have no idea how her skin, her eyes, her entire face is so transcendent, but it always is.

"You are hard to look at," I say. "You're so pretty."

Geo rolls her eyes. "Good morning to you too, miss exaggerator."

"I'm starving. How about you?"

Geo shrugs. "An omelet, maybe. Ethan says those are their cook's specialty."

"I had one yesterday and it's not bad at all, but I'm trying the French toast today. He makes it with lemon curd, I hear."

"How was it with Rob yesterday? I noticed you ducked out early."

I try not to grit my teeth. "It was amazing, except..." I'm not sure how much to tell Geo.

"Except what?"

"Have you ever kissed him?" I blurt out.

Geo's mouth drops open. "You're kidding, right?"

I shake my head.

"Never." Geo covers my hand with hers. "Rob didn't even tell me he had a crush on me until I was already in love with your brother. Trust me when I say, I never felt that way about him. But beyond that, I don't think Rob ever loved me for real."

I seriously doubt that.

"I mean it," Geo says. "Paisley has a whole long theory, but it boils down to this. Rob's the consummate giver, and I needed him."

"Explain more," I say.

"You know how Rob and I met?" Geo asks.

I shake my head again.

"I was about to be pelted in the head with a kickball," she says. "One of the kids on our block didn't want a girl to play, and I was trying to force my way into the game. Before I could even dodge the ball, someone hit it off course and spared me. Then Rob, who had intercepted the ball, shoved the bully on the ground and told him that if the kid didn't let girls play, the bully wasn't going to be playing either."

"So he's always been protective."

"Always, but it's more than that. Rob protects anyone who needs it. Kids, women, weaker men. He's a champion of people who don't have champions, but for people he loves, he goes further. He will give up anything, do anything, to help them reach their goals."

"He told me he joined the Marines for Mark."

Geo nods. "He did. And he played basketball for his dad. And he left Miami for me. And he's running the dealerships for his whole family."

"I knew that."

"He loved me because I needed someone to love me. I was so broken after Mark died, that I closed up like a clam, tight as could be. I let no one in. Then when I started to loosen up a bit, my mom got sick. Then my dad died. Rob took the kickball defense to a whole new level. He checked on me all the time. He took me to see my mom. He handled everything about the funeral for my dad. He took me out to dinner every Monday. His dealerships became my first and my largest client, paying me enough to cover all my bills and then some. He was everything I needed, on top of being what his family needed. Rob would have just kept giving to me until it killed him."

That's a little discouraging to hear. "And you're saying that means he *didn't* love you."

Geo sighs. "No I mean, he does. He'd have done the same thing for his sisters, Beth, Jennifer or Christine. He'd do the same for his mom. He loves me the same way he loves them, unconditionally."

"Great."

"But he's different with you. He wanted to sit by you tonight. He ditches my wedding rehearsal celebration with you, to spare you any discomfort." Geo meets my eye pointedly. "He's got a higher priority now than me."

"He told me he loved me last night," I confess.

Geo beams. "I knew it. I could tell. And Brekka, I swear, what Rob would do for me pales in comparison to what he'll do for you."

"We have a lot to work out," I say. "We don't even live in the same place."

"Snap and he'll move to Colorado, I know it's true."

Geo's flippant remark upsets me. He wouldn't really just follow me around like a puppy dog, right? I don't want that. I don't want someone who obeys my orders and lives his entire life just to stare at me with devotion in his eyes. I want a partner, a supportive one yes, but a man.

"What's wrong?" Geo asks. "You look kind of nauseated."

"Nothing," I say. "Nothing's wrong. Except I don't think you're quite right about the moving thing. We only just said I love you. It's not like either of us is moving any time soon."

The waiter comes and takes our order, but when he leaves, Geo taps her lip. "This is the last thing I'll say about it, but Trig moved after knowing me for a few weeks, and Rob's way more giving than Trig at his baseline. I'm just saying, don't rule out the possibility. It's so much easier to get to know someone when they're spending every day in the same place as you. And you'd kind of be doing him a favor. He hates running those car dealerships."

Geo's words stick with me all through breakfast, and when I return to my room to change. I'm wearing a red one-piece swimsuit with loose board shorts over it, when I hear a knock at my door. I open it to Rob's smiling face, and my anxiety melts away like a pat of butter on hot toast.

"Ready to go?" he asks.

In answer, I wheel through the doorway. We head for the elevators.

"Did you sleep alright?" I ask.

"I did," he says. "The hotel bed is much nicer than mine at home."

I laugh. "It's terrible compared to mine. Maybe I need to toss out my amazing, super expensive mattress. It makes traveling a trial, no matter where I stay."

"Rich people problems," Rob says. "I feel for you, really I do. And I'm sure the food poisoning you get from only using silver and gold spoons is rough, too."

I'd like to whap his arm, but it's a foot and a half too high to reach. I'm trying to be positive, and I should be grateful I'm able to move thanks to Gladys, but I still hate being unable to walk.

I glance at his backpack. "Where are we going?"

He smirks. "You weren't so happy about my surprise last time. This time I thought I'd let you pick. I have two options. First, we go to a beach and relax. I've been working on how to gracefully manage our dear friend Gladys."

The elevator dings.

"And my other option?"

He steps into the elevator and puts his hand over the doors while I wheel inside. "Behind door two is a hike, just the two of us. It's about five miles. And before you freak out and say no, let me explain. It's an amazing hike. I've done my research. It's called the Wai Koa Loop Trail."

"I can't do a hike," I say. "It's not practical."

"You could if you let me carry you," he says. "And I've been practicing. You had your physical therapy, and I had mine. If I want to experience things with you." He drops to one knee to face me. "And I do." He kisses me quickly on the mouth. "I needed to prepare. So I went for jogs, daily, with a backpack loaded with a hundred pounds. Five miles with a hundred pounds is nothing compared to basic training, trust me on that."

My very own Marine. My heart lifts. He's been training so he'll be ready to spend time with me. It shouldn't be this hard, but he doesn't seem annoyed or frustrated. Just excited, like a puppy or like Luke's son Chase at the prospect of the Flash shoes.

I frown. "Carrying a person is different than running with weights."

He grins and taps my nose. "I knew you'd say that." The elevator dings and we exit, but he stops at the sofa in the lobby, opens his backpack and pulls out a pile of black straps. "I made two harnesses. A beach one I can explain later, and this one. It goes around my back and shoulders like this." He wraps it around and then clips something in the front. "Then your legs hook on here. I know you can't hold them around my waist, but you can wrap your arms around my neck. And once your legs are secured, it leaves my hands free, and spreads your weight evenly."

My throat closes off and tears threaten. I gulp in air to beat them back. "You, uh, you made this? So we could go for a hike?"

He nods. "I want you to know that I don't care. We can head for the beach, and I think that's great. But with me, you'll always have options. We aren't limited. Together, the world is completely open to us. We can do anything we can dream up."

I want to go to the beach. It sounds easier, relaxing even, but he's clearly put forth a lot of effort for this. I don't want to disappoint him.

"Let's do the hike," I say.

Rob beams at me, and stuffs his harness back into his bag. I follow him outside and we hail a cab. Rob helps me transfer into the cab and then breaks Gladys down and stores her in the trunk. It's only five minutes to Wai Koa. Rob pays the cab driver and unloads Gladys for me.

"Where are we going to leave her?" I ask.

"That depends on you," he says. "This trail is also a bike trail, so you can probably do most of it with her. Or I can load you up right away. I don't mind either way, but since you don't have handles, I won't be able to push you easily."

"Wait, is that mini golf?" I ask.

"Yep, Anaina Hou Community Park is a privately owned property, and the mini golf spot is where we sign a waiver so they don't worry we'll sue them. It's also a mahogany farm. Cool, right?"

I transfer into Gladys and wheel away from the cab a little reluctantly. "What's our plan to get back to the hotel?"

Rob waves at the cabbie. "He's going to come back for us in an hour and a half. If we aren't done yet, which we likely won't be, he'll wait."

I have to give Rob credit. He did his homework. "Alright, well, what's your suggestion, since you're the one spearheading this date."

He beams at my use of the word date. "Our fourth official date, if you're counting, which I am."

His attitude may be contagious.

"But since you asked, and since it's summer and that's the dry season here, I'd suggest you move on your own steam through the Kilauea Woods and past the Mahogany Plantation. If you're willing to let me carry you past that, I can make the loop around from the Junction, past the Community Gardens, the fruit farms, and the Lagoon. I doubt the Stone Dam is open, but if it is, photos of that look amazing. Then we head past the guava orchard, and on out. There's a restaurant that's sometimes open if you're hungry or need to use the facilities. I'd be happy to jog back down and grab Gladys for you."

"You did think this through," I say.

He shrugs. "I believe in planning ahead whenever possible."

"Let's go, then."

There are ruts where bikes have churned the mud in rainy season, but it's not too bad to navigate in Gladys. The ground is open, and lush as Hawaii is known to be, especially Kauai. By the time we reach the Kilauea Woods, I've broken out in a sweat, but it's worth it. When we approach the Mahogany forest, maybe a mile past the entry, the sight of hundreds and hundreds of Mahogany trees planted in perfect rows, shooting upward from the path absolutely floors me. I stop moving and take it in. Eighty-six thousand Honduran Mahogany trees on two hundred acres. Breathtaking.

No one else is on the trail, and it's utterly quiet. The air is heavy, but fresh, and the temperature is perfect, which Kauai is sort of known for, so I'm not surprised.

Rob doesn't ask whether I'm alright. He simply squats down next to me and looks at the trees, soaking it in silently. When I start forward again, he does too. Never pressuring, never coaxing or rushing me, and not blathering to fill the air. It's comforting and calm and I love every second of it.

I love Rob.

I said it last night, but I'd say it again today, over and over. I'd never in a million years have chosen this activity, this nightmare of an event that challenges me and the box I fit into now, but I'm glad I came. I'm glad that tonight, when guests ask me what I did today, I can tell them we hiked the Wai Koa Loop.

How Trig's mouth will drop.

I encounter a few muddy spots as we near the Junction, and I'm happy enough to retire Gladys to the security of a large flowering bush. "Not that anyone's going to steal a wheelchair," I say.

But if they did, I'd be devastated.

"Better to make sure there's no temptation or confusion," Rob says. "Water won't hurt her, right?"

"Nope." I sit calmly on the ground while Rob stows Gladys, and attaches his harness. He hands me a water bottle while I wait.

"Where'd that come from?" I ask.

"The harness doesn't fill the entire backpack, goose."

"Goose?"

"Worse than Kiki?" he asks. "Or better?"

I love that he's trying on nicknames for me. "I didn't hate Kiki," I say, "but goose is better." I have no idea why it's better, but it is. Maybe because it's something people say to kids with fondness, and I never had that. Mom never called us any silly names, and my dad called me sweetheart consistently. Still does. I wish he didn't use the same nickname for all his girlfriends. It feels like he can't keep more than one term of endearment straight, and I hate being lumped in with them.

"Let's try it for a while, then," he says, "Goose."

I giggle.

He squats in front of me. "Ready?"

I reach my arms around his neck and he lifts me up, fastening my legs into the straps one at a time. "You sure you're down for this?" I ask. "A hundred pounds gets heavy pretty quick."

He laughs. "You know there are porters in Peru who carry more than this and they weigh a third less than I do."

I sigh. "If you're sure."

"Trust me. This will be a good workout, but nothing that I'm unprepared for. Wai Koa's not a hard hike, and there's basically no elevation."

I squeeze my arms around his enormous shoulders and kiss his cheek. "Alright, my big ox, let's go then."

"An ox and a goose?" he asks. "It makes no sense, so of course I love it."

So do I.

But not as much as I love the feel of Rob carrying me at a jog along the trail.

"The Stone Dam," he says, not even sounding winded, "is supposed to be the coolest thing on this entire hike, but it's been down for renovations or something for a while. I guess the trail gets too slippery."

From the safety of Rob's back, I watch the foliage fly past. From flowering plants to palm trees and fiery red trees I've never seen before, the trail boasts some stunning vegetation. I only wish I knew more about plants. I can identify a few of the fruit trees when we pass the Kauai Fresh Farms. And the Lagoon isn't quite what I'd expected, but even if it's small, it's still lovely.

When a tiny blue sign comes into sight, I read it out loud. "Don't lose your head."

Fifty yards down, there's another sign.

"To gain a minute," Rob reads.

Another sign up ahead. I read, "You need your head."

Rob laughs when he sees the last one. "Your brain is in it." His shoulders shake. "Not the wittiest author, but entertaining, at least. And hey, it rhymes."

It's not hot, but it's a little muggy, and Rob's shirt dampens everywhere I'm touching him. Hardly surprising with the way his legs are pumping and his back muscles rippling. Watching him jog reminds me of the perfect movement of a clock.

"How are you holding up?" I ask Rob.

"Am I grossing you out?" he asks. "I'm sorry. I maybe should have warned you that I'm a sweaty guy, but I was worried it would scare you off."

I laugh. "I love it. You're perfect."

"Not even close, but if you're not shuddering, I'll take it."

I watch his legs pounding beneath us, his arms shifting back and forth, the muscles in his neck, and his pulse. I wish I could capture every bit of it. I pull out my phone and take a selfie. Once he realizes what I'm doing, he stops and turns so the foliage is behind us. When he smiles for me, something inside of me melts.

I snap way too many photos, and I keep my phone out

after that. I wish I'd thought to photograph the Mahogany forest, but I don't mention it, or Rob will jog us back. I know he will.

Wonder of wonders, the Stone Dam is open.

"It's been dry," Rob crows. "That must be why!"

He doesn't hesitate to take us down that off-shooting trail, and when the Stone Dam opens up to view, I gasp. "The sign says each stone was broken down by hand and laid individually in place."

It looks like a long, gorgeous waterfall, with two large triangles jutting out at one-third and two-thirds of the way across. The water spills down over them at a diagonal, pouring out further and then dropping straight off on the sides.

"Amazing." I sigh.

Rob turns and takes a selfie of the two of us, my arms around his neck, my face smiling, the dam in the background.

"I didn't really want to come," I say.

Rob nearly drops my phone. "Why did you? I said the beach was fine, but honestly I'd have been okay sitting at the hotel. I just wanted to be with you."

"I thought you wanted to hike. You made a special harness."

He returns my phone with a sigh. "You've got to tell me what *you* want to do. I'd have picked the beach myself. Closer and easier to coordinate."

I laugh. "Neither of us wanted to come, and here we are. We're a terrible pair, huh?"

Rob can't twist his head like Gumby to kiss my lips, but he drops a kiss against my cheek. "I think we're a great pair, and I'm glad we got confused and came. If nothing else, that photo's going to look amazing framed on my desk at work."

That thought warms my heart. My photo, proudly displayed on his desk, for everyone to see. His girlfriend Brekka. Not a secret, not a phantom or just some girl he's flirting with. His girlfriend on his back, in front of a dam, on a hike.

"You are going to send me all these, right?" he asks.

"What will I get in exchange?"

"What did you have in mind?" He starts to jog again, moving slowly toward the exit. "Name something and the answer is yes."

I can't think of anything at first. "Let me have a little time to contemplate a fair price."

"The travails of having so much money that you literally buy anything you can possibly imagine. You realize, this means you'll be absolutely impossible to shop for."

"Oh, my brother might have mentioned that a time or two."

"I'm creative. Did I mention that?" Rob asks.

"You might have," I say. "But I'm pretty creative too. Because I think I know what I want. I want you to move to Colorado."

The second the words fly out, I want to snatch them back. It's almost exactly what Geo told me to ask for, and what I swore I wouldn't ever say. After all, I don't want him to move to Colorado just because I asked.

Rob doesn't speak.

Now I'm worried it might be worse if he refuses me. I swallow and close my eyes.

"Look at the guava orchards," he says. "Aren't they spectacular?"

I respond, but I can't recall what I say two minutes later. Who cares about guava orchards? I ruined our entire afternoon with my completely inappropriate demand.

A few moments later, we reach the Junction and I see

the bush where Gladys is waiting. Rob sets me down, but I stop him from assembling her for me. I scoot over until I'm next to her and assemble her myself. I need to do it alone, with my hands, and not have it done for me. By the time she's assembled, I lever myself up and onto her seat, and I'm wheeling toward the exit.

How could I have taken something so perfect and smashed it to bits? It's such a Brekka thing to do. Broken girl who smashes everything. It's so obvious and predictable.

Rob jumps in front of me on the path, his hands splayed in front of him. "What's going on right now?"

I pull up short, barely in time to keep from barreling over him. "What?"

"You and I are jogging along, having what I thought was an amazing time. Then you completely close off and won't meet my eye. And somehow we've entered the Indie 500 and you're sprinting to get back to the mini golf place. Is there some timeline I didn't hear about? Because by my watch, we've got four hours yet until the ceremony, which is plenty of time to drive back to the hotel, shower and get ready, even if I were doing my hair all curly and fancy and putting on make-up I didn't need."

I frown. "You think I don't need make-up?"

He sighs. "I stuck my foot in it on that one. I'm sure whatever you do will be lovely, with make-up or without. But my point is, what did I do or say wrong?"

Does he really have no idea? He's not that clueless, right?

"I asked you to move to Colorado. You ignored me."

"Oh, you were serious?" His eyebrows lift. "I thought you were kidding."

I close my eyes. Why didn't that possibility occur to me? Of course he'd assume I was kidding. Trading a few selfies for a cross-country move isn't a reasonable suggestion. I could kick Geo for planting this idea in my head to begin with. Or, you know, I suppose I can't kick her. But if I could move my legs, I sure would.

Rob folds his arms in front of me and nods. "If you're really asking me, then yes, I'll move to Colorado. I'd need to wait until I could transition my job to a manager who I trust. My family will understand since there's a compelling reason for me to leave. And you are the most compelling reason of all."

Geo's a genius, and I hate her for it. Because now that Rob's willing to do exactly what I asked, I realize I don't want him to move to Colorado. Not at all.

✽ 24 ✽

BREKKA

My mom made insane demands of my dad. I don't recall all of them since I'm the youngest child, but I remember enough. Mom would insist on Parisian food. Brought to her. Dad would fly to Paris and back, but by the time he made it back, she'd have eaten a sandwich and gone to bed. Somehow it was his fault for taking so long on a plane.

Once Mom wanted Dad to plan a perfect family vacation. She was sick of always having to set up everything herself. He talked to Disneyland and booked an entire day for our family. No one else would be present. I have no idea what that cost. Millions, I'm sure, and then Mom had a meeting come up. Dad tried to explain what he'd planned, but it only enraged Mom. She didn't want him to buy out Disney! That was frivolous and stupid, especially since the other people are part of what makes it all so magical.

If Dad went up, Mom screamed for down. If Dad said dark, Mom only wanted light. No matter what Dad gave, it was never enough. I never considered myself to be much like my mother, but now I'm not so sure. Because I asked

Rob to move to Colorado, and now that he's willing to do exactly what I said I wanted, I want him to take it all back.

Because Rob's a giver, and that makes me a taker.

Geo said it herself. He gives and gives and gives. She doesn't think he resents the person who takes over and over, but how can she be sure? And even if he doesn't resent me now, he will. First it's move to Colorado, give up your family, your friends, and your job. Then what? Give up your normal hikes. Your normal counters and floors and mobility. Then it's give up your vacation plans, since I've got to work. Then it's up when he says down. Dark when he says light. Parisian food, until it takes too long and I'm sleeping alone and we're yelling at each other.

I'd almost rather die than turn into my mother.

I finally realize that I love Rob, and then I discover that he and I may be fatally flawed. I can't even stand, but if he won't stand up to me, we're doomed. He needs to be able to demand something for himself. He needs to ask me to move to Atlanta.

Because if he doesn't, we're doomed.

"When would you want me to move?" he asks. "Is October soon enough?"

"Actually, I might have been a little hasty."

He tilts his head like he's misheard me. "I'm sorry?"

"Now that we're talking about it, I don't think you moving to Colorado is a great plan."

He nods his head slowly. "It's fast, that's for sure."

"Right. Too fast, don't you think?" Say no, say no. It's not too soon. It's the wrong direction. It's all Rob's sacrifice and none of mine.

"But eventually, you see this going that way?" he asks.

Does he mean with him moving to Colorado? Or with one of us moving? "I'm not sure."

Rob kneels in front of me again. "Do you see yourself with me in five years? Ten?"

I do. I absolutely do. "I'm not sure. I mean, we don't even live in the same state. And we don't have much in common."

Rob's face shutters like a beach home preparing for a hurricane. "That's true, we don't."

He stands up and doesn't say another word while we head for the entrance of the park. The cab is waiting for us when we reach the main road. Rob helps me transfer and loads Gladys up without saying a word. He doesn't slide over next to me on the seat, and he doesn't take my hand.

What did I say?

We don't live in the same state. Simple statement of fact, and the topic of our entire conversation. Then I said we don't have much in common. I close my eyes. Because he's not even a college grad. He's not rich. He's a Marine who sells cars.

Oh, Rob.

I reach for his arm, but when my fingers brush his forearm, he flinches and I shrink back to my side.

I open my mouth to say something, but I'm not sure what to say. Even if I coax him back into talking to me and touching me and kissing me, which I want desperately, unless Rob changes who he is, unless Rob can suddenly demand what he needs, I'm not sure this will ever work. After all, my parents must have loved one another at some point, right? They didn't start their marriage twisted and damaged like they are now.

When we reach the hotel, I still haven't figured out what I can say to repair the breach. Or whether I should even try.

"I had a great time," I finally blurt out.

"Me too." Rob turns toward me, his eyes soft. "Thank you for coming."

My heart yearns for him to pick me up and carry me up to my room and throw me down on my stupidly hard mattress. I want him to toss his rules out the window, and tell me he needs me in his life, in Colorado or Georgia or on Mars. I want him to convince me that it doesn't matter what I think, or what I fear, or how different we are, or how messed up my parents have become.

But he's Rob.

Rob doesn't conquer or dominate or force. It's not who he is, and it's not who he'll ever be. Rob carries, and lifts and supports. He can't be what I'm wishing for. It would destroy everything I love about him all at once. I turn away from him and that wounds him even more.

What's wrong with me?

Rob walks alongside me all the way to my room. Once I've opened the door, he half bows to me, like I'm royalty and he's my honor guard or something, and walks back down the hall. It feels like someone's shredding my heart, one ventricle at a time. Why can't Rob demand what he needs? Why can't he insist I meet him halfway? I'll do it, I want to scream. Just tell me what you want, so I know we won't turn into carbon copies of the unhappiest marriage I've ever seen.

But he doesn't, of course. Rob would never demand anything like that of me.

So I wheel into my big, gorgeous suite and sob into my pillow until the very last moment. Then I drag myself up and put my makeup on, and change into my sky blue sundress. I wheel myself to the door, and then down the hall. I take up my place at Geo and Trig's wedding like a robot, smiling when I should, and murmuring the right things to everyone.

It's not until I see Geo walking down the aisle that something cracks my shell. My brother is getting married to the girl of his dreams, to someone I adore. I'm so happy for them. And so I set aside my despair. I set aside my fears and my selfishness and I watch as Geo, the most show stopping, the most generous, the most peerless bride I've ever seen walks serenely down the aisle.

Her colors are perfect. Sky blue and black and silver. Her eyes shine brighter than the sapphires on the collar around her neck, a custom designed piece from Trig. Her hair falls in an ebony cascade down her back, a stark contrast to the snowy white of her veil and gown. She's not dressed like a cupcake: no frills, or beads, or embroidery, and not a speck of lace. No, her pure white, sleeveless silk gown fits her simply, a shining sheath that hugs her immaculate figure and drops to a long, draped train that flows out behind her like a smoothly shimmering waterfall. She clasps a simple bouquet of blue delphinium and delicate white snowdrops in her hands.

But her eyes never leave Trig's face, and he's beaming like he's President of the World. It's everything I ever wanted for my older brother.

They each prepared their own vows. Trig goes first.

"From the very moment I clapped eyes on you, I haven't wanted anyone else. But as incomparable as you are on the outside, your parents named you perfectly. You're truly like a geode. Your exterior is practically dirty and scuffed and dull compared to the sparkle, the magic and the brilliant beauty hiding inside of your head and heart. I have no idea why you put up with me and all my fumbly, bumbly mistakes, but for some reason you do, and I wake up every single day marveling that you've agreed to live with my flaws forever."

Trig takes Geo's hand in his.

"Thank you for helping me see when I'm being an idiot, and forgiving me when it takes me a while to grasp that insight. I promise to cherish your outside and your inside every single day, every single hour, and every single breath for the rest of my life."

Trig leans down and brushes his lips against hers. The priest shakes his head, but Trig shrugs, unrepentant.

Geo rests one hand softly on Trig's chest and looks into his eyes.

"Bernard Thornton the Third."

The audience laughs softly.

"You lived the first half of your life with that name, and you rocked it, I'm sure, because that's what you do. You were born into privilege, but you didn't throw any opportunities away. You worked hard even when you didn't have to. You excelled at math and then you did what you always do. You took a name for yourself, you made a place for yourself, and then you improved on what you'd done before. Always striving, always improving. And you noticed the amazing people around you along the way. When I met you, you were already impressive. You were a force to be reckoned with, but the man I fell in love with was a man who became more than that. You're more now than a guy who works hard and sees insightfully."

She presses her hand against his chest and gazes into his eyes for a moment. It's magical to see a tiny sliver of the bond they share.

I'm not the only one who sighs.

Geo continues. "You've always been someone who cared deeply for your family. Your parents, and especially your beloved sister. But when you decided you loved me, you were willing to do literally anything it took to make your life something I would fit within, including impoverishing yourself, so to speak."

The audience laughs again.

"And if someone had told me that one day, my grand gesture from a guy would be that he'd throw buckets of money away for me, I'd have been sure they lost their mind. But what you showed me that day is that, no matter what, highs or lows, dark or light, you're with me. You're by my side forever. Rich or poor, handsome or ugly. I know it in my bones, and for someone without a lot of family." Geo glances at Rob and the video camera behind him where her mom's watching. "For someone like me, that means the world. Thank you for walking beside me on this beautiful earth and making it a little more lovely. You've given me all you had, and I can't wait to share everything we will create together."

I glance at Rob, but he's staring at Geo, almost stoically. I turn away before I break down and cry. It hurts to think about him leaving tomorrow and not texting me every day. Not calling me every day. And not flying out to see me, or touching my face, or kissing my lips.

What's wrong with me? After Trig and Geo head to the dance floor for their first dance, I'm ready to wheel over to where Rob's standing and tell him I went temporarily insane. Maybe we can table the whole moving thing for a while. Call and text like we were, and travel back and forth when we find time.

Except before I reach him, he takes Paisley's hand and leads her out on the dance floor. I watch them spin and twirl and I realize that what I said was true.

Rob and I don't have much in common, but he's not the one with the negative balance sheet. That's me. Because he may not have an Ivy League degree, but he's got legs that work. He's got a strong back, and a stellar face that turns heads everywhere we go. And even more than that, unlike mine, Rob's heart is open and ready. Rob's steady and solid and supportive, and he deserves someone who can give him all the things I never will.

Because between my broken back and my twisted parents, I'm shouldering a tremendous bundle of insecurities. Rob will be stuck carrying them on his back forever. I'll always be a dead weight like I was today, figuratively speaking and quite literally. I'll always freak out for no reason, or spin out because he's not manly enough, when really I'm the one who's got issues. So I turn back to the wedding party and start to mingle with my family and old friends. I joke, I laugh and I try to look like I'm celebrating.

And when it comes time for gifts, I give Trig and Geo mine without reservation.

"I know most people aren't too excited for paperwork," I say as Trig opens a fat envelope. "And you're no exception, which is why you usually try to shuttle it all onto my desk."

"You're a whiz with paperwork and legalese," Trig says.

He's not wrong. "But this paperwork, well, I figure you'll forgive me. Because a few months back, I helped you execute your grand gesture to win Geo over to your side, dumping buckets and buckets of money into my own pocket in the process. But just in case your future children aren't quite so magnanimous, I thought you might want a second stab at securing that money for them."

Geo looks over the paperwork Trig's spreading on his lap.

"What is this?" she asks.

"It's a reversion document," I say. "It gives Trig's half of the Thornton Trust back to your future children, should you ever have any. My mom's still the Trustee, but eventually, that responsibility will revert to you and Trig, until your children reach thirty years of age anyway."

I don't bother mentioning that if I never give birth to

my own heir, his kids will get my trust funds, too. I glance at Rob, and he's staring back at me longingly. My resolve wavers. How bad could it be to keep the best thing in my life... in my life?

But it's not fair to him. He's not going to change, and I'm not going to want someone who won't ask for what they need, who won't demand that I give them what they want. Because I'll always demand what I want. It's hard-wired into my brain thanks to my mom.

So I wheel back to my room alone that night. When I reach my room and check my phone, I have one text message.

I MISS YOU.

My fingers want to text Rob back so badly. I shut my phone off so they don't give in. Because I know what my fingers don't yet grasp. This will get easier with time. The pain will ease, and it's for the best. I'm walking away, er, wheeling away, because it's what Rob needs. And I want Rob to have what he needs.

I only wish I could be the one to give it to him.

25

ROB

"I don't understand what happened," my sister Christine says. "You told her you loved her. She said she loved you back. She asked you to move, and you agreed to do it."

I nod my head. This is where Brekka lost me, too. "Yep. That's what happened. We had the best day I've ever had, maybe in my whole life. She was laughing, I was laughing. I think I convinced her that her paraplegia doesn't matter to me. It won't get in our way."

"Okay." Christine sits down at my table.

I take the seat across from her and pass a sandwich her way.

"Peanut butter and jelly?" She raises her eyebrows dubiously.

"You brought the jelly," I say. "It would be rude not to try it, right?"

Christine laughs and takes a bite. She and I always ate PB&Js, while Jennifer and Beth loved ham and cheese. Which is probably why she's always been my favorite. Of course, Beth's the only sister who likes to jog, which is why she's my favorite. And Jennifer's the only one who loves to play Monopoly, so that's why she's my favorite.

"Alright, so you're moving to Colorado, and then, bam? She dumps you?"

I shrug. "I don't know whether she dumped me or not, honestly. I texted her during the wedding, but she didn't have her phone. She didn't reply that night, but I'm sure she was beat. The next morning, she sent a few messages back. She said she missed me, too. She sent me a ton of photos." I flip my phone around and show her the selfies we took of our hike.

"She does look happy here," Christine says. "Really happy."

"It was a lot of fun. And we were talking about the future. And now I'm lucky to get a half dozen texts a day."

"Are they flirty?"

"I have no idea anymore." I slump in my chair and tap my phone to get into my texts. "It's been five days since the wedding, and I sent her these."

BOUGHT A DRAGON FRUIT AT THE GROCERY STORE. ISN'T AS GOOD AS IT WAS IN KAUAI. BUT IT COST SEVENTEEN DOLLARS, SO THAT'S THE SAME.

Brekka sent me a laughing face.

OF COURSE, MAYBE I WOULDN'T BE SO CRABBY ABOUT IT IF I SLEPT ON A SOLID GOLD BED LAST NIGHT LIKE SOMEONE ELSE I KNOW.

More laughing with tears emojis.

I HOPE IT'S NOT AS HOT IN COLORADO. BY SEVEN TONIGHT, I'LL BE READY TO SERVE MYSELF ON A BUN WITH BARBECUE SAUCE.

Christine smirks at me. "You'll be ready to serve yourself?"

I roll my eyes. "She's not giving me much to work with."

"But you're working a little too hard."

I WISH I WERE IN ATLANTA. IT'S HOT HERE TOO, BUT AT LEAST I'D HAVE A HOT GUY AROUND IN GA.

"See?" I point at the text. "She's flirting back, and telling me she misses me. But she's not on a plane headed out here, which she could be since she owns one." I drop my face into my hands and groan. "Why can't I just see inside her head?"

"Because that would be super creepy," Christine says. "And I'm going to pretend you didn't just ask that."

"I feel like I'm wasting time now. I want to be with her, and she wants to be with me, I know it. And here we are, marking time in our respective places, not being together."

"Would you really drop everything and move, just like that?"

I nod. "I mean, I'd miss you guys, but did you hear the part where she has a plane? She hardly ever uses it. I can come visit whenever. Weekly dinners, if you still want. Or you can come see me."

"But who would run the dealerships?"

I shake my head. "I don't know, but if I knew she wanted me there, I would figure something out. I won't leave you guys in the lurch, I swear."

"What about me?" Christine asks softly.

"I wouldn't leave you either, I promise. I wasn't even talking about going until the Fall."

"No, I mean, what about me to take over? I know my degree is in public relations," she says, "and I'm not like a whiz with management like you, but I've always been fascinated by the business side of the dealerships. I've always thought it might be a challenge..." She exhales. "This isn't coming out right and if I can't pitch you, how will I ever convince Dad?"

I yank Christine out of her chair and into a bear hug. "You're hired. Oh my word, Christine, if I had any idea. You are hired!"

Her eyes bulge. "Huh?"

"You'll be brilliant! I've asked Dad for years if anyone else in the family had any desire to run things and he's been adamant that no one had even the slightest interest."

Christine frowns. "Are you sure?"

"I hate running everything. Let's get you started tomorrow."

"If you tell Mom and Dad it's my fault you're moving—"

"Let's not jump ahead," I say. "I have no reason to move right now. I don't even have a fifth date lined up."

She laughs. "That girl has some other hang up she hasn't disclosed like a secret husband or something, but once her divorce comes through, you guys are going to work."

"A secret husband?" I tilt my head.

"You clearly haven't been paying attention during all the romantic comedies I made you watch. The fake husband is a joke, but there's something in the equation we don't see. Once that is solved for..." Christine jabs her finger at my phone. "Look at her face in that one with the waterfall behind her. That's pure joy."

I hope Christine's right. Not about the husband, but about the joy. Before she can leave, I screw up the courage to ask her for a favor. "You'll be coming to work with me every day now, right?"

"As soon as I can quit my job," she says. "That's right."

"Your major is public relations, isn't it?"

She bobs her head. "Well, I started out in marketing and shifted gears, but yeah."

"I've been thinking that if I could ever figure out who else could run Franklin, I might try my hand at something else."

She claps. "Are you finally going to sell your art?"

My what? "No, my furniture. Wait, what art?"

She throws her hands into the air. "Your furniture *is* art. It's about time. And whatever you want me to do, I'm in. I'll do it. You want me to help you market it, yes, I'll do that. You want help picking a storefront, I'll do that too. I'm in like Flynn."

"Who's Flynn?"

"Never mind," she says. "I mean that I'll do it."

Well that was easy. "The thing is, I had this idea a few weeks ago, and I wonder if it might help me at the same time."

"What's the idea?" she asks.

"You know my friend Clive?"

She nods. "Your hot friend Clive, you mean?"

I shelve that comment for later consideration. "That's who I mean, yes."

"What about him?"

I tell her my plan. She claps even louder this time. "Oh my gosh, yes. You have to do that. But it's not me you need help from first."

"Who?"

"Doesn't Geo have some new friends? An accountant who's married to a billionaire business mogul?"

Mary and Luke. "Yep, something like that."

"And you're friends with them, too?"

I bob my head up and down. "I guess so."

"The accountant can help you with that first part, and the billionaire will have contacts."

"He's not quite a billionaire," I say. "I think he's close, but not quite that rich."

She waves at me dismissively. "Details. The point is, he's connected, and you need that." She picks up her phone and dials Geo.

I grab her arm. "What are you doing?"

"Moving this thing forward before you change your mind." I hear Geo answer, faintly. Christine taps the speakerphone button.

"Hey Geo. Christine and Rob here."

"Oh hey, Christine. How's it going?"

"I know you're on your honeymoon. I wasn't sure if you'd answer."

I hear scuffling coming from her receiver. "Hang on, Trig. In a second," Geo says. "Yeah, I've always got time for my favorite adoptive sister."

Christine beams at me. "And your favorite brother, right?"

"Of course," Geo says. "What's up?"

"Rob quit his job, and I'm taking over."

"Wow," Geo says. "For real?"

"Yep," Christine says. "Mom and Dad don't know about the coup yet, but they'll find out soon enough."

"Okay. And where do I come in?"

"Well, my brother's now an unemployed loser, one step from the poor house. He's thinking maybe with your contacts, you could help us locate a space so he could sell some of his—"

"Yes," Geo cuts Christine off. "I'm in. The jewelry box he made for my wedding gift is exquisite. And the desk he made for my mom, every single member of the staff gushes about it incessantly. But he doesn't want a space to sell from. Shops are mundane, every day, boring. What we need is an exhibit at a gallery. His furniture is art, and we need to market it that way."

Christine puts her hand on her hip and points at me with the other hand. "Told you," she mouths.

"I'll be back in a few days. Let's get together for lunch,

the three of us, and start hammering the details of this out."

"Do you think Mary would mind if I called her?" I ask. "I know she runs that charity, and I was thinking of starting one, too. I want to call it Cultivate, and it'll be a charity that helps wheelchair users obtain the help they need to modify their houses, their kitchens and bathrooms, and to acquire the tools they might want to pursue careers and hobbies. Accessible workplaces, extreme wheelchairs for hikes, power chairs, car modifications, and on and on. Accessibility for places they want to go that aren't accessible, that kind of thing."

"You split your proceeds half and half," Geo says. "And then people go mad to support a new artist *and* a worthwhile charity. It's brilliant. I love everything about it. What does Brekka think?"

"It's a surprise," I say quickly. "Let's not tell her."

"Uh, okay. That's kind of weird, but we can talk about that later. We're late for a tour. I've got to run!" Geo hangs up, but for the first time in days, I'm smiling.

'You realize you're going to have to tell Mom and Dad, right?" Christine says. "Because you're the only one who has a prayer of surviving the seismic shift we've started."

My smile melts. "How about we tell them together," I suggest.

She sighs. "Fine. We've always been better together."

I beam at Christine, because she's right. Family is always stronger together.

26

BREKKA

I'm like the addict who can't quite flush her cocaine stash.

I know I need to stop texting Rob, because we're on a collision course for the same misery my parents currently enjoy. But he's so funny and I love him so much. Every day, I wonder whether today's the day. Maybe today he'll ask me to move to Atlanta for him. Maybe today he'll change his stripes for spots and we can make it work.

That's why I can't seem to resist texting him. Or answering when he calls, and telling him all about my day. That's why I haven't actually broken up with him.

LOOKS PRETTY GOOD ON MY DESK, he texts. He attaches an image of our Stone Dam selfie in a silver frame. The worst part is that it does look good. We look amazing in that photo. Perfect, even.

I'm almost done with a new proposal for Trig and it's not even ten a.m. I've taken to waking up earlier and earlier, as though I'm on Eastern time. Like I'm prepping to move myself, which I'm not, since Rob will never ask me to sacrifice for him or for us. My entire office usually rolls in around six a.m. too now, trying to impress me with keeping the same hours I keep.

THE REAL LIVE BREKKA STILL LOOKS BETTER. WHEN CAN I SEE HER?

My heart wibble wobbles in my chest. What's wrong with me? I have a wonderful guy who wants to come see me. He's offered to come and visit a dozen times. He's begged me to fly out there. I always make up excuses, but I can't really remember why anymore, not really.

CAN YOU COME VISIT THIS WEEKEND? I HAVE SOMETHING TO SHOW YOU.

My fingers hover over the phone. Rob doesn't usually send three messages in a row without some kind of response from me. Because I've reduced him to adhering to typical relationship rules, so insecure about whether I'm still invested in us. A lesser man would have thrown in the towel. But Rob's not even in the same zip code as any of the other men I've dated.

YES, I text. Then I delete it. Because I can't. If I fly to Atlanta, I'll cave. I'll tell him to move, or I'll move, or anything at all to make this work.

Although, this is *him* asking *me* to do something. He's not throwing out ultimatums, but it's a start. Maybe it's the stepping-stone to him asking me for what he needs. Maybe he's becoming vested enough in his own needs and wants to start carving out some space for himself. Could he protect us from what we might become otherwise?

WHAT'S THE SURPRISE? I finally text back.

No response. Drat.

Rob and his stupid surprises.

I hate them and I love them. No one has ever tried to surprise me other than my dad, and those are always hit and miss.

Surprise, we're going to Turkey for a week! You'll hate

the food, and no one wears deodorant. Just what teenage dreams are made of. Or surprise, I've decided to buy a three-wheeled car for you to drive! It looks bizarre and feels unsafe. Good luck. Surprise, we're skipping school for a month to go to Bora Bora. The weather is great, but of course you won't know a soul and the WiFi is spotty at best.

Mom always hated Dad's surprises. For me and Trig, sometimes they were awesome, but they were always... unreliable. Rob's surprises have all been good, so far. Even so, his propensity to insist on leaving me guessing just like my dad worries me.

My mom on the other hand, nothing's ever a surprise with her. She'll drill you to death on the details, but she won't ever take you off guard. Not with presents, which she usually calls me about weeks ahead of the event to pre-approve. Not with trips, which she's unlikely to ever plan anyway unless it's for the launch of some new company or product line. And certainly not with family business. She's always sending out memos and emails and texts updating me on the status of, well, everything. Then her assistant follows up to make sure I received the memo, email and text if I don't reply promptly.

Why did my parents ever think they might make things work? They're a circle and a square. My mom hates surprise and it fuels my father, who's always flitting from one thing to the next. My mom loves work, and growth of financial plans. My dad hates anything to do with numbers and figures. He broke out in hives once when my mom made him attend all the board meetings and weigh in on every trust decision for a month. His doctor literally diagnosed him with chronic stress fatigue.

From one month's work.

"Mail." Blake dumps a huge pile of letters into my box.

"Wait, why is there so much?" I ask.

He shifts toward the door. "Some of it might have got sorted wrong. Sorry about that." He darts out.

I exhale and begin to flip through it.

A large, recycled paper envelope catches my eye. The paper is embossed and looks almost like a wood grain. It boasts an Atlanta return address, the Callanwolde Fine Arts Center. I slide my finger under the flap and open it. Inside there's a thick, creamy invitation to the Grand Opening for the Robert Graham 'Art To Surround Us' Exhibit, and the launch of Cultivate. It's tomorrow night at seven.

I think I've discovered Rob's surprise.

I flip the invitation over and my eyes scan for details. On opening night, select pieces will be auctioned, and all proceeds will go to a new charity Robert Graham recently founded. The rest of the pieces will be available the following day at fixed prices, probably based largely on the prices set by the auction. Brilliant.

My eyes are drawn to the bottom, where gold ink outlines the word CULTIVATE.

Robert Graham, a veteran himself and a recipient of the esteemed purple heart, surrounds himself with friends and former vets who have suffered injuries that leave them unable to walk or run as they could before. He's established Cultivate as a charity intended to: 1) provide accessibility for places without, 2) modify housing and work situations to support differently abled persons, and 3) provide materials and supplies needed by applicants to pursue their dreams without limit.

Rob's selling his furniture, and he's doing it to help create a charity I know he believes in strongly. A glint of black and white gloss catches my eye. There's another paper in the envelope. I pull out the photo, an image of Clive, beaming for the camera from his wheelchair, shining cabinets at his chair height in the background.

"Rob Graham lives what he espouses. He made cabinets for my home so I could cook and clean and function independently. He's done it for three other friends as well. I'm proud to be the face of Cultivate. I can't wait to see how far this will go and how many lives we can touch." Clive Winsworth, 32, Navy veteran, President of Cultivate.

Certainty floods my chest. I've been going back and forth with my parents over that trust provision, but yesterday my attorney handed me a bazooka, and I'm ready to use it.

I text my mom. LUNCH?

True to form, she replies seconds later naming the place and time. HOTEL MONACO. HALF AN HOUR.

I text my dad next. PANZANO, LUNCH? HALF AN HOUR OR FORTY MINUTES? It's dumb to say Panzano instead of Hotel Monaco like Mom insists on calling it, but he probably knows Hotel Monaco is her favorite spot. I'm worried he'll figure out my plan. I'm hoping the actual restaurant name might throw him off the scent.

Sometimes I don't hear back from Dad for days at a time. But I'm in luck. SURE, BUT I'M BUYING.

DEAL.

I've never tricked my parents into being in the same place before, mostly because it's a terrible idea, like convincing Russia and America the other is firing nukes and standing around to see who strikes first. If I manage to pull this off, I hope I survive it.

I'm already at Hotel Monaco when my mom walks in, and I'm prepared for battle.

"I was happy to hear from you," Mom says. "I feel like you've been avoiding me ever since Trig's wedding. We haven't had lunch in weeks and weeks."

I have avoided her, mostly because I can't handle her gushing about someone I'm trying to dump.

"I'll admit, I was hoping there would be three people here today," she says.

"Oh there will be," I say, excited to surprise her. In a bad way.

Her eyes widen. "Oh, that's wonderful. I've missed Rob terribly."

My mom never misses anyone except her children. I knew Rob impressed her, but not this much. "Why do you like him?"

Mom shakes her head. "I can't say, and I know that's a little odd. I've thought about it a lot, and the only thing I can pinpoint is that he felt genuine. He clearly cared for you, and he's bright. When I researched him, what I found surprised me. He hopped around from place to place, you know. Marine, deployed, and then his injury you know and the subsequent recovery, and then back home. I can't find a clear pattern, but every person we spoke to raved about him. I couldn't find a single individual, in all that research, who had anything negative to say about Robert Graham. It's almost like he's an honest to goodness saint."

Of course she interviewed people. How embarrassing if any of them called Rob to tell him.

"Mom, you can't go around calling people he knows and grilling them."

She places her hand over mine. "For my little girl, I'd go a great deal further. But in this case, I think he really loves you. And I think he'd move heaven and earth for you. I don't even care that he's poor."

I roll my eyes. "He's not poor."

She waves her hand in the air. "Fine, worth less than two million dollars. Same thing."

Not to most people.

"But I thought about it this way. Unlike your father, who brought the trust and his family name, this Rob brings nothing. Which means he'll be grateful for everything, unlike your wretch of a father."

"What a delightful surprise to see you here, Victoria." Dad addresses Mom, but he's glaring at me.

"Wait, this is what you meant by three?" Mom practically spits the words at me.

"Dad, please sit. I'm sure you two can survive one single, solitary lunch. Since I invited you both here to settle a trust matter, I figured you'd forgive me. No time like the present to vote on my future."

"What in the world are you talking about?" Mom asks.

A waiter brings a basket of bread and I'm legitimately worried Mom and Dad might incinerate him by accident with the lasers they're shooting at one another from their eyes.

"Focus," I say. "You're here for me, so stop acting like babies."

They both completely drop their scowls as if they didn't realize they were even doing it. Maybe they didn't. Maybe it's a reflex after so many years. "Mom sent me a copy of the trust, and I hired a lawyer so I could look into my options."

"The whole thing was set up for you, darling, I'm sure we can change it however you need," my dad says.

Mom rolls her eyes. "You would say that. We're the trustees for a reason. To do what she might not be willing to do in order to protect her funds."

"For two more years," I say.

"Excuse me?" Mom asks.

"I'll be thirty in two years and five weeks," I say. "At that point, I own my shares outright. Whatever remains of Dad's share will pass to me and Trig on his death, which I hope won't be for quite some time."

Dad beams at me. "Thanks sweetheart."

"But look, the point is—"

The waiter approaches us, his hands behind his back. He should have held out a little white flag. It would have been just as obvious and possibly a little humorous.

I order the same thing as always, and so does Mom. Dad takes more than five minutes to decide, grilling the poor waiter on ingredients and the chef's preparation style. I really hope my kids aren't this fussy, if I ever have any.

"Now that we've gotten that out of the way," I say, "I'm ready to drill down to the point. I didn't invite you here because I wanted to get the restaurant burned down, or purchased in a leveraged buy out." I wink at mom. "But my attorney explained something to me. It's a weird, old school doctrine called the rule against perpetuities."

Mom's face blanks and I realize that she already knows. Somehow that makes me want to curl into a ball and cry. She's known this entire time and she didn't tell me? She didn't release my funds when she knew she could? I knew Mom ruled over Dad and the trust with an iron fist, but I never thought she'd do anything that wasn't best for me.

"Clearly Mom knows where I'm going with this, but in case you don't, Dad, let me fill you in. There's a law governing family wealth transfer that allows a testamentary trust to continue to govern parties until the latest life in being, plus twenty-one years. In our case, that's Uncle Benny, who was barely alive when this was written, and now it's been twenty-eight years since he was born. Which means... I can dissolve this any time with one simple petition to the court of jurisdiction where it was created."

I cross my arms and dare my mom to argue with me. She won't be able to resist.

"But the trust contains several tax saving measures—"

"All of which I will be able to transition," I say. "As you well know."

"Why do you want to seize control now?" Mom asks.

I glance at my dad, who would be popping buttons off his shirt if it had any, he looks so proud of me. It isn't every day that someone outsmarts my mother. His chest is puffed out, and his eyes are sparkling. "Ah, the master crosses swords with her protégé and finally, for once, the master loses!"

Oh good grief. "It's not like that," I say. "In fact, I don't even care whether we dissolve the trust. But the thing is, I don't want it."

My mom's jaw drops.

"I didn't know I had the power to give it away, since unlike Trig, I'm not thirty, and I was the last heir, right? But then I went and gave Trig's half back to his kids, so if I back out of my share, it just reverts to them too."

"Get to the point," Mom says.

"I want to donate my half to a charity called Cultivate."

Mom throws her hands in the air and starts wailing.

Dad frowns. "I understand you're charitably minded, and I appreciate it, value it even. But as you age, you'll realize that—"

"Knock it off, both of you, right now."

I glance around the room, my face heating at all the attention we've drawn.

"I'm not asking for input or sage advice from the two biggest idiots I know. I'm putting you on notice that we can do this two ways. I can bring a lawsuit against you, which will be messily splashed all over the internet, and I'll still get everything I deserve, because the law is clear. Or you can hand things over peaceably. Mom, you'll still be able to manage Dad's share and Trig's, since I'm not handing that off." I spin toward my dad. "And I'm not going to be impoverished by any means. I'll have Nometry, and the many, many gifts you've given me. Presumably, you'll continue with your extravagant gifts. I'll still be worth nearly a *billion* dollars, Dad. That's more than most people could spend in a lifetime." I don't mention that he could certainly manage. We all know that painful truth too well.

"It would take years for you to work this out in the courts." The gleam in my mother's eye bothers me. Plus, the fact that she's right. "The law may be on your side, but it's not fast. And it has costs, and I have an entire team of lawyers ready to delay this until you've come to your senses."

I sigh. "What do you want, Mother?"

"Don't donate every last cent to this charity. You can be more... measured than that and still make a tremendous difference. If I've learned anything in my life, it's that nothing needs to happen with the immediacy you feel in your youth. Donate a hundred million. Then consider other charities for the rest. What's the rush?"

"And in exchange, you'll relinquish control immediately?"

Mom shrugs. "If that's what you want. But I know you don't want to sit in all the board meetings and vote your portion. Nor do you want to lob a grenade at the entire institution."

Mom knows she'll lose everything. All of the heirs will cite the same rule, and she'll be queen of nothing.

I have more leverage than I considered. Mom's linchpin is that no one wants to do what she's doing, and no one else can do it as well. But the restructuring would be a mess. And it would prove terribly expensive.

And a hundred million is a lot of money for a start. Not close to three billion, but still a lot. It's a dynamite beginning.

"Mom, this doesn't change my plans. I'm donating my entire portion to charity. I've had more than enough leg ups from the family. I'm done with dragging that monetary baggage around. I'll keep my company, and the rest I'm donating over the next, let's say five, years."

She bobs her head. "Fine."

"Alright then."

The rest of lunch feels like a scene from a reality TV show. I mostly sit and watch as Mom and Dad bicker, but there are flashes there. Flashes of inside humor, and fond glances I never noticed before. Do Mom and Dad actually... like each other a little bit? I never noticed under the smothering blanket of anger and frustration, but it's there. A foundation of common experience, a history. And there's something else, something I can't define. I think that may be the real reason they never divorced. I'll have to think about it. But for now, I pay the check while they're talking and push back from the table.

"Well, I've got a lot of things to do. But Mom, I need that first hundred million by tomorrow."

Her jaw drops. "It's too soon. Nothing is that liquid."

"Good thing my trust manager is a miracle worker." I look pointedly at my watch. "You've got three hours until the market closes."

Mom bolts upright. "I better head out. Bernard, you've got the check?"

Dad nods.

"I already paid it," I say.

Dad frowns at me. "I said I was paying."

"You're looking for reasons to complain. It's a drop in the bucket, Dad."

He circles the table and leans over to hug me. "It's a sad day when a father can't buy his little girl a meal anymore."

They may be confused and frustrating, but my parents love me in their bizarre, misdirected ways. I'm grateful for that.

"I love you, Daddy."

"Love you too, sweetheart."

Strangely, my dad's typical endearment makes me miss being called goose.

I call my pilot on my way back to the office. "We're leaving for Atlanta first thing in the morning."

This time, I'm going to be the one surprising Rob.

❧ 27 ❧

ROB

In my wildest dreams, I never imagined this many people might attend my gallery opening. I never would have thought the venue could be a gothic-Tudor style mansion once home to Howard Candler, the president of Coca-Cola. In fact, only last night I dreamt that less than ten people turned up, mostly my direct family and Geo.

But tonight I'm swimming in a sea of suits and evening gowns, and an absolute ocean of people are admiring and touching my furniture, which is all artfully displayed thanks to the genius and hard work of Christine and Geo.

My baby sister Beth bounces up to me like a golden retriever. "Oh Rob, your tables and chairs and stuff all look amazing. And to think, Mom used to try and convince her friends to ask you to make them a coffee table. She'd tell them how badly you needed the moral support."

Whenever Beth smiles for real, her eyes squint up so much that they practically close. They're nearly slits right now, and I love it. I pull Beth in for a hug. The first piece of furniture I ever made, a clumsily joined bookcase, is filled with books in her bedroom at home.

"My original fan."

"I'd never give that bookcase up, even if someone offered me a million dollars."

I chuckle. "No one would ever pay a hundred dollars for that wobbly hunk of junk, but you'd be a fool not to take it if they did."

"Then call me a fool."

My dad and mom's heads appear around the corner. Mom's eyes are wide, looking at the guests more than the pieces.

"Where did all these people come from," she whispers once she's close enough.

I smile. "I don't know any of them."

"Why are they here?" my dad asks. "If you don't even know them?"

Geo turns around from the person she was schmoozing to answer him. "We tapped into a guest list comprised of Luke's, Paul's, Trig's, and my contacts. That formed our core group, but then we've been marketing the heck out of this, and it has grown."

"You could've used our company list," Dad says gruffly. "Then we might have known someone."

"I didn't want to take advantage." I shuffle my feet. "Or alienate anyone."

"I can't believe you've been able to manage preparing all this, and all your work," Dad says. "It's impressive, son. Very impressive."

Now or never. "Well, actually, about that. Christine's been lending a hand at work so I could spend my extra time on this."

Dad turns to look at the back of her head. "Christine, you say?"

"Yep. She told me she's always had an interest." I clear my throat. "Actually, she mentioned that she had even asked you about it once."

"Pah," Dad says. "She's a public relations major. What does she know about selling cars?"

"I majored in nothing," I say. "And I've managed alright."

"You've got heaps of life experience and natural charisma."

I'm suddenly glad Christine isn't near enough to hear what we're saying. She might pop good old dad on the nose. "Dad, Christine's taking over for me. She's picked things up quickly, and since you put the whole business in a family limited partnership years ago, we all have shares to vote. Me, Beth and Christine are all on board for sure. That's enough."

Dad splutters.

Mom's smile takes me by surprise. "Correction. You, Beth, Christine, *and me* are all on board. I doubt her twin would vote against her, which means Jennifer's probably a lock too." Mom takes Dad's arm in hers. "I believe that's called a super majority, darling. You probably ought to make peace with it, rather than making us look like the old fools you and I both are. Let's grab something to drink." She leads him around the corner toward the bar, but winks at me over her shoulder as she does.

I might have underestimated my mother all these years.

"It's unbelievable he has all these pieces," one woman behind me is telling Beth. "How did he create so many?"

The Callanwolde is twenty-seven thousand square feet, and much of that is currently showcasing my work. Geo had the brilliant idea to dedicate thirty pieces to the charity and have this grand opening to drum up excitement for them.

The gallery director, Francis Tate, turns the corner with a woman on his arm. She's much shorter than he is, but she's wearing a very tall hat, and the feathers keep brushing his nose.

"Can I order the other pieces tonight?" the woman asks Tate.

His face looks pinched, as though he's answered this question before. "The ones that aren't up for auction, do you mean?"

She grins and nods. "Yes, exactly. Can't I order those tonight?"

"Tonight's auction is to benefit Mr. Graham's new charity, as you well know. But if you'll tell me which particular item you're interested in, I'll make a note and call you first thing."

"All of them," the woman says. "Don't you know who I am?" She puts a hand on her ample hip. "Andrea Vanderblat."

The name means nothing to me, but Tate's jaw drops. "As I said, I'll make a note of your number."

"I don't want you to make a note. I'll pay five million for the entire lot, but you must agree to that right now."

"Ma'am, it's not up for sale yet," Tate says.

I nearly choke. Why isn't the moron taking the offer? Who cares what the rules are? We made the rules. Take the money!

Geo beams at me.

"Did you hear him turn her down?" I hiss. "What's going on?"

She claps her hands and whispers. "Your pieces are skyrocketing on the bidding. Having Luke and Paul and Trig invite all their friends was brilliant. These people compete, and when you add alcohol to the mix." She giggles. "Plus, it's all for charity, so they can write it off."

"Not the pieces I sell tomorrow." I frown. "Do they know that?"

"I really need to win that nursery set," Mary says a few feet away.

Luke pats her shoulder. "I told you, I've bid on it three times. I just don't feel good about spending more than we spent on our house for a crib and nightstand."

Mary's eyes widen. "No, neither do I. I had no idea it had gone that high."

Luke rolls his eyes.

I step closer to them. "Umm, you're shopping for a crib?"

Mary beams. "We aren't supposed to tell anyone yet. I'm only seven weeks along."

Geo squeals! "Oh my gosh, Mary, I took a test just last night."

Wait. A test?

The two girls are hugging and screaming. Geo's pregnant? And Mary?

"Trig is going to kill me for saying anything," Geo gushes, "but we might have babies at the same time!"

"I'd be happy to make you each a nursery suite," I say. "My gift."

A man behind me with a scarf tied around his neck, an honest to goodness scarf, says, "Wait, you're taking custom commissions?"

Another woman, this one with five inch, magenta heels and a matching sheath dress touches my arm. "You are? Oh my goodness! I had this idea for a birch wood settee, with an ivory silk cushion. I must have you make it. Tell me you will. When could it be ready? My mother's coming down to visit in three weeks. Is there any chance you could have it ready by then? I'll gladly pay a rush fee."

Suddenly people are shouting at me from all sides. Women, men, yelling things over one another.

Tate lifts his arms in the air. "Calm down, everyone. We are not taking custom orders. There's been a misunderstanding, that's all."

"But I heard Andrea Vanderblat already bought the entire collection," someone in the next room shouts.

What in the world?

"No one bought the entire collection," Mr. Tate says, "but I'm willing to have my staff open up the rest of the pieces for auction tonight, if you'd like that."

Loud cheers from everyone.

"Alright, I'll take that as a yes. My staff will be listing the additional pieces one by one over the next forty-five minutes to an hour. Please be patient."

Geo and Beth each take one of my arms and jostle me out of the room.

"This is better than you could have dreamed," Beth whispers.

"No kidding," I mutter.

"Your parents certainly won't be able to argue that you're not doing the right thing now," Geo says. "And I am going to hold you to that pledge to make us a nursery suite, but I don't expect you to do it for free."

I pull Geo toward me for a hug. "Pregnant? I can't believe it!"

"I know," she gushes. "Me either. But Trig and I are both so happy. We haven't told anyone though, so..."

"Don't tell Brekka?" I ask.

Geo bobs her head.

"Don't tell Brekka what?" Trig asks. "That tall skinny man said you two were back here." He smiles at Beth. "Hey Beth. How's it going?"

Beth shrugs. "Same old, same old. I'm not engaged, or

pregnant, or selling truckloads of overpriced furniture, or anything, but I'm good."

Trig pins Geo with a stare.

She moans. "It slipped out, okay? Mary's pregnant and, I just, look, you can't be mad. I'm too excited."

Trig slings an arm around Geo's shoulder. "Prepare yourself, Rob. You can't stay mad at the woman you love for very long, no matter what she does. And I'm discovering it's even harder when you know she's going to have a baby."

I grin at them. "Congratulations. I was just telling Geo I'd be happy to custom design some furniture for your nursery."

"Well, I'm sure we'll be delighted to sell our jet and use the proceeds to buy a crib from you."

I laugh. "Hardly. And no matter what Geo says, it will be my gift."

Trig shakes his head. "I could turn around and sell that jewelry box for a hundred times what I paid for it right now. And you already gave us the cabinet and the table for our wedding present. It's too much. Especially now that I know your stuff sells for hundreds of thousands. Congratulations, Rob."

"Thanks."

"What did Brekka say about all this?"

I shake my head. "She didn't bite. I asked her to come. Several times in fact, but she said she couldn't make it."

Trig's tilts his head and looks at me like I'm wearing polyester.

"Uh, you sure?"

"What does that mean?" I ask.

Trig grins his sideways grin. "It means I just saw her outside, wheeling around and drooling over some kind of buffet table."

My heart rate spikes and my hands tremble. "No, you didn't."

He slashes his finger in the shape of an x over his chest. "Cross my selfish little heart."

I shoot out of the room, eyes scanning, but everyone is so dang tall. I can't see past the crush of people. How could Brekka navigate through this stupid exhibit at all?

"Rob?"

Her voice stops my heart dead. I'm sure I'll slump to my knees any second and then keel over. Except somehow my feet turn around, and my head turns around and my heart starts beating again, and suddenly, there she is. Her perfect smile, her fringy hair falling in her eyes, and her delicate hands folded in her lap.

I push past the woman who's talking to me, and the man who's pointing at something and asking me a question.

"Pardon me," I say absently. "I need a moment."

I kneel in front of Brekka and cup her face in my hands. The rest of the room dissolves, and the chatter falls quiet all around me. "You came."

She bobs her head, the skin of her cheeks sliding past the palms of my hands, silky smooth against work-worn rough. "I came."

"How did you know? I wanted to surprise you, but you said you were busy."

She laughs, the sound like a songbird trilling with joy. "This time I'm the one surprising you for once. Was it a good surprise?"

"The best." Then I lean down and kiss her, claiming her mouth with mine. Telling her with the urgency of my kiss that I needed her here. I needed her to see my success, because without her it doesn't mean anything. I broke with my family and struck out on my own because she told me I could. She's been there encouraging me, every step of the way as the voice in my head, telling me to try try try.

At first, there's only her mouth, and my fist in her hair, and my fingers on her knee. The barest touch of her hand tracing my jaw. Her lips against mine. And then I notice other things. Like cheering and laughing that's somehow surrounding us.

I pull back and Brekka blushes bright red. Everyone in the room is staring at us.

"The wife, I assume?" Andrea Vanderblat asks with a gargantuan grin.

"That's Brekka Thornton," someone else murmurs. "Victoria's daughter."

"Bernard's daughter," someone else says.

"She's married? I thought she died."

I roll my eyes. "Apparently a few other people are interested in your surprise, too." I stand up.

"Brekka Thornton's my girlfriend, not my wife. Not yet anyway."

Everyone claps and cheers.

"I'll be sure to let everyone know when our status changes," I say. "Maybe a twitter blast. How's that?"

More cheering. Oh, please.

Brekka's grinning at me when I glance back down, so at least she's not upset.

I head back for the side room, Brekka right behind me. Once we're there, I drop down to one knee again. "Sorry about that. I forgot where we were momentarily."

"The mark of a successful surprise." She glances down at her lap and wrings her hands. "I'm still your girlfriend?" Her voice is small, too small.

I take her hands in mine, my large fingers enveloping hers entirely. "If you want to be."

She looks back at me, her dark, full lashes framing eyes full of hope. "It's all I want."

"Then why have you been hiding?" I ask. "What did I do?"

"You didn't do anything." She shakes her head. "And I'm not hiding, not exactly."

"Are you ever going to tell me what's going on, then?"

"I am. That's why I came this weekend. Well, that and to buy some outrageously priced furniture, apparently."

I beam at her. "I have no idea what's going on. It's like a house full of barracudas, and I'm the recipient of all their violent energy."

"That's an apt description of my social circle," she says. "And I said it was outrageously priced. I didn't say it wasn't worth every penny."

"Well, even if you don't get something tonight, I saved one thing back at the shop that I thought you might like."

Her eyes light up. "You did?"

I nod my head. "I'd love to show it to you, if you have time."

She nods. "Absolutely."

"Maybe we can go back there and talk."

Someone taps on the doorframe and I turn. Mr. Tate pokes his head around the corner. "Got a second?"

What now? "Yeah?"

"We're closing the auction on the charity items in ten minutes. We extended it half an hour as a courtesy."

"Courtesy to whom?" I ask.

"Last minute bidders," he says.

I shake my head. "I don't understand. Won't there always be last minute bidders?"

"These bids were called in."

"What?" I ask. "From where?"

"Many of our guests tonight have been posting on social

media." Mr. Tate beams. "To say you're trending is an understatement."

"Okay," I say. "Well, that's good."

"I thought you might like to be there for a press release," he says. "Your face is good branding, and several of the major networks have sent camera crews. They'd like you to announce the amount you're donating. Your friend Clive is also here, ready to accept your donation on behalf of Cultivate."

I turn toward Brekka. She beams at me. "Go, I'll be here when you're done. I'm so proud of you, Rob. For all of it. Plus, it sounds like I have some last minute bids to make now that there's time."

She follows me out the door, but I head for the dining room we designated as the pressroom, and Brekka turns toward the main living area. I wonder what she's bidding on, but when I reach the press area any thoughts in my brain evaporate. I'm immediately bombarded with questions.

"What gave you the idea for Cultivate?" a woman with hair like a helmet asks.

"When I was stationed in Libya, our unit was hit with an IED. I was thrown to the road, and debris landed on my chest. It broke my back."

The room falls surprisingly quiet.

"Through equal parts luck, hard work, and dedication by a group of military surgeons, my break was stabilized and then it healed. My broken spine has refused and I'm fine today. I can do anything."

"Could you play quarterback in the NFL?" a man with a hugely wide mouth asks.

"Anything I could do before, which sadly means that I'm as bad at football as I always was."

People in the room snicker.

"But I do have complete range of motion. It's miraculous to me, even now. But some of my friends weren't as lucky as me." I put my hand on Clive's shoulder. "Many former warriors in our nation's military are now fighting battles of their own every day at home. The wounds they received in combat continue to plague them."

"What about your girlfriend?" a man with long thin fingers, and a bright white smile asks.

I bob my head. "My girlfriend was in an automobile accident. She's also a wheelchair user today. And you know, there are hosts of other people who deal with similar difficulties. I have neighbors, friends and family who use wheelchairs and have prosthetic limbs, and I'm not the exception. I'm the rule. People who use wheelchairs are all around us. Many people have suffered injuries in combat, or are dealing with medical conditions. Differently abled people face a barrage of problems most of us never even notice. Many, many places still aren't accessible. My buddy Clive teaches," I pause. "Or, I suppose I should say, before he accepted my offer to be the new President of Cultivate, he *taught* physical education. It's not typically a job performed by a person who uses a wheelchair. Not because a wheelchair user can't do it, but because it's not something people typically make accommodations for, which is a shame."

"When we completed our rehab," Clive says, cameras snapping as he speaks for the first time, "we were told to look for jobs we could complete at home. Even for those of us able to live independently, we're directed that it's just simpler. I was strongly encouraged to go into customer service or computer programming. Everyone wanted me to do something I could do while sitting in a wheelchair in my family room."

"One of my goals with Cultivate," I say, "is to help

people to see, all people, the tremendous value that disabled people can bring to the world around them, if we're able to approach things from a new perspective. And not because they are wheelchair users, not at all. Not because they've risen above their great difficulty, but because of the people they were before, and now and the people they always would have been. They're people exactly like you and me, with the exception of needing a few accommodations. Although, instead of seeing the changes we need to make as accommodations, I wish we could think of them as opportunities to improve. I know no one likes change."

"Believe me," Clive says. "I don't like it either. But I didn't have a choice."

"In a moment," I say, "I'll have the honor to announce the amount of donations we were able to raise through the sale of some furniture I made in my shop at home. Each piece is different, unique, and one of a kind. And all the people Cultivate strives to care for, to benefit, and to enrich, are different and unique too. They aren't like everyone you see in your normal routine, but they're just as beautiful as each piece of furniture." I turn to face Tate. "Isn't this where you wanted to play that reel of the images of what we put up for auction?"

Tate nods. "And I thought I'd surprise everyone with a little announcement of my own. Thanks in large part to the tremendous response from donors tonight, the gallery is planning to donate its entire commission as well. Therefore, one hundred percent of the income from the sale of these beautiful items will go to fund Cultivate, a charity the Callanwolde stands behind one hundred percent."

I'm floored. He's donating their twenty percent cut? I don't know how to react.

Tate starts the video, and flashes of furniture I made over the past years in the quiet of my own shop appear, one by one. A coffee table with glass blown in between the joined parts of a split tree. A nightstand with the word Sleep burned into the top, then covered in iridescent glaze. A dining table formed from a single cross cut slab. A breakfast table with stump slab seats. A bookcase with carved scrollwork running up the sides, featuring butterflies and flowers I treated with a chemical stain, making them iridescent. A delicate china hutch. A set of end tables. A lamp stand. A rocking chair. On and on, the images flash. More coffee tables. An entry table, and my favorite piece of the night. A breakfast table made of the same inosculated ash I used for Trig and Geo's wedding gift, and delicate, individual chairs made of ash as well. The finish is rubbed, and the legs took me days and days to carve, those of the table matching the chairs.

"While the slide was playing," Tate announces, "the network informed me that we've had viewers, hundreds of viewers in fact, who have called asking to donate as well. We wanted to let you know, the website recently set up for Cultivate is available at the web address flashing in the strip at the bottom of the screen. If you'd like to donate, they welcome that. Every donation helps. And now, I've got an envelope here for Rob. We wanted him to read the amount he was able to raise, as well as the single largest donation out loud for all of you today. Live, so we can experience his success right here with him."

I take the envelope with steady hands. I'm surprised about how utterly calm I feel. I'm conscious that this is all happening in front of thousands of people, but I can't see anyone other than the representatives from the press and a handful of cameramen, so it feels pretty surreal. "Well," I say. "When I had this idea, I wasn't sure if anyone would turn out other than my mom, so I'm pleased, no matter what this number is."

"Tell them your pie-in-the-sky goal," Clive says.

"Good idea," Tate says.

"Well," I say, "Clive and I went over his expenses. He's going to work for the same salary he was being paid as a teacher, forty-thousand dollars a year, and since he's got VA coverage, we don't even have to pay for his health insurance." I wink. "Which is really why I gave him the job. He's cheaper than anyone else would be."

Clive rolls his eyes.

"By my calculations, if I could manage to raise a hundred and fifty-thousand, we'd have enough to run for a year and a half, especially if people like me are willing to donate their time to help effectuate the modifications to the individual applicant's homes."

"I'm not sure whether anyone mentioned this yet," Clive says, "though I know it was on the invitations. I thought maybe we should explain on air that Rob here spent weeks and weeks of weekends at my house, and donated all the supplies to redo my cabinets at a level I could easily reach. He's done it for several other friends from our injured veteran trauma support group as well."

I swallow. "But the material point is that, in addition to people donating any money they are willing to donate, we will be looking for people willing to volunteer time or skills. The more donations of any type we receive, the further these donations of cash will go."

"Exactly," Clive says.

I pull the paper out of the envelope and start to read. "It says that we raised one hundred and four—" I cut off. There must be a typo. I turn toward Tate and drop my voice. "This can't be right. Is there a typo?"

Tate shakes his head and jerks his head toward the cameras.

"Uh, okay, well, it says we raised one hundred and four million, three hundred and forty-three thousand and fifty dollars."

Clive's mouth opens and his eyes widen like teacups.

I whisper at Clive again. "Are you sure it's not one hundred and four thousand? It's less than my pie in the sky dream, but it's still tremendous. More than I had any reason to hope."

Tate points at the paper. "Keep reading, hot shot."

I look back down at the paper, my hands shaking so badly I can hardly read the figures. "It says the single largest donation was for the breakfast table and chairs made of inosculated Ash. The donation was made by Brekka Thornton, who paid one hundred million dollars on behalf of the Aldertree Thornton Family Trust."

I drop the paper.

Brekka.

"Even without your girlfriend's tremendous support," the woman with the helmet hair says, "you still raised four million and three hundred and forty-three thousand. How does that feel?"

"Three hundred and forty-three thousand *and fifty*," Clive says. "Every dollar counts."

I have no idea what to say.

One of Tate's employees hands Clive a laptop.

Clive makes a strangled sound. "I was logged in to the system so that they could provide the information for donations on the air," he says. "And look!"

He spins the laptop around toward me.

Our fund shows that we've already had almost half a million in funds donated from individuals through the website.

"I'm utterly speechless," I say into the camera. "It's one thing for the very wealthy to support a cause and take a write off. But to know that all of you viewers believe as strongly in this cause as I do? To see you all supporting us tonight, well, it's overwhelming to say the least."

A whimpering sound to my side draws my attention and I notice that my friend who's a former football player, who normally sports a classically good looking profile, has turned to look at the ground. Because his face has scrunched up in an ugly way.

Clive is crying. On national television.

"Well, it's time for us to conclude this interview," Tate says. "Because I have word that Mr. Graham has a special phone call. From the oval office. Apparently the President is planning to redecorate, and she would love to commission her new desk and filing cabinet from a veteran. Her favorite cousin is also a wheelchair user, you know."

I can't hold back my tears either. I have no idea how long Clive and I are crying on a live feed before they finally cut off, but the donations roll in even faster after that.

❧ 28 ❧

BREKKA

Mary and Luke jump up and down and cheer at 10:31 p.m.

"What's going on?" I ask.

"We won the nursery suite," Mary gushes. "It was way, way more than we should have spent, but I pointed out to Luke…"

"It's for charity," he says. "Which means the whole amount is deductible and goes to fund a good cause."

"We are going to pay almost nothing in taxes this year," Mary says. "And our baby is going to have the cutest crib in the world."

Luke spins Mary in a circle. "So what if we need to eat Ramen for a few months?"

She hits his arm. "Knock it off."

They're having a baby? "When are you due?"

Mary's grin widens more than I thought possible. "March twelfth."

"Very exciting." I can't quite inject true energy into my tone, and I hope they don't notice. I am happy for them, but something contracts inside me, a longing. I want to have a child. I want a baby in my arms, and they already have two. A third before I'm even married seems... greedy.

"Have you seen Geo tonight?" Mary asks.

I shake my head, but her words spark something inside of me. Why would she ask me about Geo, my recently married sister-in-law, after a conversation about babies? I look around the room without luck.

"Pardon me," I say. "I ought to look for her."

Mary winks at me, and I redouble my efforts to squeeze past the people all around me and find my brother. If there's news, I better not be finding out after Mary and Luke. I finally see them, their eyes on a monitor in the corner of the room, the back of Geo's head leaning against Trig's chest, his arms wrapped around her, both of them watching something earnestly.

I move toward them, but once I'm close, I realize what they're watching. It's the ten o'clock news. And my beautiful, handsome, All American boyfriend is talking to everyone who's tuning in.

"—Clive and I went over his expenses. He's going to work for the same salary he was being paid as a teacher, forty-thousand dollars a year, and since he's got VA coverage, we don't even have to pay for his health insurance." When he winks, I imagine girls all over the world sighing and giggling.

"Which is really why I gave him the job," Rob says. "He's cheaper than anyone else would be."

Clive rolls his eyes.

Rob looks so earnest. He's about to announce whether they met their goals on national television. And I realize that my donation, my bid, isn't anonymous.

My stomach ties in knots and I wheel toward Geo frantically.

"Geo!" I shout. "Geo!"

She races across the room to meet me. "What? Brekka, are you alright?"

I shake my head. "No, no, I'm not. Why are they announcing this on television?"

Trig shrugs. "All press is good press, right, but especially this. The more people inspired by Rob's donations and his work, the more support Cultivate will generate. It was Christine's idea, but Geo set it up."

I can't stop shaking my head, even if it's starting to give me a headache. "No, but I bid astronomically high on something."

"That's good, right?" Trig asks. "You're a supportive girlfriend."

Geo cocks her head. "Umm. Exactly how high is astronomically high?"

She gets it. I'm going to steal Rob's thunder, utterly and completely.

"A million?" Trig asks.

"Two?" Geo asks.

I shake my head, my stomach sinking like an Acme anvil.

"Oh no," Trig says. "What did you do?"

I close my eyes. "It's a long story I'll update you on later, but I might have seized control of the reins of the trust and told Mom I was donating my share to charity."

Trig's jaw drops. "You didn't donate three billion dollars though, right? Tell me you didn't."

I exhale. "No, it's not that bad. But a hundred million."

Geo frowns. "That's way too much."

Or maybe no one will find out, I think.

"—It was made by Brekka Thornton, who paid one hundred million dollars from the Aldertree Thornton Family Trust."

Trig whistles. "Mom will like the good PR, at least."

I drop my face into my hands. "I've completely ruined this, haven't I?"

"Maybe not," Geo says. "I mean, obviously Cultivate is poised to be a huge success, and it shows the world you support your boyfriend."

Trig snorts. "And it completely cuts the legs out from under Rob and what he was trying to do. If his girlfriend can come in and drop, what did they say? Like twenty-five times what he earned, just by writing a check?"

"Oh no, oh no, oh no." I realize I'm muttering under my breath and click my teeth shut.

"It's going to be fine," Geo says. "Rob loves you. If he's upset, he'll get over it."

Trig bites his lip. "It's kind of thousands of years of social conditioning that propels guys to want to provide for their family. That's a lot to shrug off."

"Shut up," Geo says. "You aren't helping."

"And you guys don't know everything yet. I doubt Rob's told you any details about our interactions in the six weeks since your wedding?"

Geo and Trig exchange a glance.

"What would he tell us?" Geo asks.

"I might have been kind of weird at the wedding. Like, we both said I love you, and then I kind of ran away and I've been blowing him off a little. Coming for this and donating to show my support was supposed to be my grand gesture."

"It's grand," Trig says. "That's for sure."

I groan.

"Look, no need to get all melodramatic yet." Geo strokes my head soothingly. "Wait to freak out until you talk to Rob and find out how he feels. He's pretty evolved, for a guy." She glares at Trig.

He shrugs. "I'm not very evolved, but at least I admit

that. Maybe our kids will get your genes in that regard. We can hope, anyway."

"Speaking of your kids." I lift my eyebrows.

"Oh, come on. Who said something?" Geo asks.

Trig and I both glare at her.

"We took one test last night, right before bed," Trig whispers. "Geo promised me she wouldn't tell anyone, and now she's practically taken out an ad in the national news."

"At least I didn't give anyone a hundred million dollars," Geo mutters.

I laugh. We're all a bunch of idiots. "Well, congratulations, you two." My eyes fill with tears. My brother's having a baby! And I'll be an aunt. Even if I never have children of my own, I can squeeze his little cherub as much as I want.

Now I want to move to Atlanta even more. Not that I've been asked. Not that I'll ever be asked, more than likely. I'll be lucky if Rob doesn't throw me out the second I show up at his door.

"Where did you leave things before the press announcement?" Trig asks. "I'm assuming he didn't know you were coming tonight?"

I shake my head. "I surprised him." The tears in my eyes change from joy to despair. "And now he's not going to want me to come over anymore."

"You're supposed to see him later?" Geo asks. "That's good. You can explain. You didn't mean to make it public. You had no idea they were going to read anything on national news. It's not your fault he looked stupid."

"He didn't look stupid," I wail. "He looked gorgeous and perfect and amazing. He looked better than anyone I've ever seen in my life."

"I did?" Rob asks.

My heart surges in my chest and I worry it might pop out of my body and flop around on the floor, spurting blood and making a huge mess. I remind myself this isn't a Quentin Tarantino film, and my heart is safely beating inside of my rib cage.

I nod dumbly at Rob from across the room. "You did. You do. You always do." Everyone milling around falls silent. Again. What's wrong with me tonight? People shift out of the way as Rob strides toward me. He takes my hand in his and bends over to kiss the back of it.

"Tate says I can head home. You still want to come?"

"You still want me to?" I hate the wobble in my voice.

Rob cocks his head sideways and lifts one eyebrow. "Of course."

I squeeze his hand before he lets go so I can wheel my way toward the door.

I glance back at Trig and Geo, and Trig mouths, "Good luck!" and grins stupidly. Geo actually throws me an honest to goodness thumbs up, like she's running for Mayor or something.

When we reach the parking lot, I follow him a dozen yards before I realize we're headed for Little Debbie.

"You came here in your old Chevy?"

He shrugs. "What else would I drive? I only use the Ram when I'm hauling stuff, and the gallery worked out transportation of everything last week."

This unassuming, classic-car loving artist in front of me floors me every day. He's so humble. He's so kind. He's thoughtful and caring. What was wrong with me? How could I ever think he could turn into my father? He would never resent me for asking him to move, would he? I search his face for signs of anger, frustration, disappointment or inadequacy.

I can't read him, not at all.

He doesn't speak as he helps me into Little Debbie and loads Gladys into the back. I think about how far we've come since we met in May. He needs no direction, but manages her like a pro. I don't object to his help. In fact, it's nice to surrender for a second and to let someone else do something for me. It might even be nice to have a partner in the daily struggle.

A tear rolls down my cheek and I brush it away before Rob can notice. It's a good thing I opted for the waterproof mascara today.

"I'm happy you came tonight," Rob says.

"You are?" I hope he doesn't notice when I draw a ragged breath to steady myself. "I mean, I'm so glad that you are."

Rob has just put the truck in gear, but he turns toward me sharply. He rams it back into neutral and turns in his seat. "I love you, Brekka. I think I've loved you since May. That's more than three months now. I love your heart, your fire, and your stubbornness. I love it all. I'm always happy to see you. No matter what."

I break down into tears, and he shuts Little Debbie off. He slides across the bench seat and gathers me in his arms. "What's going on?"

"Trig said I broke us," I sob.

Rob swears. "I love your brother. I really do, in spite of, well, let's leave it at that. But he's really idiotic sometimes. What in the world could he be talking about?"

"I didn't know." I hiccup loudly.

His eyes widen. "Didn't know what?"

"That you'd read it out loud!"

"Read what?"

"I mean, I didn't realize they'd make you read it out loud that I was the one who donated all that money. I'm so sorry!"

"You're sorry? For donating to my charity?" Rob licks his lips and I want to kiss him so badly it pains me. "What are you sorry for? You donated an amount beyond my wildest dreams, to a cause that matters to me. And I assume it's a cause that also matters to you."

"I s-s-stole your thunder," I say.

"You didn't." He wipes my tears carefully with his thumbs and then kisses my cheeks. "Who told you that? You made us look like a united front to the world. My girlfriend, donating generously to support her boyfriend's efforts. Surprising me, lifting me up, motivating me, like always."

I lean back against the seat so I can see his face. He's serious.

"What about a thousand years of social conditioning?"

"I have no idea what you're talking about," Rob says. "Maybe I should call Trig." He reaches for his phone, but I stop him. We've had quite enough of Trig's moronic brand of misguided help.

I bring his hand to my face. "Don't call anyone. Just kiss me."

He does. Oh, he does. And I forget all about money, and trusts, and well-intentioned, stupid family members. And I forget my own name. And then I forget I ever had a name. All that matters is Robert Graham, and the knowledge of a truth his kisses stamp deep into my bones.

He loves me. He loved me before, and he loves me still.

And I think he always will.

29

ROB

When someone taps on the window and lifts their eyebrows knowingly at us, it's time for me to stop kissing Brekka. Or I might just punch that random rich guy I don't know in his smug face. As much as I'd love to do that, it might set me back a bit on my public image, which matters now for Cultivate.

I sigh and shift away from Brekka. "Maybe we better go."

She smiles slyly. "You might be right."

I wait for her to buckle, and then I start Debbie back up. "You still up for checking out my shop? Because if you're tired, we can do that later. I can take you... where are you staying? Trig's?"

She shrugs.

"You don't have plans?"

She shakes her head. "My plans were seeing you, and now I am."

I close my eyes and remind myself that I'm a gentleman. My mom raised me right, and I love this girl. I focus on being the gentleman she needs me to be. "Well, I have a guest room if you need it."

Her eyes burn into mine.

A guest room. I have a guest room.

I focus on the road, not pressing her for information. I still can't believe she thought I'd be angry that she donated to Cultivate by buying my favorite piece. "You know, the table and chairs you bought are the twins to the ones I made for Geo and Trig, out of the inosculated ash tree I was telling you about on the day we met. I'd bought that wood a few weeks before, which is the only reason I knew the fancy word to begin with."

She smiles, but doesn't comment.

"Those trees were beautiful individually, but even stronger together."

Brekka reaches across the bench for my hand. "Sort of like us."

Exactly like us. I open my mouth to ask the question I've been afraid to ask. Then I close it again. What if she shuts down again?

But at the end of the day, I need to know. I blurt the question out before I can chicken out again. "Why did you change your mind about me moving to Colorado? What did I say or do that was wrong?"

Brekka unbuckles her seat belt and slides across the bench. She buckles up again in the middle seat and leans her head against my shoulder. "It was all my fault. It had nothing to do with you, nothing you said, and nothing you did."

"I doubt that."

"No, it was. You have parents who love each another. You grew up in a happy home. I know you worry some-times that I'm rich and you're not, but if we're valuing the things that matter, you're the wealthy one, and my family was practically bankrupt."

I don't interject, even when she pauses. I don't ask questions, or even tell her that I agree. I feel like she needs to get something out, and I don't want her to lose momentum.

"You misconstrued something I said, I think. When I said we're different, I worry you thought I meant that you don't have a college education, or didn't go Ivy League. I worry you're thinking about Nometry. Or even before, you thought I meant because I can't walk and you can. None of those are what worried me. I meant that you trust people. You live your life motivated by a desire to help, to care for, to protect people around you."

"Brekka, you're the most caring person I know. In fact, we only met because you flew across the country to defend your brother."

"Which gave you a skewed view of the kind of person I am," Brekka says. "I'm fiercely loyal to a handful of people. Actually, if I'm honest, it's less than five people. Trig's at the top of the list, and then Geo's a new addition. And I try to take care of my parents, in spite of their flaws. That's about it. After the accident, things got weird with most of the people I thought were my friends. And everyone at Nometry works for me. I'm not you, Rob. I don't have Clives all over America blessing my name. I don't donate my weekends to charity, and I don't quit jobs so I can support people I love. I'm selfish at my core, and you're a giver."

"You don't see yourself the right way."

"Maybe," Brekka says. "Or maybe I'm completely correct about this. But when you agreed so quickly, so readily, without agonizing or struggling over it, when you just up and said, 'sure, I'll move to Colorado,' I don't know. When you were ready to drop your family for me, it scared me. I think my parents may have started out that way, with my dad bowled over by my mom's strength of will, offering her the world, offering her everything he had. And my mom took it all, and then she just kept right on taking."

"That's not at all my impression of your parents," I say, "for what it's worth."

"No?"

I clear my throat. Maybe I shouldn't share this, but it's too late at this point. "We talked at the wedding, you recall, and I've talked to you and Trig a little. I think your dad met your mother and was entirely bowled over, like you said. But I think he was taken in by her competence, her tenacity, and her intelligence. The same things that impress me to the ends of the earth about you startled him. I think your dad probably hadn't spent a lot of time around women who knew what they wanted and went for it with everything they had. And your dad had been so used to always getting his way that he had no idea what would happen when he agreed to marry a force of nature like your mother. I think at first he loved it, but over time, he began to measure himself against her. Instead of being proud of her, he began to resent her for being so good at everything."

Brekka begins to cry. "He did, you're right. He hated her for being what he wasn't."

"Unless you think I'll wake up one day and wish I had a knack for business, or an ability to manage massive corporations, we might not run afoul of one another on that issue."

Brekka laughs. "Maybe not."

"But more than that, I think your dad failed in his most basic task as your mother's husband."

"What's that?" she asks.

"His job was to treasure her and to celebrate her victories. When trees intertwine, the wind brushes them back and forth. Think of the wind like issues and problems that chafe the bark away. If the trees grow together, they're both stronger. If they try to build that bark up, if they insist on going their own way, if they refuse to move." I pause. "If they refuse to yield, then bark reforms and the tree conceals a weakness at its center. Those trees aren't inosculated. They're flawed, primed to be split apart by wind and rain. Your gardener would tell you to cut them down."

Brekka squeezes my hand. "I started to bark up, didn't I?"

I nod. "You did. And it hurt me here." I tap my chest. "I know that sounds idiotic, but I want us to grow together in the wind."

"So do I," Brekka whispers.

I pull into my driveway. "I have something to show you. I don't want to freak you out, though. So if any part of you feels like running, or like barking up, tell me now and I'll wait."

She shakes her head. "I'm not scared. I feel stupid, but I'm not afraid. Every time I think you'll freak out, you don't. Every time I think you'll be angry, you're calm. Every time I expect the worst, you show me the best. And I haven't had time to tell you yet, but Rob." She chokes up. "Your furniture, well, people might have been spinning out a bit tonight, and no piece of furniture is worth a hundred million, but you have to know, that frenzy wasn't all media hype. It wasn't all posturing. Your work is ... moving. Your pieces are brilliant and delicate and refined, and utterly unlike anything I've ever seen. Now the world sees you as clearly as I do, and I'm not sure I like that."

"My other pieces were up to five and a half million all together when I left. Tate told me he'd let the auction run another hour."

"Mom will be shocked," Brekka says. "She told me she

liked you in spite of your being poor, which by her standards means you're worth less than two."

I laugh. "Your mom's been calling and interrogating people, you know."

Brekka groans. "I was hoping you didn't know. It's so humiliating."

"And even so, she's been misinformed. We've got a family partnership and we own all the dealerships together, so I was already worth more than two before tonight. But I'll let that slide. She's only protective because she loves you," I say. "She's bizarre and boundaries mean nothing to her, but she's doing it to try and protect her daughter, and I have absolutely nothing to hide."

"I know that."

I climb out of the truck and assemble Gladys, and this time, instead of transferring herself, Brekka holds her arms out to me and lets me lift her and set her in her chair. I kiss her on the top of her head and head for my shop.

"We aren't wasting any time tonight, are we?" Brekka asks.

I shake my head. "I've wasted enough time."

She grins. "Or rather, I have."

"You said it."

She laughs, a sound like she made when we stood in front of the waterfall at Stone Dam, a free sound, a joyful sound. When we finally reach my shop, and I open the door and turn on the light, seeing it so empty hits me like a slap in the face. I've sold nearly everything I ever made. My fingers itch at that thought, desperate to dive back in and start creating.

"I have a custom order," I say. "From your brother."

"You do?"

"Which means my very first custom order, and now my second, both came from Trig."

"For what?"

"I'm sure you heard that Geo and Trig are having a baby. Mary and Luke are too, and they won the crib, I hear. So I promised Geo I'd make her an even nicer one."

Brekka beams. "You better do it, too, or I'll never hear the end of it."

"You're going to be an aunt," I say. "How do you feel about that?"

"I don't think it's really sunk in yet," Brekka says. "I'm giddy, and then I forget all about it. Then you mention it, and I'm giddy again. I want to squish a baby so badly." Her eyes soften and lose their focus.

"Do you want one?"

She turns toward me slowly. "From the tips of my toes all the way to the top of my head."

"Good to know," I say. "Well, the piece I'm looking for is easy to spot, at least. Everything else has been cleared out. It's the one piece I didn't sell. It was a custom design, too, although the customer didn't know about it."

She weaves around the table saws and the drying wood, the belt sander and the sawhorses, following me until I reach the table I made. "At first I meant to make you a cabinet. It would have gone floor to ceiling, and been full of varying sizes of cupboards and drawers. Tall, short, large, tiny. There would have been drawers in the bottom, and each box and drawer would have held something different."

"This is a table," Brekka points out.

"Yep, I made you a table. A coffee table, in fact."

"Why the change?"

"Because I was at my sister's house, and her son climbed on top of a chair and pulled out a half dozen china plates, smashing them on the floor before she could stop him. They were on display, you see, and he realized they were beautiful."

"And?" Her brow draws together.

"Well, I figured one day you might want children. I decided to make this child friendly right from the starting gate."

She runs her hand across the top of the shiny, smooth, light ash wood coffee table.

"I intended to make this into a giant slab." I run my hand down the side of the ash edge. "I left it live edge, as you can see. It's finished, but the bark is still there."

"Okay," she says patiently.

I reach underneath and find the latches. "But if you loosen these, which you need to know how to do. I'll show you later." I slide the entire top part of the slab backward. It slides smoothly. "The table opens to reveal these boxes. Some large, some small. They're hidden, because sometimes we can hide them. And we can choose what to display to the world."

"Most of these are empty," Brekka points out.

"You'll notice there are twelve spaces," I say. "I figure this table will last me ten years that way. But two of these spaces are already filled."

I reach down and lift up a delicate porcelain teacup, the top part reddish brown, filtering down to deepest blue at the bottom. I hand her the teacup. "What do you notice about this?"

She takes it carefully and touches the edge. "It's broken," she says, "and repaired."

I nod. "Through a process called Kintsukuroi."

She shakes her head. "I've never heard of it."

"In America, when we break something, whether it's a dish, a bowl, or a toy, we usually throw it away. Or if we do keep it, we try and repair or glue it so that no one can see the break. We consider breakage and damage to be something to hide, to cover up, or something that destroys the value of the object."

Brekka meets my eye with a questioning glance. "But this break is repaired in gold. It shines."

"Ah, there you have the difference. But before I fully explain, let me tell you another story. On the day of your surgery, I slugged your brother in the face, nearly breaking his nose. I did it because he kept referring to you as someone who needed to be fixed. I told him you weren't broken. I didn't realize that I was wrong too until I left the hospital and took to wandering the streets of New York."

Brekka flinches, her eyes injured.

"I stumbled, angry, emotional and upset, into a pottery shop. The man there showed me something I'd never seen or heard of. Kintsugi pottery has been broken, and repaired. But the art of Kintsukuroi celebrates the breaks, because they're a part of our history. They make us more beautiful. They add to the story of who we are, and what we've overcome to become what we are."

Brekka traces the golden vein of the repair on the teacup.

I crouch down in front of her. "Brekka, you were broken in that accident, physically on T10, and metaphorically in that the landscape of your life shifted seismically. The change in your goals and dreams broke your spirit, and being limited to a chair and unable to ski as you once did destroyed your plans. Being unable to walk and run and dance wounded you deeply. I've seen the pain of that break, and the repercussions that have reverberated through your life. But I've also seen the strength deep inside of you that allowed you to heal, to repair that break, and to strengthen the rest of yourself, your mind, your body, your heart, so that you are whole. You aren't broken anymore, and in that I was correct when I yelled at Trig, but even I almost meant to hide the break. I thought you were like me. You'd glued yourself back together and Trig should stop making reference to the breakage."

I take her hand in mine. "I missed part of your incandescence too. You're more beautiful for your history and your rewrite of your future. You're kintsugi, in every sense of the word. I love everything about your break, and the healing you did to address it. I promise that every single year, I'll find something, some unique gift to give you. Something that's more beautiful for an inconsistency, or for having overcome something. And we'll put it in this table together. In that way, this table is my promise. We're better together, and together we can celebrate the twists and turns that lay before us in this life, no matter what they are. Together."

"But there are two things in the table," Brekka says.

The other thing is a blue box.

"That's true." I pick up the blue box. "Trig assured me I had to find this at Tiffany's."

Brekka's hand flies to her mouth.

"But when I went to look for gems, nothing looked quite right. They swam in front of my eyes, if I'm being honest. I went down row after row. The jeweler showed me perfect sparkly rock after perfect sparkly rock. None of them looked special enough for you."

I open the box, and she reaches for it. I shake my head. "Uh uh, not yet. I'm not quite done."

She smirks.

"What do you know about inclusions in diamonds?" I ask.

"Nothing," she says. "Just that Mom and Dad won't buy one if it has any. That's about it."

"Typical," I say. "But I did some research. Inclusions sounds like a good word. It sounds like something you'd want, and maybe that's meant to be a marketing tool. Technically, they're flaws, yes, but they don't always make something less beautiful. It took the jeweler at Tiffany's weeks, but he found this for me." I reach inside the box and pull out the ring. It's a simple solitaire in a platinum band. It cost me every dime of my liquid savings, but I think it was worth it. Plus, once I hear back from Tate, I think I'll be more than replenished. Even after taxes.

"This is a large diamond, weighing in at five and a half carats. It's a brilliant cut. But it's not flawless, because right in the center is something called a knot inclusion. But instead of being dark or cloudy, the inclusion on this is colored golden. It looks like a rose to me."

I hand it to her and she looks at the stone carefully.

"It's something that's technically a flaw, but if that doesn't look the same color as your eyes, I'm blind. And it looks like a flower. That gem won't sparkle as much as some of the others, but if there's another stone with that kind of hidden value, I won't ever find it."

"I hope you got a discount," Brekka says.

"I did," he says. "In fact, the only way someone like me could ever afford a five and a half carat, otherwise flawless diamond like that, is that the people of the earth around me are morons and they fail to see its true value. They don't know that it's worth a billion times what the normal, boring, sparkly diamonds are worth. They undervalue it, like you've undervalued yourself. But I'm here to tell you that I'm a delighted man to find two such bargains in my lifetime."

Brekka beams at me.

I drop down to one knee and take her hands in mine. "And I'm not on one knee to be eye level with you this time, or not only for that. I'm kneeling down in front of you, my unique, breath stealing Brekka, my fire filled little dragon, to ask you if you'll marry me. Will you be my kintsugi, my beautifully broken and expertly repaired wife?"

She leaps toward me, her arms circling my neck. "I like that nickname even more than goose. And yes, I'll marry you, you big ox. But only if you beg me to move to Atlanta first."

"Please, please, please," I beg. "Uproot your life, your company, and your home. Anger your parents and move to Atlanta, Georgia to live with me forever and ever."

"Yes, oh yes, I will." She kisses me until I believe her.

30

BREKKA

Rob helps me transfer into my sit ski and fasten all the straps.

"Are you sure this is a good idea?" I ask. "I mean, the wedding is in a month and a half. If I get injured..."

Rob smiles. "You're so cute when you're nervous. You always get crabby. And yes. I'm sure my idea is a brilliant one. If you didn't want to do this, you'd have sold that ski lodge already."

"I have memories that have nothing to do with skiing at that lodge."

He shakes his head. "You can't lie to me. I know every time."

Stupid Rob. He kisses me and all my anger evaporates. He does it regularly. I don't know why I worried before. He wins every argument.

"No fair," I say. "You can't kiss me when we're fighting."

"You didn't get the memo?" He kisses me again. "All's fair in love and war. Plus, I'm doing this with you, and I'm going to be so bad that I'm sure to make you look good, no matter how rusty you are."

"You have two legs."

"I have a broken back, and my surgeon said nothing risky, so if I can do it, so can you."

Vail's pretty accommodating of handicapped skiers, and even has a lift that I can ride on each run. Eventually, I sigh and give in.

"Fine, let's do this." Maybe once I've gone down the run, the anxiety that's formed a tight little ball in my belly will go away.

Rob and I angle ourselves downhill and oh! The feelings! I'm sliding down the ice on my single ski, turning and gliding, the wind in my hair, the cold air flooding my lungs and I'm alive. More alive than I've been in, well, in five years.

When I stop at the bottom, my heart's racing and the smile is frozen on my face. But wait, where's Rob? In my fear, and then my glee and elation, I forgot it was Rob's first time on skis. I'm a horrible fiancée. I twist my head all the way around. Where is he?

I squint and squint until I finally make him out, near the top of the hill in a heap, skis pointing both upward and sideways. Uh oh.

It's nearly ten minutes before Rob makes his way back down the hill to where I'm waiting.

"Thanks for ditching me," Rob grumbles.

"Are you alright?" I ask.

"Everything but my pride seems to be intact," Rob says. "Thanks to the advice from this sweet little eight year old, here." He gestures toward a girl in a purple ski suit with bunnies on it. "She's been skiing for five years. Five. Years." He shakes his head. "I'm guessing you want to go again?"

I nod and grin. "Maybe something a little harder this time."

He sighs, but he tugs me toward the lift. I'll be sure to finish right by it next time. "I'm thinking this may need to be a brother sister bonding thing from here on out. Because if you go up much harder runs, they'll need to carry me down in a body bag."

I laugh. "You're so melodramatic."

By the end of the day, Rob's doing much better, and I've skied my first black diamond in five years. The feeling is inexplicable, like my first slice of cherry pie. Or my first time down a water slide. Or something better. It's almost as good as the first time I ever kissed Rob.

And he brought me here. He made me do this.

"Brekka?" a voice from my past asks.

I turn and meet the eyes of my old coach, Rocket McKinnon. "Hey Rocket."

His voice is just as craggy as it ever was, and his eyes crinkle up when he smiles in exactly the same way I remember. But he's got more gray in his hair, and more lines criss-crossing his forehead. "You're skiing again?"

I expected disdain, or judgment, or pity. All I see in Rocket's eyes is exhilaration, excitement and joy.

I nod mutely.

"I would love to be your trainer. Please, please consider me. I know I haven't coached any Paralympic athletes, but I was made for this, I swear."

When Rob asked me to marry him, my heart swelled almost to the point of bursting. When I moved Nometry and myself to Atlanta, and I began to see the love of my life every day, my heart learned to live with an unbelievable level of joy, day in and day out. We picked out a house on the same road as Trig and Geo. I've been watching as Geo's belly grows, and my love for Rob has grown right alongside it. Trig and Rob have even started having boys' nights once a month so that Geo and I can have a girls' night. I have no idea what they do, but there haven't been any more black eyes or broken noses.

And now, a part of me that I thought had died and been buried springs back to life. I'm free in a way I never hoped to be free again. And my old coach, my old life, my old dreams are staring me in the face and asking me to come out and play. A Paralympic Athlete. Another shot at a gold medal.

"Yes," I say. "I think I might like that."

Rocket beams at me. "Girl, you and me are going to destroy these mountains, and there's no limit to where we can go."

He's right. Rob tumbles down the mountain then, to stand at my side.

"Hey," he mumbles. "It didn't take me quite as long this time." He brushes the snow off his hand and holds it out. "I'm Rob Graham, Brekka's fiancé. Nice to meet you."

Rocket shakes his hand. "I'm her old coach, Rocket McKinnon. I've asked her to let me coach her again."

Rob beams at me. "Well, that's wonderful. Did she agree to it?"

"She sure did. And I see great things ahead of us." He turns toward me. "What finally got you back out here?"

I lean my poles against my sit ski and take Rob's hand in mine. "When I broke my back, I thought my life was over. I let my dreams die, including my Olympic hopes. But Rob showed me that I'm as free as I choose to be. He helped me find my freedom again, and my peace with the world. He helped me find liberty."

"Well, I saw you take that last run, and I owe you a big thank you, Sir Rob. I've never seen anyone with as much grace on the snow as your Brekka, and she hasn't lost a bit of it. If anything, she looks surer of herself. Maybe we can all grab dinner and talk about some details."

"I'd like that," Rob says.

"I've been following you, you know," Rocket says. "I'm sure you're busy with your work stuff. But if we can find some time around that, I think you could get those gold medals yet."

"I better get started designing a display case." Rob grabs me and kisses me, right in front of Rocket and everyone else. "I love you my little kintsugi. I couldn't possibly be prouder of you."

"I know," I say. "You helped free me, and then you went beyond that. Life took my legs, but you've given me wings."

"I'm pretty tired from all this flying," Rob says. "But I bet I have enough energy left for one more run. Want to show your old coach that you've still got what it takes to smoke him?"

Oh, how Rob gets me. "Absolutely, I do."

And then with Rob at my side, or perhaps trailing a few hundred yards behind, I do it.

THE END

If you enjoyed the fourth book in The Finding Home Series, grab the FIFTH book, Paisley's story, Finding Holly, which is out now.

If you would like one of my books for FREE, you can grab Already Gone when you sign up for my newsletter here: www.BridgetEBakerWrites.com.

Finally, if you enjoyed reading Finding Liberty, please, please, please leave me a review on your platform of choice!!!! It makes a tremendous difference when you do. Thanks in advance!

And if you'd like to join a fun group of readers (and me!) on a facebook group, check us out right here: https://www. facebook.com/groups/750807222376182 Bonus: I've decided to write some short stories, one for each series, that will be made available FREE, exclusively in my reader group. So if you want an extra peek at your favorite characters, come grab them there.

✹ 31 ✹

SAMPLE OF FINDING HOLLY

I enjoy simple things.

A hot cup of coffee. A fluffy cat curled up on my lap. A perfectly shaved snow cone. Disappearing into a good book. So when someone walks by my window holding a bag marked "Pleasant Pie," my eyes widen. The new pie place around the corner I have been stalking is *open.* I slide into my ridiculously comfortable Brooks sneakers, still so new the shoelaces are crisp, and jog right over.

The cold wind rushes around me as I close the door, clearly as excited as I am about all the gorgeous pies behind the glass counter. "If I ran all the way here from Holden Street, I probably burned enough calories to eat a slice of pie, right?" I ask.

The cashier's creepy perma-smile wavers. "Uh, isn't Holden Street like right there?" She leans forward to look out the window at the street signs. How does she know the location where she works? I mean, really.

"Right," I say, "that's true. But I forgot to mention that live on the third floor."

The cashier, who I'm beginning to think is kind of

dopey, tucks her black hair behind her ear. "I'm not, like, a nutritionist, or whatever, but—" She points at the glass cabinet. "The calories are listed by each slice. I doubt you burned more than ten calories getting here."

Hmm. "I don't actually care whether I burned enough. Your job is to give me a somewhat convincing laugh and then *not* point out that your pie has exactly—" I squint. "Nineteen bazillion calories per slice. Because you want me to buy it. All of it."

"If you buy all of it, what will I do the rest of the day?"

Oh for the love. "You want me to buy some of it, though, right?"

"Of course." She nods her head. "Did you want a slice?"

"I ran all the way here, so yeah, I do." Ran might be a stretch, but my legs moved up and down, propelling my body forward. I'm not one to quibble over variances in speed. "Actually, since I've never tried any of your pies, I might need two."

Her name tag says Judy, but I'm going to call her Judgy McJudgerson, because her eyebrows shoot up like jumping beans and her mouth drops.

"Coconut Cream and Muddy Bottom Pecan." I want to try the cherry too, but. . . you know what? She's not my boss, who is actually much nicer than this lady. "I'll take a cherry, too."

"To go?" she chirps.

"No." I stick out my bottom lip. "I'll be eating them all here. Alone." And I'm totally going to stuff my face in front of her until I pop.

"Can I get a name?" she asks flatly.

"Paisley," I say.

I sit down at the table near the window so I can watch as people pass outside. March in Atlanta is a strange time. Some days are sunny and close to seventy degrees. Other days, like today, are in the forties. And today, to add insult to injury, it's drizzling. I shiver a little thinking about it and hunker down into my fluffy, hooded jacket. They say you burn more calories when it's cold, so I probably totally burned this slice off already.

I have no idea what is taking so long, but at least I'm amply entertained. Some of the people walking past have absolutely no idea it's cold today. One woman jogs past, and doesn't even slow down to acknowledge the pie, wearing shorts that barely cover her rear, a tank top, and ear muffs. No lie. Because without cute pink puffs, her *ears* might be cold.

The cashier brings me a plate just as Miss Earmuffs turns the corner. "Thanks Judgey," I say.

"Oh, no, it's Judy," she says.

"Right," I say. "My mistake."

I wish Mary was here to make me feel guilty for teasing the pie lady and less guilty about stuffing my face. But Mary has fallen into a tax and wedding planning hole. Trudy would have made a hilarious joke about Miss Earmuffs that would have left my side hurting from laugher, but she's too busy studying and job hunting. Plus, even if she had time, Troy shouldn't really be gobbling down buckets of pie. And if Geo were here, she'd order three pieces of pie and the waitress would goggle at her looks, and gush about how she could stay so svelte and gorgeous while eating whatever she wants. To make matters worse, Geo would eat it, and stay exactly every speck as gorgeous and skinny as she is.

I poke at my pie, wondering exactly how much more my thighs will jiggle if I eat it all. I take my first bite of the Muddy Bottom Pecan and decide it's worth it. No matter how much cellulite this turns into after it's processed, it's worth it. As I'm stuffing my first bite of cherry into my mouth, a tall, handsome, dark haired guy walks by the window.

He stops dead, and my mouth drops open.

I'm not goggling over his looks, although they are almost as striking as my friend Geo's and that's uncommon. You don't often see men with hair as black as pitch and eyes as green as plastic Easter grass. His irises are the exact shade of that grass that comes in big bags to stuff the bottom of little kids' baskets. I know, because when Geo taught me about Easter egg baskets and I saw the stuff for the first time, I thought, I've seen that before. Which is why the eyes aren't throwing me right now. No, it's the man himself.

He's definitely not supposed to be here.

His ridiculously green eyes widen and his mouth shapes into a perfect 'O' in front of me. He looks absolutely nothing like me. Which would be uncommon if we were full siblings, but we only share a mother. And he looks exactly like his father, judging from the photos.

My brother Cole wastes no time ducking into the pie shop and practically sprinting over to my table. "What are you doing here?"

I don't laugh at the absurdity of his question. Trust him to spring that on me, as though I'm the one who's out of place. "Here?" I point at the table on which my three pieces of pie rest. "As in, inside a shop that sells delicious, scrumptious, calorie-laden pie?"

Cole opens his mouth, but before he can answer, I continue. "Or do you mean, what am I doing in Atlanta? Because that's what I wanted to ask *you,* since you didn't bother to tell me you had any plans of crossing the ocean that usually separates us."

Cole rolls his stupidly-beautiful eyes. "If I told you I was coming, you'd have made up some excuse."

"Excuse?" I pretend I don't understand what he's saying.

He sits down next to me and picks up my fork.

I swat at his hand. "Hey, that's mine."

"You're going to eat three pieces of pie all by yourself?" He's even judgier than Judge Judy.

Ooh, that's better than Judgey McJudgerson, not that Cole would get it. "Look, I can do whatever I want. You aren't the prince of Atlanta."

"I kind of expected a hug, maybe, or a little cooing. After all, I haven't seen you in two years."

I stand up and pull him close for a hug. Before I let go, I whisper in his ear, "I'm happy to see you, but get your own dang pie, or I might send you back home today."

Cole laughs and walks over to the counter. I notice Judge Judy doesn't hassle him for ordering two slices. In fact, she practically trips over her feet carrying his pie over. It reaches the table seconds after he returns, but she doesn't make much effort to return to the cash register.

"Umm, did my brother forget to pay for that?" I glance up at her. "Maybe you're waiting here to make sure he doesn't cheat the restaurant?"

"Oh." Judge Judy giggles. "No, he paid." She still doesn't leave.

Ohmygosh, I forgot how obnoxious it is to hang out with Cole. "Well." I lift my eyebrows.

"He's your brother?" she asks.

"My much older brother who doesn't live here and already has a wife, a girlfriend *and* an ex-wife," I lie. "Now scram."

Cole's dreamy eyes dance when she leaves.

"I should punch you," I say.

He frowns. "Why?"

"A black eye might ugly you up a little."

He lifts one dark eyebrow. "I don't follow. Maybe it's my English. Ugly me, as a verb?"

I sigh. "I have this friend, Geo. She's like, slap-your-mom beautiful."

"I wouldn't slap our mom—"

"She is the female version of you, okay?"

His brow furrows.

"Only she's a girl. So she brings droves of guys to my side, and she can't keep them all, can she?"

He opens his mouth, but I dive right back in. "No, she can not. But you, your looks are terrible for me. They draw catty women with their claws out, right up until they realize I'm your sister." Actually, I have a newfound appreciation for Rob's patience. To hang out with Geo as long as he did, he must have the forbearance of a saint.

"Tell me more about this Geo," Cole says.

I roll my eyes. "She's engaged. Look, focus. Why are you here?" I ask.

Cole has just stuffed a very impolitely sized bite of chocolate silk pie into his mouth. He points at the bulge in his cheek and cocks his head sideways.

I suppress a laugh while he chews.

"Don't you mean, 'How long can you stay? I miss you so very very much, darling Cole'?"

"Right," I say. "What I meant to say was, oh beloved Cole, how long can you stay with me on this trip on which you came to visit me, uninvited and at a bad time?" I clap my hands together and paste a slightly pained smile on my face. "I do hope it's a terribly long time."

Cole frowns. "I know you're kidding, but it's starting to sting anyway. Are you really upset I'm here?"

I sigh. "You know I'm happy to see you. I'm sorry if I'm crabby. Lady friend over there just called me a pig."

"Three pieces of pie." Cole looks at my plate pointedly.

"I only ordered two at first," I say. "And her job is to sell me pie."

"Three slices."

"I meant to take them to go," I say, "but I wanted to try a few. When she judged me for it, I don't know. I couldn't help myself."

"Typical." Cole smiles. "I've called you a dozen times in the past few weeks, and you've returned my calls twice. And even then, you could only talk for a few minutes. You can't be that busy."

"What's going on, Cole? It's tax season in America, so believe it or not, I'm actually pretty busy."

"And you don't want to come home to visit. It's been almost a decade."

I blow air out of my mouth in frustration. "It hasn't been that long, and you know I don't want to go home. Mom and Dad will just guilt trip me."

"You can't walk out on your family forever."

"Why not?" I ask softly. "Noel did."

Cole flinches. "It's not the same."

"No, it's not." I shove my plate away with way too much partially eaten pie away. I can't eat a bite more, not now. "But it turns out, I don't even need to go home to take a guilt trip."

"Mom and Dad miss you." Cole taps a fork on his plate and stares at the lemon chiffon pie like it might try to walk away. His words are so quiet I can barely hear them. "I miss you too."

My heart trembles a little, but I tell it to shut up. Missing someone is hard, but you survive. In fact, with time it becomes easier and easier. "Then it's good you're here," I say. "I'm slammed at work, but Mary won't mind if I leave a little bit early each day to see you."

I eat another bite of pie so that I can say I'm full, but I

have no idea which pie I'm even eating. Then I stand up. "Well, I think I might have over ordered. I'm heading home. You ready?"

Cole wipes his mouth on a napkin, folds it in half and sets it next to his plate. Then he stands up, pushes his chair back under the table and nods. "Now I am."

"Where's your suitcase?" I ask.

"Lost on the flight. I gave them your address, and they insist they'll deliver it shortly."

"Stupid airlines," I say. "You may never see that bag again."

He shrugs. "It's not like I brought the crown jewels or anything."

I laugh. "More like your dumb plaid pajamas and that ratty old lamb."

Cole's nostrils flare. "I did not bring Lamby."

I can't help making fun of a grown man who still loves a stuffed animal. "Too big of a risk." I nod slowly. "I totally understand."

The walk back home takes less than two minutes. "So how many calories do you think we just burned?" I ask when we reach the third floor.

"Doing what?" Cole asks.

"On the trip from the pie shop to my apartment," I say. "Duh."

Cole frowns.

"Seriously. You think it was two hundred? Three?"

He laughs. "You're crazy."

"And we're related, so what does that say about you?" I bump the door open with my hip.

"What was that?" he asks.

"Oh, nothing, a sticky door, that's all."

Cole follows me through my front door and into my

living room. "Oh Pais, this place is an even bigger dump than your last apartment."

I drop my purse on the floor. "Well excuse me if my house is not spotless. I had no idea you were coming, so it's not like I can be faulted for not picking up." I glance around at the throw pillows on the floor. The pizza box by the edge of the sofa. The empty, almost empty and nearly full water cups strewn across every surface haphazardly, like zits on a teenager. "I'll pick up, okay? It'll take me fifteen minutes."

"I'm not talking about it being messy."

Of course he isn't. He's talking about my plaid sofa that doesn't even almost match my orange arm chair. He's criticizing the wonky-legged kitchen table with five chairs, none of which match. "It's eclectic. That's a thing in America. They call it shabby-chic."

"A little heavy on the shabby. You're not poor," he says. "Your trust—"

"What's wrong Cole?" I plop down on my comfortable sofa and scoop up a few pillows to block the part where the cushioning on the arm has shifted, exposing the frame. "You wouldn't have surprised me like this if something wasn't wrong."

He sits on the edge of my oversized armchair. "Dad's sick."

"You couldn't have told me that on the phone?"

"It's time to come home, Paisley." Cole's eyes bore into mine. "It's time to stop hiding here and come back. We need you."

Oh please. "Now they're sending you here to make heartfelt pleas?" I shake my head. "Tell Mom and Dad that I'm not hiding, and if they want to see me, they can big fat get on a plane and come here themselves."

"Big fat?"

"It's an American expression. It means, suck it up and do it."

"Suck it up?" Cole asks.

Oh come on. "Look, Dad's not really sick. Mom would have called if he was."

"Dad has macular degeneration and can barely see his hand in front of his face."

"That hardly sounds life threatening." I try to ignore the pangs of guilt, but they're a little more insistent.

"He didn't want me to tell you this, but he's also suffering from heart failure. The doctors aren't sure how much longer he will be around. I'm not trying to alarm you. It could be years, it could be months."

I open my mouth to argue, but I can't think of a thing to say. Dad's big and strong and larger than life. He's getting close to seventy, sure, but that's nothing. That's not so old anymore.

"All Mom wanted for her birthday was for me to convince you to come home."

I miss those tiny pangs of guilt. Now they're like waves of guilt, crashing over my head. "Fine. Fine, I'll come home."

Cole beams at me, his perfectly white teeth practically blinding me.

"But I can't come right now. My boss is mired in the middle of an avalanche of work, and her wedding is in a few weeks. Plus, did I mention she's one of my closest friends?"

"Wait, are you offering to come home for a visit? Or did you mean you'd come back permanently?"

I grit my teeth. "For a visit. We can't keep arguing about this. I'm not fifteen years old. I'm an adult, and Mom and Dad can't make me do anything."

"When Dad dies, you have to come back," Cole says

simply. "And it would be a shame if you missed being with him for what little time he has left."

"I'm sorry he's sick," I say. "I'm sorry you've had to deal with all of it alone. I'm really, really sorry, okay?"

Cole nods.

"I'll come for a few weeks, alright? After tax season, and after the wedding, I'll come for a really long trip."

"We need more than one visit. With Dad being sick." He shakes his head. "Business is bad. Dad's bringing some investors in to check things out."

"Investors?" I ask. "Or consultants?"

Cole shrugs. "Investors, I think. Dad says we need someone to buy in, and if they have ideas on how to run it, even better."

"Berg Telecom has made telephones for a hundred years," I say. "Our clients are loyal."

"No one buys phones anymore," Cole says.

I lift my phone. "Really?"

"We make landlines," he says. "We haven't ever been able to secure a manufacturing contract for cellular phones, and our plants don't have the technology—"

"What do you think I'm going to do about it?" I stand up and walk across the room to my window. "I'm a *secretary* Cole."

"You're not," he says. "You're pretending to be a secretary."

"I went to college here in the United States," I say, "and graduated with a degree in microbiology. I never used it. I needed a job immediately, because, well, you know why—so they wouldn't deport me. I've been working as Mary's executive assistant for years and years. It's who I really am. It's what I really do. I actually love my job."

Cole stands up and crosses the room until he's standing right next to me. "You can move away. You can insist that everyone call you by your middle name. You can sit on used plaid couches and heinous orange chairs. You can even live in an apartment with threadbare carpet. You can work as an assistant to some woman you respect and admire, while doing a job that you could do half asleep. None of those things changes who you really are, and it's not a secretary."

I set my jaw.

"Since I'm a half-brother, you're Dad's only heir. At some point you're going to have to move home and take over for him, Holly Paisley von Liechtenstein. You're the Hereditary Princess of Liechtenstein, whether you like it or not."

৩২৫৩

I f you enjoyed that sample, grab Finding Holly now!

ACKNOWLEDGMENTS

My husband is the best man I have ever known. He supports me and lifts me up, and he is patient with my many shortcomings. I love him every single day.

My kids are so great about letting me write and edit and only rarely complaining.

My writing friends are simply the best.

Dr. Rohit Vasan, you were SO patient with all my questions and invaluable for the medical side of Rob and Brekka.

To my sensitivity readers: thank you. I know I was annoying and clueless, and you were so patient. I am not naming you because I know I need to stand behind my own words and any errors in them, but I appreciate your help and guidance more than you know.

To my ARC team and my readers and my fans, your reviews and your words and your support mean the WORLD to me. Thank you!

And to my mom, last this time, but never least, thank you for your unfailing support and enthusiasm and wonderful feedback. THANK YOU!

Bridget loves her husband (every day) and all five of her kids (most days). She's a lawyer, but does as little legal work as possible. She has a yappy dog and backyard chickens. She makes cookies waaaaay too often and believes they should be their own food group. To keep from blowing up like a puffer fish, she kick boxes every day. So if you don't like her books, her kids, or her cookies, maybe don't tell her in person.

Suppressed (2)

Redeemed (3)

Renounced (4)

The Anchored Series:

Anchored (1)

Adrift (2)

Awoken (3—releasing July 15, 2021)

Capsized (4—releasing September 15, 2021)

A stand alone YA romantic suspense:

Already Gone

Children's Picture Book

Yuck! What's for Dinner?

www.ingramcontent.com/pod-product-compliance
Lightning Source LLC
Chambersburg PA
CBHW031616180726
48284CB00005B/1575